"Brennan shows a deft co[...]
mal and otherworldly in [...]
its kind since Dean Koontz and Stephen King were still
writing about monsters. There's no shortage of those here
and the result is a new genre classic."
—*Providence Sunday Journal*

"An exciting supernatural adventure." —Mindful Musings

"Top-notch character development . . . equally top-notch
plot at work. . . . Allison Brennan outdid herself. *Original
Sin* delivers all the supernatural chills and thrills in an
edge-of-your-seat story that you need to read late at night
for full effect." —Leontine Book Realm

"Darkly powerful [and] shiver inducing!"
—*RT Book Reviews*

"An action-pack[...] thriller filled with demons and evil
witches that [...] your spine [...]. . . A nice
introduct[...] paranormal [...] if you are a fan of
thrillers. Fans of horror [...] like Koontz and King
should take a look." —Blog[...] Reviews

"*Original Sin* is the start to what promises to be an
amazing paranormal series. . . . I'm pretty sure that
Moira will be on my list of top-five heroines of 2010.
She's that good. . . . So far, this is the best book I've read
in 2010." —Book Binge

"A terrific mixture of suspense, mystery and a lot of
action with a hint of romance . . . I found myself repeatedly surprised by the turns in the plot. I have definitely
been pulled into the world of the Seven Deadly Sins."
—Fantasy Dreamers Ramblings

"A Perfect 10!" —*Romance Reviews Today*

ALSO BY ALLISON BRENNAN

Original Sin

Sudden Death
Fatal Secrets
Cutting Edge

Killing Fear
Tempting Evil
Playing Dead

Speak No Evil
See No Evil
Fear No Evil

The Prey
The Hunt
The Kill

CARNAL SIN

the Seven Deadly Sins

ALLISON BRENNAN

BALLANTINE BOOKS • NEW YORK

A Ballantine Books Mass Market Original

Copyright © 2010 by Allison Brennan
Excerpt from *Love Me to Death* copyright © 2010 by Allison Brennan

Published in the United States by Ballantine Books, an imprint of The Random House Publishing Group, a division of Random House, Inc., New York.

BALLANTINE and colophon are trademarks of Random House, Inc.

This book contains an excerpt from the forthcoming book *Love Me to Death* by Allison Brennan. This excerpt has been set for this edition only and may not reflect the final content of the forthcoming edition.

ISBN 978-0-345-51168-3

Cover photograph: © Jessica Hills Photography

Printed in the United States of America

www.ballantinebooks.com

9 8 7 6 5 4 3 2 1

For the amazing writers
who share Murdershewrites.com,
as we celebrate five years on the Web

ACKNOWLEDGMENTS

Though writing is a solitary profession, writers often seek out others for help and guidance. I have been blessed with many people willing to share their knowledge to help me write the best book possible.

First and foremost, my editor, Charlotte Herscher, who always sees the big picture when I'm immersed in the details. Without Charlotte my books would certainly suffer. The rest of the Ballantine team have been hugely supportive and I appreciate each and every one. And of course my agent, Kim Whalen. I wouldn't be here without her!

Special thanks go to CJ Lyons, doctor and author, who patiently walked me through how the brain works and didn't think I was crazy for wanting a scientific explanation to support supernatural deaths; Wally Lind with Crime Scene Writers for always taking the time to answer the most arcane questions I have; LAPD Officer Kathy Bennett, a fellow writer, who went above and beyond to help with the details related to Los Angeles and the LAPD; L.A. County Coroner's Office, especially Chief Coroner Investigator & CO Craig Harvey, for information specific to the L.A. morgue: I may have stretched a few truths for story purposes, but hope I didn't break anything important!

Major appreciation for my husband, Dan, who not only helped immensely with setting details, but tolerated my odd hours with minimal fuss; my kids for keeping me grounded in what's really important—sports, reading, video games, and *Buffy* reruns; and my mom for her never-ending support.

And where would any of us be without emotional support? I owe my pals big-time for their support this past year, in particular Toni McGee Causey, Roxanne St. Claire, and Karin Tabke. You are all incredible women I greatly admire. You listen, offer advice, commiserate, celebrate with me, and motivate me to get back to work when I slack off. Without you, I don't think I would have made it through this book in one piece. I love you all.

Lust's passion will be served;
it demands, it militates, it tyrannizes.

—Marquis de Sade

PROLOGUE

One Week Ago

Kent Galion had it bad for the blonde.

With dark, sultry eyes she stared back at him down her long, elegant nose. And when she passed with a tray of drinks for the rowdy frat boys in the corner, she purposely brushed against him. He'd been watching her all night and they'd shared the secret look, eyes that whispered *I want you*.

What woman wouldn't want Kent Galion? When he was labeled one of Los Angeles's ten most eligible bachelors, they commented on his Midas touch and *GQ* good looks. At forty, he was fit and in his prime. He owned this club and more, the king of the West Side. Any of the staff would serve him in his bed or theirs, and often made that clear, but he rarely took any of them up on their offers. Two years ago he'd dated a sexy cocktail waitress, and that had ended up in a long-term business relationship. He still didn't know why he'd let his dick lead him down that hazardous road—he'd put up most of the risk, but they were in business fifty/fifty. At least Wendy handled the day-to-day management that he detested. The arrangement had been a sore point between him and his younger brother, but Marcus had always been stuffy and conservative.

Kent glanced around the dark, trendy club but didn't see Wendy. *Where was she?* She'd be able to satisfy this deep craving he had; there was nothing she said no to.

He'd always enjoyed women, but just lately his sexual appetite had been insatiable. It was like the good old days of being bad. He'd been hungering in ways he used to before he had responsibilities and a business empire to run. Still, he'd managed to resist the girls at the club until it had become impossible to avoid them. Two nights ago . . .

Sweat broke out on his forehead. He blocked the memory from his mind, certain it wasn't as bad as he remembered. He'd tried calling Stephanie the morning after, but she wouldn't answer her cell. And she hadn't come in to work today. Maybe it was her night off. He didn't concern himself with the staff schedule.

"Who's the new girl?" Kent asked the bartender. He sipped his customary club soda and lime. Kent didn't drink; alcohol made smart men stupid.

Ike glanced at the curvy blonde Kent had been coveting all night.

"Rachel Prince. She's been here a couple months."

Kent hadn't seen her before, but then again he usually did the rounds only once a month. For some reason, this week he couldn't seem to stay away from Velocity, his newest and most successful club.

Rachel smiled at Kent as she walked by on her way to the cash register. Ike leaned over. "She's the type who'd love your money," he warned.

"I like her ass."

"Just saying."

Kent had dealt with plenty of women who'd slept with him to get at his money. He'd had a vasectomy five years ago, so no one could trap him that way—he already had an ex-wife and two kids he paid plenty for. Fortunately, they were on the East Coast and he didn't have to deal with them except to write a check every month. His ex had remarried, and the new guy was better than Kent had been at all that domestic bullshit.

Of course Rachel Prince wanted him. He was rich, and he owned the place where she worked. She would be grateful for his attention and would express that gratitude on her back, on her stomach, on her knees—any way he wanted it. His dick hardened and he shifted on the stool to relieve the pressure. It didn't help.

Kent waited until Rachel took a break, then he walked to the back of the club and found her alone in the employee break room. Velocity staff had classy outfits—the females wore sexy black dresses that hinted at everything but showed nothing except a little cleavage. On Rachel, the short skirt revealed long, perfectly curved legs.

"Hello, Rachel," he said. He could still feel the dance music's beat throbbing from the front of the club.

"Hi, Mr. Galion."

"Kent."

She smiled, her brown eyes assessing him. She licked her painted red lips.

He'd come in here with the intention of asking her to come home with him tonight. But seeing her like this, alone, staring at him with blatant lust, she might as well have been wearing a sign that said FUCK ME NOW.

Kent broke out in a sweat. He stepped toward her. She stepped back. That irritated him. "Come here," he said.

"I only have ten minutes. You shouldn't be back here."

"I own this place."

"But this is the girls' dressing room."

He turned and locked the door. "I saw you looking at me."

"I—I didn't mean to."

Why was she acting nervous? This was all set up earlier when their eyes first met, silently agreeing to rough-and-ready sex. The thought that he'd have to wait to satisfy this burning pained him. His head ached. He didn't want to wait; no dancing around the table in the ridiculous game women insisted on playing. It would happen here; it would happen now.

He moved fast and grabbed her, harder than he meant to. "You agreed."

"I don't know what you mean. Let me go. Please." She wasn't shouting or pushing him away. They were just words; they meant nothing.

He kissed her neck, one hand squeezing her breast. She tensed, and he pushed her against the wall. "I need you," he whispered. He sucked her neck, remembering being a horny teenager giving hickies to every girl he screwed. He'd branded them, shown everyone the sluts they were.

"Stop! Please stop." Was Rachel crying? He didn't want to look.

She doesn't want you. She doesn't want this.

Kent's head pounded. He pictured another blonde, Stephanie, sobbing. Saw the bruises.

Where was Stephanie?

You killed her, asshole.

"No!" He moaned, gripping the woman with his fists, trying to block the memory.

Rachel thought he was talking to her, that he wasn't

going to stop, and she stammered something he couldn't understand. He had to stop. This wasn't right. He didn't need to force himself on any woman; they came to him willingly. He'd never forced himself . . .

Stephanie. You raped her and killed her.

Stephanie had come home with him voluntarily. She'd wanted him to fuck her. Wanted him . . .

She didn't want you to tie her down. She didn't want to be manhandled. She begged you to stop.

He hadn't been able to get enough of her. He had to tie her down or she would have run away.

You killed her.

Stephanie's dead green eyes stared at him.

You killed me.

He shook his head as Rachel opened her mouth to scream. He covered her mouth with his hand. "I don't want to do this, please, help me, I need you!" His heart raced and he grabbed her dress, pulling it down to see her breasts. One popped free and he bit into it, her taste exotic.

She kneed him in the balls and he went down on his knees, rage building that she would *hurt* him, that she would *deny* him, that he wouldn't be able to satisfy this painful craving. He would die if he didn't fuck her. He would die.

Rachel ran to the door, shouting, but the walls were thick. No one heard her over the deafening music. She fumbled with the doorknob. He'd locked the door. It gave him time to grab her.

She spun away from his grasp.

Let her go, let her go!

She stumbled toward the back door, the employee entrance. Pushed it open.

Get her!

Kent chased after her, caught her in the alley, and pushed her against the wall with such violence that she lost her balance and fell to the ground.

"Please don't, Mr. Galion, don't—"

He didn't hear her pleas. He didn't smell the garbage from the bin, or see the graffiti staining the dark brick walls.

All he saw was this female, his prize, his satisfaction. After he unzipped his pants, he reached down and ripped off her dress, taking satisfaction in the sound of the fabric tearing.

She fought back, but he didn't feel the scratches on his face or the dampness of her tears or the sticky blood on the side of her face where he'd slammed her into the wall. All he felt was a driving urge to screw the blonde, shutting out the last whisper of his conscience that told him to let her go.

"You're mine," he growled, twisting her arm so hard it snapped.

Detective Grant Nelson was nursing his first beer of the night, enjoying the alternative music as well as the attractive women. He'd gotten off duty two hours ago, gone home, showered and changed, and headed straight to Velocity for some much-needed R&R as he began his weekend off. His hair still felt damp on the back of his neck. He hadn't bothered shaving, and suspected that's why he was getting so many sideways glances from girls too young for him. His stubble, darker than his light brown hair, made him look dangerous, and for some reason the twenty-somethings liked hard-edged cops.

Julie Schroeder, the club's assistant manager—who was also his ex-girlfriend—made her way through the crowded floor of the popular, neon-lit club until she reached him. They'd broken up months ago, but Grant maintained a cordial relationship with all his ex-girlfriends, and he and Julie still got together on occasion. Truth be told, he had a hard time staying away from her, though they both knew that together they were a lethal combination.

"Julie." He leaned close to her ear so she could hear him, touching the small of her back just firmly enough that she'd know he'd come here alone—and hoped not to leave alone. "How you doing?"

"We have some trouble in the back," she said.

He put his beer down and slid off the stool. He glanced around as he followed Julie through the club, but didn't spot any other cops in the room. But that wasn't surprising; Velocity wasn't a blue bar. That's why Grant liked it—to keep his work separate from his fun.

Except when there was trouble. Now he sure wouldn't mind some backup.

Julie said, "One of my staff complained earlier this week that Kent Galion was making inappropriate overtures, and I told her to take the rest of the night off and I'd talk to him. I was sure it was all a misunderstanding, but last night a different waitress made the same complaint. I tried talking to him after that, but he wasn't paying attention. Acted distracted. Then I saw him follow Rachel back to the break room. Now the door's locked."

"*Kent Galion?*" Grant found it hard to believe. Kent owned Velocity, among other clubs in Westwood and the surrounding area, and he was a respectable citizen,

one of L.A.'s top businessmen, even voted Most Eligible
Bachelor by one of the local magazines a few years back.

"Normally I wouldn't be worried, he's generally a nice
guy, but there were three complaints, and then Ike said
he wasn't acting like himself tonight. Thought he might
be sick or something."

"Three complaints?"

"Stephanie said he'd propositioned her Monday night.
On Wednesday she left early; I told her to get her head
on straight. I feel bad, but Kent? She hasn't come back,
missed her shift tonight. I probably pissed her off."

Grant tried the door. "Key?"

"I tried. Something's blocking the door."

"Call nine-one-one. Get Ike and try to get in this way.
I'm going to grab Reggie and go around the alley."

Grant ran back through the club and tagged the
bouncer, appreciating the 300-pound, six feet three
inches of solid black muscle for backup. "There's trouble in the alley," he said in a low voice. Reggie didn't
question, just followed.

They sprinted down the alley, Grant in the lead. Hearing a woman scream, he picked up speed.

In the cone of light under the security lights above the
employee entrance, he saw Kent yank a woman back behind a dumpster and backhand her. He didn't have time
to think about why Kent Galion, a man he'd known so-
cially for years, was attacking a woman. It made no
sense—drugs? Alcohol? Likely both, but he'd never seen
Kent drink, let alone do drugs.

Grant shouted, "Freeze! Police! Freeze, Galion!"

Kent didn't hear him, and instantly Grant thought
PCP. Kent's pants were down around his ankles and he

held Rachel tightly to him. A completely fucked situation. But Grant had to get the girl to safety. He didn't see a weapon in Kent's hands, but that didn't mean he didn't have a small knife or gun.

"Kent!" Grant shouted.

Kent turned to him, eyes wild and sweat beading on his brow, his expression not unlike that of a trapped animal—odd, considering he was the predator and the waitress was the prey.

Grant rushed and tackled Kent as if he were back playing college football, slamming the bastard onto the rough concrete alleyway. They rolled, and Grant winced as his shoulder twisted beneath him, but he didn't let Kent up. He maneuvered on top and took advantage of Kent's vulnerable position of wearing no pants to slam a knee into the asshole's groin and hold it there. "You fucking pervert," Grant growled at him. "What were you thinking?"

He didn't have his handcuffs on him, but he rolled Kent onto his stomach and stood, pulling his gun and pointing it at Galion's head. "Don't move."

He glanced over his shoulder. Reggie had taken off his T-shirt and put it on the half-nude waitress, his beefy arm around her. "Rachel?" Grant said. "You okay?"

She was bleeding from a head wound and pale as a ghost, eyes wide, her entire body shaking while she cradled her broken arm. In shock or close to it.

"You got him?" Reggie asked.

"Keep her warm," Grant told Reggie as he turned his attention back to Kent Galion.

Galion wasn't moving. Shit, shit, *shit*!

"Officer Nelson?" Reggie said.

Grant ignored the bouncer and squatted next to

Galion, feeling for a pulse with one hand, his entire body tense. At first he couldn't feel anything, then realized that the pulse was so rapid he couldn't count individual beats. Kent was hot as a furnace.

"Dammit, Kent, what shit are you on?" he muttered.

Julie and Ike came out through the back door. "A table blocked the—" Ike saw Galion on the ground. "My God, what happened?"

"What was he drinking?" Drugs and alcohol were a piss-poor combination.

"Club soda."

"He's cranked on something." Grant had seen enough perps on PCP and meth and a dozen other hard-core narcotics to know an OD when he saw one. "Get wet towels, he's burning up; make sure an ambulance is on the way. Tell them possible drug overdose. Did you call nine-one-one?"

Julie nodded, then went to Rachel and took the traumatized barmaid from Reggie.

"He followed me, Julie, he was looking at me all night, he said—he said I'd agreed to have sex!" Rachel sobbed. "I didn't, I didn't do anything to make him think that, I swear Julie, I didn't—"

"Shh, I know, honey, it's okay. It's going to be okay," Julie said as she led the girl back into the club.

Grant grabbed the towels that Ike had brought out and tried to get Galion's temperature down.

Don't you dare croak. Don't do it.

Galion began to convulse.

"Where's the damn ambulance?" Grant demanded a moment before he heard the sirens.

Kent Galion died en route to the hospital.

ONE

Present Day

Moira O'Donnell woke up with blood on her hands.

Her heart raced as she sat upright in the strange bed, staring at the dark-red blood *drip, drip, dripping* onto the white sheets, disappearing as each thick drop spread. She swallowed the scream that fought to escape.

She blinked and the blood was gone. The panicked rage faded. She almost—almost, but not quite—forgot the feeling of her hand clenching the heavy, balanced dagger. Almost forgot the sickening sound of the blade slicing through tendons, hitting bone, cutting out an invisible soul and throwing it to demons that tore it to shreds, feeding.

It's not real. It's not real. It's not real.

She repeated the mantra, reminding herself that it was only a nightmare, that she'd certainly never killed a person.

The fear from the dream stayed; it always did. Moira lived with fear day in and day out, sometimes buried so deep she *almost* could believe it was gone. When she lied to herself.

As the nightmare faded, her vision blurred. The dim early morning light coming from the edges of the closed blinds looked cloudy and surreal, like her nightmare.

She felt a vision coming on . . . but that wasn't possible. She'd never been fully awake for a vision before; they'd always hit her in the moment of unease immediately following a nightmare, before she could claw her way back to consciousness.

She was awake—knew she was awake—but everything around her was foggy, while her mind started a movie she didn't want to see. Moira's gut reaction was to stop the onslaught of images, but she couldn't even if she'd tried. In a rush, her mind flooded with thoughts not her own, sights she'd never witnessed, feelings she'd never had. No vision had ever been anything like this. Not this physical sense of evil seeping into every pore, filling her until she wanted to scream.

She flew across the continent and back, tired. Bored. Frustrated. There were many places she could stay, but none of them appealed to her. It was all too easy. The desires of the body were weak, and she was anything but weak. She wanted freedom, but wasn't free. She wanted vengeance, and she could have it—have everything— when she was free.

Freedom! Her time was now. She grew stronger with each passing day.

Yet, her spirit was caught by something stronger than she. She resisted, angry. But she was tied to the earth, and the harder she fought, the weaker she became. Spinning, spinning, spinning out of control, shrinking . . .

A weak, dark-haired woman sat in the circle, waiting for her. She fought the entrapment, but she'd been in the astral plane, and her anchor had called her back.

Someone trapped her! She stretched and fought and vowed revenge on her captor. The mind that shared this body was foolish. She suppressed it. Brutally, without remorse.

Moira screamed as pain filled her head. For a split second, she thought she was possessed. She tasted the hot sulphur on her tongue, felt an evil presence under her skin; then it was gone. The vision, the pain, everything. Everything but the fear.

Her body shook violently. From the corner of her eye she saw movement—something was in her room. She jumped out of bed, knife in hand without even thinking about reaching under her pillow for her weapon. She held it in front of her to ward off dark magic or a demon, making quick, confident strides toward the enemy.

"Moira!"

Rafe. She swallowed, blinked, tried to regain her focus as she wobbled on her feet. He grabbed her wrist and her vision cleared. She had been inches from him. What if she'd hurt him? What if she'd been trapped in a vision and killed him?

"You were looking right at me, but you didn't see me," he said quietly.

She shook her head to clear her foggy mind and sat back heavily on the edge of her bed.

She had to get her mind wrapped around what had just happened. The nightmare, waking up, the vision— being only inches from Rafe before she recognized him.

Maybe she had been asleep. That made her more dangerous to those she cared about.

She'd been in Santa Louisa for nearly a month, but the last two weeks she'd been doing *nothing*. Anthony Zaccardi, Santa Louisa's own resident demonologist, had his books and research, trying to track down the Seven

Deadly Sins. Rafe had his physical therapy and retraining. And what did she have? Exercise until her body ached. Nightmares that reminded her of her deadly flaws. Visions almost daily for the past two weeks that left her drained and on edge. And *still* no trace of her mother, Fiona O'Donnell, or Fiona's lover, Matthew Walker. In the last seven years she'd never stayed in any one place this long, except when training to become a demon hunter at Olivet. At least there she'd worked her ass off, too exhausted to go stir-crazy.

"I'm okay," she said, but not fast enough.

Rafe didn't believe her, but he didn't need words to ask. He never did. His dark, bottomless blue eyes questioned her, compelling the truth from her lips.

"I had another vision," she admitted.

That she could say it out loud showed she'd accepted the fact she was a freak. She'd always known it, but now? Well, it sounded even crazier. But Rafe didn't think so, which was both comforting and scary as hell. They were so much alike . . . yet so different. She was scared to death of what might happen if she dropped her shields. There was no future for her; she couldn't lose her focus.

"I think . . ." How could she explain? "One of them— one of the demons—found a host." That wasn't quite right, but she didn't understand everything she'd felt and heard and thought. "Or something like that." It sounded lame. It *was* lame.

"Anthony doesn't believe they're seeking to possess anyone."

"Anthony doesn't know everything," she snapped.

Rafe walked over to the dresser and leaned against it,

crossing his arms over his chest. Already, two weeks after he miraculously awakened from his coma—if that's what it was that had kept him unconscious for ten weeks—he'd regained his color and much of his strength. They were staying at Anthony and Skye's place—hardly big enough for the four of them—with Rafe sleeping on the couch. She needed to get out of this place. Not just because she itched to find her mother again, but because the close proximity to Rafe was too distracting. Not to mention Anthony's need to control both of them day and night, and Skye's constant questions. Moira liked the cop, but there were some things better left outside of the law. If Sheriff Skye McPherson knew even half the laws Moira had broken . . .

Rafe *still* didn't say anything. Damn, how annoying was that? He just pinned her with his sharp eyes, his unshaven square jaw locked, waiting for her to tell him the truth.

"I know it's not possible," she began—*hoping* it wasn't possible—"I just—it felt—" She hesitated, then said what she truly feared. "It felt like I was looking through the demon's eyes. I tasted Hell on my tongue, my blood burned. But—I think—" She bit her lip.

"What?"

"She was pure evil, Rafe. Powerful. And really pissed off. She felt trapped, and somehow she blamed *me*." She gave him a half smile. "Stupid, I know."

Rafe didn't smile, nor did he say anything—why was he always so damn quiet? Why couldn't he get angry like Anthony or frustrated like Skye? Instead, he was *calm*.

"I won't let anyone hurt you, demon or human."

He barely whispered, but she heard every word as if his voice etched them directly onto her bones. Every hair on her skin rose. He appeared unflappable, but his stoicism was a ruse—he was a tightly controlled bundle of energy, his restlessness tangible but unseen. His words had movement and weight. He never had to raise his voice to be heard, and *everyone* listened.

She wanted to believe him. He meant what he said, but he wasn't strong enough to protect her—or anyone—from the Seven. Neither was she; none of them were. They'd nearly died battling the demon Envy, and they had even lost one of their own. A loss she feared would be repeated until there was no one left standing.

Despair had moved in with her fear, but she fought it, questioning whether they were her own feelings or left from residual contact with the Seven. Was their power still present even though they had long left Santa Louisa?

All but the demon Envy, trapped in a tabernacle at St. Francis de Sales in downtown Santa Louisa, in a vault that Moira had commented was the supernatural equivalent of Fort Knox. Anthony hadn't been amused. He never was.

But Rafe had smiled at her joke behind Anthony's back, and winked at her, another reason why she was drawn to him. He liked her quick wit, and he made her smile.

"For nearly two weeks, I've been doing nothing but waiting for something we can't even identify," she said. "How can we stop the Seven Deadly Sins if we don't know where they are? Do we have to wait until someone drops dead? Do we have to wait until we hear on the news that Greed is working its evil magic on Wall Street

or people are dying because they're too slothful to eat?
And dammit, where did Fiona go? I can't *feel* her magic
anymore. They're just *gone,* and I'm waiting for them to
come after me! And what if—"

She stopped. When had she become a sniveling brat?
She had to put the fear aside or it would bite her in the
ass. Yeah, she was worried—so was everyone else. She
had to stop feeling sorry for herself, accept her fate, and
move forward. Maybe if she repeated the mantra
enough she could make it happen.

"Moira, what is it?" Rafe asked, his concern apparent.

She gave voice to her hidden fear. Maybe by speaking
it aloud she could stop it from seeming so real. "What if
the Seven have infected me?"

He looked at her tenderly and shook his head. "They
haven't. *You* would know."

"But I *don't* know."

He smiled. "This is a silly conversation, Moira."

She shook her head, biting back a smile.

"I saw that," he said, and sat next to her. He took her
hand and kissed it. "Come on, smile."

Moira started to smile, mostly because Rafe could be
so endearing even when he annoyed her, but he kissed
her hand again, holding her palm to his lips a moment
too long. He stared at the scar from the demon attack
two weeks ago, the scar he'd given her to save them all,
and his face darkened. He squeezed her fingers tight, almost too tight, and pulled her to his chest.

She had no time to protest as Rafe's lips covered hers,
as one hand held hers between them and the other
pressed against her back, holding her still. She tried to

turn away, but his mouth followed, sliding down her cheek, to her neck, to the oh-so-sensitive spot behind her ear. A startled gasp escaped her throat and it sounded like she was enjoying this, like she wanted Rafe.

And she did. She'd been keeping her distance because every time she got too close, every time he touched her—innocently or not—she remembered that kiss. That damn, incredible, heated kiss two weeks ago that affected her so deeply that she *still* warmed at the memory.

It wasn't a memory anymore. It was happening again, only this time Rafe wasn't injured, and this time they weren't about to go to battle against a demon. She could make no excuses about the risk of the moment, the fears of life or death fueling their sex drive, because right now they sat in her bedroom—on her bed—and Rafe was not slowing down.

"Rafe—" Her voice cracked when his hand moved up under her shirt and touched her breast. Her body betrayed her, her hand shot out and wrapped around Rafe's neck, pulling his mouth back to hers. Waves of conflicting emotions, of lust and fear, of desire and doubt, battled. They shouldn't be doing this. Moira couldn't do this. There was too much at stake.

She refused to open her heart because Rafe could die. Worse, he could die because of her.

She'd already lost the first man she ever loved. She couldn't love again. And with Rafe, sex wouldn't be a hot and heavy one-night stand.

"Rafe—" Resolved, she put her hands between them and pushed. Hard. He got the point and let her go, a frown hardening his handsome face.

"I, um—" she stuttered, her face flushed. "You want to go to the gym?" That was lame. She swallowed nervously, took a deep breath, and regained her composure. "Well?"

"Every time I get close to you, you take me to the gym. Or for a run. Anything to avoid talking about what you feel when I touch you. What I feel when I think of you. Why I can't get you out of my mind. You look at me when you think I'm sleeping. I know you're worried. About what?"

"This isn't the time—"

"It's never the time for you," Rafe said, frustrated.

Movement in the hall startled her, Moira jumped when Anthony appeared in the bedroom doorway. What if he'd walked by two minutes ago? He did not like Moira and Rafe spending time together. Did he suspect they had this attraction? He looked as if he hadn't slept the night before, with bags under his bloodshot eyes. Anthony had been clocking a lot of hours at the mission reading old books, many handwritten and in ancient languages.

"Rico's plane just landed," he said. "He'll be here in twenty minutes." He glanced at Rafe. "I need to talk to you."

She raised an eyebrow at Anthony. "Secrets already?"

He didn't answer her.

She pushed by him. "Whatever. I'm going for a run."

"Be back in twenty minutes," he repeated.

Moira paused, staring at Anthony. She wanted to say so much to him—that she was sorry about everything that had happened seven years ago, that she missed Father Philip as much as he did, that she wished he'd trust her, that she needed his experience if they were going to stop the Seven Deadly Sins.

But he wouldn't even look at her, the distrust and dislike rolling off him. He hated her. He'd never admit it; it would be so un-Christian for him to *hate* anyone. She didn't know why his disdain hurt so damn much.

Moira left the house and set off on her jog at a brisk, steady pace, pushing aside Anthony's animosity, her growing and unwanted feelings for Rafe, and her confusion over her most recent vision. She focused on running, breathing, one foot ahead of the other. As she ran, her head began to clear.

She loved to run through the early morning fog, the cold, damp sea air burning and cleansing her lungs as if she were running through purgatory, pain and pleasure. She'd been staying at Skye and Anthony's for two weeks now and knew the cliffs along the shore almost as well as she knew the paths at Olivet, where she'd lived for more than a year.

But even now, she couldn't think of herself as a demon hunter, because the only reason she'd been trained to banish demons from Earth was to clear the field to pursue her mother, the evil witch who used demons and magic to protect herself from St. Michael's Order. Moira, in turn, had to be able to protect herself from whatever her mother—or her half sister—tossed her way so she could live to battle them again.

As she ran she realized she was heading north, toward the ruins two miles away where it had all started. Two weeks ago Fiona had cracked open the gates of Hell long enough to release the Seven Deadly Sins, incarnate demons who should never have been allowed to escape the bowels of the underworld.

Moira had been to the ruins only once after she'd found Rafe hiding in a nearby cabin, though she knew Anthony often ventured out here alone. But he didn't see what she saw; he didn't feel the evil slithering over every cell in his body like she did when she neared the ruins.

She felt as if she were drowning in evil, sinking lower and lower until demons could grab her soul and torture her until the end of time. It was enough to drive most people crazy. Maybe only the truly deranged would endlessly fight demons in a losing battle. Normal people—sane people—certainly didn't seek out incarnate evil.

As Moira neared the ruins, she saw evergreen bushes that had turned black, and the cypress trees that dotted the central coast going from canopies of dark winter green to shriveled, leafless, gnarled wood. There were no birds chirping, no animals scurrying under the dead bushes. Three dead seagulls lay rotting near the edge of where the coven's circle had been cast. Had they flown too close to the evil that still radiated from the ground? Were they thrown off course, or dragged down against their will?

Moira realized one thing about her visions: they almost always led her back *here,* to the ruins. She'd been fighting them for two weeks, but this morning's vision had brought her here. There was something she could learn from the scorched earth.

While the residual dark magic had all but disappeared, due largely to Anthony's daily prayers over this spot, evil remained. Here, the gateway to Hell could be opened without much effort. And not just here—there was a new gateway at the former Good Shepherd Church, courtesy of Matthew Walker. Santa Louisa was becoming a beacon for evil. Moira wouldn't be surprised if some trickster demon changed the welcome sign on the highway:

WELCOME TO SATAN'S LOUISA
HOME OF THE SEVEN DEADLY SINS

All remnants of the coven's circle were gone. No more hexagram, no more spells, no more candles or herbs. But Moira knew where the center had been and avoided it, as if she could be dragged down into the pit right then and there.

Here, the Seven Deadly Sins had been released from Hell and if not for Rafe, they would have been trapped in the *arca,* a flesh-and-blood person who Fiona was happy to sacrifice to the underworld for her own selfish plans for immortality. As long as Fiona O'Donnell lived forever, everyone else could die.

"I'll find you, Fiona," Moira whispered into the still fog. "I'll find you and kill you."

She breathed deeply, focusing all her senses the way Rico had taught her. Looking within and around, not calling on supernatural forces for answers, because the price was always higher than any human should have to pay; instead, she relaxed, Psalm 23 running quietly, automatically, through her mind. Natural forces surrounded her, trying to provide answers when Moira didn't even know the right question to ask.

As I walk through the dark valley . . .

Of course she had plenty of questions. *Where is Fiona? Where is her coven? Why can't I find her?*

Moira walked around the edge of where the circle had been, focusing all internal thought, her whole senses, into her vision from this morning. Her visions always related to Fiona. At least, until two weeks ago, they'd always led her to where Fiona *had* been.

Her mother must have been involved in whatever demonic ritual resulted in that dark-haired woman being possessed in her vision. While Moira's visions scared her, they were invariably grounded in what was happening on Earth and she could use them to seek answers. The vision this morning felt more intense, as if she were a participant and not just an observer.

Could it be her visions were less about Fiona and more about the demons that Fiona brought forth? This morning she'd been looking through the eyes of the demon. She'd been terrified and tried to avoid seeing anything, but it was there in the back of her mind.

Do not be afraid.

She heard Father Philip's quiet, deep voice as if the priest were standing beside her. She blinked back sudden tears. Father wouldn't want her wallowing in self-pity and fear; he'd expect her to suck it up and do what needed to be done. Right now that meant analyzing her vision, focusing on what she'd seen but failed to process because of her fear.

She'd seen what the demon saw. The dark-haired woman. Where was she? In a business. There were other people around. No one Moira could see clearly, but she felt the voices—music—vibrating in the background. Voices . . . people . . . dancing . . . drinking. A club. A place where people went to see and be seen, to find a one-night stand when they lied to themselves that they were looking for true love.

Moira never lied to herself. She'd found her one true love and now he was dead. One-night stands had been all that had kept her physically connected to the rest of humanity, fortunate souls who didn't live their lives wrapped in guilt and the terrifying knowledge of things Moira wished she'd never known. That monsters—

demons—were real; that ghosts were lost souls and some were out for revenge; that magic came from Hell and no matter what your intentions, you had to pay the piper in blood. The piper's name was Satan.

The hair on the back of her neck rose and her skin tingled. She might have believed it was a chill from standing still too long after running, but she knew better.

Someone was watching her. Approaching her. Getting closer.

She opened her eyes, pulled her knife from her pocket, and whirled around.

Rico Cortese grabbed her wrist as she was about to cut him. "I thought you'd forgotten everything I taught you."

"I would have pulled back in time." She hoped.

"I know." The Olivet instructor assessed her with a half smile. "At least you're still in one piece, kid."

"So are you," she replied.

He wore all black and looked more like a Mafia thug than a man of God. His dark Italian complexion was marred by a scar across his temple, and he was built like a Marine. Moira supposed it was to be expected, since Rico led St. Michael's version of Special Forces. Not so much an army for God as an army against Satan.

Rico gave her a tight hug, then kissed her on the cheek. "It's good to see you. I've been worried."

"Like you said, I'm in one piece."

She'd forgotten how much she loved Rico, even if she'd wanted to kill him—often—during training. He'd forced her to work harder, think deeper, and feel far too much, all to break her apart and mold her into a warrior. In the end, when she thought she'd been torn apart one too many times and would never be anything but a pawn in a game she didn't understand, he showed her that she was stronger than she'd believed possible.

But it was hugely different, and ten times harder, being in the actual battle than training for a hypothetical one. People didn't die during training, and now there were no second chances.

He stepped back and she asked, "How did you know I was here?"

"I didn't. I came here first so I could see the ruins first-hand."

"And what are your conclusions?"

He looked around the cliffs. "I know you're standing outside where the circle was cast by Fiona's coven. I saw where the plants began to die. I know there were demons here—powerful demons—by the evidence. The corruption of the soil, the dead earth. But"—he stared at her gravely—"I don't sense Hell. I don't feel the heat or see the rivers of fire. I'm aware of the evil because of what I see—it's overwhelming if you know the signs—but that is nothing compared to what *you* feel."

"How do you know what I feel?" she whispered.

"Before he was killed, Father Philip told me every-thing. There are no secrets. All I have to do is look at you and see the fear in your eyes."

Her hands clenched and unclenched as she shifted her weight from the right to the left foot. Rico watched her fidget, himself standing still as a statue. It always made her nervous how Rico saw deeper inside her than she wanted. "Fear is your worst enemy, Moira. You need to take control of your emotions."

"I can't." She gritted her teeth. "You weren't there."

He hadn't been talking about the ruins and neither was she. One mention of Father Philip and she was mentally transported back to their battle against the demon Envy.

"You're not the first person to have faced an incarnate demon."

"Well, that takes away the warm fuzzies. I no longer feel special."

"You forget I know you."

"I haven't forgotten." He knew her weaknesses and doubts, what made her cry and what made her angry. She hated that.

"Show me your arm," he demanded.

She put her hand on her hip. "No *please*? Where are your manners?"

He stared. Without humor, he said, "Please."

Her heart was racing. Why did she care if he saw the scar? Why did she care what he thought, or if she'd screwed up? He might banish her, he might hate her, but he wouldn't kill her. At least she didn't think he'd kill her.

She angrily took off her jacket and dropped it to the ground. In the cold salt air, goose bumps rose from her sweaty skin. She held out her arm and Rico took her hand, turned it so he could inspect her injury. Considering the ferocity of the attack, it was amazing that there were only two small, round scars; one on her wrist and one near the inside of her elbow, where the demon's jagged teeth had punctured deep into her flesh. The marks were faded as if she'd hurt herself as a kid—not been bitten by a rabid demon dog just two weeks ago.

"Tell me what happened."

"I told you—"

He squeezed her wrist. "Everything."

She jerked her arm away. "I did my research and figured out where Fiona was keeping Rafe. I found him in a double demon trap—Rafe was locked in a circle to protect him from the demon dog, and the demon was trapped in the room circling him, to prevent Rafe from leaving."

"What did the demon look like?"

"Ugly as sin. Like a Cerberus, but with one head. Four legs, but his tail wasn't wagging. It was spiked, like a stumpy dragon tail with thorns. I ran through his domain and into the trap with Rafe. I had to get Rafe out before Fiona returned. Not to mention that Fiona and her band of merry magicians were setting up their own ritual to regain control of the Seven. I stabbed the beast with a poison dart. He croaked, but not before the hellion bit me."

"What happened to your arm at that point?"

"It hurt like it was being burned in the fucking flames of Hell. What else?" Her breathing quickened as Rico drew out her anger. Meanwhile, he was a damn emotional iceberg. He had to be. He'd tried to train her to be just as cool but failed in that regard. She'd never learned to perfect the hard, uncaring exterior that most Olivet graduates maintained.

He didn't respond. She closed her eyes, picturing herself back in the middle of that round room that had reeked of sulphur and rot. "It bit me as I plunged the poison dart into its chest. It convulsed and died in the corner. And no matter what Anthony says, it was dead, not just unconscious. And don't ask me why it didn't turn to ash or disappear into the underworld—I don't know, and at the time I didn't think about it because we had more pressing issues."

"Your arm?"

"It hurt, it bled, it bubbled like acid. I wrapped it in a shirt, then Rafe and I got the hell out of Dodge. When I took the shirt off, it was—well, the little teeth marks were mostly gone, and *poof*! I had these two deep red punctures. By the next day they were scars, and now they're like this."

There was an awkward silence as he fully concentrated.

"Show me your hand."

"Hand?"

"Don't be obtuse. The hand that Raphael cut open and stuffed in the demon Envy's gut."

She felt the blood drain from her face. Rico Cortese was watching her, observant as a hawk. She held out her left hand and he took firm hold of her wrist.

Rafe hadn't cut through any tendons and the throbbing pain had disappeared, but she'd have a scar for life—unlike the scars on her arm, which would soon completely vanish.

He stared for a long minute. Moira snapped, "Take a fucking picture."

Rico dropped her hand, removed a small box from his inside jacket pocket, and handed it to her. "Open it."

She did. Inside was a syringe and vial. Before she quite knew what he intended to do, Rico took a rubber tie from his pocket.

"What?" Moira began, looking from the syringe to Rico, then back again. "You—want my blood?"

"Please make a fist."

Moira didn't want to comply. Tears burned in her eyes. "What's going on?" she demanded. Rico tied the rubber around her upper arm, tapped her vein, rubbed an alcohol wipe over the spot, and inserted the needle. Blood flowed into a vial.

He wasn't going to tell her. She hated him right then. What a fool she was! A guinea pig, a lab rat, for what she didn't even know. Why had she done any of this? Why hadn't she just run away after Peter died and never returned to St. Michael's? Never gone to Olivet? She could have fought Fiona on her own terms, and so what if Moira had died and gone to Hell? At least she would have taken Fiona with her. Peter's death would have been avenged. Now Moira was tied to St. Michael's Order, and they wanted her blood.

Rico released the rubber strap. "Relax."

"Right." She swallowed heavily as he swapped out one vial and replaced it with another empty tube. He took three samples, put them in the box, closed it, and put it back in his jacket. She glared at him. "What are you going to do with my blood?"

Rico's expression softened just a fraction, and she knew him well enough to read that he regretted what he had to do.

But duty always won.

"I'm proud of you," Rico said as he put a small Band-Aid over the puncture.

That was the last thing she'd expected him to say. She put her jacket back on.

"You didn't answer my question." Moira's imagination ran the gamut of possibilities. Did she have some demonic virus? Had the demon infected her when it bit her? Or when Rafe sliced open her hand? Did they think the Seven Deadly Sins had affected her or her judgment? Were they working on a cure? She almost laughed at the thought, as if St. Michael's would look beyond their battle toward a medical cure for losing one's soul to a demon.

"I don't have the answers you want."

He turned away, signaling the conversation was over. She almost pushed him—verbally and physically. She wanted answers, and she'd fight to get them. But there was something subtle in Rico's expression that had her backing down.

Instead of pushing, she said, "We should go back. I'm sure Anthony is wondering why you're late."

"I'm not late."

She glanced at her watch. "He said twenty minutes—oh, about forty minutes ago."

"Anthony will wait." He turned back to face her. "Your emotions are dangerous not only to you, Moira, but to others. You care far too much. In our war, casualties are unfortunate but necessary. You can't think logically if you act solely on your feelings or your loyalties are divided. There is a balance; you must find it. I thought I'd taught you better."

"And you can forget Father Philip that easily? *Snap*, no feelings? No damn *grief*? I'm still human, just the way God made me, *right*?"

Rico reddened. She'd rarely seen him react to her needling. "I will say this once. I loved Father Philip and I grieve for our loss." His voice quivered on the last sentence; then he said with firmness, "But I will not allow pain, sorrow, hatred, or rage to stop me from my sacred duty."

Moira touched his arm, wishing she hadn't pushed him. "I know you cared; I was out of line."

He dipped his head and squeezed her fingers. "I cannot expect you to control your emotions any better than you have. You weren't raised on the island."

In other words, she was an outsider. Loneliness washed over her. Why did she think something had changed? Why did she think she belonged? She was as alone now as she'd been the day Peter died. One year of bliss in a lifetime filled with pain, loss, and violence.

"I must ask you," he continued, "did Raphael use magic?"

Another unexpected question. Rico was full of surprises.

She answered as truthfully as she could, but still felt as though she was betraying both Rafe and Rico. She didn't want to lie, but what was the truth?

"I don't know." She didn't like the look on Rico's face. Though he didn't display any emotion she could identify, she knew Rico well enough to know that he was concerned about something—almost *worried*. Very unlike him. "Why do you think he did?"

"I read Anthony's report. There are questions. Anthony may be too close to Raphael to . . . be impartial. And he doesn't understand magic like you do."

"There was so much magic flying around I could barely discern individual spells, let alone who was wielding the power. It was awful." She paused, then asked Rico the question that had been on her mind since the moment she first saw him. That it effectively changed the subject was an added benefit. "Have you heard anything about Fiona? Where she's hiding?"

He shook his head. "You will be the first to know, Moira. I can search for her all I want, but you'll be the one to find her. You know that. For seven years, you've been the only one who could."

"Oh, joy."

He took both her hands and held them. How unlike Rico, showing compassion. "I am not going to lie to you, Moira. Our war will get harder. Defeating Fiona is only part of the whole. You must destroy the *Conoscenza*."

"That damn book!" She looked around at the dead earth. That book—the Book of Knowledge, the ancient *grimoire* filled with spells allegedly written in demon blood—was supposed to have been destroyed more than a century ago. But Fiona had searched for it and found it, believing it would give her the key to immortality. And perhaps it would. Fiona didn't care about the cost; she didn't care about anything but her own selfish desires. The Seven Deadly Sins she'd released from Hell were only the beginning, and Moira would do everything in her power to stop her.

Except use magic. Her attempt to stop Fiona with magic before had left the only person she'd ever loved dead, and Moira herself somehow connected to the underworld in ways she certainly didn't understand. She doubted even Rico or Father Philip understood. Which was why everyone was wary around her. Suspicious, like Anthony.

"Have you figured out how I'm supposed to get rid of this book?"

"No. But Dr. Lieber has agreed to meet with Anthony. We hope to have answers very soon."

She should be happy with the news, but the way Rico said it, a blanket of foreboding suffocated her.

"Terrific!" she said with fake enthusiasm. "I can hardly wait."

"Moira, please be careful."

"Always." She winked at him. "I'm running back to the house. See if you can keep up."

She ran, not waiting for an answer to her unspoken challenge, sure he wasn't telling her everything, but not knowing whether it was because he didn't want to or whether his silence was due to orders from a higher power. She wished she knew exactly who was calling the shots. She hated being a pawn.

Either way, Rico was keeping secrets from her and those secrets were going to hurt her.

Or get her killed.

TWO

After seventeen years on the force, the last nine as detective, Detective Grant Nelson trusted his gut instincts. They were rarely wrong. While he would wait for the evidence, Grant was confident that the death of George Erickson was the result of sex games turned deadly.

Grant assessed the murder scene. Private home in upscale Westwood, wife out for the night with friends, bedroom set up for a romantic tryst with candles, champagne, and the sultry voice of Patsy Cline playing in the background.

And of course the dead guy, on his back buck naked on the fully made bed, with no visible cause of death. Heart attack or OD; Grant opted for heart attack because there was no vomit or signs of violent convulsions, no obvious signs of drug use or abuse. Did the mistress panic and bail? If so, they'd probably pick up her prints. Or did Erickson collapse from the exhaustion of his sexcapade? Walk the woman out, then drop dead of a heart attack? Or maybe the wife caught him sleeping off a drunk, realized she hadn't been the recipient of the mood music and champagne, and suffocated him with a pillow. Whichever scenario, they had some legwork ahead of them to put together the pieces. This was the part of police work Grant enjoyed—the puzzle.

"Only one glass of champagne." Grant's new partner,

Jeff Johnston, walked slowly around the room. Johnston, who looked like the football lineman he'd been in college, had been a uniformed officer in the Devonshire Division before his recent promotion. He peered into the trash can in the corner. "Scratch that. There's another glass in a million pieces. Think CSI can put Humpty Dumpty back together again and print it?"

Grant stared at the shattered crystal. Why toss the glass? Another puzzle piece for him to fit. Not reporting the death is one thing; covering up her identity quite another. Could be a hooker with a rap sheet.

CSI and the deputy coroner arrived. Grant and Jeff left them to process the scene while they sought out the deceased's wife. Officer Ann Timmons had been consoling Mrs. Pamela Erickson. She stood and approached them when Grant and Jeff entered the living room.

She rolled her eyes. "Good luck."

Odd, Grant thought as Timmons met up with her partner on the front porch.

Pamela Erickson was pretty—though on the skinny side—with red-rimmed eyes and her long brown hair up in the back. She was pissed off.

"Who's the bimbo that walked out on my husband?" she demanded. "What woman *does* that? Walks out on someone who's dying?"

Grant sized her up. He'd interviewed hundreds of next-of-kin and he'd seen all sorts of reactions to death. But this was a shade different. Why did the wife assume Erickson was dying while his mistress was still in the room?

"We don't know for certain that anyone was here with your husband," he said, though he didn't believe that for a minute. "Or, if someone was here, whether Mr. Er-ickson was dead before or after she left."

She stared at him. "You can't be that dense—I found him. I saw the bedroom. *Someone* was with George last night and it wasn't me!"

"Did you know your husband was having an affair?"

She laughed, a tinge of bitterness lacing her humor. "He wasn't having an *affair*. He was fucking around. Of course I knew it. He wouldn't screw around behind my back."

Swingers. Married couples who had an agreement they'd sleep around. Grant knew something about that. He'd never seen it end well—it sure as hell hadn't worked for him and his failed marriage—but it was accepted practice these days among the movers and shakers in L.A., and had spread to suburbia. "Do you know who he was with last night?"

"No."

"And I'm guessing you weren't out with friends?"

She glared at him. "I'm not going to be judged by a *cop* on how George and I lived. We *respected* each other, which is a hell of a lot more than I can say about some marriages!"

"If there's anything suspicious about your husband's death," Grant said, "I'll need to verify your alibi."

It may have hit Pamela Erickson at that moment that maybe her husband *hadn't* died of natural causes. Her lower lip trembled and she swallowed, looking from Grant to Jeff and back to Grant. "Someone hurt him on purpose? B-But, George?"

"Was he well liked?"

"Everyone loved George! He's the nicest guy on the planet. He makes me laugh, which is why I married him.

We have a good time. We like each other. The sex is good. We're *happy*. People love him at work. He's a lawyer—not stuffy and stuck-up, but a good lawyer."

"Criminal defense?"

She blinked, not expecting the question. "No. Copyright law. He works for musicians and indie labels, to protect artists from piracy. He loves music. That's why he goes to—"

She stopped, and Jeff prompted. "Goes where, Mrs. Erickson?"

"Velocity. A club in Westwood that has up-and-coming bands playing Thursday nights. I usually go with him, it's our night out, but my ex-husband came to town unexpectedly and George told me to go out with Adam."

Tears fell. They seemed real, but Grant was cynical—he couldn't rule out Pamela Erickson as a suspect until he verified her statement and alibi. "George never brought anyone home before. This was our place. Adam and I went back to his hotel. If I had been with George instead, he would still be alive." She sobbed. "I'm going to miss him so much."

Grant abruptly walked out while Jeff gave the standard thanks, got her contact information, and followed him.

Velocity.

Shit.

"What's going on, Grant?" Jeff's posture was casual, but his eyes were all cop and looking closely at Grant. Was he acting that guilty? And hell, what was he guilty of? He was single and he had been off duty last night. And just because he went to the club didn't mean he had gone there to get laid. Even if he did get laid.

"Hell if I know," Grant said. "Could be just what it looks like." But something seemed . . . not what it looked like.

"You're thinking something."

"Did you hear about that college kid who died half-naked in the alley behind Velocity Wednesday night?"

"The case Cole Pierce pulled?"

"Yeah. I'll call Pierce, see if there are other similarities. Two deaths in two nights? Both patrons of the same club?"

"But that was a frat boy; this guy's a respected lawyer."

Grant stared at the wall without seeing anything. Just a week ago Velocity's owner, Kent Galion, had been pumped up on something unidentifiable and died after attacking a waitress.

"Do you think there's a connection?" Jeff asked. It made no sense, but *damn* it was a strange coincidence. "Maybe they knew each other."

It was something to consider, but from what Grant remembered hearing from the night watch was that there was nothing unusual about the college student's death. It was being looked at as an OD . . . yet that's exactly what Grant was thinking about Erickson. OD or heart attack. What if someone was dealing bad drugs out of Velocity? Julie was going to have a shit fit, but Grant realized he couldn't tell her about it. He'd have to talk to Narcotics, see if they were looking into something—and push the damn coroner's office off their asses and give him the tox screen on the frat boy. Pierce would be happy to share with Grant—anything to get out from under their towering workload.

Grant said, "I was at Velocity last night. I didn't see

anything and don't recognize the victim. I got there late and walked Julie out. After Galion lost his head last week, I've been worried about her safety."

"I thought you and Julie broke up."

He shrugged, avoiding looking his partner in the eye. "We're friendly. She might know who Erickson went off with—she has a good eye, but if there's a connection, we need to keep Julie out of it. If this is a drug case, we'll need to bring in the narcs."

"What if the motive is financial?" Jeff looked around the house and whistled. "Erickson was loaded."

"We'll talk to the widow, make sure nothing is missing, check into his finances. I'll talk to Pierce, get him to bump the other case to us, and you can follow up on the money angle. I'll talk to Narcotics. And it might help our case if we go down to the morgue and put some pressure on whoever is doing the autopsy on our stiff. See if I can rush both reports and expand the drug and tox screenings."

If there was a connection, the coroner could prioritize the bloodwork and additional tests. If the cases were drug related, they could get the DEA or FBI involved, get them to pay some of the lab costs. And the FBI lab had greater capabilities than Los Angeles.

Jeff looked at his notes. "Wife says Erickson left the house just before eight to catch the first set of a new band, told her to enjoy herself with her ex-husband and he'd see her in the morning. That told her, according to Mrs. Erickson, that either he expected her to screw her ex or he would be out screwing."

"She said that?"

"Not in so many words," Jeff said. "I read between the lines."

"You don't approve."

"It's not my job to approve or disapprove."

"But?" Grant prompted.

"I don't get them." Jeff glanced over his shoulder to make sure the wife couldn't hear him, and said in a low voice, "She never said she loved him. She *liked* him. She *respected* him. He made her laugh. But everyone else *loved* George Erickson. No one would want to kill him. Why get married?"

Grant didn't want to tread into that territory. Jeff was still new to the Pacific Division; he probably didn't know Grant's reputation, however deserved it was . . . or wasn't.

Why did he care what the big black ex-jock thought of him? They didn't have to be friends. Jeff was a decent cop, with sharp instincts; Grant liked working with him because he *appeared* to be a dumb jock, and the appearance loosened people—especially suspects—into talking. It helped. But Jeff was anything but a dumb cop, and Grant didn't want anyone scrutinizing his life. Maybe because he didn't like looking too closely at it himself.

"I did marriage once," Grant said, trying to lighten the conversation, though he felt as if the weight of the world was on his shoulders and he didn't know why. "Didn't work out. I'm through."

"Cynical much?" Jeff joked.

"You got a few years under your belt answering domestic calls. Is there any such thing as a perfect marriage?"

"Doubt it," Jeff said, "but my parents have been married for forty-two years and I still catch them copping a feel when they don't think anyone's looking."

"Too much, Johnston." They walked out front where the deputy coroner pushed George Erickson's body, tucked and zipped into a black body bag, to the meat wagon.

What happened last night, George? Too much fun for the ticker?

"Hey, Nelson!" Timmons approached. "Just got a call in from Glendale PD wanting to talk to you."

"About what?" He didn't have any active cases that crossed into Glendale's jurisdiction.

"A stiff found in some dude's freezer. The detective in charge said you might want to come over—the house is Kent Galion's and the dead woman is Stephanie Frazier, a waitress from Velocity."

If people had told a younger Fern Archer that she'd not only work at the morgue but *like* her job, she'd have laughed them right out the door, telling them to sober up. *She* was going to be a photographer, thank you very much, and she didn't like dead things.

Shows what you really know about yourself when you're a kid.

Ironically, it was her love of photography that had landed her in the morgue in the first place, when she trailed a pathologist for an assignment called "Day in the Life." Don Takasugi hadn't wanted a smart-ass black girl with a nose ring in *his* lab, regardless of the coroner's agreement with Pierce College, and he'd gone out of his way to shock her.

Instead, Fern had found her true calling. For all of Don's antics that day, when she saw the compassion and respect he showed for the dead, it reminded her of her Grandpa T-Rex—nicknamed such because of his temper and build—who was as mean as a pit bull, except when he cared for her dying grandmother.

The next week she signed up for an internship at the morgue. She got her AA in human biology, and Don hired her a year later. He still tried to shock her with his dark humor, and though he was her toughest critic—both of her job and her photography—she also knew that she was his favorite.

"What are you doing?" Don's voice broke into her thoughts.

Fern jumped and nearly dropped her camera. She glanced around the morgue's intake room, where she was processing the latest arrival, laid out on a gurney in front of her. "He just came in. Wife found him naked and dead in their bedroom after an apparent night of hanky-panky."

"What are you doing with the camera?" he asked again as if she needed clarification, rather than simply more time to come up with a plausible lie.

"I'm just . . ." She bit her lip. "It's the birthmark." She couldn't lie to save her soul. Her mama always told her that when she lied, her skin darkened. Fern didn't know how that was possible—her skin was quite black naturally, thank you very much—but her mama always seemed to know exactly when Fern was lying.

"What about it?"

"It's pretty darn near the same mark as the guy who came in yesterday morning *and* the guy who came in Friday night with the brain."

"The brain" was an intriguing case because Don hadn't seen anything quite like the enlarged brain stem, and if Don hadn't seen it before, Fern certainly hadn't. While the guy's body had been cremated, his brain was stored in a room off the main floor, awaiting the neuro specialist who came in twice a month to inspect unusual brains, primarily for genetic abnormalities.

"The same birthmark?" Don asked skeptically. "We had dozens of bodies come through here yesterday."

"Forty-seven," she said without even thinking. "And I thought I'd seen the mark before, thought it was a tat. Now?"

"It has to be a tattoo," Don said. "Identical birthmarks? Unlikely."

Damn near impossible. She showed him the backside of her camera and flipped through photos until she came to the digital copy of the birthmark she'd taken before "the brain" was sent for cremation. "See?" She put the camera next to the corpse's body.

The supervising pathologist frowned. "Test it for ink."

"Been there, done that."

He glanced at her sharply. "Why? It's not protocol."

"Remember that memo we got two weeks ago?"

"You'll need to be more specific, Ms. Archer."

She inwardly cringed at his irritated tone. "From the Santa Louisa Coroner's Office. To contact them if a body came through with an unusual birthmark. They attached a photo."

"That wasn't the same image."

Not *exactly,* but to Fern it was just too weird. And the fact that Don had remembered it without prompting told her that he also thought the whole thing was bizarre. "Have you ever seen a birthmark that looked like this? Even a little bit?" She looked at him with what her daddy called her *Yes, Fern, anything you want* gaze. "Do you want to call Santa Louisa or should I?"

He shook his head, and she thought she was going to have to dig in her heels. She didn't want to go above Don—she didn't know if she would—she just wanted him to let her run with it. It seemed important to her.

"Go ahead," he finally said, "but we have bodies stacking up in the crypt, so put the camera away and get back to work as soon as you hang up the phone."

THREE

Rafe hadn't heard Moira laugh often enough in the two weeks he'd known her, so when she entered laughing through the sliding glass doors into the kitchen, he turned with a smile.

He froze when he saw Rico Cortese running two steps behind her.

"Beat you!" Moira exclaimed as she stepped across the threshold.

"You cheated," Rico said, his voice serious but his eyes not quite as hardened as Rafe remembered. Rico smiled—actually *smiled*—at Moira.

"Yes I did, and I won." She raised an eyebrow. "I'm surprised you didn't catch on, considering I simply used one of your own tricks on you."

"I didn't teach you that particular maneuver."

She shrugged. "I improvised." She winked at Rafe. "Victory is *so* sweet. I'm going to shower and then—"

Anthony stepped into the kitchen and told Moira, "You're late." He then spotted Rico. For a moment he seemed perplexed that Moira and Rico had come in together; then he said, "Rico—good to see you again."

"We have some time," Rico said. "I had a stop to make."

Behind Anthony, Skye entered the room. Anthony's

girlfriend was pretty in a no-nonsense kind of way—long blond hair pulled loosely back, tall and athletic, with sharp green eyes that seemed to see more than what was in front of her. She said, "So you're the infamous Rico Cortese."

"Very pleased to meet you, Sheriff." Rico extended his hand.

Rafe resisted the urge to roll his eyes. He knew what Rico was thinking—that Skye McPherson was distracting Anthony from his duty. Rico had long advocated that Olivet's demon hunters shun personal relationships, even though they'd never taken a vow of celibacy. That Anthony was living "in sin" with the sheriff must irk Rico, even though Anthony wasn't a hunter.

Anthony said, "May I get you some coffee? Water?"

Moira said, "Water would be great, thanks, Anthony." She smiled widely though her eyes were cold, knowing Anthony had addressed Rico.

Anthony opened his mouth, then closed it. The animosity between the two had grown even though they'd successfully worked together to trap the demon Envy two weeks ago. The tension grated on all of them, but Rafe didn't know how to get Anthony to lighten up on Moira—or how to suggest to Moira that she not push his buttons all the time.

"Right." Moira pointed a finger at Anthony. "I'll get it myself." She crossed to the refrigerator and took out two water bottles. She tossed one to Rico without looking and the trainer caught it with ease, his reflexes almost feline. There was an easy camaraderie between Rico and Moira, which got under Rafe's skin. He averted his eyes, kept his face impassive. The fact that Rico had trained Moira, and befriended her, didn't change the depth or complexity of Rafe's relationship with her. Given their past, it was natural that Rico and Moira had gotten close.

How close?

"I'll be back in ten minutes," Moira said, leaving the room.

Rafe leaned against the counter.

Rico stared pointedly at Rafe, putting him even more on edge. "Raphael. I see you've returned to the land of the living."

Rafe gave a nod. "You haven't changed."

"You have."

Rico's style was cool and hard to read. His comment was full of double meaning.

Rafe had fought his own battles with Rico over the years. Some might chalk it up to a difference in opinion, like Anthony, who had worked with both of them and had respect for each man. But Rafe knew how his former trainer thought: as far as Rico was concerned, those who died in the battle against evil were martyrs, heroes, saints. Rico trained his men—and Moira—well, but in the end, they all knew they would die fighting.

There were no old men who'd graduated from Olivet. That Moira was one of Rico's hunters increasingly bothered Rafe.

Skye broke the awkward silence. "Will you be staying the night?" she asked Rico.

He shook his head. "The sooner I transport the demon to Olivet, the better for everyone."

Rafe watched Skye assess the situation as any experienced cop would. He wondered what she thought of Rico.

"Why are you moving it in the first place?" Skye

asked. "Not that I'm complaining—I'd rather have the creature as far from Santa Louisa as possible. But Anthony said the vault at St. Francis is strong enough to hold it."

Rico nodded. "It is. But Olivet's facilities are far more extensive and better equipped to contain the demon. And we have guards. Father Isaac at St. Francis is devout and capable, but his age makes him vulnerable. I want to minimize his risk."

"And what are you going to do once you get it there?" Skye asked.

"Keep it restrained until we find out how to send it back to Hell. Or kill it."

"Demons can't be killed," Anthony said.

"We can't be certain of that. Based on the evidence I've seen, Moira killed the demon that imprisoned Raphael. We're exploring every possible solution to this crisis. We have no choice. The last time the Seven reigned on Earth, virtually every man involved in banishing them back to the underworld died."

Skye tensed. "This has happened before?"

Anthony said, "Nearly a thousand years ago. It's documented in the *Book of the Unknown Martyr* Father Philip brought with him before—"

Anthony paused. Father's death had been hard on him. As hard on him as on Moira. And still, Rafe realized, Anthony wouldn't talk to Moira about it.

Rico said, "In the Martyr's book, there is a lot written about the *Conoscenza*. We also know from the Unknown Martyr that his battle was not the first. This has all happened before and it will continue to happen until the *Conoscenza* is destroyed. In this age, we can't afford to lose everyone. This is but one battle in a war that will last until the end-time."

And that, Rafe realized, was the truth that unified them. St. Michael's Order was founded on the core principle that inaction in the face of evil was the greatest sin.

"How did they do it a thousand years ago?" Skye asked. "They had to have been successful."

"They were. They sent the Seven back to Hell. But we don't know how, because everyone involved died in the process. The book ends with only an incomplete plan. We don't know what they did, only that they believed they could destroy the *Conoscenza* with fire. Yet, it resurfaced twice in the last eight hundred years, and each time was allegedly burned. And it still survived."

"It sounds impossible," Skye whispered.

"The *Conoscenza* is written by demons with demon blood, on paper made from human remains," Rico said matter-of-factly.

Skye paled, and Rafe wanted to shake some compassion into Rico.

Rico continued, "I read your report, Anthony, and Moira's." He turned to Rafe. "I didn't get one from you."

Rafe looked Rico in the eye. "I didn't realize I answered to you."

Rico said, "It would be helpful to know from your point of view what happened at the Mission last November. Your recovery is very important to St. Michael's, as is anything you remember during your coma, and upon waking."

Skye straightened her back, and Rafe wondered whether she'd known Anthony had sent Rico her police reports. Rafe wondered if they were public.

To Rico, he said, "You know what happened."

"I still have questions."

"Then ask them."

His refusal to bow down to Saint Rico irritated the trainer, though he hid it well. Rafe suppressed a grin. The man needed to be taken down a notch. He wasn't a saint yet.

Rico said, "We'll get to that later. Anthony, I have an assignment for you."

"Of course. What do you need?" Anthony sat at the table and the others followed his lead.

"We have battles all over the world," Rico said. "Our Order is spread thin. Losing Father Philip was a severe blow—he was our spiritual center. He was our advocate. He was the reason the Order had quiet sanction from the Vatican to continue our thousand-year mission. I went to the sanctuary in Italy to solidify our position and ensure that we wouldn't have to go underground, as the Order has had to do from time to time. That's when I convinced Dr. Lieber to meet with you."

Anthony said, "That's good news. I've been trying to reach him for the last two weeks. But I haven't heard that St. Michael's is worried about going into hiding. Has something changed?"

"For now, nothing. But make no mistake about it: we have been put on notice. We must be discreet. We must be swift. This age—with the Internet and instant information, instant news—it both helps us tremendously and severely threatens us."

Moira returned, her dark hair wet from her shower. She'd pulled it into a tight ponytail, water still dripping down her back, her black high-necked shirt molding to her skin. She didn't sit with them at the table, but perched on the edge of the buffet—both physically above the men and separated from them. Rafe wished she'd join them, and hoped she didn't think that because she was the only female hunter she didn't have equal say, or because Anthony dismissed her that she wasn't part of the group. But he realized that Moira had the best vantage point. She could see everyone at once.

Moira said, "Speaking of the Internet, I've been monitoring the message boards and there's been increased chatter about paranormal activities. Most are garbage, but I've been following up on a few. In fact, I was planning on heading to San Francisco to check out a coven that may have been connected to Walker while he was up there."

Rafe stiffened and Anthony glared at her. They hadn't known she was planning a trip. There was no way Rafe was letting Moira run off on her own. He had confidence she could handle most anything that came her way—she was unusually resourceful—but she was still threatened by Fiona O'Donnell and Matthew Walker, who had nearly killed her.

Rico said, "The situation has changed. No one goes on any assignment alone. And right now, I don't have anyone to spare, especially with Anthony's trip to Italy."

"What?" Anthony asked.

"I told you that Dr. Lieber has agreed to meet with you. John is driving him from Switzerland as we speak. You'll meet him at St. Michael's."

"With all due respect, Rico, I have a lot of work to do here."

"Dr. Lieber takes precedence. He refuses to fly, and will speak only with you. There's no other option."

Moira said, "I can still check out the situation in San Francisco. I don't need backup—I've been on my own for the last seven years, and a few days by myself isn't going to kill me."

"I'll go with you," Rafe said.

"We will discuss it later," Rico said in such a tone that Rafe knew he'd never consider sending Rafe with Moira. Was it because he didn't trust him? Because Rafe hadn't finished the training at Olivet? Or because Rico just didn't like him? The feeling was mutual.

Rico continued, "Ensuring that the demon you captured is secure is our number one priority, followed by Anthony's trip to Italy. Dr. Lieber is a brilliant man, if extremely paranoid, and while I don't think he *knows* the answers, I believe he has information that could lead us to the solution on how to send the Seven Deadly Sins back where they belong."

"How long will he be gone?" Skye asked. She was trying to sound nonchalant, but Rafe sensed she was upset about Anthony leaving.

"Two or three days. I don't want him away from Santa Louisa too long. We've decided that the Santa Louisa mission is, for now, one of our most important bases. We must continue rebuilding. We need a place for our people to regroup. We've lost many in the battle. And many like Father Isaac, who've provided sanctuary in the States, have grown fearful in the face of threats and adversity. Some of our allies have closed their doors to us."

Moira said, "What do you expect? They don't see the point of fighting when they think they just have to be good little children, and when the end comes they worry about their own souls and no one else!"

"Moira!" Anthony said harshly. "That's enough."

Rafe leaned forward and said softly, "She's right and you know it."

If Rico noticed the friction, he said nothing, commenting instead on the state of the mission. "I've been authorized to provide any resources necessary to restore the mission as quickly as possible, and Anthony is the best to oversee the project."

"So Anthony is going to Italy," Moira said, "and you're taking the demon to Olivet. What do Rafe and I do? Sit around and twiddle our thumbs?"

Rico said, "You will continue to do what you need to do."

"Can you be a little more vague?" Rafe said.

"Raphael, we need to find out exactly what happened to you during your coma, or you could be a risk to all of us."

Rafe slowly rose from his seat. "I am not a risk."

"That's not what he meant," Moira intervened. "Rico."

"But that *is* what I meant," Rico said flatly. "I appreciate loyalty, but for ten weeks the coven had Rafe under their thumb. We don't know what they did to him, and we need to know. I have every available man searching for members of Fiona's coven. Any luck with Richard Bertram?"

Skye said, "I'm still working on a supeona for destroying Rafe's medical records, but Bertram claims it was an accident."

Rico dismissed her legal authority, and Rafe saw it irritated the sheriff. Rico said, "Make no mistake: our primary responsibility is to capture the Seven before we lose more lives. And second? Find and destroy the *Conoscenza*." He looked at Moira. Something crossed his face, but when Rafe tried to figure out what had disturbed Rico, the trainer's cold, blank expression returned.

For a split second, Rafe thought Rico had looked scared.

"That's my job," Moira said lightly, belying the seriousness of the conversation.

"Yes it is," Rico said softly.

Something was wrong, and it bothered Rafe that he couldn't put his finger on it. It had to do with Moira, and by extension her safety. He would damn well figure out what was going on.

Skye's phone vibrated on the table, and she grabbed it up and excused herself, walking outside onto the deck.

"Where's the girl now?" Rico asked, changing the subject.

"The girl?" Rafe asked.

"The *arca*."

"Her name is Lily," Rafe said.

Anthony shot him a glance. Rafe wasn't about to back down. Rico could damn well think of Lily as a person. When she was thought of as anything less, she'd become expendable, a martyr to the cause. Rafe wasn't going to let that happen to the teenager that Father Philip died to save.

"She's with Deputy Hank Santos," Anthony said. "He has assisted us."

"I read your report," Rico said impatiently. "Santos was affected by one of the demons; he may be susceptible again."

"Jared is keeping an eye on the situation," Moira said.

"The girl's—" Rico hesitated, then said, "*Lily's* boyfriend? So we have hormones involved? Can we trust his judgment, considering he was willing to participate in an occult ritual ostensibly to save his girlfriend?"

"He understands the situation now," Moira said. "He's not going to make the same mistake."

"All it takes is one mistake. He either exercised poor judgment or he was under the influence of a spell. Either way, he's weak."

"He's not weak," Moira defended Jared. "Young, but not weak. I'll work with him."

"Then he's your responsibility," Rico said, showing his irritation and his true colors. Rico did not like mistakes, not even one. "You'd better keep him in line."

"One mistake is all it takes to die," Rico had told Rafe during his training at Olivet. *"One mistake and people you care about die. One mistake and you lose your soul."*

Skye stepped back into the room and cleared her throat. "If you're done bickering, I have some news. Rod—Dr. Rod Fielding, the coroner," she added for Rico's benefit, "got a call from the Los Angeles morgue. Three confirmed demon's marks in L.A." She held out her BlackBerry to show Rico.

He glanced at the digital photograph and asked, "What do you think?"

Anthony held out his hand, but Rico handed the phone to Moira. A wash of unease ran down Rafe's neck from the anger coming off Anthony. No one else seemed to notice.

"Fuck," Moira said and handed Anthony the phone. "Not identical to the others, but close."

Skye said, "The L.A. coroner will allow me to view the bodies, but they won't send them up here."

"I'll go with you," Anthony said.

"You're going to St. Michael's," Rico reminded him. "Your flight leaves today."

"Skye can't go to L.A. alone," Anthony said. "She doesn't know what she'll face, she doesn't have the training—"

Skye said, "Rod Fielding and I are going to view the bodies, talk to the coroner and the investigating officers, find out about the victims. Rod wants to show the L.A. coroner the brains of two of our victims. Apparently, one of the L.A. vics has a similar anomaly. I'll be back tonight—it's only a three-hour drive."

"What if you locate Fiona's coven? It's too great a risk, and if the marks prove to be true demon's marks, we'll know that one of the Seven is in L.A. It's too dangerous to go there alone—for any of us."

Rico said, "Moira will go with her."

"I'll go as well," Rafe added.

"No." Rico didn't even look at Rafe when he spoke. "There's no need for you to go. Moira is a trained hunter."

Rafe bit back his displeasure, wanted to argue, but Moira was looking at him, silently asking him why he was being so hostile. Rafe didn't like seeing Moira worried about him, but her eyes betrayed her concern. She'd been apprehensive about him and the memories he had—memories that weren't his. They didn't speak of it often, and Anthony had dismissed Rafe's recollections as remnants of his magic-induced coma. At least Anthony pretended he wasn't concerned. But Rafe didn't like being the brunt of scrutiny, and he didn't want Moira or anyone looking at him as though he were crazy. Or worse, that he was somehow being used by the coven.

Then she said, "Rafe should come with us to L.A. We can cover more ground with the three of us there, and leave Dr. Fielding to talk shop with the coroner."

Rico didn't look happy that she'd contradicted him, and Rafe held back a grin.

"That's fine with me," Skye said. "But we should get going. It's a long drive."

Moira walked around the table. "Is this what it's going to be like?" Everyone turned to look at her, unsure of what exactly she was driving at. Her eyes settled on Rafe's. "We won't know where the damn demons are until people start dying?"

Skye said, "My thoughts exactly." She glanced at her watch. "I need to swing by the station and let them know I'll be out all day, clear up a few things."

"I'll get my stuff together," Moira said and left the room.

Skye asked, "How do we know which demon is at work and where it is?"

"That's easy," Rafe said. "Look at the deaths and find out what the victims were doing when they died. That will lead us to the demon."

Anthony nodded in agreement. "When we trapped Envy, it was because we figured out the common denominator of the four people who died. Once we know what connects the victims in L.A., we can devise a plan on how to trap it."

"With another tabernacle?" Skye asked.

"That," Anthony said, "is one thing I'm uncertain

about. I hope Dr. Lieber has the answers. At this point, I'd be happy with a theory."

Moira returned wearing her custom leather jacket, her satchel with the tools of her trade draped over her shoulder.

"I'm ready when you are, Sheriff. And Rico?" She paused until Rico looked at her. "If you learn anything from my blood, let me know."

After she walked out, Rafe glared at Rico. What was he planning for Moira?

FOUR

Grant Nelson had been staring at the dead young woman for several minutes when Johnston said, "Nelson? You okay?"

Grant turned his back on Stephanie Frazier's frozen remains, her body folded improbably into Kent Galion's freezer. He didn't work Missing Persons, but he'd heard from Julie at Velocity that Stephanie had been missing since she'd complained about Galion hitting on her Wednesday night.

Missing Persons hadn't taken Stephanie's disappearance seriously until her roommate, a flight attendant, came home a week after Julie had last spoken to Stephanie and said her car was in the garage, she hadn't fed her cat for days, and none of her clothing was missing. While Missing Persons was retracing her last steps, two neighbors came forward and stated that Stephanie was last seen in the passenger seat of a black Mercedes.

Galion drove a 2009 Mercedes coupe.

Because of Grant's involvement with Galion's case, Missing Persons contacted him after the body was found in Galion's Glendale home.

"It makes no sense," Grant said as much to himself as to Johnston. "Why did Galion do this?"

Johnston wasn't so sure. "We don't know he—"

"Like hell we don't! He attacked a waitress at Velocity last Friday. I wouldn't have believed it except I saw it. So did Julie and the bouncer. Galion broke the girl's arm."

After what Grant had witnessed, it wasn't difficult to believe that Galion had killed Stephanie Frazier and stuffed her in his extra freezer.

"Galion has a brother; maybe—"

Grant knew where Johnston was going with the questions, but that didn't mean he was right. Grant trusted his gut, and his gut told him all the evidence would point to Galion—*Kent* Galion, not Marcus—as being the killer. But he also knew they had to cover all the bases. "Work with Glendale PD on the case, check into the brother, anyone else who had access to the house. It's not our case, but I want to know what they find."

"Roger that," Johnston said. "And for what it's worth? I think your instincts are right on the money. But it doesn't hurt to rule out the brother."

Grant strode over to the head of the CSU. "How do you handle a frozen body?"

Isabelle Juarez looked at him over the top of her reading glasses. "Since we can assume foul play—most people don't accidentally die naked in a freezer," she added sarcastically, "we'll transport the freezer with the body intact to the coroner's office and thaw her out there in a controlled environment in order to preserve potential evidence."

"How long does that take?"

"We don't want to warm her up too quickly because that'll mess with time of death and bacterial evidence, so probably twenty-four hours. I'll let you know."

"Any sign of assault?"

"We haven't processed the entire house," she replied. "It's been cleaned recently. But we'll go over the house with a fine-toothed comb. I know you'll need everything for a case like this."

"Our chief suspect's dead. This is Kent Galion's house. The victim's been missing since Wednesday night, and I have witnesses who place her in the same make and model car as Galion's."

Juarez nodded as she put the information together. "Right, I heard about that. Galion died in the alley behind Velocity. Attacked a waitress and was killed by a cop."

Grant bristled—he hadn't killed Galion, he'd used proper force for the circumstances—but he felt no need to explain any of it to the CSU.

"That makes this very interesting," she continued, sticking her glasses in her pocket and pointing to one of her team to finish photographing the freezer.

Interesting.

Grant wouldn't have used that word.

Rafe wanted to talk with Moira, but he didn't know where she'd gone. He took a few minutes to pack for their trip, and when he returned to the kitchen Rico was there alone. Rafe glanced out the back window and saw Anthony and Skye standing close together on the cliffs, far beyond the deck.

He didn't mince words. "What did Moira mean about her blood?"

"She shouldn't have said anything," Rico said.

Rafe glanced at Rico as he leaned against the kitchen counter. The man was the best damn trainer on the planet. He was also arrogant, cunning, and rigid. There were no gray areas with Rico, no weakness, no slacking. If you didn't perform 100 percent every minute of every day, his criticism was wicked.

"Spit it out, Rico. I know what you're thinking."

Rico didn't show agitation or surprise. "I doubt that."

"You don't trust me. You still think I was somehow party to the priests' murders at the mission."

Just saying it out loud caused the acid in Rafe's stomach to bubble and burn. Guilt warred with the injustice of Rico's silent accusations.

"I know you would have given your life to save any one of those men." Rico's words stunned Rafe into silence. "However, you're correct that I don't trust you."

"What's going on?" Rafe asked, though he wasn't quite sure what he was asking. The pressure of the last two weeks—awakening from his drug-induced coma, saving the young Lily Ellis, stopping the coven, losing Father Philip, and then the rigorous physical therapy to regain his strength—weighed on him. Not to mention that while everyone else had had months to mourn the deaths of the twelve priests last November, in Rafe's mind only two weeks had passed.

"You could have been a brilliant theologian or demonologist, but you left St. Michael's for St. John's. You could have been a great priest, but you left St. John's for Olivet. You could have been a top warrior, but you left Olivet to return to the seminary. Yet you never took your vows, leaving St. John's for Santa Louisa de los Padres." Rico assessed him. "How can I trust you? You have no direction, no true allegiance. It's as if you're waiting for something, unable to commit. At your age, that's unacceptable."

Rafe's blood boiled. "I am loyal to St. Michael's."

Rico didn't respond. "Dammit, Rico, how dare you doubt my devotion!"

"Moira has never lied to me until today. She's protecting you."

"Don't be an idiot. Moira isn't protecting me from *you*."

Moira lied to Rico? What had she said? Rafe had never asked her to keep any secrets, though they had skirted around some of their concerns about what happened to him in the hospital while he was in the coma. Was that what she didn't want to tell Rico?

"Then explain to me how you learned to stop the *Conoscenza* ritual. How you knew the language."

"I don't know. The words just came to me." Rico's disapproval and doubt mirrored Rafe's own heart, but he pushed it aside. He wished he knew how he'd been able to save Lily Ellis, the *arca*, the teenager who would have been sacrificed to house the Seven Deadly Sins in her body for Fiona and her coven to use at will. He'd just . . . known. And he hadn't stopped the ritual; he'd only saved Lily and prevented the coven from trapping the demons. They'd been released into the world, and people were still probably dying because of it.

He had some ideas about his knowledge, but those ideas terrified him. From his dreams—his nightmares—Rafe knew things he should not know. And sometimes he had the sense that he wasn't quite himself anymore. But he couldn't tell Rico any of this. Because deep down, while he never doubted Rico's loyalty to the demon hunters he trained, he also knew that Rico was ruthless. Any members of the Order who showed signs of mental instability were sent back to Italy for "observation," but they were really in a glorified prison. Even with all the screening and protection and training, some members snapped.

"Anthony is protecting you, I understand," Rico said. "You and Anthony have always been close, and I appreciate the support you've given each other over the years. So if Anthony is somewhat *blind* to what's been going on, I can take his comments and report with a grain of salt. But Moira?" Rico slammed his palm on the counter, a rare physical burst of anger. "She's *never* lied to me. But she did it fully knowing what she was doing. I know her better than she knows herself, and I will not tolerate her hedging."

"What are you going to do? Toss her in a dungeon?"

Rafe was being flip, but Rico's sharp reaction surprised him. "Don't you dare suggest that I'm anything like her evil mother."

What did that mean? What had Fiona done to Moira—and what did Rico know about it? Rico's comment reminded Rafe that he didn't know Moira as well as Rico did.

"You've distracted Moira long enough," Rico continued. "Stay away from her. She has a vital job to do and she can't do it if her loyalties are torn."

"Is that the real reason you don't want me going to Los Angeles?"

"I can see right in front of me what's going on," Rico said. "Moira is preoccupied with your problems, your coma, your dreams. She's worried and not fully focused on finding Fiona and Matthew Walker. She's not focused on destroying the *Conoscenza*."

Rafe defended her. "She is consumed by her search for her mother!"

Rico shook his head. "If she wavers, even a fraction,

she'll die before she gets a chance to complete her mission. And if that happens? There's no one else. No one that we know of who can destroy the book."

"That's all she is to you? A tool?"

"Isn't that all any of us are? That's why you've been wandering, Raphael. You refuse to accept that you have a calling more important than yourself. Moira is not you. She's accepted her charge, and she's willing to do what it takes to stop evil on Earth."

"Even if she has to die." Rafe realized why Moira would not acknowledge their intense, growing feelings for each other. She believed she would die. She was trying to protect herself, and him as well. But he didn't want that kind of protection. "You weren't there during the last battle. You have no idea how bravely Moira performed. Nothing can distract her from her goal; you trained her well." Rafe sounded as bitter as he felt. But he would not let Moira die.

"Yes I did," Rico said with complete confidence. "But make no mistake, Raphael—her situation is extremely dangerous and any distractions will prove fatal. I don't know what you did to ingratiate yourself with Moira, to get her to *lie* for you. I don't want you going to Los Angeles. Stay away from her."

"Like hell I will. Moira and I are a good team. We worked together trapping Envy. You can even ask Anthony."

"Moira doesn't need a partner."

"Doesn't that go against everything you taught us at Olivet?"

"I am Moira's partner."

"You?" Rafe laughed. "From way up in Montana? I can see how well you protected her two weeks ago when

Matthew Walker nearly killed her. Or from the Cerberus who attacked her. Or from the demon—"

Rico pushed off from the counter and was only a foot away from Rafe, his jaw tight and his dark eyes narrow. "I will be there when it counts."

Rafe didn't back down. "It counted *then*."

"Stay away from her."

"No." Why was Rico so fixated on Rafe partnering with Moira? They had the same goal: stopping the Seven Deadly Sins. And no one else cared about Moira the way Rafe did. He didn't want her to die. He wondered if Rico or Anthony felt the same.

"I'll have you recalled," Rico threatened.

"I dare you."

"The cardinal won't protect you if he thinks you're stopping Moira in any way from completing her mission."

Suddenly, everything came clear. Rico's attitude, his efforts to keep Rafe from partnering with Moira. His harder-than-usual animosity. Before he could stop the words from spilling out, Rafe said, "You're in love with her."

Rico's eyes widened in shock. He hadn't realized it, but Rafe saw it as clear as day. Rico was playing the dominant male, trying to chase Rafe away from Moira because he considered her his territory.

Rafe wasn't about to be chased away from anyone he cared about, *especially* Moira.

Rico said in a low voice, "You've been lying to everyone, Raphael, and maybe you're even lying to yourself. Anthony told me how you cut open Moira's hand during the battle with Envy. You claimed it was because the demon at the witch's house died after biting her, and you were taking a leap of faith. Good excuse, which Anthony bought hook, line, and sinker. But we both know there's more to it than that."

Rico thought Rafe cut Moira as some sort of excuse? A cover for nefarious activity?

"I don't know what the hell you're talking about, Rico. What I told Anthony was the truth."

"The truth?" Rico said. "I don't think you know the truth."

Rico was baiting him and Rafe tried not to jump.

"You took Moira's blood because you think it's a weapon."

"Isn't that what you used it for? None of us even suspected her blood might hold the answers."

"It was just a theory, I didn't know it would work. We were all going to die. I had to do something."

"But you knew exactly what to do."

"That's why you want her blood. You're going to test my theory, try to hurt a demon with it."

"It's not a theory if you're using magic."

"I'm not going to tell you again that I'm not."

"I don't believe you."

"Go to Hell."

"You're playing a dangerous game, Raphael."

"I'm not playing. I've never been more serious in my life."

"If anything happens to Moira under your watch, I will kill you," Rico said. He strode toward the sliding glass door, but Rafe wasn't letting him have the last word.

"The same goes for you, Rico. And I'm betting that

your plans for Moira have more to do with her *dying* than mine."

Rico hesitated a moment, then continued out the door without looking back.

Rafe stared after him. *You're on notice, buddy.*

FIVE

Rico and Anthony retrieved the tabernacle that housed the demon Envy from St. Francis de Sales Church, and Anthony drove Rico to the small Santa Louisa airfield where Rico had landed his private plane earlier that morning.

Rico always kept his emotions under tight rein, which was why most people thought he was heartless. In many ways, he was; his vocation required it. He had no time for the pleasantries that were customary among people. Like Anthony and the others, he'd been abandoned as an infant at St. Michael's doorstep and raised by the priests and monks in the fortress they called home. He'd been trained to be a warrior for God. He knew nothing else. He didn't want to know anything else. His calling was clear, and he had never doubted it once in his thirty-seven years. Never.

Which was why Raphael was able to get under his skin. Ex-hunter, ex-seminarian, the guy was full of doubt and questions. And he had the audacity to question Rico about the single most important, most dangerous battle they'd faced this century—which also could be the last. Raphael had never understood that he was a soldier, and soldiers take orders. Though he didn't agree with them, Rico had accepted Raphael's choices. Until now. Raphael was spreading his doubts to others, including Anthony. The cardinal had always supported Raphael's rash decisions, so Rico had kept quiet. But now Moira was showing shades of Raphael's influence.

Without her doing exactly what she was supposed to do, they would lose. All her training, all the time Rico spent working with her so she would have the mental and physical strength to do what now very much needed to be done, would be wasted.

He hadn't enjoyed being the lead trainer. He had to break down his people to ensure that they could not be broken when in battle. It was grueling work. Rico survived only because he knew it was necessary to ensure the survival of the human race. Few people wanted to go to war. But in the battle between the underworld and humanity, the underworld would never stop coming for them. It was relentless. Vicious. Evil.

So Rico accepted his calling, but there were times he despised what he had to do. Such as when he had put Moira in a dungeon not unlike the one her mother had kept her in for nine days. Being physically trapped was Moira's greatest fear. Rico had to put her in the same situation so she could learn to survive if it happened to her again.

God, how she had suffered! Rico had wanted to pull her out time and time again, but he didn't. He couldn't. And she was stronger for it. She had survived jail when trapped there two weeks ago. She was still claustrophobic, but she now had the tools to overcome it. She had to be able to survive anything Fiona or the demons put in her path.

There was more at stake here than their lives! That Raphael didn't see and understand that was far more disturbing than anything the fool had done—or not done—to date. If Raphael corrupted Moira, turned her away from her mission, there would be chaos.

And all Rico had done to prepare her would be for naught.

"Would you like me to inspect your plane?" Anthony asked as he pulled up to the airstrip.

"I'll do it," Rico said. "You need to catch that plane to Italy, and you have a long drive to San Francisco."

"I understand the importance of this trip, but the timing is very bad," Anthony said.

Rico was in no mood to listen to anyone else question orders. That it was coming from Anthony—who had always been loyal and righteous—was especially disturbing. "Your personal life is inconsequential, Anthony. I shouldn't have to tell you that."

Anthony tensed. "I have not allowed my personal life to interfere with my mission."

"Any personal life interferes. I hope you understand that when you are forced to make a choice."

"You can't be telling me I have to choose between Skye and St. Michael's!"

"Not now. But you know as well as I do that the time will come when a choice is inevitable. Every one of us who has become . . . *involved*," he emphasized, "has had to choose between the Order and their personal relationships. It's never been pleasant, and usually it's deadly."

"You don't have to tell me that," Anthony said with anger. "Before he was killed, Peter was my brother."

"Yes. Peter. He was not just your brother, he was a brother to us all. But your affection for him clouded your judgment then, just like your affection for Raphael is clouding your judgment now."

"What does that mean?"

"It means exactly what I said. You are blind when it comes to Raphael. We don't know what happened to him at the hospital, what those magicians might have done to him. What he's doing now. If you stop and look at everything that has happened these last two weeks—objectively, not with rose-colored glasses—you'll see that he is teetering on the edge. I don't know which way he's going to fall. But Raphael will fall, and he'll take others with him."

Anthony slammed his fist on the steering wheel. "It's her fault!"

Rico's gut twisted. He couldn't share everything with Anthony—yet. But soon he'd have to know. For now, he said, "I understand why you have animosity toward Moira, but she's essential to our mission. Without her, we can't beat Fiona or destroy the *Conoscenza*."

"She's not that good."

Rico disagreed, but arguing with Anthony on that point would be fruitless. "There are things we don't fully know at this point, but the research is extensive and your meeting with Dr. Lieber is essential to filling the gaps in our knowledge."

"What research? It would help if you kept me informed!"

"I would tell you everything I know, Anthony, except it would cloud your judgment. I don't want you going into the meeting with any preconceived ideas. After Italy, you'll fly to Olivet. We'll meet and combine information. I still have some work to do but will have answers by the time you return to the States."

"Does your 'work' have something to do with taking Moira's blood?"

"Yes," he said simply.

Anthony expected more from him, but Rico remained silent.

"I need to leave or I'll miss my flight," Anthony said after a moment.

"Be careful, Anthony. These are dangerous times."

Rico retrieved the tabernacle and watched as Anthony drove away. Too fast. In anger.

Anthony's anger had always been his weak spot.

Rico walked to his plane. He secured the demon in his hold, which he'd spiritually reinforced to prevent any possible escape. Still, flying alone with the demon tested even his steely resolve.

But he always did what was necessary, no matter what the risk or cost.

SIX

Moira had never been to a morgue before.

She'd seen dead people, but she hadn't hung around to see what happened to the bodies *after* they died.

And she kinda, sorta—okay, *absolutely*—wished she did not know now.

Skye didn't seem to have the same problem Moira had walking through rows of the dead in a very cold, very large, very sterile room in the Los Angeles County Morgue, following a petite black girl with a nose ring named Fern. Fern . . . something. Moira had been so floored by the atmosphere, she didn't even remember the girl's name. Fern called this cavernous room the crypt—just the *name* freaked Moira out. Dead people covered with sheets, gurneys stacked three high that could be summoned by the touch of a button.

"I want to be cremated," Moira said suddenly.

Fern shot her a glance and a grin. "You'd still probably have to come through a place like this first."

"Great." She plastered a smile on her face, but it didn't feel natural and Skye shot her an odd look. Somewhere between concern and surprise. Moira could practically hear Skye saying:

You nearly died facing down an incarnate demon, but a few dead people freak you out?

Moira didn't know why she was getting the heebie-jeebies. She wasn't normally skittish. But the hair on her arms rose, and she couldn't stop thinking about the dungeon her mother had locked her in, the first time she'd tried to escape Fiona's coven. It had been cold—not this cold, but cold enough. And the smell was similar—not the antiseptic, overly clean scent of the crypt, but the underlying, subtle scent of death. Of decomposing bodies. That they were in a room that could be easily locked, where they could be trapped with the dead, terrified her. Another type of prison. A place Fiona would love to keep her while she mentally tortured her.

"Moira." Skye put a hand on her shoulder and Moira jumped.

"Fine. I'm fine."

Skye didn't believe her; who would? Moira was probably as pale as the corpses. She mentally closed down her senses—Rico would be pissed, but Moira didn't want to feel any of the spirits that might be lingering. She was too jittery, like this morning when she came within inches of hurting Rafe after her vision. She didn't think she would have—she'd been acting on what Rico called her mental muscle, instincts plus training that kept her alive.

But *something* was off here, and while it wasn't magic, it creeped her out. So she'd turned her senses off, flipping a mental switch. Rico could go pound salt for all she cared. He'd stolen her blood, after all; she could shut off the power to keep her sanity in this place of the dead.

I should have stayed with Rafe and Dr. Fielding. They'd gone to meet the M.E. who had identified anomalies in a brain similar to what Dr. Fielding found in the victims of the demon Envy. But a room full of human organs had sounded worse than the crypt.

Fern said, "I still have two of the bodies, but I don't know how long I can keep one of them. The family is calling, it's been two days, and the autopsy ruled heart attack, though we're running additional tox screens because the detective in charge thinks it might be drug related. We don't normally keep the body once we're done, and the family wants to ship him back to Michigan."

"Two—I thought you said you had three bodies," Skye said.

"Two bodies, but I have photos from a third that came in last week. The body I called you about is scheduled for autopsy this afternoon." She glanced at her watch. "I'm prepping him in an hour."

"Would it be all right if we observe?" Skye asked. Moira suppressed a shiver at the thought of watching a body being cut open.

"I don't see why not, but I gotta clear it with my boss."

The first victim still in the morgue was a twenty-two-year-old who'd been found dead in an alley behind a local nightclub with his pants down around his ankles. No visible sign of death, and the first officer on scene had called it a possible OD. Not unlikely, Skye had told Moira, considering the prevalent drug use among college students. His alcohol level was only a fraction above the legal limit.

"Drugs are bad news, but add alcohol to the mix and there's a brain-cell-killing cocktail that's damn effective."

Fern pulled the sheet off a corpse. "This is Craig Monroe, the twenty-two-year-old college student from UCLA."

Skye said, "He was found partly naked in an alley behind a club?"

"Velocity, a club in Westwood."

"Have you gotten the drug screen back yet?"

"Not the secondary screen. He was cleared of the obvious—no nose candy, no needle marks, his lungs were clear—not a smoker, legal or illegal. Nothing in his stomach but a few beers, nuts, and a well-digested pepperoni and mushroom pizza."

Moira was never eating pizza again.

"Coroner is ruling a heart attack, but it's by process of elimination. With fifty or so bodies coming through here each day, sometimes that's the best we can do." Fern motioned to Skye. "Help me turn the body."

Moira stepped back. She wasn't going to touch the corpse. The thought nearly paralyzed her. The fear was highly unusual, and she didn't know why. Did it have anything to do with burying Father Philip last week?

Don't think about that, don't go there, don't remember that he's dead. That he'd been in a place like this.

She turned away and breathed deep, calming breaths. That made it worse. She had sharp senses, and couldn't help but breathe in the preservatives the coroner used to keep the dead from rotting. And the slow decay in the cold room. And the vile antiseptic that kept the place as sanitary as possible with hundreds of dead bodies lined up like B-movie zombies ready to rise and conquer the world.

You'd better stop it, girl, or you're going to puke all over the place.

Right. Big, bad demon hunter Moira O'Donnell scared of a couple hundred corpses. She was okay. If she repeated the mantra enough, maybe she could buy in to it.

She heard them moving the body behind her and couldn't block out the sound. She closed her eyes.

"Dammit," Skye mumbled. "Moira, look."

Moira forced herself to open her eyes and turn around. She tried to avoid looking at the bluish-white skin, and focused only on the demon's mark on the dead guy's lower back.

"See? The birthmark is freaky on its own, but it matches the photo I sent you, and it matches the mark on the new guy," Fern said.

"Can we see the new corpse?" Skye asked.

"It's the same, but if you want to, sure." She gently rolled the body back to its original position and covered it again. They returned to the front of the crypt.

Fern removed the sheet and turned the body attached to the tag that read *Erickson, G.* followed by a number. The mark on Erickson's body was exactly the same, in nearly the same place. "So what is it?" Fern asked the question she'd been itching to ask from the beginning.

Skye looked at Moira. "It's not identical to the others."

"Of course it is," Fern interrupted. "Just like the stiff over there *and* the photograph."

"I mean to the bodies in Santa Louisa."

"So you have seen this before?" Fern was curious. "What does it mean? It's not a tattoo; I can find no ink in the skin graft. But we're considering a type of caustic material may have caused the mark, like a brand, but there is no dead skin to indicate a burn. And then—"

Two men entered the crypt and swiftly strode toward them. One was black and broad, well over six feet tall;

the other, of average height, was a white guy with an athletic build and a pissed expression across his *GQ* face. They both wore plainclothes with a badge on their belts and guns at their side.

"Takasugi said you brought in another cop to view my body? Without my permission?" *GQ* said.

Fern bristled but didn't back down. "Detective Nelson, I followed morgue protocols."

Skye said, "Ms. Archer didn't know that I was coming down. She spoke with my medical examiner, and I came with him to verify information that may be related to one of my cases." She stepped forward and extended her hand. "Sheriff Skye McPherson, Santa Louisa County."

"Detective Grant Nelson; my partner, Detective Johnston." He shook her hand, glanced at Moira, then looked at the uncovered body. "What's that tattoo? I haven't seen a gang tat like that. Jeff?"

Detective Johnston shook his head.

Nelson said to Skye, "Proper procedure would be you calling *me* or my superior if you want information on a case, not dropping by the morgue. Long drive just to look at a tattoo when we could have sent you photos."

"I called the Sheriff's Department," Skye said, "as a courtesy because I didn't know anything about the case or who had jurisdiction."

Fern stood up to the cop, though she couldn't be more than five foot two. "I called Santa Louisa. And it's not a tat. It's a birthmark."

"You tested it? I've never seen a birthmark like that."

"No ink, though I've sent the grafts to the lab. But the odd thing is that the birthmark matches the college student who came in yesterday, and the guy last week who died while in custody."

"What guy?" Nelson said.

"Galion."

Nelson blanched. He held it back well, but Moira was watching him closely. She was trying to gather the courage to open her senses again. She didn't know if he was just a powerful personality or if he was driven by something supernatural. This cop may not have worked the second victim's case, but two out of three? Warning sirens shrieked in Moira's head.

Nelson turned to Skye. "And you know what this is?"

Skye didn't say anything for a moment, and Moira couldn't blame her. What could she say? That their victims had been touched by a demon and that had likely contributed to their death?

Skye cleared her throat. "I'm not sure. But I had four bodies with similar marks on their backs."

"Naked men?" Nelson asked.

"No."

"Then it's not the same—" He cut himself off.

"You were going to say killer," Moira said.

Grant Nelson shook his head. "I don't want to get into this here. I came for the autopsy."

"I'd like to observe," Skye said.

Nelson just shook his head. "Are you going to share your cases with me?"

She hesitated. "Mine are a bit complicated."

"Right. I share, you don't. Look, Sheriff McPherson, Santa Louisa is a county of what? Thirty thousand? My division, one of twenty-one in the city, has over ten times that number. I'm dealing with multiple jurisdictions and there's nothing to connect these victims. I just got another case dumped on me because of the possible connection, so if you can give me something that *helps* then I'm all ears. Otherwise, I don't have time to play show-and-tell."

"You're lying," Moira said.

"O'Donnell!" Skye snapped.

Moira shook her head. "He said that there's nothing to connect these victims, but there is."

"We don't know that," Nelson said.

"You think you know."

"I don't know who the hell you think you are, but you're not going to walk into the middle of my investigation and tell me what I know and don't know."

Skye straightened. "Can we take this outside? I'll tell you everything I have, and maybe we can help each other."

Moira couldn't imagine that Skye was going to tell this cop the truth, but she didn't say anything. These two dead guys were connected somehow to one of the demons—or one of Fiona's witches. Had Fiona relocated here in Los Angeles? Definitely possible, it was a big place. Easy to blend in. Of the twelve who had been at the ritual two weeks ago, one was dead and two were in prison. One was walking freely around Santa Louisa because Skye had no cause to put Dr. Richard Bertram in prison—which angered Moira to no end. The guy was guilty of being a witch, of being party to summoning the Seven Deadly Sins from Hell, but there were no laws against these crimes. And try proving any of it in court! Skye was trying to get Bertram on something else—such as drugging Rafe into a coma—but they still had no proof of that. Rafe's medical records were missing or had been destroyed.

Nelson agreed. "Five minutes, you first." He glanced at Moira. "I didn't catch your name."

"Moira O'Donnell." He stared at her, looking her up and down, trying to intimidate her with his unblinking gaze. She straightened her spine and stared right back at him. She'd faced down an incarnate demon; no way some arrogant cop was going to bully her.

He said, "You're not a cop."

"Nope."

Skye said, "She's a consultant. An expert on cults."

Moira barely restrained her surprise at Skye's easy and blatant lie.

"Cults?" Johnston asked. "You think this is some sort of cult killing?"

"Outside," Skye said.

"I'm going to prep the body," Fern said. "Thirty minutes and we'll begin in the main room."

Skye had piqued the interest of the two detectives. They led the way out, and Moira whispered, "Cult?"

"I'd sure as hell call Fiona's coven a cult, wouldn't you?"

She had a point. Moira bit the inside of her cheek to keep from laughing out loud.

Skye said, "Don't get cocky, we're not out of the woods yet. Nelson doesn't want to share, and I can't tell him the truth, so we're going to have to play this carefully." She slowed and said softly, "Did you feel anything from the corpses?"

"They're dead."

"But—"

"Magic? No. They're *dead*. Any spell on them would have ended as soon as they croaked. But they definitely did have some contact with one of Fiona's coven. Or—"

"Or what?"

"A demon, up close and personal. And in a city this

big, I don't know how we're going to track the coven or a demon. I know one thing, though—I need to go to that club, Velocity."

"Not alone."

"Skye, I hate to tell you, but you're a cop. You look like a cop, act like a cop. I can blend in. I'll get a cab, meet up with you in a couple hours. And honestly, I don't want to watch those bodies being sliced and diced. Being in that room alone freaked me out."

"I didn't think anything freaked you out."

"You'd be surprised."

"You and Rafe go, take my truck. Rod has the van, so I won't be stranded." She glanced at Moira. "Why did you call the detective a liar? That's really fucking with my position. I want him to play nice; calling him on the carpet isn't helping."

"He knows there's a connection." She frowned. She wasn't psychic; how did she know that? Rafe said she was an empath, and while she hadn't wanted to believe it, it made sense based on various times when she sensed facts about people after meeting them. Detective Nelson had entered the room and Moira simply knew that he *thought* that the dead were connected. She couldn't read his mind, it was more his emotional state; he *felt* the connection deep down.

Skye said to Grant as soon as they left the crypt, "We had four victims with similar marks on their bodies. Our coroner is working on how the marks were made; he's thinking some sort of laser."

Skye was lying through her teeth, but it sounded good. Moira was impressed.

"A laser?" Nelson asked, skeptical.

"I'm not a doctor, but my M.E. thinks a laser on a low

setting or possibly ultraviolet radiation could cause those type of markings."

Nelson said, "Possibly? So if this is a cult, are these victims members or innocent?"

"I'm not sure."

"There's nothing that connects the victims—nothing. Other than they are males and were involved in a sexual situation immediately prior to death."

"They were having sex when they died?"

"Inconclusive at this point. Monroe had ejaculated minutes prior to his death. I'll find out about Erickson during the autopsy."

"Were there any vaginal fluids or cells on their persons?"

"Galion was about to commit felony rape when he was apprehended, but hadn't penetrated. We have witnesses to his assault. Monroe had his pants down when he was found, and while there was no vaginal evidence, the coroner found female saliva on his penis. They're processing it for DNA now, but that takes time. The last one, Erickson, is who we're viewing today."

"Anything else?"

He didn't say anything.

Skye asked, "Did they have anything else in common? Where they ate, worked, lived, played?"

"That's it," Moira said, watching the detective closely.

Nelson avoided Moira's eyes and said through clenched teeth, "All three vics have a connection to Velocity, a popular nightclub. Monroe was found dead in the alley, and Erickson had been to the club earlier the night he died."

"Where was he found?"

"In his bedroom by his wife. The room was set up for a romantic scene, but his wife was out for the night."

"He was having an affair."

"They were swingers. The wife was with her ex-husband in his hotel room; he confirmed it, as did the manager and security footage."

"And did—"

Nelson cut her off. "This is my case, Sheriff."

"I'm not taking your case. I'm just trying to help—"

"Stay out of it."

"I—"

"I don't need your help. You'll fuck things up if you go pissing around the club and my investigation. I'll let you observe the autopsy, and if you can provide any further information about this supposed cult—give me something to follow up on—then great. But after we're done here, I expect you to be heading back up north." He glared at her pointedly. "I wouldn't want you to get stuck in rush-hour traffic."

Rafe could speak, read, and understand Latin, Greek, and Aramaic, but he couldn't decipher the complex medical conversation between Rod Fielding and the L.A. head pathologist, the tall and appropriately cadaverous Don Takasugi. The smell of formaldehyde didn't seem to bother the pathologists, but Rafe felt slightly ill—though he wasn't sure whether his discomfort was from the cloying scent of preservative or the visual of human organs soaking in it.

As soon as Rafe walked into the room he felt uneasy. He tried to convince himself it was the sight of the organs and the smell, but even that stopped bothering him after a few minutes. As his senses adjusted to the overpowering visual and olfactory assault, he accepted that maybe it was something else that disturbed him.

Static was the only way he could describe it. Very faint, as if a radio was tuned to a distant station in the next room, barely audible, the occasional half-heard word more grating than the static itself. When he tried to listen to the sound, his head ached. When he didn't consciously listen, it was like fingernails on the chalkboard: every skin cell tingled.

He tried to hide his discomfort while half listening to the scientists discuss the anomalies in the two brains that Fielding had brought with him.

One came from Chris Kidd, a high school senior who'd died of a brain aneurism, though Fielding wasn't confident in that diagnosis. The other belonged to Mrs. Barbara Rucker, the high school secretary who'd pushed a pregnant woman down the stairs, then crashed her car at high speed, seemingly on purpose. Because Fielding was a scientist, and his boss, Sheriff Skye McPherson, believed in evidence, they were both seeking scientific, medical answers for the deaths in Santa Louisa two weeks ago. While they acknowledged on the surface that a demon had been responsible, neither *completely* accepted that answer. It was as if they wanted, or *needed*, to know exactly how the demons affected their victims.

As far as Rafe was concerned, he had all the necessary answers. The Seven Deadly Sins had spread far and wide, drawn to people or places that celebrated their vice. Perhaps they were connected to the missing coven, which would mean Fiona and her minions were nearby. Or, if they were free from the bondage of Hell and the witches who'd summoned them, they may have another reason for targeting the areas they did. Either way, the demon

touched a victim—physically or simply by proximity—
and the individual's conscience was stripped away, resulting in the deadly sin taking over all thoughts and
actions. In Santa Louisa, Envy had created chaos. Loot-
ing, riots, and violence. Once the demon was trapped,
however, those affected seemed to regain their restraint
and were able to withstand the temptations of unrestrained envy.

But the town wasn't the same as before. Skye wouldn't
admit it, but Rafe saw it. He'd lived there as an outsider
for months before the demons came to town, and he
saw—and felt—the changes. Before the demons swept
through Santa Louisa, the quiet community nestled between the ocean and the Los Padres Mountains had
been filled with kindness. Neighbors helping one another. Picnics in the park. Kids playing ball in the parks
and riding bikes down the street, carefree. Rafe had
been comforted by the small-town normalcy of Santa
Louisa, the way everyone knew everyone else.

Now? The violence the demon Envy created had torn
families and friendships apart. The jail was full, the
court docket nearly exploding as people were held ac-
countable for the crimes they committed after Envy
stripped away their conscience. The distrust and lingering sense of envy and the anger it spawned among so
many people, even those not directly affected by the
demon, cast an invisible shadow over everything.

Rafe felt it, even if Skye was in denial. And it greatly
disturbed him.

"Amazing," Takasugi was saying. "And you didn't
notice this on gross examination? I'll need to go back
and look at the craniums of my other bodies."

"This first victim had pronounced neovascularization

of the brain stem with secondary aneurysm formation. He collapsed two hours after a basketball game, and died approximately thirty minutes later. In the second victim, I didn't see anything to warrant the same diagnosis, until I did a micro exam two days ago. But both seem to have new blood vessels feeding into the brain stem, and an enlarged amygdala."

"The brain stem?" Rafe spoke up for the first time.

The scientists seemed to have forgotten he was in the room. "Yes," Fielding said, eyeing Rafe curiously.

Rafe shook his head. He had a thought, but his training was in psychology, not forensics. He waited for more information.

"The amygdala has a primary role in the processing of memory and emotional reactions," Fielding explained. "That there are new and extensive blood vessels going from the amygdala to the brain stem is unusual."

"Highly unusual," Takasugi concurred.

"And that might make someone act irrationally?" Rafe said, carefully choosing his words. Psychology was an imperfect science—human beings couldn't be pigeon-holed in established boxes—but there was always a cause for human sociopathy. Sometimes hereditary, but usually environmental. Sometimes nature, but mostly nurture. Or lack thereof.

Human conscience helped people overcome their primal urge toward violence, lust, and greed. But without such restraints, there'd be no end to the anarchy. It made the release of the Seven Deadly Sins even more nefarious. Demons on Earth were bad, but what if people acted just like them? There would be violence without remorse, scorched earth, destruction across the globe.

Chaos. End-time.

Takasugi said, "The brain is the most complex organ in the human body and there's more that we don't know than we do know. The amygdala is also involved in pheromone production, epinephrine, and other natural chemical responses. A deformed or damaged amygdala could manifest any number of presentations, from headaches to irrational behavior to chemical imbalances—"

"And death?" Rafe said. Chris Kidd, the senior, hadn't committed any envy-related crimes, but he had the same demon mark as the other victims.

"Possibly."

Fielding said, "Mrs. Rucker acted irrational and out of character prior to intentionally crashing her car. Her death was due to the trauma of the crash, so I only did a cursory exam of her brain at the time. But when the other bodies came in with similar marks, I went back and reexamined what I could. One of the victims had already been cremated, another buried, but these two I still had access to."

Fielding glanced at Rafe. Ned Nichols had been cremated—or, technically, salted and burned in a crematorium—after Nichols manifested as a vengeful spirit. Fielding had never felt right about doing that, not only because it was against the law without next-of-kin authorization, but because he had jeopardized his career and reputation by acting without said authorization.

Takasugi removed Mrs. Rucker's brain from its container and placed it in a sterile tray. Rafe stepped back, queasy. He didn't generally have a weak stomach—he'd fought off one big-ass demon that wasn't pretty—but this was different.

"Amazing," Takasugi repeated. "I have a brain that

looks remarkably similar to this in one of our recent corpses."

"Do you still have the body?" Fielding asked.

"No, it was released to the family—an ex-wife and his children. They buried him, I believe, but I'll have to check the files. However, we kept the brain for further research considering the anomaly."

"Ugh, that's so gross!"

Rafe turned and saw Moira standing in the doorway behind him, staring distastefully at the brain displayed on the exam table.

"Almost as gross as the crypt," she added.

Moira didn't look like herself. Sarcastic, sure, but her eyes were troubled and her skin was pale. Rafe caught her eye, but her expression was unreadable.

Fielding introduced Moira to Takasugi. "Where's Sheriff McPherson?"

"I bailed before the autopsy," Moira said. "Main room, if you want to watch the festivities. Can I borrow Rafe?"

"What's wrong?" Rafe asked.

"Nothing." She smiled at the two scientists. "Dr. Fielding, don't leave without Skye, okay? She gave me the keys to her truck." She held them up.

Rafe snatched them from her hand. "You don't have a license."

"Yes I do. Just not in the States."

He raised an eyebrow.

"Okay, so it's expired, but I know how to drive better than you."

"I'm driving. Skye doesn't need any more trouble."

She rolled her eyes. "Fine."

Rafe thanked the men and left them to science. He had

the information he needed—only he wasn't quite sure what it meant yet. He walked out of the room with Moira. "Learn anything?" he asked.

"Plenty. I'll fill you in on the way. You?"

"I think I know how the demon is operating."

She stopped walking as they reached the main doors. "That's huge! How?"

"The brain stem is the most primitive part of our brain. The most basic part, and the most important. The amygdala is bigger than it's supposed to be in the victims, and it's feeding off an increase of blood to the brain stem. The amygdala is responsible for human emotional responses. What if the demon takes away something—a barrier of some sort, a biological or spiritual control valve? That explains why these people have no restraint. And it explains the basketball player in Santa Louisa."

"Chris Kidd? How?"

"He didn't act on his impulses."

"We don't know that he had them. He was marked, but maybe it hadn't manifested yet."

"What if he was fighting the impulse? What if the process was somehow incomplete or imperfect and Kidd was resisting? What if his conscience was stronger than the others, and he fought back? His blood vessels ruptured. That didn't happen to the others."

"So what does that mean, Rafe? If someone doesn't fight the urge to act on envy or lust or pride, they kill someone and then die? If they do fight the urge, they still die? Where does that leave us? Tilting at windmills?"

Rafe didn't have the answers. "I don't know."

"Well, Don Quixote, that certainly makes me sleep

better at night," Moira said as she walked out of the morgue.

"Moira—wait."

She stopped but didn't turn around. Rafe put his hands on her shoulders. "What had you so freaked when you saw me in there?"

"Freaked? Not me."

"You weren't yourself."

"Okay, fine. The corpses were creeping me out. Satisfied?"

"That just means you're human."

"Oh, joy."

Rafe turned her to face him. "Give yourself a break. You're not superhuman."

She mocked surprise. "What? You mean I have to give back the cape and golden lasso?"

He smiled and touched her chin. "I didn't say you weren't a superhero."

He'd said it to make her feel better, but she turned away. "I'm not."

"Moira—"

"Dammit, Rafe! Look what we're up against. I don't see this ever ending." She shook her head, then looked at the blue sky. "I hate this! If God wanted to help us in this battle, He'd leave clearer instructions."

"We just need to figure them out," Rafe said.

"I'd rather have a rule book, thank you very much." She glanced back at him. "Let's go."

"Where are we going?"

"Velocity. It's a club in West L.A., and so far, it's the only connection between all the victims. Maybe we'll get lucky and catch the demon before anyone else dies."

SEVEN

"There's nothing for you here," Detective Grant Nelson told Skye after the autopsy was complete. "If we learn anything more, we'll let you know."

Skye bit back her anger. Antagonizing this homicide cop wasn't going to win her friends. She needed him on her side. Or at a minimum, to not stand in her way. "I'd appreciate it," she said, keeping her voice calm.

"Where's your cult expert?" he asked, shooting his partner a sly grin.

"Getting air," Skye said. "She'll be back shortly."

"I have to get back to work," he said, glancing at his BlackBerry with a frown. "But I'll call."

I get your point. He wanted Skye out of town. Cops didn't like others invading their territory, and as far as Grant Nelson was concerned, she was a small-town sheriff and he was a big-city detective. He showed her the common courtesy between colleagues, but nothing more.

Jeff Johnston, his rookie partner, gave her a warmer goodbye and said in a low voice out of Grant's earshot, "His bark is worse than his bite. I'll make sure he lets you know what's up with these deaths."

"Thanks."

When she was certain the detectives were gone, Skye

went back to where the pathologist Fern Archer was sewing up the body of George Erickson, the swinger.

"Nelson made it clear I couldn't talk to you without him in the room," Fern grumbled.

"That's fine; I don't want to talk to you about his case."

Fern smiled widely. "What can I do for you, then?"

"A favor? If you get another body with a similar mark on it, would you call me?" Skye put her card down on the stainless-steel table behind Fern.

"Sure." Fern bit her lip. "You think this really is a cult?"

"Of a sort. These deaths are somehow connected to the bodies in Santa Louisa."

"My boss is signing the death certificate as a cardiac arrest."

"But you said there were no signs of heart failure."

"I said heart *disease*. But there's no other explanation. His heart just stopped."

"But you don't have the toxicology reports back."

"We have the prelims. We have a lab right here, can run standard screens 24/7. No drugs, low alcohol, no common poisons. And there're no signs of trauma, aneurysms, anything that could be a contributing cause. But then I heard that my boss is talking to your coroner about the dead guy's brain. Want to clue me in?"

Fern had been more than helpful, so Skye told her, "Dr. Fielding found something unusual about the brain stem, and wanted a second opinion. Dr. Takasugi was very kind to help."

"And?"

"And they're not done."

"Don can be tight-lipped sometimes," Fern grumbled.

"I'll let you know if anything interesting pops up."

She grinned. "Thanks."

Skye resisted the urge to smile. She liked the petite black girl—she was spunky and held her own against the arrogant Detective Grant Nelson. "If you ever want to move out of a big city into small-town America, let me know."

Fern beamed.

Skye added, "Seems that the victims have only one thing in common: they were horny men."

"Oh, maybe a scorned woman or stalker?" Fern grinned. "I like that. Female stalkers aren't that common."

Skye raised an eyebrow, and Fern said, "I read crime novels, what can I say?"

"Maybe you should have been a cop," Skye said.

The intercom system beeped. "Fern, you still back there?"

"Yes," she replied.

"You got to come to Receiving. You'll never believe this. Bring your camera."

Skye raised an eyebrow.

Fern said, "Let's see what's going on. Should be fun." For a young woman who worked in the morgue, Fern seemed almost happy-go-lucky.

Skye followed her to the receiving room. A City of Glendale crime-scene van had backed up to the main double-door entrance. One of the investigators was signing paperwork at the desk while five people stood around a white freezer with a police seal on it.

Fern said, "There's a body in there, isn't there?"

"Bingo," the investigator said without looking up from his paperwork.

"Amazing," Fern said. "What's the story?"

"Found by the housekeepers when they were cleaning out Kent Galion's place. We don't know for sure he killed her, but she's been missing more than a week. It's just a matter of putting together the evidence. If she was frozen right after death, the evidence should be well-preserved."

"Wow, I haven't had one of these before." Fern sounded excited. "Let's get the freezer weighed, then take it to the decomp room and let it thaw in a controlled environment. Hopefully we can autopsy in twenty-four."

Skye went over to the investigator and showed her badge. "Would you mind if I take a look at the file?" she asked.

"Help yourself," he said.

She flipped through the crime-scene notes, then turned to Fern. "Did you say earlier that Kent Galion was the name of the other body with the demon's mark?"

"I did; he's long buried."

"He attacked someone?"

"Galion was the owner of Velocity. Think that's the connection? Because the college kid died in the alley?"

"Nelson said Erickson was also at Velocity the night he died."

Skye jotted down the victim's and the suspect's addresses, trying to act nonchalant. She might have to risk ticking off Detective Nelson, because Skye needed Moira to check out the houses. One of them might lead to Fiona's coven.

Her phone vibrated. "Thanks," she said, handing the file back to the crime-scene investigator.

"Find what you were looking for?"

"Just curious," she said. She mouthed *thank you* to Fern, then stepped out of the building and answered her phone.

"McPherson."

"Skye. It's Anthony."

Her heart fluttered just a bit, enough to remind her that she already missed him. "Where are you?"

"New York. I have a few minutes before boarding. I wanted to hear your voice."

"I'm glad."

"What's going on in L.A.?"

"Three men have turned up dead, apparent heart attack, but with demon marks on their backs. Rafe and Moira are checking out the only connection between the three, a nightclub they were at immediately before they died."

"Where are you?"

"At the coroner's, waiting for Rod. I was just about to call Moira and give her some addresses to check out using her—" Skye was at a loss on how to describe Moira's ability to feel the presence of magic.

"Be careful, sweetheart."

"You, too." Quieter, she added, "I love you."

"I love you, too, Skye. And I'm worried. I wish I were there."

"Me, too, but more so we can have our house to ourselves. It's getting crowded."

"I've been trying to find Moira a place to stay, but—"

"Only Moira?"

"Rafe needs time to heal."

"Rafe is fine."

"Skye, the situation is complicated."

"I'm not obtuse, Anthony. I understand the complexities of the situation."

"Skye—"

"We'll talk about it when you come home."

"I'll call as soon as I land in Sicily. I need to board. *Mi amore*, please be careful."

She hung up the phone and rested it against her forehead. She didn't want to snap at him, especially now, but for the last two weeks Anthony had been pulling away from her. He didn't realize it, and she knew it had nothing to do with his love for her. His love was one of the few things in which she had complete confidence. It was more what he didn't say, the pressure St. Michael's had placed on him since Father Philip died. Struggling with Moira O'Donnell's presence. Several times when Anthony and Moira verbally sparred, Skye had the feeling Anthony wanted to slug her, yet Anthony wouldn't hit a woman. He believed in chivalry—in opening doors, in the small, sweet gestures that showed his deep respect for women, coupled with the way he treated her in bed, insisting that her pleasure was more important than his. For a macho guy, Anthony was a true gentleman. *Except* with Moira.

She called Moira. "I'm texting you the address of the first known victim of the demon, and the address of a woman he allegedly killed before he died. Can you check them out and do your thing?"

"You mean check for magic."

"Right." Skye shifted on her feet. She still had a hard

time talking about demons and magic as if that were a normal part of her job.

"Will do, as soon as we finish with Velocity."

"Are you there yet?"

"Hardly. There are so many flippin' cars on the road we should have walked."

EIGHT

Almost immediately after Moira hung up the phone with Skye, the text message came in with two addresses. She had no idea where they were, but Skye had a GPS in her truck. But first things first: Velocity.

Moira reluctantly let Rafe drive to the nightclub. She itched to get behind the wheel, but Skye frowned on her driving because she didn't have a legal license. Moira was trying to play by the rules since the sheriff was letting her live in her house—and she liked her—but it was becoming increasingly difficult. She'd been on her own for so long that she was beginning to feel claustrophobic under the watchful eyes of Anthony and Skye.

Not to mention Rafe Cooper. But that was a whole different issue.

"You think the club has something to do with the deaths?" Rafe said after Moira told him what happened to the victims. Something occurred to her and she sent Skye another text.

Did the police talk to the women who were with Monroe and Erickson? Who are they?

"Three men—all involved in sexual acts," Moira said. "You know what we're dealing with here."

"You think it's Lust." Rafe pondered that for a moment as they stalled in highway traffic.

"Envy killed by having people act on their deep-seated envy of others . . . Lust must be targeting people predisposed to being unable to control their physical desires. Most of us control lust, even when we're attracted to someone. Even when we know that person is attracted to us."

Rafe glanced at her, and Moira pretended not to notice.

She glanced at her phone. "Skye says the cops don't know who the two men were with the night they died." She stared out the windshield. "What if Lust came to town and the people she touches act out? It would explain the man who attacked the waitress. And why the married guy took a woman home from the same club."

Rafe didn't say anything for several minutes, which was fine with Moira. She didn't want to talk about lust or attraction with Rafe.

Why Los Angeles? Proximity to Santa Louisa? Because this was where Fiona was hiding out? Or something else? She hated that no matter what they did, they'd never know where the Seven Deadly Sins were until someone died. There had to be a better way, but every idea they explored hadn't panned out. She scoured the online paranormal message boards, looking for clues, but so far every possible lead turned out to be a dud. She itched to go on the road, follow up in person, but not until today had there been even a hint of the Seven Deadly Sins in action.

Maybe if she had more control over her visions . . . if she could find some way to use them to find the demons *before* someone died. But the only way Moira knew how to do that was through magic, and if she touched magic again, Fiona would be able to track her, whereas for now Moira was invisible to Fiona's psychic eye. Worse, using magic would open Moira up to possession again. She recalled the last desperate moments with Peter, whom she'd loved so passionately. Who would she kill next time?

Rafe?

Her stomach flip-flopped and she involuntarily grabbed the door handle. When she realized she was gripping the vinyl so hard her knuckles were white, she let go. Rico was right. Fear was her worst enemy. It was going to get her killed.

Rafe broke the long silence. "Why did you let Rico take your blood?"

Moira hadn't been expecting that question.

"I didn't have much of a choice."

"He tied you down and took it against your will?"

"Shit, Rafe, you know how it is. Would you refuse an order?"

"He ordered you?"

She frowned, more than a little bit angry with this conversation. "So he wants my blood. It's not like he's going to drink it. Let him play his cloak-and-dagger games. It doesn't hurt me."

"And then you announce it to take a jab at Rico— which I admit was fun to watch—but maybe you should have told me in private so we could do something about it. He's keeping far too many secrets that can get you hurt. Do you know why he took your blood?"

"I have some ideas, but I didn't know I was supposed to give you a blow-by-blow of everything that happens in my life," she snapped, knowing she was overreacting, but her heart was pounding and she didn't know why.

"It's not like you've been eager to tell me more about these memories of yours."

"It's not the same thing, and you know it!"

"Yes, it *is* the same thing, because it has to do with trust."

"So that's why you didn't tell me? Because you don't trust me?" Rafe couldn't keep the hurt out of his voice, and that upset Moira, but she still wasn't backing down.

"Rico took my blood because *you* cut my hand and stuffed it in the guts of that damn demon. He wants to know if my blood is 'special.'" She said the word derogatorily. Of course it was *special*. She'd been conceived to serve the underworld. For all she knew, a demon was her father.

She dry-heaved.

"Moira—"

"Stop." She put her forehead against the cool glass of the passenger-side window.

"I don't want to see you hurt."

"Too late."

"That's not what I mean."

"This war is dangerous, Rafe."

"Rico is using you."

"Maybe that's the only way to save my soul."

"Don't talk like that!" This was a futile conversation, but Rafe wouldn't let it go. "Rico doesn't care about anyone, only his cause."

"His cause is *my* cause," Moira said.

"Stopping Fiona is only one part of it, and you know that."

"If you're worried that I'm a pawn in Rico's game, don't be. I know what the stakes are. If I'm a pawn in anyone's master plan, it's the Big Guy upstairs, and you damn well know it. You, me, Anthony, all of us. All I can do is what I can do. Find Fiona. Stop her. Destroy the *Conoscenza* so no other magician can use it to summon the Seven Deadly Sins or whatever other evil purposes the book has."

"And if you die?"

"We are all going to die someday. So what?"

"No!" He slammed his hand on the steering wheel, making Moira jump.

"This shouldn't be a surprise to you, Rafe," she said quietly. "You were raised knowing that you'd die a martyr."

"I'm not going to let you die."

"It's not your call."

"But it's Rico's?"

That Rafe sounded jealous was too simple. His emotions were more complex than simple jealousy, Moira realized, not that he had anyone to be jealous *of*. And Rico? They'd been arguing about something while she was getting ready this morning, but neither of them had raised his voice and she hadn't been able to hear anything they said. Not for lack of trying.

"That's the street," Moira said, gesturing to the right.

He made the turn too fast, earning a foul gesture from an elderly woman walking four tiny dogs.

Rafe passed Velocity, which was two blocks off Wilshire Boulevard and only a couple of miles from the south entrance of UCLA. He then turned around and parked in a garage up the street from the club. All without speaking.

She glanced at him, confused and ticked off at his reaction and a little sheepish. She hadn't wanted to give in to Rico's demands this morning! But what choice did she have? While it was an odd and unnerving request, if there was something in her tainted blood that could help or hinder them in this battle, didn't she owe it to them to give it up? Besides, Rico had trained her. He was essentially her commanding officer. And while she didn't like to take orders from anyone, if she did, it would be from Rico.

"Fifteen dollars *an hour*?" Moira said, changing the subject as Rafe took a ticket from the machine. "It took us nearly forty minutes to get here—I swear, I don't know how the people around here can stand all these other people—and now fifteen bucks to park?"

"This conversation is not over, Moira," Rafe said through clenched teeth as he turned off the engine. He jumped out of the car and slammed his door shut.

Moira got out of her door and said, "That's what you always say, but it's *done*. Can we just do this?"

He grabbed her arm and pulled her against his chest. "You can't die."

The anger and fear on his face was surpassed only by raw pain. She wanted to pull away, to tell him to stop manhandling her, but she couldn't. Rafe's intensity unnerved her, had her at a loss and bordering panic. She didn't want these feelings for Rafe, but they were growing.

"Rafe—"

He kissed her. This was no tame, sweet embrace; it was fierce. Moira froze, stunned by the depth of his emotion. Then Rafe's hands reached for the back of her neck, holding tight, as if he feared she was going to bolt. And she wanted to; she wanted to run far away from Rafe's feelings. From what he wanted from her. Emotions overwhelmed her, his and hers. Fear. Desire. A deep yearning for something intangible, a freedom neither of them had. Her stomach fluttered and she returned his kiss, mirroring Rafe's passion with her own deep longing.

His body pressed against hers, pushing her against the truck. Her hands were on his shoulders, and her mind told her to push him away, that now was not the time to do this, she couldn't *think* and she had to focus. The club. The demon. The men who'd died.

But she couldn't think, Rafe's need becoming her own, drawing out of her everything she'd been denying him, denying herself. From the minute she first laid eyes on him, unconscious, dressed in stolen medical scrubs, huddled in the corner of an abandoned cabin, she'd been irrevocably part of him as he was of her, far more than two demon hunters trying to undo the damage her witch of a mother had done.

Her arms wrapped around his neck as his mouth dove deeper into hers, his tongue mimicking lovemaking, and every cell in her body warmed to the brink of combustion.

Moira let the heat flow within her, Rafe's hard, athletic body pressed firmly against hers, his leg maneuvering between hers, the friction making her shudder and cling to him. Her mind was mush, her body did all the thinking for her, and its thoughts were focused on one thing: getting naked with Rafe.

His hands were under her shirt, rubbing her bare back, while he kissed her in that one spot behind her ear that he'd discovered earlier, the erotic soft spot that made her melt when his tongue fought it.

The sound of a distant car made her jump and she

looked around, disoriented. They were making out in an L.A. parking garage in the middle of the day. Did they lust for each other so much they lost all sense of time and place?

Lust.

She pushed him away, not meaning to push hard, but he jumped back. His breathing was as uneven as hers.

"We can't do this."

"Moira, you can't deny the way we feel about each other. Don't even try; you'll be lying."

"It's not real."

He froze, energy rippling under his muscles. "What?" His voice was low but the anger rolled off him, so dark it was nearly visible.

"We're near the club. It's the influence of the demon. We both think it's Lust here."

"Bullshit. I can't believe you're using the demon as an excuse for your feelings!"

"I'm not! I just can't think; that's not like me."

"Maybe because you're *overthinking.*"

"Stop!"

"What are you scared of?"

She turned away and walked briskly down the ramp toward the street. Scared? What *wasn't* she scared of?

"Moira!" Rafe followed her.

"Leave it alone."

"No."

She spun around and pushed him. Though she was strong, he didn't budge. "I can't do this now! I need my senses, all of them, under my control, and when you push me like this, I lose control. I feel raw, open, and exposed. I can't let it overwhelm me. Please. Just leave it."

On the verge of tears, she turned around so he couldn't see her face.

He said nothing for a long minute. Moira worked on controlling her breathing, stuffing her feelings deep inside, focusing on her sixth sense, the sense that felt magical energy. The sense that felt what no one else could see.

He touched her shoulders gently and whispered in her ear, "I understand."

Somehow, that admission unnerved her more than their argument.

"But I want you to know that this isn't simple lust. Together, we have far more than a physical attraction. We'll talk about it more. Sooner rather than later." He kissed the back of her neck, and Moira almost leaned against him. Almost gave in to a moment of bliss that she didn't deserve. Rafe understood her. No one else did. No one else even tried.

But she didn't give in to temptation. How could she when so much was at stake? When at risk was not only her life, but the lives of scores of innocents?

Rafe dropped his hands and led the way out of the parking garage.

NINE

Grant sat in the interview room at police headquarters with Nina Hardwick, a plump, attractive woman in her late thirties. Under any other circumstances, he wouldn't have given the hysterical woman more than two minutes of his time, but Nina Hardwick was not a typical woman. She was a well-respected lawyer for the Board of Supervisors, and they'd crossed paths several times over the years.

Nina had always seemed by-the-book. That she'd admitted to an affair with the married George Erickson, regardless of his open marriage arrangement, surprised Grant. But his bewilderment turned to shock when Nina made strong accusations against her dead lover's wife.

"Pamela Erickson killed George," Nina said. "You can't let her get away with it!"

Sitting across the table from her, he tried for sincerity. "Nina—it's okay that I call you Nina?"

She looked down her nose at him. "Cut the good-cop crap, Grant, I think we're past the formalities. I'm not crazy."

"Mrs. Erickson has a solid alibi."

"I don't care if she was at a dinner with the governor, president, and pope! She killed him as sure as I graduated *summa cum laude* from USC. She doesn't have to actually be there to kill him, right? She could have poisoned him, or hired someone, or—"

Grant cut her off, "I just came from the autopsy." He had a hundred things to do and the day was nearly over. And while he'd certainly go over Erickson's case again, he had nothing that pointed to Pamela Erickson as a killer. "There are no physical signs of foul play. We should know more after the weekend. If he was poisoned, we'll know from the bloodwork. Full panel."

She dismissed his comments with a regal wave of her unadorned hand. "You don't get it, Grant. She doesn't need to poison him. She's a witch."

Grant rubbed his temple. "Nina, it's been a long day and I just came from the morgue. Pamela Erickson has an alibi, and I have her on security camera, not just a witness. Jeff and I have talked to half a dozen people who confirmed that the Ericksons had an open marriage. I haven't talked to everyone on the list, but by Monday I don't expect to learn anything different. You were having an affair with him, I can understand why you're upset, but there were signs he was with a different woman last night."

She slammed her hand on the table. "He wasn't!"

He raised an eyebrow. "Were you with George last night?"

She stared at him, obviously stunned. "*What?*" She shook her head. "Grant Nelson, I swear—"

"I'm a cop, Nina. You just admitted to an affair with a married man and are accusing his wife of murder. We know he was with someone last night, someone who walked out while he was dead or dying. Was that you?"

She stifled a sob. "No."

"I assume you have an alibi," he said softly.

"I was in Sacramento for the last two days. County business. My flight came into Burbank at eleven-thirty this morning. I heard about George on the noon news as I was driving to the office."

Pretty damn solid, Grant thought, even though he hadn't believed for a second that Nina had killed Erickson. "Nina, if he cheated on his wife with you, he could have cheated on you with someone else. Believe me, I know what I speak about. I wasn't faithful to my ex-wife, or my mistress."

Nina leaned forward in her chair, her hands clasped on the table, her knuckles white with the pressure. She spoke slowly as if he were a child. "Grant. George's marriage was only open on one side."

Grant frowned. "Excuse me?"

"George let Pam fool around because that's what Pam wanted. I swear, he was under a spell when he married her. I've known George for years, since I interned in his offices while I was in law school. We were friends for a long time—he's ten years older, I never thought we'd get involved—but about a year ago I ran into him at a political fund-raiser. He was upset. He explained their arrangement and how he didn't know why he'd ever agreed to it, because it wasn't how he was raised. He said he loved Pam . . . but when he said it, somehow he didn't mean it. I think he *knew* he didn't mean it.

"We started talking, and I was going to help him divorce her. One thing led to another and we fell in love. It was an affair of the heart long before it became sexual. Pam found out and had a meltdown. George was not allowed to cheat on her, but she could screw any number of men. That's when I hired the private investigator."

She reached below the table into her briefcase and pulled out a half-inch manila folder. "He found some very interesting things about Pamela Levin Erickson."

The folder was standard P.I. issue. Photographs of the subject, timed and dated notes, detailed observations. He flipped through the folder more to humor Nina than because he expected to find anything. He stopped when he came to a photo of an orgy. Two women and one man who couldn't be identified in the picture, his face blocked by one of the women. Pam Erickson was naked and very much an active participant.

"Interesting, hmm?" Nina said.

"This doesn't prove anything."

"Turn to the next one."

This picture was of the same scene but a wider shot. The three participants were in the middle of some sort of odd circle with candles surrounding them. Several partially clothed women were observing the orgy.

Grant recognized Wendy Donovan, the manager of Velocity. She stood inside the circle wearing a sheer gown, watching. She held something in her hands, but Grant couldn't tell what it was. It seemed to reflect the light of the candles.

He swallowed uneasily, then cleared his throat.

"She's a witch," Nina said.

He straightened. "You mean a *witch*? I thought you meant something else."

"I generally mean what I say, Grant. She's a witch. A real witch. I know it's hard to believe, and if I hadn't seen these pictures and followed up with my own research I'd never have paid the P.I. I hired, Carson Felix."

"Felix?" Carson Felix had been one of the most respected private investigators in the city. The city had often hired him for contract work, and he'd often been retained by the rich and famous. He'd investigated everything from cheating spouses to kidnappings to embezzlement.

And he was dead.

"Well, you know what happened to him," Nina said.

"He committed suicide two months ago."

"Bullshit. He *supposedly* committed suicide—"

"There were multiple witnesses. He'd been acting depressed for weeks and left his office desolate. A dozen people saw him take a nosedive off the San Pedro Bridge."

"He was driven to do it. I don't know how she did it, but Pam had to have found out he'd taken pictures of their sick rituals."

"It might not be our thing, but—"

"Don't feed me a line about privacy in the bedroom. I was having an affair with a married man, I'm no saint, but dammit, it wasn't just the orgies. Even Felix was scared. He gave me that report and said he was through, that they were *evil*. Felix, who helped you guys with some badass killers and never batted an eye? Calling a group of naked women *evil*? *Quitting* an assignment? Felix was freaked out. There's something going on!"

"I'll look into it," he said. He hadn't planned on following up on anything Nina said, but that there was yet another connection to Velocity disturbed him.

"Be careful, Grant. These people are crazy, but they're smart. And they obviously know how to get people to do things they wouldn't otherwise do."

"Nina, why aren't you worried about your own safety?"

"Because Pam didn't know who George was sleeping

with, just that he was having an affair. We were extremely discreet."

"And she couldn't have hired a P.I.?"

"If she knew who I was, there's no doubt I'd be dead, too. Unless—" She hesitated.

"Unless what? I'm losing my patience."

"Read Felix's file. He suggests that Pam belongs to a female coven of witches. Maybe they have some sort of principle that they don't go after other women."

"Coven," he said flatly.

"Don't look at me like I'm a crazy scorned woman. I didn't believe any of this crap for a long time. I have my guard up; make sure you do, too."

Grant didn't know what to believe. He wouldn't have even considered any of it, except Nina was someone he knew and respected. After she left, he took Carson Felix's file to Jeff's desk, where his partner was updating reports.

"I don't know if Nina is smoking crack or onto something," Grant said, "but even if her theory is wrong, Pamela Erickson needs to stay on our list." He handed Jeff the file. "Do not let this out of your sight. I want every person in that file identified. Name, last known address, place of employment, criminal records. And, verify Nina's alibi. I doubt she's lying, but we have to check."

Grant retrieved the one clear picture of Wendy Donovan, Velocity's manager, and put it in his own file folder. In this case, it would be better to just ask. In person.

Skye sat on a bench one hundred feet outside the main doors leading to the morgue. It reeked of cigarettes, the ashtray overflowing. But it was the only place to sit outside.

She didn't want to sit, so she stood and paced.

She missed Anthony so much it hurt. Especially now. Somehow, when he was at her side, she felt as if she could do anything. That with all the crap hitting the fan, they'd make it through. Without him, she saw the mess she called her life. The lies and deception to her staff. The manipulation. Breaking the law. Her career was in jeopardy, and with it her reputation and very likely her freedom.

"Skye, what's wrong?"

She hadn't heard Rod Fielding approach. Rod had heard all this before; he was one of the few people she could confide in because he was one of only two members of her staff who knew exactly what was going on. She didn't want to dump on him again. Instead, she asked, "What'd you learn?"

"Don Takasugi, the supervising pathologist, knows his stuff. I've left the two brains with him and he's going to dissect them himself. He normally has a neuroscientist come in, but he's personally curious."

"Rod, I don't have to tell you that—"

He put his hand up. "I understand that we could be run out as laughingstocks, lose our jobs and pensions if we talk about what *really* happened to those victims, but we might not have a choice. The micro exam on Rucker showed an enlarged amygdala—the memory and emotional center of the brain. The cerebral cortex is extremely complicated, but if this is how the *demon*"— he whispered the word—"is affecting people I might be able to come up with an antidote, or at least a way to slow the growth of the affected cells. But I can't do it on my own. I don't have the skills."

"And just who would you bring in?"

"I don't know. I've been thinking about it all day. I was hoping Anthony might know someone."

"He just boarded his connecting flight out of New York. I'll talk to him when he lands."

"Learn anything at the autopsy? Want me to go back in and talk to Takasugi?" Rod asked.

"There's nothing we don't already know."

Her phone rang—Assistant Sheriff Hank Santos.

"McPherson," she answered.

"That bastard Truxel," he said, his voice low. "He just let Elizabeth Ellis out of jail."

Elizabeth Ellis was Lily's mother, and had been a willing participant in a violent ritual that nearly cost Lily her life. The D.A. had been a thorn in her side from the beginning of this mess, which started with Rafe's coma following the murder-suicide at the mission. "What?"

"He dropped all charges against her."

"He can't do that! Lily's pressing charges."

"He said she wasn't a credible witness."

"But my statement—"

"Heresay."

There was no use drilling Hank. There was nothing he could do about the situation, and nothing Skye could do from L.A.

But a free Elizabeth Ellis put Lily at risk. "Take Lily to my house. I'll be back tonight and take responsibility for her protection."

"Do you really think that Mrs. Ellis is going to hurt her own daughter?"

Skye didn't know—but Rafe had been adamant that

Lily was still in danger. "I can't risk it. I'll keep her this weekend, and hopefully by Monday Anthony will be back from Italy and we'll come up with a better solution. Keep a close eye on her."

"I will."

Rod shook his head, stunned. "That idiot Truxel let Ellis out of jail?" he asked when Skye hung up.

"We have to go back. I can't believe this!" That the D.A. didn't take the sworn statement of the sheriff as cause enough was a huge problem. The press was going to have a field day. And how could she protect Lily, Anthony, and her staff? Everything was spiraling out of control.

"Where did Cooper and Moira go?"

"To that nightclub, Velocity."

Skye didn't want to leave them in Los Angeles, but she didn't see how she had a choice. She felt torn and hopeless. "I hope Rafe and Moira find something at the club; otherwise we're at a dead end, and I need to get back to Santa Louisa right away."

TEN

The past is never dead. It's not even past.
—WILLIAM FAULKNER

Velocity spanned half a block, from the corner to a narrow alley wide enough for one car. Opaque black glass, embedded with blue and green neon lighting that flowed in a minimalist version of ocean waves framed the exterior on two sides. It had the simple, understated elegance only achieved with a lot of money.

"You're quiet," Rafe said.

Moira didn't address his unspoken question. She'd pushed their argument in the garage aside; she had to focus on her other senses, not the feelings between her and Rafe.

"I'll bet they charge twenty bucks a drink," Moira muttered. "And they probably don't have Guinness on tap."

"It doesn't look open."

Moira pulled out her phone and looked Velocity up. "Friday night, open from five until two. It's only three. I don't really want to hang around for the next couple hours."

A woman walked out of the building, an oversized tote over her shoulder. She wore impossibly tall heels, but when she reached the corner, she slipped them off and put on Vans.

"So we know people are inside," Rafe said.

"I can pretend I'm interviewing for a job."

"I doubt they interview right before opening."

"I can pretend I'm a health inspector."

He just stared at her and shook his head. "I've been thinking about this. The demon can go anywhere it wants, right?"

"Pretty much, though they're probably looking for easy marks."

"So why *here*?"

She thought about it. "You're right, you'd think the demon would want to spread its warm fuzzies. Why stay in one club? There're probably a hundred of these places that appeal to the raging-hormone crowd." Moira straightened. "Maybe—" She hesitated.

"What?"

"As far as we know, no one in Fiona's coven was affected by the demons. Yet we know they were in contact with Envy's victims."

Rafe nodded. "The demons could be connected to them in some way. Following them around."

"If Fiona figures this out, she'll have a way to bring the Seven back together by reuniting her coven."

"Not if we trap them first."

She glanced over at the nightclub. "Maybe Fiona *is* here."

"Moira—"

"I'm not planning anything stupid, Rafe. I just want to be prepared." She switched subjects, because Rafe seemed to understand too much about what she was thinking. She didn't want to lie to him about what she had planned when she found her mother. "Let's check out the alley. Maybe I'll sense a spell at work. Maybe that frat boy had a curse on him."

"You think you can sense the magic even after two days?"

"Possibly. After being so close to Envy, I think I can pick up on residual energy, over and beyond the foul stench the demons leave behind."

"Their scent doesn't last long."

"Probably not two days."

They walked past the building toward the alleyway that ran parallel and several blocks south of Wilshire Boulevard. Moira relaxed, focused on the energy in the area. But Rafe's close presence distracted her. She felt his emotions, and they were all directed toward her, even as he looked down the alley and assessed the area. His feelings were clogging her senses.

"Rafe, I need to go down there alone. You're messing with my head."

"Are you sure?"

She smiled, widely, hoping to alleviate Rafe's worries. No luck, he still looked concerned.

"I'll be right here."

Moira walked slowly down the alley. It went all the way through to the street on the other side, but was narrow and didn't look as if it was used for much of anything but servicing four dumpsters. A few unmarked doors on both sides of the alley suggested emergency or employee entrances.

Craig Monroe had been found with his pants around his ankles, with no outward sign of homicide. Had there been no demon's mark on the college kid's back, Moira wouldn't even be here. It would have been a human crime, not a supernatural murder.

What drew the demon to Velocity? What made it stay? Why had it not spread the deadly rages of unrestrained lust far and wide? Perhaps it wasn't as easy as simple contact. Moira realized there were far more complexities to these demons than any of them understood. What needed to happen before the demons affected someone? It had been more than two weeks since the Seven Deadly Sins had been released. Had the demon Lust been in Los Angeles since the beginning, or arrived more recently? Envy had managed to destroy many lives and families in two short days; why was Lust taking so much longer?

Moira moved farther down the alley. Though direct sunlight was nonexistent between the buildings and the stench of days-old garbage uncomfortably filled her olfactory senses, she'd nevertheless much rather be here than in the morgue watching some dead guy get cut open.

While the signs of police activity were gone—and there were no convenient chalk outlines like in the movies—Moira knew exactly where the body had been found. In the center of the alley between two dumpsters was a surprisingly clean square of stained cement. It had probably been picked clean by cops collecting evidence.

She leaned over, noting a faint stain on the gray brick wall, at approximately the height where a sitting body would rest. Her heart quickened when she considered it might be washed blood, but that was impossible. Craig Monroe hadn't had a scratch on him.

Moira touched the wall. A wave of pain spiked down her nerve endings and sent her jumping back several feet.

An odd, unsettling sensation washed over her as the pain faded. She wanted to run far away, but if she didn't figure out what was going on here in this alley, who else would? She slowed her breathing and concentrated, using her "Spidey Sense," as Rico in a rare moment of humor dubbed her sharp instincts. Intuition, a sixth sense, whatever others might name it—she had it in spades, and she'd worked hard to learn to decipher her subconscious thoughts and feelings. But it didn't come easily. And honestly, she didn't like it. Opening her senses forced her to lower her guard, making her vulnerable and defenseless. But there was no other way to know for certain whether there had been demonic or magical energy in the area.

She reached into her jacket, her weapons now within easy reach.

Her peripheral vision darkened. The air cooled around her. A light breeze swept down the alley, rustling newspapers and food wrappers that had missed their designated receptacle. The sky overhead grew darker and lights came on at either end of the alley and over doorways, except for the one door marked VELOCITY EMPLOYEE ENTRANCE.

Lights . . . why were the lights on in the middle of the day?

It was no longer day, it was night. Moira froze, rooted in her spot, staring at the dark space between the dumpsters, and realized a young man stood there. Craig Monroe.

"Damn, but you're hot," he said. "I can't believe I'm doing this here. I want to fuck your brains out."

With shimmering brown hair that seemed to sparkle in the dim light, a voluptuous woman stepped forward and kissed him. Moira couldn't see her face. She knew this was a vision—it had to be a vision; they couldn't see her. But she was awake! It seemed so real. And it was more vivid than a vision, brighter. She smelled the alley, felt the chill, and saw everything sharply—too sharply, as if altered through a prism. She glanced around her, but everything was dark. All Moira saw were lights above doorways and deep, endless shadows.

She had no sense of emotion or life from the images in front of her, as if they were ghosts.

If Craig Monroe was a ghost reliving his last moments, trapped between Heaven and Hell, this alley was now haunted. Moira was no expert on getting rid of ghosts. Demons, yes; ghosts were a whole other business. Ghosts could be dangerous, but they weren't a direct threat and they rarely roamed. Moira could contact any number of people to deal with Monroe and release his soul to wherever it was supposed to go.

Monroe didn't seem to see her, and he didn't look like a ghost. Or act like a ghost. While he stood right in front of her, she knew better than to try and touch him. She didn't want to give him an easy way to get inside her.

"I'm so hungry for you," he said with a primal growl. He was looking right at Moira, but not at her. She remained frozen, ready to run or fight.

The woman said, "What do you want?"

"Suck my dick. That's what you promised."

The woman laughed, a low, seductive sound. She kissed him and he grabbed at her, eager, greedy. Fisted her hair violently in his hands. Pushed her down to her knees so hard it had to have hurt, but the woman didn't protest. She unzipped his pants and pulled them with his boxers down to his ankles. His penis jutted out, hard and red and quivering.

"Do it!" Craig commanded.

The woman took his dick into her mouth and he groaned. Oddly, Monroe looked pained as he thrust himself into the willing woman's mouth, his hands pressing her head against him, unconcerned about whether she could breathe or whether he hurt her. His knuckles were white from the pressure, and he grunted. Moira wanted to beat him senseless for the complete disregard he showed for the woman, as if she were there solely for his pleasure.

Moira knew this wasn't real. But it *was*. It wasn't happening now, but it *had* happened. She'd heard of imprinting, where an act of violence imprinted itself on a place and certain people—empaths—could sense the crime. But she'd never heard of anyone actually *seeing* the act itself unless there was a ghost involved.

One of her hands moved to her pocket that had salt. Her other hand was wrapped around her dagger.

The color drained from Craig's face and he cried out, "What—what—" then his body jerked, his eyes bugging out in complete terror. His mouth moved but no words came out, only a high-pitched, barely audible screech that gave Moira goose bumps. No human sounded like that.

The woman rose from the filthy alley as Craig stared blindly at Moira, his body sliding down the wall as he fell, dying.

He's not seeing you. He's not seeing you.

"No—" His voice was weak. Moira didn't know if she actually heard him, or if it was her mind filling in the plea.

The woman put her hands on his head and said, "*Vestri animus est mei, adeo mihi.*"

Your soul is mine, come to me.

Craig's spirit—his soul—rose from his body. Not a ghost, but his actual soul. Moira had never seen a soul as it was ripped from a body, but she'd heard it was possible. Had nightmares about the possibility. Craig's cursed soul was a dark-gray glowing mist. It wrapped around his body, trying to get back in. The woman opened her mouth, sucking in the mist—his soul. Her entire body momentarily darkened, then it shimmered seductively. She dazzled, becoming even more beautiful than she already was, unnaturally stunning.

The demon turned and saw Moira. Her eyes widened in total surprise. Moira reached for her dagger, not understanding what was happening. Had she slipped back in time? Impossible. She almost laughed. After what she'd seen and done in her life, backtracking a couple of days seemed plausible!

Then she recognized the woman—the same brunette she'd had the vision about that morning. The woman who was possessed.

Craig Monroe had been killed two days ago. The chilling realization that Moira was sharing some sort of experience or memory with this vile demon terrified her, but she stood her ground. Swallowing her fear, she said with surprising authority, "*Deus, in nómine tuo salvum me fac, et virtúte tua age causam meam! Deus, audi—*"

The demon cut her off. "Moira, darling. You do not understand."

Moira held out the sacred blade, ready to defend herself or kill if she had to. She didn't want to take an innocent life, prayed she could save the victim the demon was using.

"*Deus, audi—*" she started again, her voice cracking.

The demon laughed. "You foolish child." She grimaced. "But now I need to find another vessel. That displeases me."

With a flick of the demon's wrist, Moira was flung across the alley and slammed against a brick wall. She fell to the filthy ground with a thud. Trying to rise, her vision blurred and her head ached. She closed her eyes. A wave of heat crossed over her and she tried in vain to stand, then she collapsed.

I just need a minute . . .

ELEVEN

Rafe ran toward Moira as she flew across the alley and hit the brick wall. Intense rage and deep-seated fear filled his mind even as his instincts had him scanning the area for threats. Moira tried to rise, then collapsed. She wasn't moving by the time he'd reached her side.

Rafe glanced at the wall where Moira had been staring. There was nothing there. He'd known something was wrong, but she'd made it perfectly clear she needed space to concentrate, and his presence distracted her. If he had gotten there sooner, she wouldn't have been hurt.

Her charge is extremely dangerous and any distractions will prove fatal.

Rico's warning came unbidden, and Rafe scowled, pushing the thought from his mind. But Rico had planted the seed, and now Rafe feared his former trainer was right.

He knelt next to Moira and checked her pulse. Strong. Rapid, but steady. Thank God. She was unconscious, though, and that worried him. "Moira? It's Rafe." Her face had a nasty scrape from where she'd fallen, and there was a bump on the back of her head. He pulled his hand from her hair and came away with a smear of blood, but there didn't appear to be a deep cut.

Dammit, he shouldn't have let her go down the alley alone!

Her knife had fallen out of her grip. He heard something behind him and quickly pocketed the dagger inside his jacket.

"Slowly move away from the body," commanded a deep voice behind Rafe. "This is the police; keep your hands where I can see them."

He hesitated. Moira's gun was partly visible.

"Now!" the cop shouted.

His back to the police officer, Rafe gently placed Moira's head on the ground, and while doing so shifted her jacket so that her gun wasn't visible. He couldn't take the chance that the cop would see him remove it from her holster. Slowly, he stood up and turned to face the cop, who had his gun drawn and aimed at Rafe.

Rafe said, "She needs help."

"Step away from the body."

"I'm not leaving her lying in this filthy alley!"

"Step away from the body," the cop repeated as he walked briskly down the alley, his eyes never leaving Rafe. "Keep your hands where I can see them."

Rafe did what the cop demanded. The cop knelt to check Moira's pulse, his gun still on Rafe.

"What happened?" the cop said.

The alley door across from Rafe opened—it was the employee entrance to the nightclub. A muscular black guy walked out. "Trouble, Detective?"

"Call an ambulance, Reggie. How long has she been out?"

Rafe said, "Two or three minutes." He started toward Moira and the cop said, "Stand back. Do you have identification?"

Rafe began to retrieve his wallet and the cop shook his head. "Back right pocket," Rafe said.

"Turn around, put your hands on the wall."

Rafe complied. The cop pulled out his wallet. "You can turn around, but keep your hands where I can see them."

"Name's Raphael Cooper. I live in Santa Louisa."

The cop's head shot up, his eyes narrowed. "Santa Louisa?"

Moira moaned and tried to get up. Rafe stepped toward her, and the cop put a hand on his chest. "Hold it, Cooper."

The detective looked again at Moira. "Moira O'Donnell," he said as he recognized her. "From the morgue." He shook his head. "Well, fuck me. I told Sheriff McPherson to stay the hell out of my case."

It would have to be Detective Grant Nelson, the lead cop in the deaths they were investigating.

"Skye didn't know we were here," Rafe said.

"I don't buy that for one minute."

Moira got up on all fours. "Please," she said, "no ambulance." She spit out saliva tinged with blood.

"Moira," Rafe said, "don't move."

"I'm fine," she mumbled.

Nelson helped Moira sit up and lean against the wall. It was obvious to Rafe he'd spotted her gun as his stance changed from helpful to suspicious.

"Tell me what happened," he demanded of Moira, watching both her and Rafe closely.

She took a deep breath, glanced at Rafe, then proceeded to lie smoothly. "I was walking down the alley and someone pushed me against the wall. I must have banged my head harder than I thought, because I went out."

"Who pushed you?"

"I don't know."

"They? How many?"

"Three boys. Older boys, in their teens."

"They just ran through the alley and pushed you down."

"They were huddled together. I think I surprised them."

"Know what they look like?"

She shook her head.

"White? Black? Purple?"

She glared at him. "White. Skinny and dressed like kids—jeans and T-shirts. It happened fast. My head hurts."

"An ambulance is on its way."

"I'm fine."

"You should be checked out."

"I said I am fine."

"Why were you here in the first place?"

"Is it a private alley?"

Rafe saw that Nelson was getting irritated with Moira's answers, so he said, "Detective, we just wanted to see the club where the kid died."

"You're not a cop. Your friend the sheriff doesn't have jurisdiction. You're interfering with a police investigation and I swear, I'm this close to taking you both to jail."

Moira paled, and Rafe wasn't going to let anyone imprison Moira again. He said, "We'll go, Detective. Sorry to have caused a problem; we didn't mean to interfere."

"Nelson," Reggie said, "the girl doesn't look too good."

The detective lost some of his hard edge. "Let's get her inside." He glanced at Rafe. "You want to help me?"

Rafe wrapped one arm around Moira, Nelson did the same on the other side, and they helped her to her feet.

"I can walk," she insisted, though she leaned heavily on Rafe. Her eyes were half closed and Rafe noticed she was trying to shake off the dizziness.

Reggie opened the employee door. "This is the break room. You can sit in here a minute."

Rafe said, "Let's get you some water."

"Cancel the ambulance. Please."

"No," Nelson said.

"Please," she said again, in her *don't-argue-with-me* tone.

"It's against my better judgment," Nelson said, then nodded to Reggie, who was back on his cell phone, shaking his head.

As soon as Moira stepped through the doorway into the break room, she felt magic. It wasn't strong, but there was enough here to have her skin tingling. She wasn't consciously searching for it; the wave hit her unexpectedly, and she shivered.

"What is it?" Rafe whispered.

"Detective," Moira said, "could I get some water?"

Reggie said, "I'll get it. I'll tell Wendy you're back here."

Damn, she didn't want to talk around the cop.

Reggie popped his head back in. "Nelson, there are two cops up front."

Detective Nelson said, "Stay here. I'm serious." He tapped Rafe's wallet. "I'm keeping this, because we're not done talking."

As soon as he left, Moira stood. When Rafe protested, she said, "I'm fine. Shaken. I had a vision. I think."

"What the hell happened out there? A ghost?"

"A demon."

He reached for his dagger, but Moira motioned for him to keep it hidden. "Not now, in the past."

"I don't understand."

"I don't, either. I thought at first it was a death imprint—everything darkened, the lights came on, and I saw Craig Monroe walk in front of me, followed by a woman. It was the same woman I had the vision about last night. The brunette."

"You're certain? The woman you thought was possessed?"

Moira nodded. She felt so cold just remembering the image of Craig Monroe dying so violently, his soul drawn out before he was gone. She sat down again to collect her thoughts.

"At first I thought she was a victim and he'd been infected. By the way he was treating her—she seemed to be willing, but he was rough and mean. She gave him oral sex, but right when . . . you know . . . something else happened. He was dying. He saw something in her face and he was scared shitless—I couldn't see her face, but I saw his." She shivered. "He begged her to stop, then she sucked his soul out of his body, swallowing it with her mouth. She's a demon—very powerful—but she was definitely in a human body." She frowned. "I didn't know she was a demon—I couldn't feel anything, no magic, no otherworldly power; it was like watching a movie. But when she spoke she said his soul was hers."

She hesitated, and Rafe prompted. "How did you get thrown against the wall if it was a death imprint?"

"It was the demon. She saw me."

"That's impossible."

She scowled. Rafe sounded as though he didn't believe

her. "I don't know how it happened! She turned and saw me. It was unreal. Like—like maybe I went back in time. I know that's not possible—dammit, I don't know what's possible anymore! But the demon saw me, looked right at me, called me by name!"

Rafe looked as though she'd slapped him. "The demon talked to you?"

Moira couldn't stop shaking. Rafe sat next to her. He put his hands on her shoulders and rubbed. "Moira, I'm not going to let anything happen to you. You're safe now."

"Safe." She closed her eyes and took a deep breath, then whispered, "I don't think we'll ever be safe."

"Have you heard of anything like this before?"

She shook her head. "I started an exorcism—I knew subconsciously that it wasn't going to work, because Monroe was already long dead and the demon wasn't there, but I thought maybe the demon was just coming back to the scene of the crime, or I was in Hell or something. I don't know! But she looked at me, laughed, said I didn't understand. Called me a fool and tossed me against the wall. Didn't touch me. Couldn't." She opened her eyes. "She knew me."

"Anthony understands how demons operate. I'll call him."

"He's still on a plane to Italy."

"We'll figure it out. It could be a mind trick, a spell—something that had you seeing Monroe's death."

"She said something else, that she had to find another vessel. I think she was angry that I'd seen her victim. But I don't know the woman. I don't know where to start looking."

Moira stood, and Rafe said, "You need to take it easy. You have a nasty bump."

"I've had worse. I need to shake it off. I don't like it here." She began to walk around the room, stopping in front of the employee lockers. She closed her eyes, her hand inches from the front of each locker as she walked by. "There's magic here." She hesitated in front of the next locker. "And here." She kept going. At the end she stopped. "There's a witch for virtually every locker! But this one belongs to the leader."

"How can you tell?"

"The strength, the power. It's in her clothes, in everything she has." She looked at the name on the locker. She blanched.

"Moira?"

"Donovan. It says Wendy Donovan. That can't be a coincidence." One of the witches in Fiona's coven who escaped during the chaos when they trapped the demon Envy was *Nicole* Donovan. She had seduced a cop and had an in with the police. Information obtained by her had helped the coven elude police. Nicole had also recruited students from Santa Louisa High into the coven and had nearly killed Moira.

The door opened and Detective Nelson walked in with a stately, beautiful woman in her thirties. The woman glared at Moira. "She looks fine to me."

"Wendy, I just need a place to talk to them and find out what happened in the alley."

Moira knew that Wendy was the head witch, the high priestess, and this was her locker. Magical energy bubbled beneath the surface of the woman's skin, ready to lash out, but she kept it under tight control.

Detective Nelson handed Moira a water bottle.

Wendy said, "First you come in here making accusations against *me* and then expect me to help *you*?"

"I explained I have to follow up on every lead."

"Lead? You can't think that the lawyer's death had anything to do with the club. We're already dealing with press issues because of what Kent did."

"I'm not going to publicize this. You know me better than that."

Wendy didn't look happy, but Moira suspected it had more to do with her presence than with Nelson's investigation. The negative energy coming from Wendy was aimed right at her. If she was a witch tied into black magic like Moira thought she was—and her sister was in fact Nicole Donovan—Wendy would know who she was, and who her mother was.

"Fine," Wendy said, "but we open in forty-five minutes, and I need you gone."

"Can we use your office?" Nelson asked.

"No," she said and walked out.

Moira said, "Hostile, isn't she?"

Nelson ignored her comment. "What were you doing in the alley?"

"We told you."

"I'm not buying it. Did McPherson send you down?"

"The deaths of Mr. Monroe and Mr. Erickson are connected," Moira said. "You saw the marks on their bodies."

"The coroner found no evidence of homicide," Nelson said.

"Then why are you still investigating?"

He hesitated. "Do you have evidence that proves the deaths were not natural?"

Neither Moira nor Rafe said anything. Detective Nelson looked tired and frustrated. Moira began to feel odd—the hair on her skin rose. She feared she was being watched, but when she surveyed the room there was nothing here. Yet . . . she trusted her instincts. Slowly she relaxed the internal barrier that protected her senses. She allowed herself to feel the magical energy building in the air.

"We might be able to help," Moira said.

"You have evidence?" He sounded sarcastic.

Moira was taking a risk telling the outsider anything, but she didn't know how else to bring him to their side. "Does Wendy Donovan have a sister named Nicole?"

The question surprised Nelson, and the answer was clear on his face even before he said yes.

"I knew it," Moira said.

"Meaning?"

Rafe answered. "Nicole Donovan is wanted for questioning as a material witness in the murder of a priest two weeks ago."

"Ask Sheriff McPherson," Moira added.

Detective Nelson stood. "Wait here," he said. "I'll be right back."

"Don't tip them off!" Moira said.

He looked at her squarely. "I have no intention of doing any such thing, but I'm going to verify your accusation."

As soon as he left, Moira said, "Do you feel something?"

"No—but I can tell you do."

"I don't know exactly what, but I think someone is in the process of casting a spell. It's not a full ritual—too subtle—but it's definitely here."

Moira went back to Wendy Donovan's locker. She

picked the lock in five seconds and Rafe said, "What are you doing?"

"We're leaving, but I need to know where I can find her."

"We should call Skye, get her over here to straighten this out. I don't want you going back to jail."

Moira closed her eyes and said, "I think—it feels to me like the spell is aimed at Detective Nelson." She looked at Rafe. "What if that's what they're doing? Trying to get him to put us in jail? Right where Fiona can get at me?"

Panic rose and she swallowed uneasily.

"Okay, let's get out of here. He's not going to be happy if we walk out but I don't see another option."

"Better we walk than if he finds our weapons." She frowned, reaching into her pocket. "My—"

"I have your dagger." Rafe slipped it from his pocket to her. She breathed in relief. "But he saw your gun. Didn't say anything; maybe he thought you're legal because you work with Skye."

"He knows I'm not a cop. I'd rather take my chances out there than here. But I want to see what's in the witch's locker. Maybe she knows where Fiona is."

She looked through all Wendy's things. "No wallet, nothing! We need to find out where she lives. Maybe Nicole is there, hiding out—dammit, she needs to answer for what she did! How do we find her? Follow her when she gets off work?"

"We should talk to Jackson Moreno."

Moira froze. She closed Wendy's locker. Jackson Moreno—she had tried to forget about him and his family. She'd been so arrogant, so damn stupid back then.

When she thought she could save everyone. When she thought everyone wanted to be saved.

"No," she said emphatically. "We don't need him. Besides, he won't want to help me."

"Jackson knows more about witches in Los Angeles than anyone else."

"I know, but—"

"He has supplies; he's supported St. Michael's for years."

"He's not one of us."

"Technically, neither are you!"

Moira bit the inside of her bottom lip. It was true, but she expected comments like that from Anthony, not from Rafe. It hurt, reminding her that she was still alone.

"I'm sorry," Rafe said immediately, his voice full of remorse. "You know I didn't mean it like that. It's obvious you have issues with Moreno. But Father Philip trusted him. What about you? Do you not trust him?"

She shook her head. "It's not that," she said softly. "I've made a lot of mistakes in the past, and there're some people I don't want to see again. But you're right—Jackson will know everything there is to know about Wendy Donovan, or know where to get the information." She held up a small book.

"What's that?"

"Wendy's spell book. It seems to be notes and ideas, not her primary *grimoire*. But it might help us figure out exactly what she's up to and how it connects to this demon."

She suddenly jumped, her neck ice-cold.

"What's wrong?"

"We have to leave now. Detective Nelson is returning. I can't go back to jail, Rafe."

"I'm not letting anyone take you anywhere." He grabbed her hand and they ran out the back door.

Rico stepped into the sanctuary of Olivet, but he didn't feel the relief he normally experienced when he arrived at the place he called home in the foothills outside Missoula. They were close enough to the city that winter posed only an inconvenience, while many other places in Montana were completely cut off.

Olivet itself was a virtual fortress, with four connected L-shaped buildings surrounding a courtyard that blossomed breathtakingly in the spring and summer. When Moira had first arrived at Olivet, for her original assessment six years ago, she'd come in May, and the only time he'd seen peace cross her face was when she walked through the lush gardens in the courtyard.

Lodging was in the main building, along with their classrooms. The other buildings were off-limits to most people. But it was the deceptively small structure in the back, connected through underground tunnels that extended deep into the mountainside, where Rico brought the tabernacle.

Tobias—one of a set of triplets left at the doors of St. Michael's as infants twenty-eight years ago—was waiting for Rico when he arrived. He and his identical brothers Darius and Joseph had unusual gifts that made them indispensible to the Order. Rico did not like the term "psychic," for it felt unholy, but it was the closest to the truth. The triplets could communicate and share information with one another telepathically, which was an invaluable gift when you needed information immediately and there was no access to phone or computers. More so, the triplets could almost see out of their brothers' eyes. Rico had done extensive testing on the brothers to make sure there was no evil at the core of their gift, and he'd even brought Moira in and had her scour for magic or demonic energy that might be too subtle for Rico to recognize the signs. But it appeared that the gifts were truly heavenly—or at least, natural and not satanic. Sometimes it was hard to discern, but gifts came from within, while magic—witchcraft—came from casting spells and calling on supernatural forces.

Darius and Joseph were on assignment, but Tobias was here, keeping guard. "The storm has worsened," Tobias said.

"Yes, but I need to go out again." Rico placed the iron box on the table. Inside was Envy, contained in the tabernacle.

"I'll secure the beast."

"Thank you."

Tobias lifted the heavy chest with ease and took it to the vault.

Rico walked down the wide hall to the small lab. He sat at a sterile table and removed a vial of Moira's blood. One blood sample he'd hidden at the mission; another he'd placed in the box with Envy. He wasn't certain why—he was guided by instinct. But if his theory was correct, if there was something in Moira's blood that killed or harmed demons, then the presence of her blood might keep the demon under better control.

Rico had been asked to obtain only one sample for testing, but he'd learned that being prepared was akin to staying alive.

A ringing phone interrupted these thoughts. He answered it with a generic "Hello."

"It's Cardinal DeLucca. Rico?"

"Yes, Cardinal."

"Is it done?"

"The demon is in the vault."

"And did you get the sample?"

"Yes." His stomach felt unusually tight and uncomfortable. Moira had looked at him with such intense betrayal that guilt flooded him even now. He'd done many difficult things in his life in the battle against evil, but every action was required to save a soul. Something as simple as drawing Moira's blood shouldn't elicit such turmoil and doubt.

He did not doubt. His faith was what made him strong.

"Have you tested it yet?"

"No."

"You should have done it as soon as you landed."

"I had to secure the demon first."

"Of course." The cardinal sounded impatient, but Rico wasn't surprised. That the Seven Deadly Sins were on the earth threatened all of them. And with their recent losses . . . including Father Philip . . . Rico's chest hitched. Philip had been their rock. The human cornerstone of St. Michael's Order. Now the others looked to him for guidance, and he felt ill-prepared to be anything but the warrior that he was. Philip had been the leader; he'd been the one who led the counsel and who, in his silence, commanded the most respect.

If it weren't for Father Philip, Moira would have been executed long ago.

"Anthony is on his way," Rico said. "He'll be landing

in Italy just after noon, your time." Which was only about nine hours from now. Which meant it was past midnight for the cardinal. "You're up late, Cardinal."

"I won't be able to rest until I know the results."

He sighed. "I'll call you within the hour."

He rose, retrieved a syringe from supplies, and drew out half the blood in the vial. He then stored the remainder in a refrigerator, capped the syringe, and left.

Tobias was dressed for the cold. Rico hadn't asked him to join him in this assignment, but Tobias knew he was needed. "You had no choice, Rico," Tobias said.

He nodded. "Let's do it quickly."

While Rico had been traveling today, Tobias had located a possessed human. The man was restrained in a demon trap in another building on the far side of the compound. Now they would see if Moira's blood was what they suspected: poison to demons.

If they were right, then all the other research they'd discovered over the years would be validated. If her blood was poison, the words of the Unknown Martyr would be fulfilled: that only blood that could kill a demon could forever destroy the *Conoscenza*. Exactly as they had believed for so long.

They would have a powerful weapon in Moira against the demons that walked on earth; though the Seven could be sent back to Hell, there were others. The battle wouldn't be over until Judgment Day. Moira's blood would be in demand by everyone in the Order. They would bleed her to save the world, and Rico would be the one to force her to comply. He knew her well enough to know that she'd never agree to be locked here in Olivet for the rest of her life, a prisoner. But they couldn't let her roam. If the covens knew the power of her blood they would kill her, or use her in far more painful and hideous ways to control the demons they summoned. Renegade groups—unaffiliated with St. Michael's but whom they had worked with from time to time—would want her for their own plans, many of which went against the creed of St. Michael's: *Protect the innocent.*

Many in St. Michael's had died protecting the innocent lambs of God, but the men of St. Michael's were preordained to this call. And others had joined them from the outside. Like Moira.

You're in love with her.

Raphael's accusation had contained more truth than Rico had known until the words were spoken.

But love didn't matter when at stake was the fate of humanity.

TWELVE

Moira bit her thumbnail as Rafe turned into Moreno's church, Grace Harvest, near the Warner Bros. studio. Four years and it hadn't changed. The trees had grown a bit, and there was a new one growing near the main doors. Long ago, GH had been a Catholic church and it still had the simple Spanish mission façade with tile roofs and mission-style arches, but the stained glass had long ago been replaced by clear windows, and the crucifix replaced with three empty crosses.

GH was an independent church and while Moreno, with his charisma and personal wealth, could have grown the ministry into a powerhouse, he'd chosen to keep it of modest size and scope.

"Are you going to tell me what your problem is with Moreno?" Rafe asked her as he parked in the empty lot near the main church entrance.

She supposed she didn't really have a choice. "Do you know him?" she asked

"Only by reputation. He's an authority on witchcraft and has been tracking the dark magic covens, particularly in the western United States. Anthony and Father Philip worked with him many times over the years."

"You know his oldest daughter disappeared with a coven four years ago."

Rafe nodded. "It's what prompted him to devote so

much of his time to St. Michael's and give sanctuary to those who wanted to leave covens."

"I'm responsible for Courtney's fall."

"You." He stared at her, his dark blue eyes black with anger. "And Courtney had nothing to do with it? You have an inflated ego. You, alone, chased her into practicing black magic."

"No, but—" She clenched her fists. "I know what you're doing, and you weren't there!"

"You're always so damn hard on yourself, Moira!" Rafe snapped, running a hand through his dark hair. It fell back over his left eye. He reminded her of an Irish barkeep—hair a little too long, eyes a little too bright, and sex appeal far too potent for her to resist.

But she *would* resist.

Just think of all the people you hurt over the years, Moira. Do you want Rafe to be one of them?

That was enough to throw a wet blanket on her libido.

"I fucked up, Rafe."

"You carry the weight of the world on your shoulders, taking the blame for all the bad choices that other people make. Dammit, why not just take the blame for Eve? After all, she took a bite of the damn apple in the first place. But that was probably your fault, too—I'm sure you could figure out a way to feel guilty about the fall of man."

Moira grabbed the vehicle's door handle and opened it. Taking her arm, Rafe pulled her back inside the truck. She glared at him, pulling her arm free.

Rafe gently touched the side of her face. His hands shook just enough that Moira realized he was still upset with her. But the look on his face had softened as he ran the back of his hand up and down her cheek.

The silence between them unnerved her. She swallowed.

"There's no use holding off the inevitable," she muttered, glancing at Moreno's church.

He took her hand and kissed it. "Let's go."

The church was unlocked, but empty. They walked around the building to Jackson Moreno's small, well-kept home. A twenty-year-old Mercedes was parked in the driveway. Jackson had the same car four years ago.

Rafe knocked on the door and Jackson answered at once. "I saw you approach," he said with a glance at Rafe, his eyes focused on Moira.

She couldn't read his expression. Jackson Moreno was conservatively handsome, in his mid-forties, with light brown hair graying at the temples. He was as tall as Rafe, trim, and wore pressed beige slacks and a crisp button-down light-blue business shirt without a tie, the sleeves rolled up to the elbows.

Moira bit the inside of her cheek, remembering that she'd seen this man cry when his daughter disappeared.

"Moira." He was surprised to see them, his gray eyes inquisitive.

"Hello, Pastor Moreno. I—we're sorry to just drop in." She cleared her throat. "This is Rafe Cooper, he's with St. Michael's."

"Cooper—Raphael Cooper." He nodded in recognition. "I've heard of you, of course. Please, come in." He opened the screen door. "And call me Jackson. I am so sorry about Father Philip. He was truly a good man."

"Thank you," Rafe said, stepping inside. Moira hesitated.

"I can't imagine that this is a social call, however. Let's go to my study."

Rafe took Moira's hand and forced her to follow Jackson through the house to his study in the back.

Nothing had changed, Moira realized. The church, the house, even Jackson Moreno himself. Time seemed to stand still, and she felt just like she had that last day four years ago before she went back to Olivet, after telling Jackson that his daughter had left for good: miserable, unworthy, and a failure.

Jackson's study was small, dark, and masculine. A modest desk seemed to disappear among three walls of stuffed bookshelves and stacks of files. It was an organized mess. A single window looked out onto the parking lot and the church beyond.

"May I bring you coffee? Tea?"

"We're okay, thank you," Moira said. "We don't have a lot of time."

Jackson motioned for them to sit on the small couch; he took the desk chair, turning it to face them.

"I can only imagine. I heard about what happened in Santa Louisa."

"Then you know we only trapped one of the demons," Rafe said.

"I don't know the details. St. Michael's Order is justifiably tight-lipped. I learned, of course, about Father Philip's death, and that the Seven Deadly Sins are out. I was contacted to keep my eyes and ears open."

"We're here because you know more about the local covens than anyone, and we have a crisis," Rafe said. "We have reason to believe that the demon Lust is in Los Angeles."

"Sadly appropriate. But how in the world did you figure it out? I haven't heard anything, and I have been listening closely."

Moira turned her phone to show an image of the mark from George Erickson's body. Jackson frowned and inspected the photo while Moira said, "This is a demon mark. It's highly detailed and unusual—similar marks were on those infected by Envy as well. Three bodies have shown up at the morgue with this mark, and all three have a connection to Velocity, a nightclub which—"

"Velocity?" Jackson's head shot up and he handed her phone back. "It's been all over the news, the gossip about Kent Galion. A shock. Are you saying he was possessed?"

Moira shook her head. "We don't think that the men who were marked were possessed, but that they were infected somehow by the demon."

"Infected? I don't understand."

"Most demons possess their victims, but the Seven Deadly Sins are incarnate," Rafe explained. "They can possess a human if they want, but they don't need to."

"And what do you mean by infect?"

Moira said, "When someone is in contact with the demon, they act on that sin."

Jackson looked skeptical. "Then why isn't everyone consumed by lust? Or greed? Or any of the other sins? Shouldn't we be hearing about an epidemic of violence?"

Rafe elaborated. "We all have a conscience," he began. "Some are better formed than others. We know little about the Seven, but we know a lot more about human nature. We sometimes call our weaknesses our personal demons. Some of us are naturally predisposed to envy, for example. We are unfathomably jealous of other people and what they have that we don't. Yet our conscience helps us battle our personal sin, keeps it in check, so we don't steal or hurt people because they have something that we want. But the same person who is envious may not have a problem with lust or laziness or pride."

Jackson nodded. "I understand. In my ministry, I counsel many people and most have a primary weakness. But that doesn't explain why there are only a few who have been affected."

"We don't understand exactly how the demon operates. If the demon needs to physically touch its victims, or how much freedom the demon has in the first place."

"Freedom?"

Moira said, "An ancient spell brought them to Earth. Rafe stopped the ritual, but they were already free. We don't know how they affect people specifically, but we just learned that one of the original witches in the coven that released them is here in L.A." She paused, gathering her thoughts. "Maybe the demons are tied somehow to the witches involved in the ritual. Or they don't have all their strength because the ritual was interrupted."

Rafe considered that. "I hadn't thought of it like that. You could be right."

"There's a lot we don't know," Moira said, frustrated. "What we do know is that when a person is marked, they're pretty much toast."

Rafe frowned. "That's not exactly right. When we capture the demon, its power over its victims is gone. They regain their conscience."

"So it appears," she said, explaining to Jackson. "We

have proof that someone was infected in Santa Louisa and he seems fine now that Envy has been locked up."

Rafe continued, "The demon goes after the easy targets. A nightclub like Velocity is full of raging hormones. If Nicole somehow brought the demon with her to L.A., it would stay because feeding on those hormones, the physical attractions, would be easy."

"Hmm. Maybe." Moira squirmed. She really didn't care much for the whys and what-fors. She just wanted to stop the demon before anyone else died.

"And this is tied to Velocity?" Jackson asked.

"No doubt. We were at the club and I felt dark magic in the employee room. But it was Wendy Donovan's locker where it was the strongest."

Jackson couldn't hide his surprise, and Moira added softly, "My skills have improved; I don't make the same mistakes—"

He held up his hand to cut her off, and her heart skipped a beat. She wanted so badly to apologize for what happened with his daughter Courtney. Four years ago, she couldn't face him for more than the few minutes it took to tell him she'd failed. To see the pain and shock and rage on his face. The accusation that she was to blame. She couldn't beg for forgiveness then . . . and now he wouldn't let her.

Jackson said, "Wendy Donovan is the high priestess of an all-female coven. Half the witches are employees at Velocity. She's also part-owner and runs the place. Her co-manager, Julie Schroeder, is also high up in the coven." He looked at them pointedly. "They're an Azabet coven."

Moira's stomach flipped.

"What does that mean?" Rafe asked.

Moira said, "They have a devotion to a succubus. Once a year they sacrifice an unfaithful man to such a demon, who steals his soul, resulting in his death."

"But there are three victims, not one," Rafe said.

"Perhaps they're working a more dangerous ritual," Moira said. "But if it's a succubus, maybe we're wrong about the demon Lust."

"It makes no sense," Rafe said. "The marks on the bodies were made by one of the Seven—they are far too similar to the marks we saw in Santa Louisa."

Moira stood and paced the small room. How could Jackson, or anyone, work in such tight quarters? "I don't know!" she exclaimed, her aggravation leaking out. "I only know that a succubus is summoned by a coven and in exchange for whatever the witches ask for, the succubus is given a soul."

"Then what happens?"

"The succubus goes back to Hell with a full stomach?" Moira threw her hands up. "Why do you think I know everything about demons? I've never called on a succubus, I've never—"

Rafe didn't move, but he caught her eye and she felt foolish. She stared at the wall. It happened to hold a picture of Jackson with Courtney and his younger daughter, Caroline. She averted her eyes, her face red with embarrassment.

Rafe said slowly, "Maybe Wendy Donovan's coven found a way to trap Lust, thus the marks on the bodies."

"That would explain what's happened," Jackson said. "Who were the victims? Kent Galion and . . . ?"

"A college student," Rafe said. "Craig Monroe died in

the alley behind the club. Moira witnessed his death imprint, saw a demon draw out his soul."

Moira looked down, still not understanding what had happened in the alley.

"The third victim was a married man who died in his home after an apparent romantic interlude while his wife was out all night with her ex-husband, according to the police reports. He'd been at Velocity earlier that evening."

Jackson said, "I have information about Wendy's coven that I'm happy to share, but I must warn you that she is extremely dangerous."

"Aren't they all?" Moira said flippantly, glancing at Jackson.

"Perhaps. But Wendy is . . . ruthless. Perhaps borderline psychopathic. At any rate, her background may prove helpful."

"Do you know where she lives?" Moira asked.

"Yes."

"That's all I need."

"I would be extremely cautious in handling Wendy," Jackson said, concerned. "I've heard a lot about her, some of the stories almost unbelievable. She's powerful and cruel."

Rafe said, "It's wise to be well prepared before acting. We should learn everything we can about her so we know how to handle the situation."

"I don't disagree, Rafe, but the longer we wait, the more power Wendy Donovan and her sister amass. If they really did find a way to trap the demon Lust—or if Lust is attracted to the coven because of their ties to the succubus—more people are going to get hurt." Moira wanted so much to take them both down. Especially

Nicole, who had stood by and watched Envy kill Father Philip.

"We'll read the files and come up with a game plan, okay?"

She nodded reluctantly. People like Anthony and Jackson were researchers—she was a hunter. Yeah, she needed information, but more than that she needed to act. She hated being cooped up. She hated being in this tiny room.

Jackson said, "I'll be right back. I only know a few of their hierarchy, but I'm confident that my information is sound. I have it in my safe." He left the room.

Rafe said, "I told you it wouldn't be as bad as you thought."

"He has class. He's being gracious. I don't deserve it."

"Moira, if you keep beating yourself up like this Fiona will know exactly how to get to you. After she used my memories of the mission against me, I've been working hard to accept what happened, accept my blame, and move on. I can't be tortured like that again. I don't know if I could survive it."

"You would." Moira began to reach for him, then dropped her hand, nervous.

"I don't know that I'd want to. And you know you'll be hard-pressed to survive another attack by Fiona if she can twist your pain and use it against you. She wants you dead, Moira. I don't think she's going to play around next time."

Jackson stood in the doorway and frowned. "Are you in danger?"

"No more so than usual," Moira said with a wry smile.

Rafe took the folder and sat back down on the couch,

Moira next to him looking over his arm at Jackson's orderly documentation.

Jackson said, "They use traditional spells with blood and hair to create potions. From what I've learned about Azabet covens in general, they offer up one of their members to serve as the demon's vessel."

"They ask to be possessed?" Rafe asked, incredulous.

"Crazy, I know," Moira muttered. "Even Fiona wouldn't risk giving up her control, no matter what it might gain her. But sacrificing someone else? No problem."

Jackson continued. "The vessel is required to drink a potion, which marks her for the demon, and during the ritual the vessel is possessed for a specified time, usually twenty-four hours."

Moira interjected, "Because the victim is already prone to stray, he's easily seduced by the demon. After sex, the succubus steals his soul and his life, then leaves the vessel. But they have three victims racked up, and it doesn't look like they're slowing down."

"Maybe she lost control of the demon," Jackson suggested.

"What happens to the witch who was possessed?" Rafe asked.

"Sometimes she doesn't remember anything," Jackson replied. "She's often physically injured—the demon uses the body in unnatural ways. The possessed can lose their mind. I'm only aware of three of these covens operating in the world right now; they aren't common."

Moira flipped through the folder. She stopped on a picture of a brunette who was all too familiar. "This is her! This is the vessel used to kill Craig Monroe."

Jackson looked. "Nadine Anson. She's been with Wendy since the beginning."

"She's one of them! We know the demon is in her right now—at least it was. We need to find her."

"Her address is in there," Jackson said. "I believe it's near Velocity, where she works."

"We need to find her and figure out what ritual they're using to trap the demon," Moira said.

Jackson said, "I'll compile the rituals they may use to trap a succubus, but it'll take me a few hours."

"If they've trapped the demon Lust, is that going to help us?" Rafe asked.

Moira said, "It can't hurt. We have to assume that they trapped the demon Lust either by accident or on purpose. The demon is using the coven for purposes we don't know. Either way, covens are surprisingly traditional. While they experiment with new spells, when they find something that works, they stick with it."

"Maybe they were experimenting," Jackson said, "and that's why this demon is killing more than one man."

"You could be right. But first, we have to find Nadine. If the demon is still in her, we can at least contain it until we figure out what to do."

They all stood, and Jackson said, "I'll go through my notes, call a few experts, and hopefully have answers for you tonight."

"The sooner the better," Moira said.

"I understand the urgency," Jackson said as he walked them to the door. Then he added, "I owe you an apology, Moira."

She jerked her head around so fast she gave herself a pinch in the neck. "Excuse me?"

"I said some things to you four years ago that I've regretted. I should have written to you, I suppose, but I thought it would be better face-to-face, so you know I'm sincere. I expected our paths to cross long before this."

"You have nothing to apologize for," Moira said softly.

"Four years ago, I turned to Philip as my last hope of saving Courtney. I put all my faith in you when he said if Courtney could be saved, you could do it. But I'd already lost my daughter. Not a day goes by that I don't pray that she'll come home, and I'll welcome her. But it was her choice to leave, and good or bad, that's what God gave us in the Garden of Eden: free will. For better or worse." Jackson took her hands and squeezed. She swallowed uneasily. "But it wasn't Courtney who was at risk," he said, looking her in the eye. "She was already gone. It was Caroline you saved."

Moira was confused. "But—I don't understand. My arrogance sent Courtney away. I was so sure I could turn her away from black magic, but I said all the wrong things. Caroline was never practicing witchcraft. I tested her right when I arrived."

"You did everything right, everything you could considering the circumstances. You said exactly the *right* things. What you didn't know, what I didn't know either until weeks later, is that Caroline had planned on going with Courtney that night. She was packed and heard everything you said in the church hall. It stopped her from making the same mistake Courtney did. I didn't lose one daughter that night; I saved a daughter. If I had lost both of them . . ." He took a deep breath. "You convinced Caroline to turn away from magic. She's in college now, majoring in psychology. I lashed out at you then because I only saw my loss; but sometimes, we don't always see the effect we have on others. I didn't see how my grief over their mother's death affected my daughters, just like I didn't see how my anger at Courtney's decision turned her against me. You tried to save her, but you couldn't because I'd already chased her away. But you did save Caroline, I believe with the help of God, and I owe you my deepest gratitude and sincerest apologies. I hope you accept them."

Tears burned behind Moira's eyelids. She wanted to argue with him; he hadn't been there, he didn't know how she'd messed up. But she hadn't known that Caroline was there.

"Of course," she whispered. "But I do take responsibility for my failures as well as my successes."

"Which is why you are as strong as you are."

"I think we have everything we need here." She handed him the folder, but he shook his head.

"Keep it. Read it over carefully, and be extremely cautious. These people are devious."

Jackson walked them to their truck. "Have you heard from Courtney?" Moira asked. "Or do you know where she is?"

"No, but I'm looking. She knows she can come home, but sometimes, we all need a reminder that God is a forgiving Father. More forgiving than I showed her before. I just want her safe, no strings attached."

It was Moira who now warned Jackson. She took his hands and squeezed. "Jackson, you be careful, too. Love is blind."

Rico returned to Olivet with a heavy heart. He didn't know why he was so uneasy. He'd known from the first report out of Santa Louisa after the demon Envy had been captured that Moira's blood was a weapon. But now he had proof. Her fate was set in stone.

He called the cardinal, who answered on the first ring. "The test was positive."

"It worked?" His voice was calm but hopeful, as if he had doubted it even though it was his own theory that had prompted the test.

"Yes. The demon died."

But the man the demon had possessed would never be the same. The victim was in a special ward of a hospital, one that housed many victims of demons. Few recovered.

"Good work, Rico. The tide is turning."

"I think we should keep this information contained for as long as possible. You understand that if it gets out, Moira will be in grave danger."

"You explained your concerns earlier, Rico. There's no need to reveal the truth at this point, but you understand that the time will certainly come."

"She'll become a prisoner; we can't do that to her."

"It will be the only way to protect her, as you well know. When the word gets out—and it will, sooner or later—rogue hunters will want her, as well as the covens. They will double their efforts."

He knew it, and he hated it. He'd do anything to protect Moira.

"God bless you, my son," the cardinal said.

Rico hung up. He didn't feel like celebrating, and for the first time in his life he did not feel blessed.

THIRTEEN

Skye sat straight in her chair at Starbucks listening to Detective Nelson rant about her interference in his crime scene. Staring across the table at him, she decided to let him get everything out. He was obviously exhausted and running on fumes.

After he told her about finding Rafe and Moira in the alley, and how they walked out after he'd ordered them to stay put, he said, "They're damn lucky I didn't haul their asses to jail. I didn't say anything, but your *consultant* was carrying concealed, and I doubt she has a concealed carry permit for that little .38 I saw."

Skye restrained a wince. She'd warned Moira about carrying the gun, but Moira was stubborn. And she certainly had every right to feel threatened. Skye, as sheriff, had offered her a CCW permit, but Moira refused to go through Live Scan fingerprinting. *"I'm not putting my prints in your system,"* she'd said.

"You could be deported if you're caught without a permit. Or put in jail."

"I'll take my chances."

"I think—"

He interrupted. "I've been working nonstop since seven a.m., when I was called to a possible homicide which may not be a homicide," Nelson snapped. "Ten hours with a sandwich on the run and not enough caffeine to keep a rat awake. I'm supposed to have the weekend off, but I already know that I'll be working for the next forty-eight hours on my own time because I have a high-ranking county attorney sitting on my ass claiming that George Erickson's fucking wife is a witch and cast a spell over him. I have a college kid who's dead but had no drugs and little alcohol in his system, and a small-town sheriff riding my ass with two sidekicks who don't obey orders!" He pinched the bridge of his nose and said, "What were they doing at Velocity? I don't buy their pathetic excuse of wanting to see where Monroe died."

"Grant," Skye said quietly, "did you say witch?"

"Witch? Oh yeah, witch. I've known Nina Hardwick for more than a decade, since she was bright and shiny out of law school working for the Board of Supervisors. It sounds fucking insane, and if it was anyone other than Nina I would have sent them on their way. But Nina's not some flighty, birdbrained witness. She's one of the most respected attorneys in the county."

"This may be the cult I was telling you about."

He stared at her blankly as he gulped coffee, but Skye knew what he was thinking, because she had thought the same thing when Anthony Zaccardi had first tried to convince her that demons existed. She hadn't really believed him until she saw her best friend possessed. Until she was thrown across the room by a bolt of energy that couldn't be seen.

She continued, being patient with Nelson because she understood how he felt. "Moira O'Donnell, my consultant, would be a good person to look into this, Detective. You're right, she should have stayed and answered your questions. And I'll make sure she talks to you. Moira is an expert on this cult, and she'd be able to tell pretty quick if Erickson's wife is involved."

Nelson shook his head. "I'm not working with a civilian. I'm not working with you. I want you to leave and take your consultant and her boyfriend with you."

It took Skye a second to realize Nelson was referring to Rafe Cooper. "I really—"

He cut her off. "I *want* you to leave, but unfortunately, I'm screwed either way. So, you bring Moira O'Donnell down to the precinct at oh-eight-hundred tomorrow morning, and we'll go from there. I want to know what happened in that alley. She said a couple of teenage boys pushed her against the wall so hard it knocked her unconscious for a good three minutes. I find the whole story hard to believe. *Impossible* to believe. So if she tells me the truth about that, maybe I'll listen to her about this cult whose members think they're witches." He shook his head. "I can't believe I just said that."

"I don't think you should be working this alone—"

"I have years of experience over you, *Sheriff*, in Los Angeles, not some hick county where the worst crime is Miss Mabel stealing Miss Edith's prize tomatoes."

"Hold it right there, Nelson. I'm damn tired of your mightier-than-thou big-city-cop attitude. You need my help, and I'm not here to trample on your case or take any glory; I could care less about taking credit for this collar. The only person I care about finding is Nicole Donovan, because she's a material witness in an ongoing investigation. You can have the rest of them. But if you want any chance of finding answers, you have to open your mind. I thought that's what L.A. was all about—open-mindedness."

He stared at her. "We're a lot more close-minded than people think. If— shit, what is it?" He pulled his ringing BlackBerry from his pocket. "What?" he answered. His face changed. "Are you one hundred percent positive? . . . Meet me at her condo and don't go in until I get there." He hung up. "Bring me Moira O'Donnell and we'll talk."

"What was that about?"

"Fingerprints all over George Erickson's bedroom belong to one of the waitresses at Velocity." He grinned humorlessly. "Murder or not, she walked out and didn't report a death. I'll find out if it's connected to Craig Monroe. One thing I'm good at, Sheriff McPherson, is getting answers." He stood. "Eight a.m. Tomorrow. If O'Donnell and Cooper aren't there, I'll have them arrested."

Skye watched him walk out and then she called Moira. Rod was on his way to pick her up so they could head back to Santa Louisa. When Nelson had called her about Moira and Rafe, she'd taken a cab to Westwood and met the detective at Starbucks while Rod continued his research at the morgue.

"What's up, Sheriff?" Moira answered.

"I just had my ass chewed out by Grant Nelson. Why did you leave when you were being questioned? You're really screwing with my authority."

"We had to—there're witches at Velocity, and they were working a spell. Did you see Nelson? Is he okay?"

"Tired, irritated, and hungry, but nothing seemed out of the ordinary."

"Good. I didn't know what they were doing exactly,

but it seemed to be aimed at him. I figured they were working to have him arrest me."

"Can spells do that?"

"If the magician's any good. It's something like mind control, but not."

Skye shook her head. Talking with Moira could be exhausting. "I promised him you and Rafe will be at the police station to finish your conversation tomorrow at eight a.m."

"I'll try—"

"You'll be there or he'll put a warrant out on you. And leave your gun in the car—you're going to get me in trouble, and yourself deported."

"I'm sorry, I understand, but—"

"I don't think you do. You run around like the law doesn't apply to you. I'm trying to help, but you make it extremely difficult!"

"Skye, what's wrong?"

Skye took a deep breath. "I have to go back to Santa Louisa. The D.A. let Elizabeth Ellis out of jail."

"What? He can't do that!" Moira said. "I should have done it my way."

"That's not the answer, and you know it. Besides, Ellis is not the one we need to worry about. Let's get these seven bastards back where they belong and worry about the human problems later. Hank and Jared are keeping a close eye on Lily. They took her to my house, and I'll be there with her tonight. But right now you have to promise me, swear on a Bible if you have to, that you'll be at the police station to meet Nelson at eight a.m. tomorrow morning and tell him what he wants to know."

"He wouldn't believe the truth."

"Maybe, maybe not."

"Skye—"

"Dammit, Moira, this is serious."

"All right."

"Promise?"

"I said yes."

"Did you check out the houses?"

"Yes—Galion's is locked up tight, gated, the works. I didn't sense anything, but we didn't go inside. I don't think there's anything strange there. Stephanie Frazier, ditto. The roommate was there, Rafe sweet-talked his way inside; I sensed nothing. From her house or her roommate."

"I thought it was a shot."

"We also met with a friend who has some information about Wendy Donovan and her cult, and we're going to follow up on that."

"Nelson just got a call about evidence in the Erickson case."

"What kind of evidence?"

"Prints all over his bedroom."

"Whose?"

"I don't know, one of the waitresses at Velocity. He's not exactly my best friend right now. He's keeping me in the dark until you come in. But he also has *another* witness named Nina Hardwick, who claims that Erickson's wife was a witch. He didn't believe it, but I think I convinced him that maybe it's the same cult we're both investigating. He's considering it." Skye rubbed the back of her neck and looked out the window. Young men and women dressed in anything from jeans and designer shirts to skimpy dresses and pressed slacks passed her on their way down the street to one of the many clubs, including Velocity.

"Where's the detective now?" Moira asked.

"On his way to the suspect's apartment."

"Alone?"

"He's meeting his partner. What's wrong, Moira?"

"You have to stop him. I know who killed Craig Monroe. It was Nadine Anson, one of the club's waitresses, and she was possessed. If that's the same woman who was with Erickson last night, that puts Detective Nelson in danger."

"Explain."

"I don't have time! I have her address."

"Hold it, Moira! How do you know who killed Craig Monroe?"

"I saw it. I can't explain how, but you have to trust me, Skye."

This situation was getting out of control. Skye wished she didn't have to leave right now. But honestly, how could she stop it? She had to focus on what she did best: being a cop. She could protect Lily. She couldn't battle demons.

Skye said, "Moira, put a lid on it with Nelson. He's a good cop, but this case is getting to him."

"I'll be good."

"Check in with me. Often."

"Roger that, Sheriff," Moira said lightly and hung up.

Skye pocketed her phone and waited for Rod Fielding. She hoped she'd made the right decision to go back to Santa Louisa.

She had a sick feeling she was leaving Moira and Rafe to the lions.

FOURTEEN

With the streetlight above illuminating him, Jeff Johnston sat on his motorcycle across from Nadine Anson's pricey condo only a mile from Velocity. Grant pulled up behind Johnston. Before Grant had even turned off the engine, his partner had hopped off his bike and handed him the report.

"Thanks," Grant mumbled through his headache. The sun had set well over an hour ago. Grant despised winter; the weather in L.A. was good, but he hated early darkness.

He read the summary, then looked at the computer printout that matched the prints—good enough for court. The prints at Erickson's also matched a partial from the dumpster next to where Craig Monroe's body was found—not admissible in court because they only had a small fraction of a print.

If Nadine Anson had been involved in the orgy with Erickson's wife as the photo that Nina Hardwick gave him suggested, she could argue that her prints were in the bedroom because she and Pam Erickson were lovers.

It was enough to bring Mrs. Erickson and Ms. Anson in for questioning, but hardly enough to get the D.A. to even glance at the case.

Grant sighed heavily. "We don't have any evidence

that George Erickson was murdered. The coroner is ruling cardiac arrest pending full drug panel."

"We can nail Anson for not reporting Erickson's death. If she could have saved him and didn't, we can get her for manslaughter. If he was dead, we could get her for not reporting the death."

"She'd plead out, get probation and time served, and the D.A. would jump at it because it wasn't premeditated. We'd be lucky to get a nickel, and she'd make too good a witness. Can't you see the defense dragging in all the sex pictures? Complete circus. She turns on the waterworks, apologizes, gets acquitted. The media would eat it up. The D.A. would never go all the way on this unless Nadine Anson or Pam Erickson planned to kill him. We need to keep looking at the wife. Maybe Nina Hardwick was right and Mrs. Erickson was jealous, spiked his vitamins, slowly poisoned him with arsenic, anything. Or blackmailed Nadine to do it. Paid her. We can get her financials Monday morning, see what comes out."

"You're stretching, Nelson."

Johnston was right, but Grant was at his wits' end and his pounding head made it worse. "I don't know what to make of this case. Cults, witches, orgies." He opened his door. "Let's go up and talk to Anson. You're sure she isn't working today?"

"Got the Velocity schedule from Julie; she's off."

Grant looked at his phone. "Great, Sheriff McPherson just sent me a message." He read, "'Moira O'Donnell is on her way to meet you at the suspect's apartment. I'm on my way back to Santa Louisa, call if you need anything.'"

He glanced at Johnston. "I never told her where I was going."

"How'd she know?"

"Maybe that friend of hers is more involved in cults than the sheriff said. Maybe she knows *exactly* what's going on. I should take *her* into custody as a material witness."

"So—what, we're gonna wait for her?"

"Hell no, I'm not running this investigation on the whims of a small-town cop. I still can't buy that this is some broom-toting female cult killing men. Why? There has to be a reason. I can *almost* buy into Nina's statement that the swinger lifestyle only went one way. I've met crazier women than Pam Erickson in my life. Georgie-boy strays, wife kills him. But why would Nadine Anson help her? And leave her prints all over the place?"

"And what about the marks on the bodies? That's damn creepy. That also ties into Craig Monroe and Galion."

Jeff had a point. "We've got a lot of work to do."

"We're working this weekend, huh?"

"If we don't, that damn sheriff and her cute little side-kick will be mucking up my investigation. And who do I call to get her off my back? The district attorney in Santa Louisa? A small county like that is going to be tight; he's not going to call her off."

Grant crossed the quiet side street, Johnston at his side. "Let's play it nice with Anson, make her comfortable. See how much we can get out of her before we push."

They identified themselves to the condo manager and were let into the lobby. After knocking on her door, it was clear that Nadine wasn't home. Her neighbor across the hall was leaving as they stood waiting.

"Nadine isn't here," he said.

Grant flashed his badge. "Do you know when she usually comes in?"

"She has Thursdays and Fridays off, but I haven't seen her in a week."

Grant asked, "Does she have a boyfriend or family in the area?"

"She's from the Midwest; I don't know much about her family. But her boyfriend is a stockbroker who lives in Los Feliz."

"Do you have his name and contact information?"

The guy seemed put out, but shrugged. He unlocked his door. "Is it important?"

"Yes. She's a material witness in an ongoing investigation," Jeff said.

"Just a minute."

He went inside and less than a minute later emerged with a name and phone number scrawled on a sticky note.

Marcus Galion, 818-555-4579.

"Galion?"

"Yeah. Kent Galion's little brother. You heard that Kent died last week? Maybe Nadine went to stay with Marcus for a while, to cheer him up. Hell, Nadine could cheer me up any night she wanted."

Grant and Jeff took the stairs down to the courtyard. "Where to now?" Jeff asked, glancing at his watch.

"Go home, but put in a call to Marcus Galion and ask him about Nadine Anson. I'll go to Velocity and talk to Julie about her. There's something here, I feel it."

*   *   *

"That's it." Moira directed Rafe toward the condo where Nadine Anson lived. "Close to Velocity."

Rafe parked across the street. "Are you sure you want to do this? That detective is never going to listen to what we have to say."

"Skye was a genius with the cult story; we'll run with that. And demons are kind of like supernatural drugs. Sort of."

Rafe grinned while shaking his head at her. "Just watch the sarcasm, like Skye said. Nelson is a hothead and frustrated. Oh shit—"

Moira followed Rafe's eyes to where Grant Nelson and his partner were leaving the condo.

"We're too late," she said. "She's probably not home. We should follow them."

"You want me to follow a cop?"

"I'm good at tailing people. Want me to drive?"

"No." He watched Nelson get into an unmarked sedan and drive away. He made an illegal U-turn down the street. Johnston jumped on a bike and did the same. "That makes us following two of them. Impossible if they split up."

"My money's on Nelson. He's not going home. My guess? He's going to try and track Nadine down at the club, or maybe a friend or boyfriend's house."

Rafe waited until the cops turned left, then made a sharp U-turn in the truck and sped up to follow.

They were on Wilshire Boulevard minutes later. Moira glanced down the street toward Velocity. "They didn't turn."

"I'm not following him to the police station," Rafe said.

"Agreed. If he goes there, we turn around and go to Wendy Donovan's house."

"How about food? I haven't eaten, and I doubt you have—since you never eat unless I tell you to. We could get a pizza."

"Whatever did I do before I saved your ass two weeks ago?"

"I have no idea."

"I didn't starve, that's for sure." She pulled an energy bar from her pocket, opened it, and split it with Rafe.

"I hate these things."

"They've kept me alive for years," she teased. "In fact—" She whipped her head around, recognizing the brunette in the red dress walking leisurely down Wilshire Boulevard. "Stop! That's Nadine! Rafe, stop!"

Rafe braked, causing cars behind to honk.

"She's beginning to drive me crazy," Rafe muttered to himself as Moira leapt from the car.

Moira ran through traffic, eliciting more honking horns, but she barely noticed. Nadine Anson was easy to spot—tall, stately, gorgeous—but it was her darkly glowing aura that had caught Moira's attention from more than a hundred feet away.

Moira didn't dwell on the fact that her instincts—her extra senses—had been growing since the Seven Deadly Sins had been released. She couldn't think about how or why, only that she *knew* that brunette in the red dress across the street was Nadine Anson even though she'd seen only one photograph of the woman.

One photograph and two visions.

It was the height of the dinner hour, and pedestrians walked in singles, pairs, and groups down the street. Moira irritated more than a few of them as she brushed past. She didn't *quite* see Nadine anymore through the people, but she saw the glow and kept focused on that.

A thunderclap—though there wasn't a cloud in the sky—jolted Moira. She kept moving forward, but no longer saw the glow. People around her were silent, looking at the sky.

"It'd better not rain—I just had my hair done!" a woman next to her said.

"I can't believe this. They said no rain all weekend!"

But raindrops didn't fall. The night sky was clear, though with all the lights Moira could make out only one or two stars in the sky.

Heart racing, Moira feared the demon that possessed Nadine was looking for more victims. She couldn't imagine what it would do with all these people in the middle of a city street. Demons didn't make grand statements; they preferred the small, quiet murders of the soul. Did they fear that if they acted too boldly they'd truly suffer the wrath of God? For a brief moment, Moira wished they would create some catastrophe so that the Big Guy would come down and banish them all forever; then guilt washed over her at the innocent lives that would be lost by such action.

In all of history, demons themselves rarely, if ever, acted among the masses. They didn't show themselves, or cause disasters. Whether by choice or design, Moira didn't know. Maybe there were guardian angels preventing the major catastrophes. Demons still used humans to do their dirty work, picking up souls one by one.

But thunder without clouds? A demon—it had to be the succubus possessing Nadine—had done something. Moira couldn't even see Nadine with all the people.

A nearby scream had Moira picking up the pace, sprinting toward a commotion on the corner of Wilshire and Westwood, an incredibly busy intersection. The lights were annoying enough, but the horns and people were making Moira claustrophobic.

And there was Nadine, standing on the corner, screaming.

"What happened to her?" Moira heard one woman asking her boyfriend as they passed Nadine in distaste.

"Help me!" Nadine screamed.

Nadine Anson screamed for help, pulling her hair so hard that clumps of golden brown came out in her hands. She definitely wasn't glowing with the demonic aura, and Moira had no idea where the demon had gone. She whirled around, looking at everyone, looking above them, trying to spot the demon's shadow, but there was none.

The demon had disappeared.

Moira realized she'd never before *seen* a glowing aura, that her senses had always been focused on her own physical reaction to things she couldn't see. She'd experienced a heightened awareness of all her other senses, but not sight—until now. She pushed the new talent aside—not just because the idea scared her, but because right now Nadine's life was in jeopardy as the woman stood too close to the curb. The honking cars didn't faze the distraught witch, nor did she seem to notice that she'd drawn a crowd.

"Where's the camera?" a teenager next to Moira asked, eagerly looking around.

This girl thought Nadine was acting? Moira stepped in front of her, to a chorus of, "Hey! I can't see!" from the girl and her friends.

"Nadine," Moira said. "Look at me!"

"Help! Oh, God, oh, God, I'm sorry!"

"Nadine, it's over. It's gone. Step away, you're going to get hurt."

Nadine was sobbing without tears. She looked too thin, too weak, as if she hadn't eaten in days. Her eyes were hollow and her skin—which had seemed so smooth and lustrous in her photograph—was splotchy and stained dark. What had the demon left behind? What had it stolen from Nadine?

Moira had been possessed once. She'd wanted to kill herself when it was over, because she'd killed the man she loved—the *demon* used her to kill the man she loved. Willing or not, Nadine couldn't have known what the demon was going to use her for or how it would affect her.

Or when the demon suddenly left, without the protection of the coven's circle, how lost and terrified she would feel.

Once the bystanders realized that this show wasn't a movie, they moved away from Nadine as if she were a leper. Nadine flinched as Moira held her hands out, palms up. "Nadine, I'm a friend."

"Stay away! Get away from me! It's your fault. You saw and didn't do anything! You didn't help me!"

Nadine pulled more hair from her head, eyes wild and bloodshot. Moira stared at her eyes. They weren't bloodshot—Nadine was crying tears of blood. Traffic sped by, causing Nadine to sway.

"I need to get you home. Nadine, let me take you home, okay?"

"I know you! I know you! Why didn't you help me? You didn't help me! Oh, God! What's wrong with me?"

"Nadine!" Moira shouted because the woman didn't seem to hear anything she was saying. "I will help you." She took another step closer and Nadine took a step back, off the curb. Another horn blared. Where was help?

While most of the people stayed far from Nadine, Grant Nelson ran up. Shock crossed his face as he watched Nadine; then he turned to Moira and asked, "What happened?"

"I saw her walking down the street and jumped out—"

"I know. I saw you get out of the truck and cause a fucking traffic jam on Wilshire at the worst time of night." Looking into Nadine's dilated pupils, he made a quick assessment. "Damn drugs."

Moira couldn't very well tell the guy Nadine had been possessed for a few days by a psycho demon who'd left her half crazy.

"My partner's calling an ambulance," Grant told her, keeping his eyes on the hysterical woman. Someone took a picture with his iPhone, and Grant nearly decked him.

"Watch it," Moira warned. "Everyone has a fucking camera-phone."

Grant told the crowd to back off, then turned to Nadine. "Nadine, it's me, Grant Nelson. You remember me, right? From Velocity?"

"I hate you!" Nadine screamed.

Moira didn't know whether Nadine was talking to Grant or the crowd. She watched Grant closely. He had a familiarity with Nadine.

"You know her?" she stated.

"I go to the club a lot. I know most of the staff."

Grant stepped forward. "Nadine, I'm here to help you. I want to help. Step back from the curb."

"Get back! Get back!" Nadine screamed. "I can't see!"

If she couldn't see, how did she know Grant was there? Moira wondered. Was she missing something?

Nadine felt around wildly.

Grant said, "Honey, it's okay. You'll be okay, I promise. Come here, I'll take care of you."

"No! No! I killed them. I didn't mean to, I didn't know it was going to be so awful, no, no, no! Don't do this to me! Don't!"

Grant mumbled, "Shit." He said to Moira out of the side of his mouth, "Circle around the other side; I'll go this way."

"She's going to get herself killed," a bystander said.

"Grab her," Moira said. "Get her away from the traffic."

Grant moved away from Nadine's line of vision and Moira distracted her by moving in the opposite direction. "Nadine, my name's Moira. I can help you. You need to let me help you."

"I know you! I know you! No, no—" Her face twisted and she put her hands on both sides of her head, her fingernails clawing her skin, drawing blood.

Grant ran toward Nadine, but she whirled around and screamed at him. "It's your fault! Go away! Leave me! God, help me, I'm dying!"

Grant got ahold of her wrist, but she scratched his face with sharp nails and he stumbled backward, unable to keep his grip.

Moira grabbed Nadine from the other side and held her tightly around the waist. Nadine threw her head back once, twice, into Moira's face and she tripped, trying to pull Nadine back with her, away from traffic, but Nadine dug her fingernails into the palm of her hand, which was still healing from the deep cut two weeks ago.

Moira saw black. Blood poured from her nose as Nadine wrenched herself from Moira's hold and ran off the curb. Grant reached for Nadine, but the crazed woman turned and lurched headlong into the traffic, slamming against a car. Brakes squealed, but not before Nadine fell onto the pavement and was run over by a bus trying in vain to stop.

Moira screamed, her hands on her face, shaky from Nadine's quick and surprisingly violent assault. Grant wore a bewildered expression, his face bleeding from where Nadine scratched him. Bystanders shouted, some woman cried hysterically, but Moira stood stock-still. She was stunned, shaken to her core.

Strong hands from behind pulled her back. She turned and found herself in Rafe's tight embrace. She held on as if he were her lifeline, and then the tears fell.

FIFTEEN

When the irritated and extremely exhausted Grant Nelson left Moira and Rafe in their hotel room after confirming that they would be at the police station at eight the next morning, Moira turned to Rafe. "If he thinks I'm going to hole up in some stupid hotel while those witches who killed Nadine set up another victim, he's delusional."

"I expected you'd come to that conclusion," Rafe said.

She frowned. "You agree, right?"

"One hundred percent. But we need a plan."

"We read Jackson's notes; we know most of the players. I understand generally how these rituals operate." She wished she knew more about them. Her mother had never called on a succubus, though Moira had heard of the rituals. Would her limited knowledge be enough? She wished she had more time.

She crossed to the window and looked out at the lights in the parking lot below. She didn't like being this high up—she'd requested a ground-floor room, but there were none available. They were on the fourth floor. She supposed if she had to jump she might survive, but she didn't want to test the theory.

They were in a hotel, not a motel, and it was damn expensive. Moira would never have stayed here in a million years, but when Nelson gave them the ultimatum of hotel or jail, Rafe said they were planning on staying at the Palomar. It was sleek and contemporary, and Moira felt that she didn't belong. She was used to sleeping in rooms that rented by the hour, places where she could dump salt across every opening and no one would say anything. She didn't fit in this high-class environment, but surprisingly, Rafe seemed comfortable and at ease.

Moira couldn't explain Nadine's bizarre behavior, but she wasn't wholly surprised. The demon had had complete control over Nadine, but Nadine was awake during the entire possession. Demons don't eat or sleep; they feed on human souls. What could that do to a human being for a week?

Rafe had given Nadine last rites and anointed her with oil to prevent her spirit from wandering the earth lost and vengeful, but neither he nor Moira knew if it would work, or where her soul might be trapped.

Moira's cell phone rang. "It's Jackson. Finally," she said and answered it, putting it on speaker so Rafe could hear.

"Hey, Jackson, Rafe and I are both here."

"I have some information that might help," he said. "I found the chalice that Wendy's coven is using."

"You have it?"

"A photograph. I'd rather discuss this in person; it's rather complex and we need a plan."

"*We* need a plan," Moira said, "Rafe and me. You're not joining this expedition to Wendy's house. You have a daughter, someone who relies on you. I'm not risking your life, too. Besides, Rafe and I are trained—"

Jackson cut her off. "I sent Caroline out of the area to

stay with her grandmother. You need my help. Let me show you everything I've found and we can figure out what to do. But I think we can get rid of this thing tonight."

"Halleluia," Moira said. "We're at the Palomar. How fast can you get here?"

"Thirty minutes."

She glanced at the clock. It was just after ten p.m. It had already been a long day, and promised to be even longer.

"Hurry," she said and hung up.

"I'm confused on one point," Rafe said.

"Only one?"

"Wendy's coven uses a succubus. How would they know how to trap one of the Seven when even Fiona couldn't do it?"

Good point. Moira considered. "Fiona thought she knew how to trap the Seven one at a time. She had Lily on the altar, was going to give her body to Envy until we stopped her. Nicole Donovan was there—she must have learned the ritual. Shared it with her psycho sister Wendy."

"But the demon left Nadine's body when you were chasing her, so it wasn't trapped. Why did it allow itself to be contained at all? After facing down Envy two weeks ago, I don't think any of those bastards are going to willingly be controlled by a mortal."

Moira frowned and turned from the window. "I don't know—but since a succubus is all about sex and stealing the souls of men, maybe the demon Lust is playing the game because it amuses her. Or—" She hesitated.

"Or what?"

"In my vision she said she had to find another vessel."

"You mean, that vision that threw you against the alley wall." He stepped over so he could touch her face. She knew she must look like death warmed over after the attack in the alley and Nadine head-butting her. Her hand still stung, though Rafe had bandaged it—and kissed it—for her.

She swallowed nervously, the proximity to Rafe clouding her thoughts, and said, "She may have been drawn out and contained in another vessel."

"Spontaneously?"

"I don't know! Demons are like yo-yos. They can sometimes be pulled back to the point where they entered the earth. Like they're attached to an invisible umbilical cord that leads right back to whichever Hell's gateway they walked through."

"If that's the case, why can't we draw all of them back to the cliffs in Santa Louisa and send them back from there?"

She considered. "We may have to do just that. But Anthony is certain that if the Seven are brought together we won't be able to defeat them. There's so much we don't know!"

"I hope Dr. Lieber has the answers we need," Rafe said quietly. "We should seal the room."

"He's still there."

"Who?"

She nodded toward the parking lot before closing the curtains. "Grant Nelson. He's sitting in his car looking at this window." She accepted the bag of salt that Rafe handed her. "I'd hate to imagine what housekeeping will think when they come in tomorrow morning." She smiled wistfully at the thought. She'd accepted that she wasn't like most people—she was strange and peculiar. Usually she didn't care what anyone thought because she'd always been alone, cut off from normal people, if not physically, then emotionally. Yet now, thanks to Rafe, she felt almost like part of society . . . almost. Would this invisible barrier ever disappear?

She focused on the task at hand. "You put up the crucifixes; don't forget the vents."

"You okay, Moira?" Rafe asked, concern in his tone.

"Just peachy."

They worked in silence for several tense minutes. Moira fidgeted, uncomfortable and tired and hating this feeling that she didn't fit.

"Did Nadine see you?" Rafe asked quietly.

"See me? She said she couldn't see, but it was obvious that she—"

"No, before the demon disappeared. Before the thunder."

Moira paused. "I think she saw me as I was crossing the street."

"What if the demon didn't want a confrontation with you?"

"Me? Why the hell not? I didn't stop Envy from attacking you, me, Father—" She coughed as emotion thickened her voice.

"But it could have a plan, and we weakened Envy enough for Anthony to draw it into the trap. If it thought you could do it damage—" He cut himself off.

"What? Spill it, Rafe. What are you thinking?"

"Rico wanted your blood for something. Aren't you curious why?"

"No," she lied.

Rafe just stared at her, obviously not believing her.

"One thing at a time, Rafe! I don't want to put my thoughts back there and think what might be wrong with me—"

"Why would you think anything's wrong with you?"

"My *blood*? It's just sick. I don't want to think about what he's doing." But of course she couldn't stop thinking about it now that Rafe brought up the subject. She looked down at her hand where Rafe had sliced it open and stuck it in the burning guts of the demon Envy. It hurt from Nadine's attack earlier, but nothing she'd ever experienced had been as shockingly painful as sticking her hand inside the demon.

"If it's my blood—my tainted blood—that has the answers? What does that make me? Inhuman?"

Rafe took her hand and kissed it. "Don't do that."

She shook her head and tried to pull her hand away, but Rafe didn't let go. "If my blood is the answer, then take it. We end this now."

"We didn't kill Envy; we slowed it down so it could be captured. We don't know what will contain Lust. And I'm not risking your life until we have a solid plan."

Rafe kissed her on the top of her head, her forehead, her temple. "You're scared," he whispered in her ear. "So am I."

"I live my life in fear. I know what's out there. I want to run away so badly, but there's no place to hide. I can die cowering in a dark room or I can die fighting."

"Death is not the only option."

She stared at him. He was only inches from her. "Eventually it is," she said. "Or I can join my mother and sacrifice people so I, too, can be immortal," she added sarcastically. "Did I do enough to save Nadine? I keep playing the scene over and over and don't know what else I could have done."

Rafe stepped closer and she tried to step back, but the dresser was in her way. His proximity had her hormones rushing every which way, making her confused and nervous. She turned around, facing the mirror, Rafe right behind her. The power of his gaze in the reflection held her captive.

Rafe had never met anyone outside of St. Michael's who had more internal fortitude than Moira. He'd never met anyone in or out of St. Michael's who cared as much about the fate of others. But it wasn't just what she was willing to do in this supernatural battle; Moira had an inner spark, a strength that belied her stated willingness to die for humanity. She would never go down without a fight, and she wanted to live. He saw it in the way she recognized and appreciated beauty in the world, even when they were surrounded by ugliness and evil. She gave him hope; she gave him strength; she made Rafe a better human being. Only with Moira did he feel he wasn't stumbling on the path drawn for him by St. Michael's, God, or the devil.

If Moira hadn't found him two weeks ago, he would have died. He owed her his life, but he also felt deep inside that she'd also saved his soul.

"You did everything you could, Moira." His fingers trailed up her face, gently skirting the bruises, brushing aside a curl that had escaped her hair tie. "You were faced with something you'd never faced before, and you acted because you care."

"I don't want to care," she whispered.

"It's not a choice. It's in your heart."

She cast her brilliant blue eyes downward, breaking

the lock on his gaze. "I've spent my life not caring, just doing what needs to be done."

"That's a lie."

Her body tensed under his hands. Her head shot up, a flash of fire in her eyes as she glared at him in the mirror. Good. They'd need that fire, that confidence, when they walked into Wendy's lair tonight.

"You don't know me."

She tried to step to the side, but he wouldn't let her pass, trapping her against the dresser. She was going to listen to him. "You haven't spent your life not caring, you've spent your life *trying* not to care. But I know you, Moira—stop." He put a finger on her lips when she opened her mouth to argue. "I see who you really are, underneath the armor. You care, and it hurts because you can't save everyone. But still, you go on, every day, fighting a battle you didn't start, you never wanted, because it's the right thing to do. Most people ignore evil. Of those who believe in evil, few do anything but kneel and pray. Most people shy away from those in need— like those bystanders watching Nadine go crazy and kill herself. And while we need everyone doing what they can, most aren't willing to put their lives on the line to save any soul but their own. I admire you more than you can possibly know. You give me strength, Moira, strength I never knew I had."

Moira was speechless. Rafe's impassioned expression touched her deep inside, in a place she didn't know still existed. A door opened in her heart, just a crack, but Rafe's foot was in the way and she couldn't slam it shut. A door that had been locked tight for seven years, since the day Peter died.

"Rafe—" Her voice sounded rough around the edges.

He leaned over and kissed her neck, his breath a whisper across her skin. He kissed her again, lightly, moving to her jawline, a tickle, a hint of something more, a promise. Confident and unyielding even in the delicacy of his touch. His thumb brushed across her lips and she kissed it, drawing it into her mouth. He tasted salty and warm and sexy.

She gasped when his other hand moved up her shirt and pulled her tightly against him, his hand under her breasts. His firm chest against her back, his pelvis rigid against her rear, she felt both wildly free and deliciously trapped. His kisses became more urgent, against the back of her neck, to the side, and she tilted her head back against his shoulder, giving him access to her throat. He bent over her shoulder and licked her throat greedily, then stepped forward, pressing her thighs against the dresser with the weight of his body.

Moira's thoughts fell away as all she wanted was Rafe's body on hers. His legs were on either side of hers, his penis hard against her backside. His mouth on her neck, her jaw, her ear. She turned her head to kiss him, and he responded with a groan as he adjusted his position, his body mimicking lovemaking though they were fully clothed. The dresser moved and she used her arms to brace herself. Rafe had her bra undone and was kneading her breasts, pleasure winning over pain. She gasped as his thumbs rubbed her nipples, at first gently, then harder until she squirmed, her breath coming in short bursts.

There was no reason, there were no thoughts, as Rafe unzipped her jeans, his fingers slipping under her panties.

This was it, she'd been apprehensive about this moment, but she was ready to risk everything for Rafe. Even her heart. She tensed, shaking, but didn't try to stop him.

Rafe slowly removed his fingers before they touched that one spot that needed attention. He eased up her zipper and used both hands to close the button. She opened her eyes and looked at Rafe's reflection. Their skin glowed with perspiration; her face was flushed. Her neck was red from Rafe's stubble, and one breast peeked out from her shirt. Rafe didn't say a word, but stepped back and rehooked her bra, unhurried, and pulled her shirt back down.

"Rafe—" She didn't know what to say.

He wrapped his arms around her, rested his chin on the top of her head and let out a long breath.

That sensation, of renewal and discovery, besieged her and she swayed, her knees suddenly weak. He held her steady.

"I know what you're thinking," he said. "You're wrong."

"You don't know what I'm thinking," she said, pushing backward, but he didn't let go. She wasn't thinking at all, she only felt, and her senses were overwhelmed by their combined emotions.

He whispered in her ear as he kissed it. She shivered, wanting him to keep going, wanting him to stop. He said, "You're trying to find any excuse to deny these feelings we have for each other. I know you, Moira. You don't believe me, but I know you. Deny all you want, convince yourself that I would settle for only one night. But the way I feel for you isn't fleeting. It's not a whim. It's certainly not supernatural. It's my heart. It beats for you, Moira."

He dropped his arms, and she realized she'd been holding her breath. She really didn't like how Rafe saw her for who she was. It made her vulnerable. She turned around, was about to say something, but he kissed her lightly on the lips, his fingers barely touching her chin, and all words disappeared.

"I'm sure he's gone by now."

For a split second, Moira didn't know who Rafe was talking about. Then she shook her head to clear it and stepped away from him.

Breathe. Again. Better.

She looked out the window. Grant Nelson's unmarked sedan was indeed gone. "You're right."

She turned back to Rafe, and he handed over her backpack so she could recheck her supplies—though she knew everything was there.

She felt momentarily light-headed. When the sensation went away she had a new, odd feeling that she didn't have time to analyze—and didn't know if she wanted to.

She cleared her throat and grabbed a water bottle off the counter, drained half of it in one long gulp, then handed the rest to Rafe.

A knock on the door had her sighing in relief.

"Duty calls," she said.

Rafe looked through the peephole. "It's Jackson."

"Twenty-nine minutes," she said as Rafe opened the door. "Right on time."

SIXTEEN

It was after eleven by the time Grant finished the report on Nadine Anson's death and started for home. He'd written most of it while sitting outside the Palomar. He didn't know why he thought those two from Santa Louisa would be up to something, but he didn't feel right leaving them on their own. He hoped they'd screw like rabbits and leave his case alone.

Grant didn't consciously make the detour toward Velocity. It wasn't out of his way, since he lived just the other side of the 405 in West L.A. He was so exhausted he was practically asleep on his feet, but he wanted to talk to Julie about Nadine. He wished he could have told her in person, but he'd been tied up on the scene, then wanted to make sure Moira O'Donnell and her boyfriend actually checked into the hotel as they said they would. He had a dozen questions and every time he thought he had an answer, another ten questions popped up.

He squirmed at the thought of the two of them in a solitary hotel room. He didn't particularly like Raphael Cooper. He was too quiet, for one thing, and watched everything with sharp eyes. Grant didn't like being scrutinized by anyone, particularly Cooper. And he was always standing just behind Moira, like a bodyguard ready to pounce on any man who wandered too close.

He squeezed his eyes shut and wondered where that thought had come from. Moira was certainly his type, all that thick wavy hair and athletic body and sarcastic mouth. But he didn't go after attached women. He shouldn't even be thinking about getting her naked beneath him, but it had been on his mind since he'd met her, though that didn't mean much. Grant usually assessed women as potential lovers. But when he'd seen Moira unconscious and vulnerable in the alley behind Velocity . . . he'd wanted her.

The line outside Velocity was long, but as a regular and a cop Grant had access whenever he wanted and he used his privilege tonight.

He looked around for Julie but didn't see her. Sitting at the bar, as far from the dance floor as he could get, he rubbed his temples. A bitch of a migraine had solidified its position dead center after he watched Nadine Anson lose her mind, then her life. It made no sense, and he had been running through the scene over and over again trying to understand what happened to her. But all it did was make his migraine worse.

He should feel elated—she'd confessed right there with witnesses that she'd killed "them." Not specifically *who*, but Nadine's prints were all over George Erickson's house. It was enough that his chief would close the case and tell him to pick up one of the other fifty case files sitting on his desk.

But Grant didn't feel satisfied with closing the case with so many unanswered questions. This case—these *cases*—disturbed him. He was a good cop, but he cut corners like most. Knew what lines he could cross and which he couldn't. Had he cut a corner he shouldn't have? Had he let his friendship with the staff here at Velocity cloud his judgment?

"On the house," Ike said, sliding over Grant's off-duty beverage of choice, a bottle of Heineken. "You look like you need a couple shots of whiskey." He nodded toward the bandage on Grant's face. "I heard what happened."

"I had paperwork up the ass, otherwise I would have come in earlier."

Ike waved off his apology. "You want to get good and drunk, I'll get you a cab, no problem."

He shook his head. "Nah. Just this one for me. Early morning. I wanted to talk to Julie. Is she still here?"

"Yeah. Wendy let some of the girls off early, but Julie said she'd stay. I think she's waiting for you."

Grant shifted on the stool. His and Julie's on-again/off-again relationship wasn't doing either of them any good, but he couldn't say goodbye. Sure, they weren't together anymore—they screwed around with others—but neither of them had claimed they wanted to keep their friendship strictly platonic. Grant didn't want a relationship with anyone. He already had one failed marriage and more failed relationships than he could count on his fingers and toes combined. What he and Julie had was an agreement, though he wasn't entirely comfortable with it. She deserved better. He hoped she found someone who treated her with the respect and love she deserved. Grant cared for her—but she was too good for him. Most women were. Fortunately for his libido, they didn't seem to know it.

"Tell her I'm here, okay?"

Ike gave him a thumbs-up and walked away. Thank God; Grant didn't want to talk anymore. The throbbing dance music, which he could usually push to the back of his mind, was punishing with its heavy bass. He tried to focus on the eye candy that filled the trendy club. Like that blonde at the bar being hit on by two guys. Early twenties, small but perky tits, a little chunky around the hips, but he didn't mind. She caught his eye and he winked. She smiled, enjoying putting on the show, touching one of the men flirting with her.

Slut.

Another blonde walked by and hesitated beside him. He ignored her, though she was hotter than Ms. Perky-Tits. His thoughts disturbed him. He never thought of women as sluts. Some were too loose for his tastes, but they were few and far between. He didn't expect them to behave better than he did.

Sheriff Skye McPherson was a blonde. Quite a looker, too, better than most of the women in his division. But she was a cop. Physically, Grant would be happy to have her in his bed, but he didn't date anyone in law enforcement. Period. They were either man-haters or too damn competitive. He wanted someone who was strong and self-sufficient, but also soft and feminine. Gorgeous, but unpretentious; independent, but affectionate.

Someone like Moira O'Donnell. Someone exactly like Moira O'Donnell.

She'd been on his mind since Grant saw her in the morgue early in the afternoon. Gorgeous, check. Definitely not conceited or pretentious. Didn't flaunt her good looks like the sluts who frequented Velocity. In fact, Grant suspected that Moira wouldn't set foot in Velocity for fun. He imagined that she enjoyed beer by the pint and rowdy laughter and would know exactly how to please him. She was physically sculpted—he'd seen her muscles, her lean, hard, flat stomach, and pictured what it would be like to have her ride him all night long. No strings attached.

Self-sufficient and independent, check. But he saw her lean on that long-haired jerk who wouldn't leave her side. Raphael Cooper. What kind of name was *Raphael*? Or *Rafe*? A sissy name. And he let her just run the show. Overprotective. She could do so much better than that loser. He didn't even have a job. Grant had checked on him. He'd been in a fucking coma until two weeks ago. She probably felt sorry for him; that's why she was at his side. Maybe they weren't involved.

They're sharing a hotel room.

Grant pushed that thought aside, rubbing the back of his neck, feeling hot and cold at the same time, trying not to picture Moira O'Donnell screwing the too quiet, pompous, overprotective asshole.

She needed someone like Grant.

He would show Moira O'Donnell who was on top, and she'd enjoy every minute.

"Grant?"

He blinked, then saw Julie standing next to him, concern on her face. Guilt coursed through his body; he'd been thinking about fucking another woman while waiting for the one he'd been screwing most every weekend for the last six months. He had a flash of Julie *and* Moira in his bed, and his cock tightened uncomfortably.

He flushed. Why was he here?

Nadine.

"What's wrong?" Julie's voice cracked.

Wrong. "You heard about Nadine." He cleared his throat and focused. He was a cop first. "I'm so sorry, Julie."

Julie's green eyes brimmed with tears. "I was stunned.

Still am. I don't think it's sunk in yet. What happened, Grant? The cop who talked to Wendy and me said she committed suicide? I don't believe it. I—"

"I was there. She was on drugs. I don't think she walked into the traffic on purpose; it was like she was hallucinating."

She touched his face. "You were hurt."

"It's fine."

Julie stared at him. He took her hand. Her skin was so soft. He squeezed. "I'm sorry."

"I want to go home—Wendy said I could, she called in a few people. I just—I don't want to be alone."

"Come to my place." He kissed her forehead. Her scent made him shiver; why hadn't he noticed how good she smelled before? He pulled her to him, hugged her tightly, breathed in her hair. Kissed her neck, held her.

"Please—my place. You still have some of your things there. And I have that massage oil you like so much." She touched his face. "Do you have a headache? You don't look so good."

"A migraine."

She kissed him. "You know I can get rid of it for you."

Julie was inventive in bed, and would do anything he asked. He nodded. "Let's go."

"Let me get my purse."

"I'll come with you."

"You don't—"

"I want to."

He wasn't letting her out of his sight.

In the employee room, he locked the door. "Julie, come here." He unzipped his pants.

What are you doing? Not here—

"Grant—"

"Please. It'll make us both feel better."

A cloud crossed Julie's face, but he pushed her doubt aside.

"You know I make you feel better."

She nodded. "We have to be fast." Her bottom lip quivered.

"Then kneel."

She obeyed him and took his cock in her mouth. He held her there, not thinking about Julie, not thinking about anything but the rush of blood through his veins, the throbbing, his need. He orgasmed hard and fast, but didn't feel the wave of satisfaction he always enjoyed. His entire body was on edge, uncomfortable.

Julie pushed herself away. He hadn't realized he was still holding on to the back of her head. "Grant," she panted. "I couldn't breathe!"

"Sorry," he mumbled. "Let's go."

"Are you okay? Grant, you're—"

"It's been a long fucking day and I just want to screw you in bed, okay?"

She looked like she was going to cry. He felt like slapping her.

Grant frowned. He'd never hit a woman in his life. What was he thinking? He rubbed his temples.

Julie rushed over to him. "I'll take care of you, Grant. You'll be okay. I won't let anything hurt you. Let's go."

He didn't remember how they got to her place, but the next thing he remembered was Julie, naked beneath him, crying.

"You're familiar with how the succubus operates, correct?" Jackson asked after Rafe closed the hotel door. "And her male counterpart, the incubus?"

"Generally. They're demons who have sex with humans. But most alleged succubus attacks were human in nature," Rafe said. "People who claimed they were attacked by such a demon in order to cover up affairs, for example. From everything I've heard, they don't generally kill their victims. Sometimes drive them insane, but not steal their souls."

"True. But covens like Wendy's use the demons for their own gain, summoning them for an exchange—a soul for something of value."

"They don't need a succubus for that," Moira said.

"No, but Wendy's coven is a sex coven, and they have a devotion to a specific demon. The things of value can be anything, but are usually information from the supernatural world—new and improved spells, the location of powerful occult objects. Sometimes they seek something more immediate and tangible, like a house or money. The demons can't just conjure up such things, but they can make certain things happen that benefit the witch."

"Like if someone wants a new house, their aunt may die and leave it to them?" Rafe asked.

"Exactly. I've been researching Wendy Donovan ever since you left this afternoon. She owns fifty percent of Velocity and several other clubs that belonged to Kent Galion. But there is no record of her buying into it. Galion is carrying a small loan, but her share is worth at least twenty times the loan."

"He just gave it to her?" Moira grabbed a water bottle off the top of the dresser. It wasn't until she opened it that she noticed the *Enjoy me for five dollars* label.

"I was skeptical," Jackson continued, "but then I called a friend in public records and he confirmed the corporate records and lien amounts. She owns her house outright. It's worth at least two million dollars—the Hollywood Hills is a coveted area."

"She bought it?"

"No. Three years ago, she was engaged to a popular rock star, Kyle Dane. He bought the house, but had her put on the deed with right of survivorship when she moved in. When he died, his insurance paid off the mortgage. It's hers, free and clear." Jackson sat at the table in the corner, his gaze sweeping the room and pausing on the salt traps and strategically placed crucifixes.

Rafe sat across from Jackson. "How did he die?"

"Heart attack, after a concert. He'd been ill for weeks and his doctors advised him against touring—this was all in the major papers, I did a Google search."

"So it was no big surprise when he dropped dead," Rafe said.

"Except," Moira interjected, "he was engaged to a witch who summons demons." She didn't dare sit for fear her exhaustion would overpower her. Instead, she leaned against the dresser.

"Where does Lust come in?" Rafe asked.

"I wish I knew," Jackson said. "But since succubi are sex demons and Lust by definition feeds on the human sex drive, they must be connected."

They had to be, but Moira didn't know how. "Do you have a picture of the chalice you mentioned on the phone?"

He unfolded a computer printout. "I got this from a friend of mine in London. This is what I think Wendy has."

It was a detailed drawing of a squat, bowl-like chalice

with a glass ball nestled in the shallow curve. The base was wider than the cup and curved upward.

"Such a chalice is often used in sex magic. If there's no demon involved, the glass ball isn't necessary. The witches will collect bodily fluids—blood, semen, saliva— in the bowl and offer it up. They are essentially asking for favors, more like a prayer than an order. But with this specific chalice, the blood of the victims is dripped into the base. The glass is essential to open the doorway to Hell. When the demon is first summoned, it's brought through the chalice—"

Moira said, "Like Fiona used a human vessel to bring forth the Seven Deadly Sins."

"Right," Jackson said. "But a succubus ritual isn't usually quite as deadly—or dangerous. With the right ritual, the chalice becomes a mobile doorway to Hell. The demon comes in, is channeled into a woman—or if an incubus, a man—and goes about the business of stealing the marked soul.

"The thing is, when the soul is claimed, the demon is supposed to leave the human vessel and snap back into the bowl. The coven then completes the ritual, and the demon goes back to Hell."

"Something went wrong with Wendy's ritual this time," Rafe said.

"Damn straight," Moira said. "We have to be prepared. If the demon left Nadine's body because it was being drawn back into the original gateway—the chalice— that means it could still be at Wendy's house."

"Are you certain this is the demon Lust?" Jackson asked.

"There's no other explanation," Moira said. "The

marks on the bodies too closely resemble the marks left by the demon Envy."

"But I've heard that demon marks are common when practicing black magic," Jackson said.

Moira didn't respond, and Rafe knew she was upset. She'd been marked by a demon once, and it had nearly killed her. The mark was gone, but it still affected her. She never talked about it with him, and he realized that at some point he was going to have to get her to tell him exactly what happened all those years ago.

"These marks," Rafe said when Moira didn't respond, "are unique. They look more like birthmarks, with a thin dark red line inside forming a satanic mark, similar to what you see in occult rituals, but at the same time different than anything we've seen before."

Moira said, "Other demon marks are small, simple brands. The Seven Deadly Sins mark their victims with far more elaborate designs."

"If the demon is trapped in the chalice, we can put it in a vault, correct?" Jackson said.

"It would be unstable," Moira said. "We need something sacred to trap it completely."

Jackson said, "I brought an iron box with me; it will hold the chalice."

"If it's all we have," Moira said.

"There's another idea—something more permanent than storing it in a vault."

Moira and Rafe both looked at Jackson. "We're all ears," Moira said.

"In theory, if the demon is trapped in the chalice, it should go back to Hell. At that point, while it's trapped, we melt the chalice and that portal will be closed forever."

Moira frowned. "That destroys the chalice, but are you certain it will also destroy the demon?"

"I don't see why it wouldn't."

Moira was skeptical on that point, and Rafe asked her, "What are you thinking?"

"This is the demon Lust we're talking about. It's not going to let itself get melted."

"It may not have a choice."

"We need to talk to Anthony before we do anything like that," Moira said. "And if the demon is out and about somewhere? Not trapped in the chalice?"

"I don't know."

"So we can't melt the vessel until the demon is trapped."

"Maybe we can—maybe that would kill it."

"More likely, if you destroy the portal, its bonds are broken and it's free."

"We can use traditional exorcisms," Rafe said.

"Without the chalice, there's nothing keeping the demon here. It can go anywhere, do anything, kill anyone," Moira said.

Jackson said, "I found an exorcism that will draw back the demon and close the portal."

Moira held out her hand. "Let me see it."

Jackson reluctantly handed it over. She read it, shaking her head. "No, no, no!"

"But it's the only way—"

"Moira?" Rafe said.

"It's a spell, not an exorcism. Exorcisms work one way—sending demons to Hell. Spells summon the demon to you." Moira was agitated.

"But it could save someone's life!" Jackson said.

Moira threw up her hands. "You of all people should know better! I don't care how good or noble our motivation is in stopping this demon, I will not resort to spells and witchcraft to trap it. It can only end in blood."

"So we wait until the coven calls the demon back?"

"I'd say yes, but that means letting someone else die. Maybe more than one person. I can't do that. The only thing we can do is control the chalice. Get it away from Wendy and her coven. Then, find who the demon is possessing and perform a *real* exorcism. An exorcism will force the demon back into the chalice, and then we can lock it up or melt it."

She glanced at her watch. "Anthony should be in Italy soon. We need his input. I don't know anyone else who'll know where to get the answers about whether we melt the damn thing with the demon inside or not, or what we can use to imprison Lust. Anthony can be a jerk, but he knows more about specific demons than I do. All those books he reads."

She was trying to make light of the situation, but Rafe felt her concerns. He strode to the dresser and stood with her. Moira needed to know he was with her one hundred percent.

"Wendy will protect that damn thing with everything she's got," Moira said, changing the subject.

"How will we know if the demon is inside the chalice?" Rafe asked.

"The glass changes color," Jackson said. "But that's also easy for a witch to fake."

Moira said, "I'll know."

"If they value it so much, won't they lock it up?"

"No reason to," Moira said. "They probably have a hidden altar—either a locked room or a room behind a false wall. I can find it. Protective magic will be stronger the closer we get to the chalice." She frowned, and Rafe reached over and took her hand. He didn't say anything, but she squeezed back.

She cleared her throat. "So what's your plan?"

"We wait until everyone inside is asleep. Then we go in and steal the chalice. Put it in Jackson's iron box, and then . . . what?"

"I have a vault," Jackson said. "I can keep it there. It will be safe, at least for a while."

"See?" Rafe smiled. "A plan."

"Waiting. My favorite thing," Moira said sarcastically as the three of them left the hotel room.

As soon as Anthony landed in Italy and worked his way through customs, he called Skye even though it was nearly two in the morning in California. He'd promised he'd call when he landed, and if he woke her he'd say good night and remind her that he loved her.

He simply wanted to hear her voice.

Skye picked up on the first ring. "Anthony?"

"Good morning. Why are you awake so late, love?"

"I can't sleep." She sounded exhausted.

"What's wrong?"

"What isn't wrong?"

Anthony stopped walking through the airport and found a place against the wall where he could stand without being bumped by other passengers. "Tell me. Is it the situation in L.A.?"

"Partly, but Rafe and Moira are working on it. They're consulting with Jackson Moreno. Know him?"

"Yes, very well." He breathed marginally easier. "He's trustworthy."

"Good, because I had to come home. Truxel dropped the charges against Elizabeth Ellis. She's out of jail."

"And Lily?"

"She's here with me. Then there's the press—" She stopped.

Anthony heard the tension and stress in Skye's voice.

"I'm not going to complain."

"You can tell me anything, Skye."

"I know. You do your thing, come back soon, okay?"

Anthony spotted John Vasco from St. Michael's crossing the baggage claim area. Anthony raised a finger and John nodded.

"Of course," Anthony said quietly. "As soon as possible. Are you okay, Skye?"

"I'd be better if you were here."

"I miss you, *mia amore*."

"Ditto."

"Be careful. I'll be home as soon as I can. I love you."

"Love you, too. I hope this trip of yours is worth it, that we have the answers we need to stop these . . . *things*."

She still had a hard time talking about demons.

"So do I."

He reluctantly cut off the call. John approached. Anthony hugged his brother-in-arms. At forty-three, John was the oldest living demon hunter out of St. Michael's. He'd backed off most assignments and acted more like a bodyguard than a hunter, but he still worked in the field when needed. He said little, and his loyalty was legendary. He'd risked his life to save both his comrades and innocent strangers, and never once complained or questioned his duty.

"Good to see you," Anthony said.

John stepped back, his expression grim. "Dr. Lieber is dead."

SEVENTEEN

Rafe drove by Wendy Donovan's house in the Holly-wood Hills and there was no activity. They drove far around the hillside, then turned around and came back. Still no activity.

"Maybe they're at the club," Jackson said.

"Wendy left early," Rafe said.

"Oh yeah, right about the time their good friend Nadine had a fatal accident with a demon." Moira rolled her eyes.

Rafe parked down the hill, out of sight from the house. The three of them walked along the edge of the road and stopped in a cluster of trees across from Wendy's driveway to inspect the property. The house looked deceptively small from the front as the entrance was on the top floor and the structure went down three stories, terraced to complement the cliffside. It was after midnight. The house was quiet, but not completely dark. Dim lights on each floor—the subtlety of a night-light—highlighted each curtained window. No movement or sounds came from the house.

Rafe didn't like the risk they were taking, but waiting until Wendy Donovan went to work tomorrow ran the risk of there being another innocent victim. And considering what had happened when the demon left Nadine

Anson's body, whoever hosted the demon would be at similar risk.

Moira had been unusually quiet and physically tense as they waited, and Rafe gave her some breathing room, keeping his eyes and ears open, concerned for her safety. She was exhausted, and if they had any other choice, he would have taken her back to the hotel to sleep.

"They protected the house from evil spirits," Moira whispered. "The spells grew as we got closer, but right here it's stronger. They must have left an opening for the demon. We find that opening and that'll be the room where they have the altar and spirit trap."

"And the chalice."

"Right." She shivered. "They've been doing this for years; they have it down. The spells are strong. But they have settled in the house."

"Settled?" Rafe asked.

She frowned. "I—I don't know. It feels heavier at the bottom than the top. I wish I could explain it better."

Jackson said, "This is the top story—there are two more beneath it. Does that mean their altar is on the bottom floor?"

Moira didn't say anything for a minute. Then, "Wait here."

She started across the street before Rafe could stop her.

"Moira!" he whispered loudly.

She put her finger up in the air behind her and disappeared in the roadside shrubs that framed the front of the house.

"Dammit," Rafe said. He wanted to go after her, but he knew—he *hoped*—she wasn't going to do something stupid.

Moira wasn't reckless, even though she repeatedly risked her life. He had to count on that now.

Time passed slowly as he waited, and Jackson said, "Should we follow her?"

Rafe glanced at his watch. He was getting antsy as well, but it had been only two minutes. "Give her another minute."

Moira came back in less than that. "The altar is on the bottom floor. That entire space is like a psychic fortress. But there is definitely a hole in the far corner. That has to be where their demon trap is."

"We should go down the cliff and in through the bottom," Jackson said.

Moira shook her head. "They'll know. There's no easy way to get to the bottom-floor balcony without more equipment than we have, or making a shitload of noise. And breaching that fortress could very well alert them. We go in from the top, work our way down."

"But doesn't that put us more at risk?" Jackson said. "Greater chance of encountering someone?"

"I didn't sense any movement inside. There are no bright lights anywhere in the house. If they have an alarm, we're screwed."

"Not necessarily," Rafe said.

She raised her eyebrow. "Oh? Holding out on me?"

"I have a bit of skill in that area. I'm about as good with security systems as you are at picking locks."

"That good, really?"

Rafe liked that Moira was bantering with him again and not deadly serious. She would perform better—and safer—if she relaxed.

Moira picked the lock on Wendy's front door quickly, and Rafe inspected the entry for evidence of an alarm.

No sensors, no pads, no wires to indicate an alarm system.

"Clear," he whispered.

He closed the door soundlessly and surveyed the space. Their eyes were already adjusted to the absence of light and they listened intently. An antique clock—several of them, by the sound—tick-tocked in a room to the left. The entry itself opened into a large square gathering room. To the left was a grand dining room that sat at least a dozen, with pillars instead of walls separating it from the entry and the hall.

To the rear was a vast kitchen and great room, and a wall full of windows looking out into the dark valley dotted with lights from other people's grand houses. To the right was a hall with several dark, closed rooms.

Without speaking, Moira pointed down the hall. There was a staircase that led downstairs, and Rafe nodded.

As they descended, Moira tensed again, but she kept moving, leading the way. Jackson took up the rear.

They didn't stop on the second level, but continued silently down. At the base of the stairs was an office of sorts, only ten feet wide but twice that in length, the far-side sliding doors leading to the balcony. It looked as though it had been divided off from the rest of the floor. Two desks, bookshelves, and a few chairs filled the space. Double doors led to another room.

They stopped at the base of the landing and listened.

Silence.

Moira pointed to Jackson with her dagger and motioned for him to stay and watch the stairs, then gestured toward the closed doors. Rafe understood. They stood on either side of the doors and Rafe cautiously opened the knob on his side. Moira opened the other door. Incense wafted through the open door—myrrh and sandalwood and something else Rafe couldn't identify right off. He peered through the crack. It was pitch black in there.

A memory rushed into his head and he froze.

Screams of agony pierced the silence as Samuel Ackerman's two closest friends were tortured by a demon. The sound shredded Samuel's heart.

"Stop, stop! Please leave them alone."

The witch turned to him, satisfied he would give her what she wanted. "Samuel. You know better. What will you do for me?"

"Don't do this, Susan. Please, stop."

"You stole from me."

"You know what you're doing is wrong. How could you turn your back on God? On what is good in the world?"

"Who's to say what is good? What has God ever done for me?" She waved her arm toward the living room where a succubus and incubus tortured William and Tessa Burns. They'd been stripped naked, unable to move, unable to stop the horrid acts of sexual violence being done to them. Samuel was spared only because for him, it was worse torture to watch. He had brought this down on his friends because he'd tried to do the right thing. William and Tessa knew more about the supernatural than he did. He hadn't believed in such evil until he'd witnessed Susan's horrid acts. He realized now that she'd been born without a conscience; that was the only explanation for her actions.

He'd stolen the chalice, and now . . .

"I have everything I want because I have the knowl-

edge," Susan said. "I have power. I need the chalice you stole from me."

He hesitated. Susan chanted in ancient Latin, then said, "Kali, the soul of William Burns has been pledged, and is freely given by your mistress; take what you will!"

William screamed as the succubus kissed him, sucking his soul out of his body until he died. It took a long minute, and through it all Samuel prayed for deliverance, begged God to stop this.

God did not answer. Instead, Susan laughed. The demon, satiated, was dismissed with an incantation from Susan's teenage daughter who watched the entire proceedings, the rapes and the soul-snatching, with rapt attention. Wendy had been such a sweet child, and now . . .

"My chalice, Samuel! Now! Or Tessa will die next."

"Raphael Cooper!" Moira hit him, her voice a harsh and worried whisper.

Rafe shook his head, his eyes still seeing the violence of his vision. Samuel Ackerman had been murdered at Santa Louisa de los Padres Mission three months ago. Why was this important—why did he remember this now?

"Rafe, please!"

"I'm sorry," he mumbled, still trying to rid his head of the horrific images. He still heard the screams of William Burns as he was sacrificed.

"Listen," she whispered.

He remained silent. They stood outside the doors. There was no movement; there were no sounds from above except for the ticking of the grandfather clock in the entryway.

Moira frowned and her hand tightened around her dagger.

He mouthed, "What's wrong?"

She shook her head, uncertain, but Rafe trusted Moira's instincts. He motioned to leave, but she shook her head again and pushed open the door.

Rafe shined his flashlight into the space. He found a light switch that had a dimmer, and put the overhead light on at the lowest possible setting.

It was a long room, three times the size of the one at the base of the landing. One wall was windows with three sliding glass doors. The scent of incense was stronger, as well as the smell of fresh candle wax. Candles sat on every available surface, both black and white, and in the center, under a spirit trap painted in black on the ceiling, was a hexagram with a solitary black candle in each of the six triangles. It looked much too similar to the trap Fiona's coven had used to summon the Seven.

There was enough space for a couple dozen people to move about. Comfortable furniture, both contemporary and feminine, was strategically placed to provide conversation and optimal viewing. The windows looked out on the brilliantly lit Los Angeles Valley.

Moira took in the room quickly, then her gaze locked on the double doors on the far side of the room.

"Mo—"

She cut him off and whispered so low he almost didn't hear her. "There's a demon in there."

Rafe's blood froze. "Let's go."

She shook her head. "This is it. We trap it now and take it with us."

"I've never known a demon to go quietly."

"Tell Jackson to get in here. We'll lock the doors and hold them off as long as we can."

"Moira—"

"Rafe, we cannot let it go!" She bit her lip, glancing at the door, her eyes narrowed.

She was right, but Rafe hadn't been expecting to face the demon tonight.

"I'll tell Jackson." Rafe stepped back through the doors.

Moira started across the room. She relaxed her senses, letting them feel the magic and evil that filled the room. She calmed her breathing, and focused on the demon behind those doors.

From the moment she'd entered the house, she'd known something was off. As she walked down the stairs, her apprehension grew. But as soon as she stepped through the doors into this chamber, she smelled it. Hell. There was a portal to the underworld right here.

The demon Envy had been able to change form at will—from human to beast, and every combination. They had all nearly died trying to contain it. She feared the demon Lust would be the same, except that it had been trapped by Wendy. That meant it was weaker. It couldn't take different forms. She hoped.

A possessed human had increased strength as well as the demons' ability to violently move people and objects with their will. But in a spirit trap, the demon would be largely impotent. This truly was their best opportunity to stop it, and while Moira didn't relish facing Wendy or Nicole Donovan, she'd do what she had to in order to leave with the demon.

She glanced over her shoulder. Where were Rafe and

Jackson? She was already across the chamber at the door, which led, she expected, to the demon. Her heart quickened with fear that someone had seen Rafe. But he would have alerted her, wouldn't he? He would have made noise, bumped something.

Then Rafe stepped through the chamber door with Jackson, who closed it quietly behind him and locked it.

"I don't like this idea," Rafe said.

"It's our only option." She held up three fingers, two, then one.

Moira opened the door. Candlelight flickered in the windowless room. The demon possessed the body of a mysterious and beautiful woman, was dressed in the Velocity uniform. She hissed at her. "I've been waiting for you, Moira."

Moira hadn't expected the familiarity, though why was she surprised? In a different form, the demon had also known Moira in the alley.

Rafe started an exorcism rite in Aramaic. Moira didn't know it by heart; Aramaic didn't come easily to her. The demon flinched, and Moira checked the security of the demon trap. It appeared sound. Moira glanced around the room. This was where Wendy cast her darkest spells. Her asthame—the dagger a witch used in rituals—was properly stored on the altar. Other tools and herbs were aligned as well.

And the chalice was on a special shelf above the altar, surrounded by black candles. It was a golden chalice about ten inches tall, the top a black glass sphere. The bottom of the chalice had a thick, curved lip, just like in the picture Jackson had showed them earlier. Two jars of blood were at either end of the altar. Moira concentrated on one of the jars, unable to sense through the thick glass whether it was human or not.

The beautiful demon hissed at the exorcism, and Rafe's voice rose. Moira skirted the spirit trap, which covered half the small room. She reached the altar and picked up the chalice.

It was ice-cold in her hands, and it weighed at least five pounds. There were demonic symbols carved around the edges, but Moira didn't have time to decipher the hieroglyphics. On the base was a sigil etched into the gold, a female demon who looked like a cross between Medusa and a serpent.

The demon screamed as Rafe invoked the names of God. As Rafe continued, the chalice warmed in Moira's hands.

"The rite is working," Moira said to Rafe.

Footsteps from upstairs told them that Wendy was now awake. Moira went to the door and called to Jackson in the front room, "Watch yourself! They're coming!"

The demon said, "Moh-rah."

"Shut up," she told the demon, knowing better than to get in a conversation with a creature like this. "Hurry, Rafe!"

Rafe was sweating profusely as he increased the pace and intensity of the exorcism.

"Moh-rah, free me. You will join me and my master."

"Fuck you."

A crash against the first set of doors told Moira their time was running out.

"Rafe!"

"Free me," the demon said. "Free me."

Moira suddenly feared they were doing something

wrong. The demon flinched, but wasn't in obvious distress, nor was it even close to leaving the woman's body. Exorcisms could be as short as five minutes or take days. With one of the Seven, it would more than likely take several days.

They barely had five minutes.

A crash in the front room shook the house. If anything happened to Jackson, what would she tell his daughter?

"We have to go, Rafe!"

Suddenly, the body inside the trap collapsed. The demon was partly freed. A hot swoosh of air tainted by the foul stench of Hell itself filled the space within the trap, floor to ceiling, the energy emanating from it enough to knock both her and Rafe down. The demon spun faster and faster, but it couldn't get out.

Moira couldn't understand how Rafe's exorcism had worked that fast. But if the demon abandoned the female body on its own, why hadn't it left Nadine earlier? What was going on here? Why wasn't it trapped in the chalice? They were way over their heads with this one. For a moment, Moira doubted if they'd even get out of there alive.

"What are you doing?" Wendy cried, flinging open the doors into the small room. "Stop right now!"

Moira didn't wait for Wendy to get her bearings. Tucking the chalice under her left arm as if she were running with a football, Moira charged at Wendy, punching her square in the stomach, then kneeing her in the nose as the witch doubled over.

Out of the corner of her eye Moira saw movement. She turned and pivoted, but it was too late. Nicole Donovan—the bitch of a witch from Fiona's coven in Santa Louisa—slammed the butt of her asthame against

Moira's head. Moira's quick reflexes minimized what could have been a killing blow, and she managed to keep hold of the chalice, but her eyesight blurred. She stumbled over Wendy as the witch tried to get up, falling to her knees.

Rafe kicked Nicole in the wrist and she dropped the knife. The demon roared from the trap, the woman's unconscious body inside the trap with it being lifted to the ceiling. Suddenly the body dropped to the ground. Then it slowly rose again.

"Rafe, the demon is killing her!" Moira screamed.

Wendy crawled into the room and began chanting a spell. Moira knew it well: it was a binding spell to tame the demon.

Moira didn't want to leave the poor possessed woman trapped with the demon, but she also didn't know how to save her.

"Moira!" Rafe shouted. "Moira! Go!"

She hesitated, but didn't see any way to reach the trapped waitress. Nicole charged Moira, and Rafe stopped the witch with a punch to the jaw.

Moira spotted Jackson trying to get up from the corner of the room. She ran over, helped him up, and handed him the chalice. "Come on, Jackson—we have to get out of here. Go—"

"Where's Rafe?"

"I'll get him, go!" she ordered the pastor.

She spun around, shook her head to clear it, and saw Nicole leap onto Rafe's back. Nicole had her asthame back in hand, its polished blade reflecting the dim light. Rafe shook her off, but then Nicole slammed headfirst into his back, knocking him to the ground.

Moira ran over and grabbed Nicole's wrist as she was

about to plunge her knife into Rafe's kidney. There was already blood on the knife—Moira's chest heaved. "Rafe!" she cried out as she wrestled with Nicole.

"I'm okay!" He scrambled to his feet and freed the knife from Nicole's grasp as Moira held her wrist down on the ground. Nicole bucked beneath her, and Moira kneed her in the stomach.

"You bitch!" Nicole gasped. "You'll be sorry. When Fiona gets her hands on you, you'll wish you were dead."

"Where is she?" Moira pinned Nicole's neck down with her arm, holding her body down with her right knee and her weight.

Nicole spat in her face. Moira pressed harder, cutting off her air supply. This bitch had watched Father Philip die at the hands of a demon she'd summoned. She didn't deserve to live.

"Moira, we have to go—!"

Moira barely heard Rafe's voice.

"Where is Fiona?" Moira shouted.

Nicole's face reddened.

Rafe pulled Moira to her feet. "Stop, Moira! Now is not the time."

Moira wanted to kill Nicole Donovan. Did that make her no better than her evil mother? Vengeance—it had driven her for so long. But was she a killer?

"Let's go." Rafe took her hand.

Wendy was consumed with controlling the demon, but the witch was strong and Moira felt the demon succumb. When the room began to fill with electricity, Moira didn't notice at first.

She glanced at Nicole, who was on the ground, catching her breath, chanting a spell.

"Right behind you," Moira said to Rafe, not wanting to find out what Nicole had up her sleeve.

They bounded up the stairs to the top floor and fled the house. Jackson was nowhere to be seen. "Dammit, I told him to get the hell out of Dodge! I knew we shouldn't have brought him!" Moira didn't want his death on her conscience. She didn't want to lose anyone else.

A slight tremor beneath their feet had them both sprinting down the street.

A vehicle rushed toward them. It was Skye's truck, Jackson at the wheel. They jumped into the backseat, tires squealing as Jackson hastened away.

"You got it!" Jackson said. "You really did. I put the chalice in the box."

Victory was bittersweet. Moira slammed her fist on the seat in front of her. "We didn't get the demon! That woman—"

Rafe took her hand and squeezed. "We did what we thought would work—it didn't. If an exorcism doesn't work, we'll figure out something else."

"What else is there?" Moira snapped. "We need to strategize, but we don't have any time."

"Listen, we got the chalice. That's one big plus for the good guys," Jackson said.

Rafe caught her eye and Moira flushed with embarrassment at her loss of control. Rafe said, "Don't beat yourself up over your rage at Nicole Donovan. I wanted to kill her myself."

"I would have if you hadn't stopped me. All I could think of was that face watching Father die."

Rafe took Moira's hand, and she felt something damp.

She flipped on the overhead light and saw blood on her fingers. She pushed aside his jacket and pulled up his T-shirt. "Why didn't you tell me you were hurt?"

"It's not fatal."

She bit back a lecture and pulled her first-aid kit from her backpack.

"Is he okay?" Jackson looked back from the driver's seat.

She inspected the injury. "Nicole did this? With her knife?"

"When she hopped on my back. She just nicked me."

"This is more than a nick," Moira mumbled. She focused on cleaning the wound and taping it up. She tried to rid her mind of the image of the possessed woman's body falling from the ceiling, but even when she blocked the mental picture she could still hear the sick thud as the body hit the floor over and over again.

"Moira, we'll find the answers," Rafe said. "We have the chalice—they won't be able to use it again."

"But the million-dollar question is, can we use it to send Lust back to Hell?"

After leaving Moira and Rafe at the hotel, Jackson ensured that the chalice was properly secured in the vault in the Grace Harvest church basement. The alarm was armed. He walked across the parking lot to the vicarage, physically exhausted but emotionally wound up.

He knew about demon hunting and had participated in a few exorcisms, but only as an assistant or bystander, and only under controlled conditions. He'd had no idea what was required, what Moira and Rafe truly had to do, or how much fortitude they needed to face off a demon that wanted them dead. They had worked in unison, completely in sync with each other. It had been amazing to watch, as well as terrifying.

At least for now, it was over.

Jackson wasn't a drinker, but tonight—this morning, rather—he poured himself a double Scotch before going to his office. He sat at his desk and booted up his computer. While waiting, he sipped his drink and consoled himself with the fact that he hadn't lied to Moira. In fact, he'd told her the truth—he was still looking for Courtney.

He would never have considered breaking and entering to obtain the information he needed—information he suspected Wendy Donovan had—but when the opportunity arose, he'd jumped at it. How could he not? His daughter's life—her eternal soul—was at stake. He couldn't stand by and not try to save her.

If Wendy Donovan's contact list and computer files didn't ultimately help him track down his daughter, at least he would have a much more comprehensive list of witches across America to add to his database. Jackson was confident he would someday find Courtney. He knew the name of the witch who had recruited his daughter, and now with Wendy's files he could track down her associates. Eventually, he would find and save his daughter.

Even if it took his last breath.

EIGHTEEN

After Moira helped Rafe recline on one of the double beds in their hotel room, she took her knife and cut away his shirt from the wound. Her field dressing had held, but the bandage was soaked bright red. He'd somehow reopened the wound. *Dammit.*

"I liked that shirt," Rafe said, eyes closed.

"You have at least six other black T-shirts," she said. Rafe was pale, but at least he hadn't lost his sense of humor. She willed her hands to remain steady as she carefully removed the dressing and inspected the injury.

The wound had stopped bleeding again, but it had gone in deep enough to have Moira debating whether to take Rafe to the hospital. What if the blade had nicked a vital organ? She must have stared too long, because Rafe said, "Forget about the hospital. I'm fine."

"You lost a lot of blood." She showed him the bandage she'd just removed. "How are you feeling? Honestly. Nicole stabbed you with her asthame. We don't know if the knife was poisoned, or cursed, or—"

"I am *fine*. Just exhausted, like you. I think I saw orange juice in the mini-fridge."

She rose and crossed the room. "I forgot there was a refrigerator. I'm so used to the generic, cash-only, fleabag motels."

She pulled out orange juice for Rafe and a water bottle for herself. Then she grabbed a mini-bottle of vodka.

"I didn't know you drank the hard stuff," Rafe teased.

"Me? Hell, no. If it's not beer, don't bother me with it. This is for you." She shoved a folded towel under him. "It's going to sting."

"Don't—" he began, but she'd already poured half the bottle over his wound. "*Shit,*" he gasped, biting down on his lip.

"I warned you. Sorry." She kissed Rafe near the cut, not realizing she'd done so until her lips touched his warm skin, tasted the alcohol on his body, and smelled the sweat from their battle with the witches.

In silence, Moira finished cleaning and taping his injury, trying to ignore Rafe's watchful eyes. "You'll live." She tried to sound flip, but it came out relieved. She finally looked at him, and he took her hand and kissed it. "Thank you."

Her racing heart was finally slowing as the adrenaline from the last hour faded. "But if you feel any sharp pains, start bleeding, get a fever—I'm taking you to the hospital. Or else back to Santa Louisa to have Dr. Fielding look at you."

"I don't need a coroner yet," he said with a half smile.

"I'm serious!" She tried to stand, to pace—worry and fear battling for primacy—but Rafe didn't let go of her hand. He pulled her down on top of him.

"I'm fine, sweetheart. But it's nice to have someone worry about me."

For a split second she thought about his wound, not wanting to reinjure it, but his bare chest was flat against her, his lips right in front of her, his eyes staring into hers.

"I'm *fine*," he whispered again.

She kissed him, not wanting to hear he was okay because she knew he wasn't. He'd been stabbed; he could have died. She shivered uncontrollably. They were partners; she'd never forgive herself if he died during one of their operations.

They were more than mere partners.

"I can't lose you," she said, her mouth moving from his lips, to his rough jaw, to his neck. "I can't," she whispered.

The thought that tonight could have been their last night on earth terrified her. For two weeks they'd been talking around their mutual attraction—every time Rafe brought it up, she avoided the conversation. She didn't want to talk about the kisses they'd shared, the hot touches, the way she missed him when they were apart, the way she knew when he entered a room even when her eyes were closed. She had kept the protective shields surrounding her heart, her emotions, erect and strong.

But tonight they crashed down around her with one simple thought:

Rafe could have died.

She didn't want to care about Rafe Cooper. She didn't want to be here in this hotel room alone with him, his arms wrapped tightly around her body, holding her close as she greedily licked his salty skin. Caring raised the stakes. Caring left her vulnerable. She didn't want to care. Or to fall in love.

But she didn't know how to stop it.

Tonight, she let go. Tonight, she touched Rafe the way she'd wanted to for weeks. She pushed aside his earlier comments about not settling for a one-night stand. She'd worry about that tomorrow.

She kissed Rafe's chest. His biceps. The soft skin on the inside of his elbow. She kissed each of his fingers in turn, slowly, wanting to know every inch of his body. She kissed his stomach and stopped when her lips brushed his bandage.

"I don't want to hurt you," she said. "Maybe—"

He grabbed her forearms and pulled her up, his mouth hard on hers, silencing her excuses. He rolled over so her back was flat on the bed and he towered above her. His voice was a low, primal growl. "If I bleed, you can stitch me up later."

Then there were no more words between them, only the heat that had been building exponentially until together, they turned combustible.

Rafe pushed aside his doubts, all anxiety over what they had faced and what they would face, and focused on Moira beneath him. Kissed her so she couldn't talk, couldn't tell him to stop, to slow down, to think. He didn't want to debate whether making love to Moira was right or wrong; it couldn't be wrong. Not when she warmed his cold heart; not when she gave him the will to live, a reason for fighting the pain of memories that weren't his, or the unspoken traumas of his own distant past.

With Moira, he could face the world and any battle the underworld threw at them.

He had to. For her. *For them.*

Rafe wanted all of Moira now, and he wanted to savor each second, every kiss, every touch. He kissed her softly, lightly, but she reached up and pulled him down to her, opening her mouth so he could fully appreciate her lush lips, her eagerness. He'd been waiting for Moira to accept not only their attraction, but the very real feelings that had been simmering from the beginning. He could have had her earlier, he'd wanted to make love to her against the dresser, on the floor, anywhere, but he'd known she wasn't fully there with him, and he wouldn't pressure her any more than she could handle.

But now, tonight, she'd made the leap. She might not know it, she might think she could talk herself out of this relationship, but she wouldn't do it. And he wouldn't let her.

"Rafe," she said, her voice muffled against his mouth. "Shirt."

He raised himself on his forearms and Moira reached down and quickly pulled off her shirt, tossing it aside. Rafe stared at her skin, her beautiful, soft skin marred by a long, jagged scar across her stomach. Rage bubbled in the pit of his stomach, an anger so hot and wicked he wanted to punch something. Instead, he leaned forward and kissed every centimeter of the scar, top to bottom, then he licked it slowly, bottom to top. Moira shivered beneath him, her hands gripping his biceps.

"A demon attack?" Rafe asked quietly, then kissed the top of the scar.

"I heal pretty well from demon attacks," she said. "That one came from my mother, after I ran away the first time."

The torment Fiona O'Donnell had imposed on Moira—physically and emotionally—was cruel and sadistic. Anyone else would have been broken under the repeated assaults. But not Moira—she was made of resilience and the strongest of wills. She was a survivor of the highest order.

"Don't think about it, Rafe," she said.

"I'm not. I'm thinking about you. How amazing you are." He kissed her. "How much you mean to me." He kissed her again, longer, savoring her tongue, drawing in her bottom lip to nibble.

His mouth traveled from her lips to her neck and back to that spot behind her ear that she loved so much when he kissed it. She gasped and reached for his belt.

He rose from the bed and stared at the beautiful woman. His beautiful woman. His Moira. He unbuckled his belt.

Moira's breath hitched as Rafe stared at her with his bottomless dark blue eyes. She watched him take off his belt, unbutton his jeans and push them—and his boxers—to the floor. His long, perfect penis stood straight out, moving as if it had a mind of its own. She reached out for him, but he turned away and walked to the end of the bed. He grabbed her by the ankles and pulled her down until he could reach her waistband. He unzipped her pants, curled his fingers under her panties, and in one fluid movement pulled them off and dropped them to the floor. He never took his eyes from hers as he lay back down on top of her.

He kissed her firmly, possessively, neither too soft nor too hard. His hands moved from her thighs, skimming past the spot she wanted him to touch, up her stomach until he found her breasts. She sucked in her breath when he slid down to take one breast in his mouth while rubbing the other. At the point past where she couldn't take the exquisite torture, but was too aroused to speak coherently, he switched sides.

Moira couldn't stop moving her hands. She was never one to sit still, and with Rafe Cooper lying naked on top of her? She needed to feel him, to remind herself that this was real, that she was worthy, that Rafe was safe. She tried to take control of the lovemaking—she didn't like giving up control in anything, even bed—so she reached down and caressed his penis, urging him to speed up.

Rafe groaned and said, "Not so fast."

"I'm ready."

"I'm past ready, sweetness." He removed her hand and brought it up above her head. He took her other hand and held it tight as well, not giving her the chance to explore his body.

"Rafe—" Her voice was low and seductive.

He kissed her again, his breath coming faster, mimicking her own urgency. She pulled her hands away from his grasp, and he held them again, on either side of her head, then adjusted his body between her legs. She opened for him, her chest rising and falling with anticipation.

Rafe stared at her and she nearly stopped breathing. The passion and intensity in his expression had her frozen.

Never had anyone looked at her with such raw desire.

He let go of one of her hands, but she didn't move. She didn't know if she could. He reached down between her legs and ran his finger lightly back and forth. It skimmed that too-sensitive spot and she shivered, the warm pit in her stomach instantly turning hot and fluid. She felt so damn needy and wanton; she leaned up to kiss him, then licked his jaw, salty with his sweat and restraint.

He groaned, his veins tight on his neck, holding himself back.

"Make love to me, Rafe," she whispered and fell back onto the bed, her arms out and open, showing him with her body how ready she was. How much she wanted this. Wanted him. Now.

He replaced his finger with his penis, and slowly—too slowly—pushed himself into her. Moira didn't want to wait. Couldn't wait. She reached down and grabbed Rafe's hard ass and pushed while she arched her pelvis forward. He thrust in completely and they both stopped moving. Moira didn't think she could breathe. Waves of emotion, physical and emotional, flooded her. Rafe's emotions and her own. She relaxed, trying to absorb them all without drowning. She was teetering on the brink when Rafe said, "I love you, Moira."

Rafe held himself in check, his physical desire for sex battling his emotional need for intimacy. He craved to show Moira deep affection and the sincerity of his love, not just say the words. But urgency propelled him, as if he was going to lose her. His heart skipped a beat and he eased himself down, sinking even deeper inside her warmth, his chest against hers, their hands locked.

"Rafe," she murmured, her breath caressing his lips.

Her voice wrapped around him and he set a slow rhythm, but together slow was not an option. They increased their sensual tempo, their bodies, slick with sweat, entangled in the dance they shared. Moira's breath quickened to match Rafe's, a gasp escaping as they tried to pace themselves. But slow wasn't working, he wanted to make the exquisite sensation continue all night, it had been so long for him, and never like this. Never had his emotions been equal to the physical act of sex. Here it was all about Moira, about him, about them together.

He moved within her, slow, steady, deep, prolonging each thrust until he tumbled over the abyss. He gathered her into his arms, held her tight as his body shook almost violently.

"Moira," he whispered. "Moira, love."

She quivered beneath him, her arms and legs wrapped around him, and she gasped twice, then her breath stopped. He let go of everything inside with a long, low-pitched groan. Everything, including his heart.

Rafe rolled onto his uninjured side, pulling Moira and the blankets with him, wrapping her up with him. He kissed her repeatedly, many small kisses everywhere on her face, her lips, her neck. Her heart thudded against his chest, and he put one hand over her breast, feeling her life beating against his palm. He slowed down his kisses, drawing each one out, savoring the taste of her salty skin, swallowing her sighs in his mouth. She nestled against him, and with a final sigh, Moira slept.

Rafe watched her. Asleep, Moira was just as beautiful, but surprisingly vulnerable. Delicate. Two words he'd never associate with her while awake.

But he had known, deep down, that Moira was vulnerable. What they did—what they must do—put her at risk. He wished foolishly that he could take her away from everything evil in the world. Pamper her. Show her the beauty of the mountains, the serenity of the meadows, the majesty of endless fields of wildflowers. He would give his life to give Moira peace in hers, peace and security she'd never had before.

Someday they would have it. He might not deserve it, but Moira did.

NINETEEN

Anthony's homecoming was more bitter than sweet.

Father Philip, the man who'd raised him from infancy, was not alive to greet him at the doors of St. Michael's. His small cottage on the island was closed and stuffy from disuse. And the monastery was virtually empty. Only fourteen men remained—ten of whom were over sixty, including the head of the sanctuary, Bishop Pietro Aretino, who seemed to have aged a decade during the three months Anthony had been away.

"Bishop." Anthony knelt on one knee and kissed the bishop's hand in respect.

"Anthony." He sounded relieved to see him, and very old.

Anthony took the old man's hands and squeezed them gently. "Father Philip rests at the mission, with the others, as you wanted."

The bishop nodded, his pale eyes glistening with unshed tears. "He knew he was going to die."

Anthony's heart skipped a beat. "Why did he leave?"

"He was called. Philip listened well, and never refused a call."

Anthony averted his eyes to avoid shedding tears. He'd wept for the only father he'd known at the funeral mass; he could weep no more. Yet they were on the cusp of change. Their numbers had thinned; every single one of their order was needed, and more. St. Michael's, which at its peak had more than two hundred men living within these walls, could not function with just fourteen. Even three months ago there were more than forty studying, researching, providing wisdom and information to the hunters that Olivet trained.

"What happened to Dr. Lieber?"

Pietro shook his head. "He was eighty-six. The journey tired him."

"Bishop, excuse me, but I find that unbelievable."

"God's ways are not our ways."

"It is a coincidence I find difficult to accept. Dr. Lieber had not left Switzerland in more than twenty years. He must have wanted to speak with me desperately to travel this far."

"The trip took more than fifteen hours. John said dear Franz slept most of the time. It was difficult, but he brought all his journals. They are now yours."

"I've read most of them. I needed his interpretation."

"The answers are there. He would not have brought them if they weren't."

"What did the magistrate say?" Anthony asked.

"They haven't said anything. They came this morning after Gideon went to retrieve Dr. Lieber for brunch and found him passed on. I suppose they'll inspect the body, whatever it is that they do, then send him home for burial. I contacted his granddaughter—"

"Granddaughter? I didn't know he had any family, that he was even married."

"Oh, yes, he simply never discussed it. He's Catholic; his wife was Jewish. One day while they lived in France, she simply disappeared, leaving him with a young daughter to raise. He moved to Switzerland, and hadn't left since—until yesterday." Pietro sighed wearily. "Later, he learned his wife was killed in a concentration camp. His daughter married and had one daughter—I don't remember her first name, Dr. Zuelle. She's an archeologist at Oxnard."

Anthony had, of course, heard of Dr. Katja Zuelle. She'd written extensively on religious artifacts in Europe and the Middle East. He'd never met her, nor known she was the reclusive, paranoid Dr. Lieber's granddaughter.

"Is she coming?"

Pietro shook his head. "Dr. Zuelle hadn't spoken to her grandfather in many years. She told me she'd contact his lawyer about his will and find out what his wishes were. We, Anthony—you and I and Philip and the others—have no family, except one another. To have blood relatives and be estranged—it saddens me deeply."

Pietro sounded depressed, very unlike the serene and stately bishop Anthony had grown up with.

John stepped into the great room and said, "The cardinal is waiting in the east library."

Anthony couldn't shield his surprise. "Cardinal DeLucca? He's here?"

"He arrived this morning to meet with Dr. Lieber," Pietro said. "He didn't have the chance."

Anthony hadn't even known the cardinal was on the island. "Bishop, John," he said quietly, "everyone must be extremely cautious. Until we know what happened to Dr. Lieber."

John nodded. Anthony realized John had the same concerns. He needed to speak to his brother in private. Ever since he had set foot in St. Michael's, something felt wrong. It could simply be the absence of Father Philip

and the empty halls. Or it could be something more nefarious. For the first time, he wanted to call upon Moira
and have her use her abilities—namely her ability to de-
tect magic—here at St. Michael's. He loathed to summon her back here, but if the Order was in jeopardy he
would do anything to save it.

Pietro seemed confused, and Anthony wondered
whether at his advanced age he might not have complete
control of his faculties. "Dr. Lieber died of natural
causes," Pietro said.

"We can't assume that. He was old, but I hope a full
autopsy is done. Bishop, do you know the magistrate
who is handling the death investigation?"

"Not personally, no."

"Whoever you trust the most, someone who understands the people and demons we face, please call him
and request a full autopsy and investigation."

"I know who to call," John said.

Anthony was relieved that John fully understood the
situation.

"Anthony, the cardinal is waiting," Pietro said.

"Of course."

"I'll take you," John said. With a slight bow toward
the bishop, the two men left the room.

"What's going on, John?" Anthony asked quietly.

"I don't know, but Rico sent almost everyone here on
assignment. Only the oldest and most infirm are left—it
puts them at risk. I told Rico I needed to stay."

"You must—this is our sanctuary. If we lose it—" Anthony didn't have to finish his sentence.

"We have no one to spare. I will stay as long as necessary. While you meet with the cardinal, I'll walk the
grounds and investigate even the most trivial signs."

"Thank you."

They parted in the main entry, and Anthony proceeded down the long, wide stone hall to the east library. It was midafternoon. On a sunny day, light would have been streaming through the stained-glass windows, but not today. Still, it was one of his favorite rooms in the monastery, where he had spent a great deal of time here over the years.

Francis Cardinal DeLucca was in his late fifties, with a full head of dark hair liberally shot through with silver. He was a stately man, physically fit, and well-respected in both the Vatican and Italy. He had been instrumental in stopping a small but vocal movement close to the previous pope that had attempted to close down St. Michael's after Peter's death at the hands of the demon who'd possessed Moira. Without the cardinal, then a bishop, running interference and using his oratory skills and extensive network and personal friendships with many of the pope's inner circle, Anthony suspected St. Michael's would have closed its doors seven years ago. That was only the most recent time St. Michael's had been at risk.

The cardinal had three priests with him, as was common when traveling. Anthony strode over to the cardinal and kissed his ring. "Cardinal."

"Anthony." He put his hand on Anthony's shoulder and gave him a blessing. "I am saddened by these events."

Anthony didn't want to discuss the situation with the other men in the room. He didn't know them, and while Cardinal DeLucca had been a crucial supporter of St. Michael's and the work they did, he wasn't of the Order.

The cardinal, as if sensing Anthony's reticence, told

the men, "I need to speak with Dr. Zaccardi about spiritual matters, if you would please wait for me in the great hall?"

Anthony shifted uncomfortably at the title of "doctor." He had his Ph.D., but he never used his title. He couldn't remember the last time anyone had addressed him as such, except jokingly at his graduation.

The priests left, and the cardinal motioned for Anthony to sit. "I asked John to bring in Dr. Lieber's papers. I have the rest of the day clear. I hope you'll allow me to help with your research."

Anthony was stunned. "Cardinal, you're a busy man."

"This is important. The fate of St. Michael's is at risk. I don't have to tell you that Father Philip's death has had lasting repercussions. Though Pietro is the titular head of the monastery, everyone knows that Philip was the strength behind the leadership. Without him, I don't know that I have the power to keep St. Michael's alive."

"What do we need to do?"

"I was hoping to convince you to return for a while. Stay here and rebuild. They need a leader, and you are a born leader, Anthony."

"Stay here? On the island?" He missed his home greatly, but he would be lost without Skye.

"I understand you have begun a new life in Santa Louisa."

"I am rebuilding the mission, but that is the least of my responsibilities right now, as I'm sure you are aware of what we are confronted with."

The cardinal nodded, then turned to look at the stained-glass windows. "These are dark days," he said.

"We haven't faced such a difficult trial in our lives, Anthony. In my support of St. Michael's, I have always believed we need the righteous acts of selfless men to maintain balance until our Lord comes again."

Anthony heard a *but*, though the cardinal didn't say the word.

"The . . . *theatrics* . . . of the release of the Seven Deadly Sins, and the subsequent recapturing of one, has led to a greater awareness of what St. Michael's Order is, what you all do. We've managed to keep much of the information under control. Yet, because of Philip's death in the States—so soon after the murders of the priests at the mission that St. Michael's administered—more people are questioning. Our opponents—those who have wanted to shut down St. Michael's for generations—are gaining a following. Your presence here would do great service to the Order and halt opposing forces. They mean well; they simply do not understand."

Anthony was stunned. The cardinal wanted him to retreat and save the monastery? Surely there were others better suited to the task than he. And how could he leave Skye and Rafe alone to battle the Seven?

The cardinal continued. "The few benefactors the Order has cultivated over the years are wavering now that Philip is gone. He had been the silent power. He was the one gifted with encouraging the faithful to open their purses. The trip he made to parishes across the world more than ten years ago brought in a substantial amount of money, but as you know, maintaining St. Michael's and Olivet separately, in addition to the travel and tools—I should not have to tell you that funds are extremely tight."

"This is about money," Anthony said, disappointed.

"Not only money."

"With all due respect, Cardinal, my abilities are better served on the battleground, not inside the fortress. Especially in these perilous times. We don't have years to stop the Seven Deadly Sins; we have months. We have captured one, and we will find the others. And to reunite Olivet with St. Michael's would be disastrous. We split the two more than one hundred years ago because a coven nearly destroyed us. It is far more difficult to take out two places, in addition to the dozens of parishes and universities where members of the Order are living and working. After—yes, I will consider returning to solidify the Order. St. Michael's was my home for many years; I miss it. But my home is now in Santa Louisa."

"And with Sheriff McPherson."

"My feelings for Skye are second to my duty." As he said it, Anthony wondered whether that was true. Could he leave Skye forever if that's what it took to save St. Michael's? He hoped to never have to make that choice.

But the cardinal wouldn't be talking to him if the situation wasn't desperate.

Anthony said, "I will make calls. I have contacts all over the world I can cultivate. I can raise the money we need."

"Perhaps that will slow the inevitable," the cardinal said without conviction.

The cardinal turned to face the two boxes that sat on the long, narrow table. "Dr. Lieber brought these here with him. Perhaps if we find the answers we need, we'll have a resurgence of support."

Anthony would have preferred to go through the material alone, but he had no choice. Keeping the cardinal on their side, as their advocate, was crucial, now more than ever.

He slid over one box to the cardinal, opened the second box for himself, and silently, they read the dead doctor's extensive notes, hoping to find the answers in these pages to save humanity.

Rafe woke when Moira sat up abruptly in bed.

He squinted. They'd fallen asleep with the lights on. He had no idea what time it was and glanced over at the clock: 6:45. He assumed a.m., since the cop who expected them at "oh-eight-hundred hours" hadn't kicked in the door and arrested them. What had they had, four hours' sleep? If that.

He turned back to Moira. "Good mor—" He stopped.

Her back was covered in scars. Some faded, some prominent; some long, some short nicks. One started at her shoulder, dark and wide, and tapered to nothing at the top of her round buttocks. He lost count at twelve . . . he remembered asking about the scar across her stomach last night.

Fiona.

Rage bubbled inside him. Rage that anyone would hurt Moira—whip her, beat her, hurt her so deeply that the scars on the outside were the least of her injuries.

"Good 'mor,' too," Moira said sleepily. She rose and stretched like a cat, beautiful in her nakedness, long and lean and muscular. She crossed the short distance to the bathroom and closed the door behind her.

Rafe couldn't rid his mind of what Moira had suffered. He had his fair share of scars, though faded and hardly noticeable. Most of them he'd received as a young child, before he turned up at St. Michael's. The cut on his cheek had been during training at Olivet. That scar irritated him because it didn't have to happen; Rico had been making a point the hard way.

Did Rico fully comprehend what Moira had suffered? Or was she simply another tool in the battle against evil? Expendable, replaceable.

Not to Rafe. He could not let her be a martyr in this cause. In any cause. There had to be another way. He would find it.

He heard the shower running, and he rose from the bed and knocked on the door.

"Moira?"

She opened the door, still naked. "You knocked?"

"It would save time and water if we showered together," Rafe said.

Moira wanted to turn Rafe away. Not because she didn't want to be with him; on the contrary, she didn't want to leave their bed. She'd wanted to stay at his side, on top of his body, under his body, anywhere near him to absorb his warmth, his strength, make love to him all day. The idea that she couldn't get enough of Rafe Cooper overwhelmed her. This was wrong on so many levels. Neither of them would live a long life, for one. Rafe distracted her, and any distraction could be fatal. Not to mention, the only other man she'd loved, she'd killed.

She shivered, unable to think about Peter.

"Rafe, maybe—"

He kissed her, covering her mouth with his, and preventing her from saying whatever she'd been about to say. Since Peter, she'd avoided getting close to anyone, knowing it would end badly. In death. His or hers. Or both of theirs. Their lives were neither stable nor safe.

So perhaps because of that precariousness, shouldn't they enjoy this moment in time? What if this was it, and today was all there was? What if she'd never again feel his urgent hands on her body, his passionate mouth exploring her lips, his arms embracing her so completely that she didn't know where she ended and he began?

She gasped when he lifted her off the ground and carried her to the shower. She wrapped her legs around his waist as hot water coursed over them.

Last night was sensual and sweet; this morning was sexy and fast, up-against-the-wall passion. Rafe supported her with the weight of his body and his hands cradling her ass. She gasped as he entered her in one deep movement, then stood there. Their bodies were tense and hard, every nerve ending raw and excitable. Moira's breath came in shallow moans as Rafe moved in and out, his mouth on hers, his tongue mimicking the rhythm of his confident thrusts. Every sensation was heightened, the sound of water pounding over them, on the tile, swirling down the drain. The steam-filled bathroom sizzled with the electricity of their lovemaking. She felt weak and strong at the same time; she longed to peak yet she never wanted this rare, powerful feeling of being more than alive to ever end.

"Moira," Rafe whispered. "Dear God, but I love you."

Waves of his passionate emotions flooded her. She couldn't respond, couldn't think. They clung to the other as if drowning, and maybe they were, the steam suffocating them like an obsession, Moira's burning need to give everything she had and take everything Rafe could give. It was so much more than she'd ever desired to share with another, and she had no choice but to give in as she tumbled over the edge of ecstasy. She could no more turn her back on Rafe than she could forget who and what she was.

If it was wrong, she would deal with the fallout. She'd always faced head-on the consequences of her actions. Today would be no different. And if there was a tomorrow . . .

Slowly, they came down off their sexual high. One minute or one hundred minutes could have passed and neither would have surprised Moira. Silently, Rafe set her on her feet, unwrapped the hotel soap, and washed her body. Tenderly, methodically. Her nerve endings raw from their near-violent union against the wall, the seductive massage relaxed her, comforted her, warmed her heart as the hot water soothed her skin.

Rafe kissed her almost reverently as he washed and rinsed her. He sat her on the edge of the tub and kneeled. She leaned against the edge of the wall and he brought her foot up and washed it, a symbol of what she meant to him. She almost panicked, not wanting anyone to love her, for it would surely end in disaster.

But looking into his blue eyes, her fears washed away, at least for this one perfect moment in time. She believed they would survive, that she could love again, that Rafe was the one for whom she was willing to risk her heart, her sanity, her life.

For the first time in seven years, she didn't want to die.

"Moira—" Rafe began as he turned off the water.

"Shh." She put her finger to his lips, then her lips to his mouth. "I'll remember this moment for the rest of my life."

She stepped from the tub, and dried off.

"Who whipped you?" Rafe asked quietly.

She often forgot about the scars on her back, mostly because she couldn't see them. But they had been hideous for years. Though fading with time, they'd never be completely gone.

"The first time I ran away my mother found me. I was sixteen, scared and stupid. She—" She cut herself off, shook her head. She left the bathroom and grabbed her only clean clothes from her backpack. She'd have to shop, find a laundry, or go home tonight.

"Moira," Rafe said, then remained silent until she turned around.

He had on his jeans and nothing else, and he was the sexiest man on the planet. His dark hair was wet, curling at his neck, water dripping down his body. He hadn't shaved, and looked dark and almost unapproachable.

She knew what he wanted and shook her head. "It was a long time ago."

He met her eyes, wouldn't let go.

Just thinking of it, she felt foolish and very afraid, even though Fiona hadn't been able to find her for seven years, not until Moira walked into her territory. Moira didn't want to remember the past, even as she lived with it every day.

"Your fear is going to get you killed."

Rico had forced her to face her fears so she could survive whatever came her way. But the dungeon . . . she had never really overcome it. She'd pretended, for Rico. But deep down, she knew her survival was a miracle. It certainly had nothing to do with her.

"My mother locked me in a dungeon for a week. In Ireland, a castle. It was cold and moldy, and she sent in monsters to—" She stopped herself again.

Rafe stepped forward. "I will never let anyone hurt you like that. I would die first."

She whispered, "That's what I'm afraid of."

He tilted her chin up. "I wish I could tell you don't be afraid. I wish I could take your fears away. But I'm here for you, for *us*, and I'm not going away."

Moira tried to push aside the hope that filled her, knowing that something was surely going to ruin this—some*thing* or some*one*. But she felt lighter, as if she might have a chance to survive this supernatural war.

Rafe took her into his arms and held her tight. Several minutes later, he said, "We should go to the police station before Detective Nelson busts down the door."

"First—" Moira bit her lip. How did she ask this? After what they'd shared this morning? She blurted out, "Rafe, I need to know about your vision."

"Vision?"

"At Wendy's house. When we were downstairs. You had a vision—I know you did. You were out of it for a good minute. You have to trust me, Rafe. And I have to trust you. I want to. Just tell me the truth."

He stepped back and stared at her. She prayed he wasn't trying to come up with a lie. Then he said, "It wasn't a vision."

"Then what was it?"

"A memory. And not mine." He leaned against the desk and crossed his arms over his bare chest. "Remember when I told you about the memories I had about Father Tucci and Father Salazar? Anthony thought they had something to do with what Dr. Bertram was doing to me in the hospital while he kept me in the coma."

"Of course I remember." It was through those memories that Rafe had unlocked the key to defeating the demon Envy. They had also nearly killed him.

"This was similar to those memories. When Fiona held me captive, they wanted information from me. I don't think they realized that I have the memories of those who were murdered at Santa Louisa."

Moira didn't know what to say. What Rafe was suggesting sounded impossible . . . yet she herself had seen the death imprint of Craig Monroe. "Like a death imprint?" she conjectured.

"When you told me about what happened in the alley, I began to wonder if the same thing could have happened at the mission. The priests had been drugged and were hallucinating. Their most horrible memories became very real to them, as if they were living through their worst trauma over again. They tried hard to purge the evil thoughts from their minds, unable to live day-to-day with the frightening images. The coven wanted to drive them to murder, and the way to do that was forcing the priests at Santa Louisa to relive over and over the evil acts they had witnessed, the violence that sent them for help in the first place. And if they were reliving that violence while I was there in the chapel—I don't know, it sounds crazy, but . . . as soon as we opened the door last night, I smelled something familiar that I couldn't identify, and I had the flash—a memory. It was like I *was* Samuel Ackerman. He never told anyone what awful thing happened to him in his past that brought him to Santa Louisa, but now I know. I know the truth." His voice hitched.

She stepped toward him, put her hand on his chest, felt his heart beating much too fast.

"It was awful—I can't—"

"Rafe, please tell me. Don't keep it bottled up inside. Isn't that why those poor men suffered? Because they suppressed everything until it drove them insane, with the help of witchcraft."

Rafe closed his eyes, not wanting to tell Moira the truth. But didn't she deserve it? And she was right. If he didn't explain to someone, it would drive him off the edge. "Father Samuel was a parish priest here in Los Angeles." Rather than fighting it, Rafe allowed himself to remember. It gushed forth from the deep recesses of his mind.

"Samuel Ackerman called Susan his sister, but they weren't blood-related. They were raised together in foster care and lost track of each other after Samuel turned eighteen and went to college. Susan came back into his life—he never knew why. At first, he was overjoyed at finding his foster sister and having a family. She had two daughters, and Samuel doted on them. Wanting a family was one of the reasons he'd turned to the Church. Sadly, when she attempted to steal consecrated hosts from his church, he discovered the truth about his sister: she was an occultist. He went to Susan's house to confront her and witnessed a shocking ritual where his sister was engaged in black sex magic. A Luciferian rite, pure evil." Rafe could see the orgy Susan and her coven had shared with a vile demon. But the demon gave them strength and power, and they grew hungry for more. The addiction to power was far deadlier than drugs. Rafe would try to block the abominable memories from his mind, but feared they would disturb him for the rest of his life. "Samuel saw the chalice and remembered hearing about such a thing from a very old priest at his seminary. It was like a tether for demons, what you call a psychic leash. He didn't know what it was for, but knew it was important to Susan's rituals. The next day he stole the chalice and went to visit William and Tessa Burns, a couple who had devoted themselves to learning about occult practices after their son disappeared with a coven.

"They knew the chalice was evil, but they didn't know what to do with it. They reached out to St. Michael's for information, but before anyone was sent to retrieve the chalice, Susan managed to track Samuel down.

"He refused to give her the chalice. She'd brought her coven with her, as well as her two daughters. Wendy and Nicole."

Moira drew in a sharp breath. "Donovan."

"Yes."

"So he gave her the chalice?"

"Two of her coven offered themselves to be possessed by a succubus and an incubus. They tormented, raped, and tortured William and Tessa. When Samuel still refused to hand over the chalice, the succubus sucked out William's soul and he died. Broken at last, Samuel relinquished the chalice to Susan.

"But she had no intention of releasing Tessa Burns. She died as well."

Moira gasped at the brutality. "Dear God."

Rafe squeezed his eyes shut and Moira stepped into his arms, holding him close.

"We must destroy the chalice, Moira," Rafe said. "As soon as possible."

"I agree—but shouldn't we talk to Anthony first? After all, the exorcism didn't work. I don't even think it was our exorcism that pulled the demon from that woman's body. I think the demon did it on its own. If that's true, how can we possibly trap it in the chalice?"

"Perhaps we need to put the chalice inside the trap."

Moira frowned. This was getting dangerously close to magic. "Maybe. But I wouldn't risk it without more information. Let's call Anthony."

Rafe glanced at the clock. "I'll call him."

An urgent knock on the door had Moira frowning. "A little early for housekeeping," Rafe whispered, picking up his dagger.

Moira walked to the door, with each step feeling a wave of magical energy on the other side. A witch. She looked through the peephole. A slender woman taller than Moira, with dark hair pulled haphazardly into a loose tie, fidgeted at the door. Her elegant features were tired and strained and she had a small, dark bruise on her cheek.

"It's a woman. She was in Jackson's files. A witch. I feel it with every pore in my body." She couldn't remember her name, but knew this woman was bad news.

Rafe had his dagger ready. Moira retrieved her own and held it out to ward off a spell. Then she relaxed, letting her senses absorb everything around her, every sound, every smell, every nearby emotion. Opening up her God-given senses without using magic to shield or protect her used to terrify her. Sometimes it still did. She felt the overwhelming sense of love and fear flowing off Rafe but consciously blocked him out, focusing on the other side of the door. There was fear there, too, but only one person.

"She's alone, and she's scared," Moira said and opened the door.

TWENTY

Ambition, cruelty, avarice, revenge, are all founded on lust.
—Marquis de Sade

Moira let the witch into the hotel room and closed the door behind her. The brunette's eyes went to the dagger in Moira's hand, and Moira made no move to sheathe it.

"Who are you and what do you want?" Moira said.

"My name is Julie Schroeder. Please, I have no one else to turn to. I need your help."

"I don't know you, and you're a witch. That's two big fat negatives against you." But the name sounded familiar—Jackson had mentioned her last night, as part of Wendy's coven.

Julie's eyes darted from Moira to Rafe, who pulled a black T-shirt—identical to the one Moira had ruined the night before while cleaning his wound—over his head. The witch was nervous and scared, but damn bold to confront them here.

"You're Moira O'Donnell," Julie said as if that revelation was an answer. "You're the only one who can reverse the spell."

"Stop right there. I don't deal with spells, period. How the hell did you find us?"

"I tried to find you through a traditional spell, but that didn't work."

"Magic doesn't work on me," Moira said. It wasn't quite true—Fiona had nearly killed her with magic two weeks ago. Still, Fiona had never been able to find Moira using her very powerful dark magic, so she very much doubted a young witch like Julie could.

"So I used old-fashioned methods. I went through my boyfriend's notes."

"Boyfriend?"

"Grant. Detective Nelson? We were together last night. After what happened to Nadine."

"You're screwing the detective?" Moira asked, stunned and worried. She'd sensed no magic in Grant Nelson. Had she missed something? Had he figured out a way to block his aura from her?

"Grant and I—we have a relationship."

"Terrific!" Moira brushed by Julie and crossed to the window. She looked down into the parking lot, expecting to see a legion of witches outside her window ready to burn her at the stake. Or worse, take her to her mother.

She wasn't 100 percent confident that her finely tuned senses always worked the way they were supposed to, but she had never once been wrong about a witch or a demon.

There was always a first time.

Taking a chance, she turned to Julie and said, "Nelson isn't a magician."

"No, of course not. My coven is female only."

"Right. Because you sacrifice male souls to a succubus. Very liberating of you."

"Please! Grant's life is in danger. I wouldn't come to you if I had any other option. Moira, you're my only hope!"

"Do I look like Obi-Wan Kenobi to you?"

Rafe put his hand on Moira's shoulder and squeezed. He said, "Julie, start at the beginning."

"Grant came to the club after Nadine died. I was supposed to take him to his place, but we went to my apartment instead. I told Wendy he insisted, but I really just wanted to save him. Wendy will kill me if she finds this out."

"And I care, why?" Moira asked.

Rafe said, "Wait—why were you supposed to take him to his house?"

"Because Wendy was going to send the succubus there. Wendy didn't want any more problems at the club. We don't have much time. The succubus can go after Grant anytime after sunset. I don't want to lose him."

"Tell him," Moira said. "Tell him he's the target of a demon and see what he does."

"Are you crazy?"

"Pot, meet kettle."

Rafe squeezed Moira's shoulder again. Damn, that hurt.

"Julie," he said, using his calm, cool, collected—and very sexy—shrink voice, "we can protect Grant, but we need to know everything about the ritual Wendy used to summon the succubus."

Moira bit back an argument. She wasn't going to help a witch, not unless Julie gave up using magic. But she couldn't let Grant Nelson die because this witch had cursed him.

Julie frowned. "I planned on sticking by him all day— but something has happened to him. I don't know what . . . he's not himself. I'm scared."

"Is he possessed?" Rafe asked.

"No. Not like that. But he's different. Last night we screwed like rabbits. That's common, but Grant wasn't the same. I don't know how to explain it, but he was rough. Cruel and crude. Then this morning I saw a mark on his back and it scared me."

Moira felt sick to her stomach. She found her phone and scrolled through her photographs. "Did it look like that?" She showed Craig Monroe's demon mark to Julie.

"Y-yes," Julie said. "That's it. So you know what it is?"

"Yes," Moira said. She stared at Julie, trying to figure out whether she was telling the truth. "Don't you?"

She shook her head. "What is it?"

"It's a demon mark. You're familiar with those, I assume."

Julie shrugged. "I've heard of them, but I've never seen one."

"Haven't been a witch long, have you?"

"What do you want from me? Are you going to reverse the spell and save Grant or not?"

"Reverse what spell?"

"Wendy's. Our coven's spell. I think when we brought Kali into our world, we must have done something wrong. Wendy wanted to strengthen the ritual, called on Kali to claim three men we'd cursed, and I think the changes she made did something. Nadine died. That shouldn't happen!"

Every vein in Moira's body froze. *Kali.* She knew that demon—knew of it, at any rate. Old, evil, powerful. The ancient Jewish people had many nightmarish stories about Kali, under a variety of different names. Az, Lilith, you name it—this badass demon went back to the fall of Lucifer. The stories Moira had heard made the Brothers Grimm appear downright cheerful.

If they summoned Kali, how did the demon Lust get into the mix?

"You're messing around with the darkest of supernatural forces. No wonder you lost control!"

Julie recoiled from Moira's outburst. Rafe grabbed her arm and pulled her to his side.

"When did you perform the ritual?" Rafe asked. Moira tried to pull her arm loose from him, but he held on tight.

"Tuesday night."

"Tuesday?" Rafe said. "Are you certain?"

"Of course—Kali claimed Monroe on Wednesday, Erickson on Thursday, and Grant was supposed to be last night, but—"

"Wait," Moira said. She mentally ran through the timeline of what she knew. "Kent Galion died Friday."

"That had nothing to do with us. I swear to you, the ritual was Tuesday night. It's a special feast for Kali; we do it the same feast day every year."

It didn't make sense to Moira. Kent Galion died on Friday—and four days later the succubus was summoned? Yet Galion, Monroe, and Erickson all had the same demon mark.

Julie continued. "We tried the men who'd betrayed us, and gave Kali a taste of their blood so she would know them."

Moira snapped, "You tried them? You're the judge and jury and use a demon to execute them? You think you and your coven are demi-gods picking and choosing who should lose their soul?"

Julie's lip quivered, but she tilted her chin up and justified their actions. "Craig cheated on his girlfriend repeatedly. He was an asshole. Belinda worked at Velocity and found out she was pregnant. Craig dumped her and told her to get an abortion. She dropped out of college and quit her job. She wasn't a witch! She was just a sweet girl who got used by a douche bag. He deserved it! I loved Belinda like a little sister and he destroyed her. She went home and her father kicked her out of the house. She was so upset, she felt so alone—" Julie looked at the ceiling and blinked back tears. "She died in a car accident. I don't know if it was suicide or not. So yes, I picked Craig because of that."

Rafe pulled Moira back and asked, "What about George Erickson? From all accounts, he was a good guy."

"That was Pamela's pick. Pam was furious because he was sleeping around."

"But they supposedly had an open marriage," Moira said.

Julie raised her eyebrow. "Open? You don't know Pam. Pam gets what she wants, but George wasn't allowed the same privileges. I felt bad about him because I liked him, but those are the rules. And Grant—" Her face clouded.

"You wanted Grant dead," Moira said flatly.

"No! He was Wendy's pick. I—I went along, because I was mad. I didn't know he'd slept with Wendy during one of our off-again times. Grant sleeps around, I know that, but he wasn't supposed to go after the girls I work with! Talk about humiliating . . . I found out he'd slept with four of them, and once back when we were still together. But . . ."

"You think you love him," Moira said. "You bitch. You're jealous and you sold his *soul* to a demon? Do you know what happens when a demon claims a soul? Do you know the pain, the emptiness, that the victim feels as his soul is ripped from his body? Skinning him alive would have been more humane!"

"Kent Galion died Friday," Rafe said quietly.

Moira took a deep breath. "I was thinking about that—but can we even believe her?"

"She's telling the truth," Rafe said. He stared at Julie.

"I swear to you," Julie said, "it was Tuesday. We had nothing to do with Kent. Wendy did not want him dead— Marcus is hugely suspicious of how she got half of Kent's business without paying for it. When he gets back into town Wendy knows she's gonna be on the hot seat."

"And," Rafe continued, "Skye told us there was a dead woman found frozen in his house, who'd been missing since last Wednesday night."

Julie said, "Stephanie. She was a waitress at Velocity. But those deaths aren't connected."

"They are," Rafe said. "Galion had the same mark on his back that Monroe and Erickson had. The same mark that Detective Nelson has."

"It's connected to Fiona," Moira said. "Not Wendy's ritual. It goes back to the Seven." She asked Julie, "When did Nicole Donovan arrive?"

Julie frowned. "Why does that matter?"

Moira snapped, "Answer the question."

"Two weeks ago. It was late Saturday night; she showed up at Velocity. Surprised Wendy. They don't get along, but Nicole moved in with her."

Moira said to Rafe, "What if she brought the demon Lust with her to Los Angeles? It's the psychic leash—maybe the Seven are connected to the coven members. And the witches are immune because they were in the protective circle when the Seven Deadly Sins were released. That's how Nicole could affect Hank Santos, but not be affected herself."

"A catalyst," Rafe murmured. "Like Typhoid Mary."

Julie interrupted. "What are you talking about?"

"Nicole didn't tell you? She was part of Fiona O'Donnell's coven that released the Seven Deadly Sins from hell. They're not your friendly neighborhood demons; they're big, bad, bold, and brazen."

"So Galion was affected before the ritual," Rafe said. "Because he spent time at Velocity. The demon Lust would feed on a place like that—the sexual tension, the physical attractions. And the connection to Nicole Donovan keeps Lust in the vicinity."

Rafe turned to Julie. "You said that Wendy changed the ritual on Tuesday?"

Julie nodded. "We wanted to give Kali more power so she wouldn't leave after one, um, soul. I thought that if she didn't get Grant last night she'd go back to the underworld, but Wendy said she's still here and stronger than before. She nearly broke out of the spirit trap last night!"

"Don't we know it," Moira murmured. "Rafe, they had to have trapped the demon Lust. We knew it was Lust, but didn't know how or why it was here. Now we do."

She turned to Julie. "Get out. I don't trust you, and we have to figure out how to save the man you claim to love so much you planned to kill him."

Rafe pulled Moira out to the balcony and whispered, "We can fight this thing. Especially since it's trapped in a body."

"We tried it last night, but it didn't work. We're not dealing with a succubus—we're facing one of the Seven. I think it's too powerful to be trapped in the chalice—remember what Jackson said? The demon goes back through the portal it came from. Lust has no connection to the chalice. I think it's like a, a—" She couldn't think of the word.

"A red herring."

"Yeah. Maybe Lust got trapped because of the spell, and is required to fulfill the terms of the agreement in order to be free." Moira blanched. "When that happens, it's loose."

"We have to find it before sunset."

"If we can believe her." She glanced through the half-closed door at Julie. She sat slumped in a chair, head in her hands. She looked beaten and defeated. But Moira didn't feel an ounce of pity. She had brought it on herself.

Rafe said, "You know as well as I do that most rituals are most effective at night."

"I don't trust her."

"She wants to save Grant Nelson. Moira—I don't trust her completely either, but she can find out who the demon is possessing. If we have that information, we can set a trap. We can control where Grant Nelson is at sunset."

"And then what?"

"Then we need to weaken it, just like we did with Envy."

"How?"

Rafe shuddered. "We'll find out from Anthony."

"And Rico. He'll have some tricks up his sleeve, I'm sure."

Rafe didn't want to call Rico, because he feared that it was Moira's life that Rico would put on the line. But Rafe had no choice. Especially if he couldn't get ahold of Anthony. "Does this sound like a workable plan?" he asked Moira.

She nodded.

They stepped back into the room.

"I don't understand," Julie lamented. "For five years we've been prosperous, we've never had any problems, no one ever died, but then Nadine—"

"No one died? What about the men you killed?"

"I mean, nobody who didn't deserve it."

"Get out."

"No! Please, you must help me. Help me save Grant!"

Moira felt Julie silently working a spell. She held out her dagger to reflect any energy sent her way. "Don't even try it, or I'll slit your throat."

Julie looked stunned. "How'd you know?"

"Like I'm going to tell you that." She said to Rafe, "We need to find Nelson."

"Oh, thank you! I can help reverse the spell. We can do it right now—"

"No. I'm not a witch."

"That's not true."

"I don't think you're in a position to call me a liar."

"But everyone says you're one of the most powerful magicians in the world."

"That would be my mother." Moira tensed. "Who's everyone?"

"It's well known. It's why—"

"Why what?"

"Wendy has been trying to get into Fiona's good favor. When Nicole was invited into her coven and not Wendy, Wendy went a little crazy. She thought if she delivered you, it would give her the in."

Rafe stepped toward Julie, his gaze narrowed, and said in a low voice, "Are you setting up Moira now?"

"I swear I'm not. In fact, I'll tell you exactly how Wendy is going to do it."

"I'm not concerned about Wendy," Moira said.

Rafe raised his voice. "Moira, you need to be concerned!"

He was worried, and Moira didn't want to worry Rafe. If he changed his focus from fighting the demon to protecting her, they'd lose. Of course this relationship of theirs, or whatever it was, was a terrible idea. She couldn't afford to lose Rafe as her partner. Together, they had a chance. Apart? They'd both end up dead.

She said, "Okay, I'll watch out for Wendy. Happy? Right now, we're late for our meeting with Detective Nelson, and now that we know he has a demon's mark, we're also running out of time. We're damned if we do, damned if we don't."

"What do you mean?" Rafe said.

"Grant was cursed by Wendy's coven, but the demon's mark is on him because he's susceptible to lust. Julie said it herself—Grant played the field, slept around. That means he's prone to attack and go postal like Kent Galion—or, if he fights it, he might end up like the basketball player in Santa Louisa, dead of an aneurism. If he can fight it until sunset, great. After that, his soul is demon food."

Julie was incensed. "How can you save Grant if you won't reverse the spell?"

"I don't know yet," Moira answered.

"I can't believe this." Julie sank down on the edge of the bed, holding her head in her hands. "Grant's going to die."

"Not if I can help it. He may not be a saint, but he doesn't deserve to die *or* lose his soul. He had no part in this except he pissed off a couple of jealous witches. Honestly, you don't deserve him."

"I love him!"

"Funny way of showing it."

Rafe touched her on the arm. "Moira, we need to go."

"We take everything with us," Moira said. "If she could track us down, Wendy can, too. We're not coming back."

"What are you going to do?" Julie asked.

"First, find your boyfriend. Then, stick with him until the demon comes for his soul. Then—we'll play it by ear." She wasn't about to share any of her ideas, however weak they were.

"Let me explain something," Moira said, crossing over to Julie and standing over her. "You are on the wrong side. I don't care what you believe, what you think, or who you are, but you are toying with dark forces, and when you play with the powers of darkness, you lose. In the end, it's Hell. We went to Wendy's in the hopes of stopping the demon from possessing another person. Unfortunately, we lost that battle, but we gained the chalice. Nicole almost killed Rafe. To say I don't like the Donovans is an understatement. The chalice must be destroyed."

"But that's how she brings the succubus to us!"

"You idiot! Even now you don't admit that you were wrong. Only when the demon threatens someone you care about do you feel a tinge of remorse. I think if the demon does get to Grant first, you'll feel bad for a day or two and then go back to your old ways."

"You're wrong, I won't—"

Moira put her hand up. "Don't lie—not to me, not to yourself. But I'll tell you something: if we can't save Grant, we can't save any of you. In Wendy's thirst for power or revenge or whatever stupid idea she had, she screwed up big-time because she got a badass demon, not the sweetly evil succubus she expected. And when the demon Lust is relieved of her imprisonment, who do you think she's going to go after?"

For the first time, Julie didn't try to justify herself or argue. Moira let the dire reality of the situation sink in, then said, "I need one thing from you, other than to stay out of my way. I need to know who's possessed."

"I don't know! After what happened to Nadine, Wendy said she was going to find someone outside of our coven."

Rafe tensed, and Moira felt the anger that had been simmering at Julie's revelations start bubbling beneath his skin. "You gave the demon an innocent woman?"

A flash of the night before: the poor possessed woman's body rising to the ceiling and dropping with a sickening thud. It turned Moira's stomach.

Julie had the decency to avert her eyes and for the first time look sincerely guilty.

Moira stepped forward and poked her in the chest. It felt good to get out her frustrations, so she poked her again. "Find out who it is and where she is, then call me. If you really want to save Grant's life, I don't want any surprises."

TWENTY-ONE

Grant had slept like shit. As a result, his migraine was even worse now than it had been last night. When he'd woken up in Julie's apartment, she was gone and the night was a blur. Unable to figure out what was wrong with him, he chalked it up to exhaustion and a bitch of a case—though deep down he suspected something far different was the cause of his migraine and fuzzy memory.

After leaving Julie's he went home, showered, and changed, arriving at headquarters after eight, with an extra-large coffee, four aspirin, and a quart of milk.

His partner was at work on the computer, but before checking in with him, Grant detoured into the break room, swallowing the aspirin down with half the quart of milk. He added milk to the coffee more to cool it down than for taste, and went back to his desk facing Jeff Johnston. Grant growled, "Tell me Cooper and O'Donnell are sitting in an interview room waiting for me."

"Haven't seen them."

"I knew it. I should have put them both behind bars until I figure out what the fuck is going on at Velocity."

Johnston looked glum. "We got another problem. Nadine Anson's suicide is all over the Internet."

"What?" Grant booted up his computer and Johnston said, "Over here; I'm already online."

Grant walked around to Johnston's desk.

"At least four people posted their cell phone videos on YouTube. Another blogged about it with a series of still pictures. The major networks posted the videos on their websites. I can't believe you didn't hear about it."

"It happened twelve hours ago; I had shitloads of paperwork and crashed after an eighteen-hour day. Didn't think that an asshole or *four* would post a woman's suicide for the fucking masses to enjoy."

Johnston clicked *Play* on one of the videos and Grant stared at the screen for the next minute and forty-nine seconds. The recording caught Nadine midscream as she pulled out a clump of hair.

Johnston swore and said, "I can't believe that jerk recorded this instead of trying to help her."

Grant's anger went from hot to boiling. Someone could have saved Nadine's life, but they'd done nothing except film her breakdown. Grant was generally a pessimist—two decades on the police force did that—but he still believed in the relative goodness of people who weren't career criminals. Watching the video squashed that myth.

People were bastards, all of them.

Grant watched the video until Nadine stepped off the curb, then he averted his eyes. He didn't want to see it again.

"Wait," Johnston said. He took the mouse and rewound the video ten seconds. "Grant, watch this."

"I don't want—" He sighed and reluctantly looked. He didn't see anything except Nadine fall and the bus that ran over her bump up and down. He heard the screams of the crowd, Moira's cry from the sidelines.

"There!" Johnston said.

Grant said, "It's just a reflection. Probably a flash."

Johnston rewound it again. "Look right next to the bus, before the ad for Disneyland."

Grant focused on the spot Johnston told him to. It was a flash, but . . . it looked like a woman stood there. A pale, dark-haired beauty. She was there for a second, then was gone.

"No one could have been standing there," Grant said. "There was a car right there a moment before. It's probably a ghost image, left over from other tapes."

Johnston glanced at him. "Boy, you're a dinosaur, Nelson. This is digital. Watch one more time," Johnston said. "I'll pause it."

"I don't know what you think we're going to get out of this," Grant said, a sick feeling in his stomach.

The woman looked familiar.

An irritated, very Irish voice behind them said, "I can't believe you're watching that damn video."

Moira was beyond furious. What was the cop doing watching Nadine die like that? Like in a movie. It was sick.

"Should I bring you some popcorn?" she added.

Rafe had his hand on her back. *Right. Watch the sarcasm.* Maybe she was going too far, but she was ticked off.

Grant turned around and said, "I'm conducting an investigation. Lay off."

Moira had been forced to watch variations of that video on the television in the hotel coffee shop until Rafe

stood on a table and turned it off because the manager
had refused to do so. Then the desk sergeant was watching the news when they arrived, and Moira had snapped
at him, too. But even if Grant was just doing his job, the
circus of the video still irritated her.

Rafe rubbed the back of her neck and whispered in
her ear, "Easy, my love."

She glanced over her shoulder at him and narrowed
her gaze to lecture him about how to address her, but his
half-smile told her he'd done it on purpose. Some of her
anxiety drained away.

Johnston said to Grant, "I took a snapshot of the
image and used that image program thing to sharpen
it."

Moira turned to where Grant's partner was sitting at
the computer and looked at the picture. The color
drained from her face. She knew exactly what they were
seeing.

An astral projection of Julie Schroeder.

"It looks like Julie," Johnston said.

"It's a reflection or something," Grant said. "Julie
wasn't there. We would have seen her. She couldn't have
been there."

Johnston shrugged. "You're probably right. But it's
weird."

Moira wasn't going to explain it to them. They
wouldn't believe her, for one thing, but the realization
that Julie Schroeder had left her body and projected herself at the scene of Nadine's breakdown changed everything. Dammit, Moira had known that Julie was lying
about something! Why did this deception surprise her?

She said, "I don't know what you both are talking

about, but I have places to go and people to see. So let's get this over with."

She still hadn't figured out how she and Rafe were going to save Grant's ass, but the one thing she *did* believe after her bizarre encounter with Julie this morning was that the witch really didn't want her boyfriend to die. Maybe Julie thought that if she killed Nadine she could break the spell. But that made no sense—the demon had already left Nadine before she died. It was the departure of the demon that sent Nadine over the edge.

Maybe Julie hadn't known the demon had jumped out of Nadine's shell. Yet she had to have seen how Nadine was suffering, even if she'd been observing from the astral plane. Julie might not have been able to hear everything, but she'd have seen the physical violence Nadine had done to herself. Maybe she'd wanted to save her.

Or she was following Grant. To protect him, expecting that the demon would be going after him next.

One thing was clear: Moira couldn't trust her. Worse, though, was that Moira had believed her when she said she didn't want Grant to die. Normally, Moira was an expert at spotting the lies. Was Julie playing both sides? Trying to save Grant Nelson while turning Moira over to Fiona?

"Let's go to the interview room," Grant said.

"Here's fine. Nothing formal. I'm helping *you*. You obviously watched the video—you have Nadine's confession and it's clear we both tried to help her. You have the marks to prove it." She pointed to the Band-Aid on his face. Then she gestured to the bruise on her cheek. "So do I."

The plan Moira and Rafe had come up with on the

drive over no longer seemed like all that hot an idea. Moira was going to suggest that she tag along with Grant while he finished his interviews, giving him her assessment of "the cult" while keeping an eye on him. Rafe was going to contact Anthony about the chalice and whether it could be used to trap the demon Lust, and if so, how they could keep that wench trapped.

"Take a seat," Grant finally said, rubbing his temples.

"Headache?" Moira asked.

"I didn't get much sleep last night." Grant scowled at his partner. "Stop it with that damn video. Either finish up the paperwork or listen." He turned to Moira and Rafe.

"First," Grant said, "I typed up the statement you gave yesterday. You'll need to read and sign it."

"Of course."

"What I want to know is why did Nadine say to you, 'I know you.' Had you ever met her before yesterday?"

"No," Moira said. She didn't know why Nadine had said that, though it likely meant that Nadine—even within her possession—still remembered everything. Which means that she'd seen Moira in the alley. Demons could impart memories and information to their human victims, if they were powerful enough and had a reason. The demon Lust was certainly powerful enough, but why would it share anything with Nadine about Moira?

"You're sure about that."

"I'm not answering questions twice. Why did she tell you that she hated you?"

Grant just shook his head. "I'll be the cop."

"Fine." Moira bit her thumbnail, pretending to be disinterested, but she watched Grant closely. She knew he had the mark on his back only because Julie had told her. She wanted to verify it, but she could hardly demand that he strip. And she remembered that when Deputy Hank Santos had been affected by Envy and unconsciously battling the demonic virus, he had a badass headache, as Grant Nelson obviously did now. Still, a killer migraine wasn't proof positive of a demonic infection.

"Yesterday," Grant said with a long sigh. "What happened in the alley?"

"I told you."

"You lied to me. Sheriff McPherson promised that you'd tell me the truth. Dammit, I want the truth!"

"Can you handle the truth?" Moira asked. Rafe put a hand on her back and squeezed. She shrugged it off. She'd dealt with people like Grant Nelson before.

"Try me."

"I saw Nadine kill Craig Monroe in the alley."

Grant stared at her in disbelief. In a low voice he said, "You were a witness and didn't come forward? Do you know that's a crime? Accessory after the fact?"

"I wasn't actually here Wednesday night. I saw her do it yesterday afternoon."

"Don't fuck with me, O'Donnell!" He slammed his palm on the desk.

"I'm kind of psychic," she said. The psychic excuse sounded good, as most people would at least consider the possibility. Why people more readily believed in psychics than demons, Moira didn't know.

"Psychic," Grant said flatly.

"I saw his death imprint."

Grant put his head in his hands. "I don't fucking believe this."

"You asked."

"I should put you in jail, but I honestly don't have the energy."

"I can prove it."

"Bullshit."

"Nadine gave him oral sex. I'm sure they took some sort of sample or whatever it is they do. Since Nadine is dead, can't you compare her DNA to whatever you found on Monroe's body?"

Jeff Johnston coughed.

"Nadine could have told you," Grant said.

"Right. I told you I never met her before yesterday on the sidewalk."

"Of course you could be lying."

"I'm trying to help you! I know Skye got a copy of the coroner's report; you want me to call her? See if there was female DNA on Monroe's dick?"

"That's how you know. Sheriff McPherson told you."

"Skye didn't tell me shit. She left yesterday because she had to deal with a crisis back in Santa Louisa. I honestly don't care if you believe me. You're the one who wanted me to come down and play nice."

Grant rubbed the back of his neck. "For the sake of argument, let's say you are psychic and you saw Nadine kill Craig Monroe . . . how?"

"That I don't know." *She ripped his soul from his body and ate it.* "Her back was to me in the vision. But I know what she was wearing—a red dress. With a high neck but backless."

Grant froze. He knew that dress; Moira saw it in his stunned expression.

Rafe whispered in Moira's ear, "Anthony's calling me back on my cell."

She nodded. Rafe excused himself and walked down the hall.

"Where's he going?" Johnston asked.

"Phone call," Moira said. "We're not under arrest; we can talk on the phone, right?"

"And how did you get hurt? You had a big welt on the back of your head."

"What I saw caused me to faint," Moira lied smoothly. "I hit my head. The bricks in that alley are uneven. And hard as a rock."

Grant leaned forward. He had an expression on his face that Moira couldn't read. It was almost . . . admiration. "Moira," he said quietly, "you don't impress me as a girl with a weak stomach. Fainting?" He shook his head.

She leaned back and stared at him tight-lipped.

"Okay," he said, "you can leave. But stay in L.A. Until I know what's going on at Velocity, I need you where I can find you. Because you're lying to me, and it's pissing me off."

"I can help you, Detective."

"With this cult. Right."

Moira fumed. "Yes, with this *cult*. I don't really care if you believe me or not, but let's look at the facts. Three men are dead. Kent Galion, Craig Monroe, and George Erickson. They *all* had the cult mark on their backs. Nadine confessed in front of dozens of people that she killed them. You'll find her DNA on Monroe's body, and you already found her prints all over Erickson's bedroom. She obviously lost it yesterday and had a mental breakdown."

"The way you say it, the case is over. Suspect dead. Case closed."

Moira opened, then closed her mouth. That wasn't what she wanted the detective to do, was it? Close the case?

But maybe that would be good. Get him out of the picture so she and Rafe could find the demon, trap it, and de facto, Grant Nelson would no longer be infected.

They had only one day. If the detective died, according to Julie Schroeder, the demon was supposed to head back to Hell. But if Rafe was right, if the demon fulfilled its obligation to Wendy's coven, the psychic leash that bound it to the chalice—or to the coven—would break. Because they weren't dealing with a succubus but Lust itself, who hadn't arrived through the chalice, it couldn't be used to send Lust to the underworld.

Moira bit her lower lip. How could she keep an eye on the detective at the same time she tracked the demon?

"I guess you're right," she said, acting dumbfounded. "Case over."

"It's done, as far as you're concerned." Grant rubbed the back of his neck again. "I have details that need answers, and I'm going to find them—which is why you're staying in L.A."

An attractive woman strode into the room, her eyes pinned on Grant. She wore tailored slacks and a blazer over her substantial hourglass figure. "Nelson, what is going on? I've been monitoring this case since I spoke to you yesterday morning and you didn't tell me that you had a suspect and now she's dead! Suicide?"

"Where did you hear that?"

"I read the police report."

"Those aren't public."

"I know." She held up an employee badge. "It helps when you work for the Board of Supervisors."

"Nina—please. I'm in the middle of an interview."

"Is it about this case?"

"I can't tell you. You put yourself in the middle of it when you told me you had an affair with the deceased."

She angrily got in Grant's face. "Dammit, Nelson! Don't blow me off. Did you look at the files I gave you? The orgies? The occult rituals? There isn't just one person responsible, and you know it."

Moira's interest piqued. She sat up. Grant shot her a look. "You can leave, Ms. O'Donnell."

"I don't think I want to now," she said.

Nina looked her up and down, then extended her hand. "Nina Hardwick, attorney for the Board of Supervisors."

Moira shook her hand, sensing the energy that made up Nina Hardwick's invisible aura. She wasn't a witch. And now she had an ally.

"I'd like to hear about the orgies and occult rituals," Moira said.

"No! This is a police investigation," Grant snapped, losing his temper.

"But you said the case was closed," Moira snapped back.

"Closed?" Nina said. "You closed it?"

"No! I didn't."

"But you said—" Moira countered.

"I was being sarcastic."

"Then you still need my help," Moira said.

"The time I call in a psychic to help me in an investigation is when I turn in my resignation."

Nina stared at Moira, eyes wide. "You're psychic?"

Moira couldn't tell whether she was skeptical or in awe. "Not exactly; I sometimes have visions of past and current events." She wasn't even lying with that statement. She liked Nina Hardwick. The woman was tough as nails and she irritated Grant Nelson. "What files?" she asked.

"Where are my files, Grant?" Nina asked. "I want to show this girl, Miss O'Donnell?"

"Moira."

"They're part of a police investigation," Grant said.

"Ah-ha! So the case isn't closed."

Grant stood up. "That's it, both of you out of here or I'm putting you in custody for interfering with a police investigation. Nina—stay out of it. You, O'Donnell— don't leave L.A. until you hear from me."

Nina was going to argue, but Moira quickly said, "Thank you, Detective Nelson. You have my number." She gave Nina a sideways glance and the woman picked up on the hint.

Nina said to Grant, "You'd better tell me exactly what you find out about Pamela Erickson and this dead suspect or I swear, I'll make your life hell."

If he lives long enough, Moira thought.

TWENTY-TWO

Julie drove her sporty convertible to Wendy's spacious house in the Hollywood Hills. She had never been so terrified in her life.

"Wendy doesn't know," she whispered to herself. She couldn't know! Then why ask her to meet now?

Julie had done everything Wendy asked of her. She'd planted the hex bag. She'd lied to Moira O'Donnell because she wanted her on her side to save Grant, but the hex bag would let Julie find him anywhere—just like the one she'd planted on Nadine. She'd gotten Rachel Prince to drink the potion so the demon could possess her. She'd tracked Nadine when Wendy couldn't reach her—how were they to know that the demon could release Nadine on its own? It wasn't supposed to happen like that. Julie wondered whether Moira O'Donnell had done it. She didn't believe for one minute that O'Donnell wasn't a full-fledged practicing witch. If she wasn't, why was she still alive? What she knew—what she could do with that knowledge—could damage covens across the globe. If she weren't a powerful witch, she would have been killed.

Julie had done everything she'd been asked—everything except turn Grant over to the succubus—so why did she feel that Wendy was lying to her?

"*We're having a meeting at my house to discuss the*

problem of Moira O'Donnell and her boyfriend. Don't be late."

Julie was early. She parked in the driveway. Pam was already there. With Nadine dead, that left their coven with eight members. Nine was the perfect number; who was Wendy going to recruit? Julie didn't see Nicole stepping up to take orders from her sister Wendy.

She took a deep breath and got out of her car. She walked around to the side of the house and down the outside stairs, to the bottom level. Glancing in through the window, she saw that the room was a mess, but there was a new circle cast on the main hardwood floor—not in front of the altar. She didn't know how Cooper and O'Donnell had gotten out alive—other than by using magic. Moira O'Donnell had incredible powers. It was the only explanation.

Why had she denied it?

She opened the door. Wendy was on the far side of the room, with her sister Nicole and Pam Erickson.

"Julie," Wendy said without turning. "I have someone for you to meet."

Julie's blood ran cold. She froze as her eyes fixed on the most beautiful woman she'd ever seen, standing naked in the center of the spirit trap.

The stranger's golden hair flowed down her back in waves of silk moving as if blown by a gentle breeze, though there were no windows or doors open in the room. Creamy, flawless skin encased graceful arms, shapely legs, and full, round breasts. Her bright eyes, as exquisite and sharp as two amethyst crystals, locked on Julie. Though she smiled, the chill in Julie's veins settled deep in her bones.

As the strangely beautiful woman moved to the edge

of the circle, Julie noticed a naked man lying on his back. His eyes were open, his contorted face frozen in shock. His penis stood straight up, impossibly long and engorged. But he didn't move. Was he dead?

It was Ike, their bartender at Velocity.

"Wh-why?" Julie asked. She wanted to be strong, but her knees shook and she couldn't move.

Run, Julie, dammit, run!

"Our friend needed sustenance, since you kept her from the sacrifice. Ike has screwed every waitress in the club; he jumped at the chance to come to my place for an orgy." She laughed.

"What are you talking about?" Wendy had always been unpredictable, but she was acting fool-crazy.

"You didn't fool me. Grant was so freaked and tired last night you could have easily taken him to his place. But no, you took him to *your* apartment, where you set up a spirit trap to protect him."

"I've always set up protections around my home! You know that."

"Yes. I do. Which was why you were supposed to take him to *his* house." She waved her hand as if swatting a gnat. "No matter." Wendy rose and faced her. Her grin terrified Julie. "Our new, very powerful friend has taught me a lot since last night. We now have an understanding." Wendy looked at the woman—the demon— with admiration and a palpable affection that turned Julie's stomach.

"I saw you, Julie." Wendy's voice turned venomous. "You're not the only one who can leave her body. I saw you leave the hotel. I watched, and then Moira O'Donnell came out. You've betrayed me. The only reason you're not dead is because in your ignorance, in your stupidity, you inadvertently gave me the key. I will wrap Moira O'Donnell up in a pretty bow and deliver her to her mother, and Fiona will place me high in her coven.

"If you survive—I don't think you will, but if you do—I will forgive you. Until then, our friend has many things to do. We've chosen you."

There would be no reasoning with Wendy. Her eyes were bright, almost drugged, and her aura was shimmering with excitement. Raw terror propelled Julie toward the door. It would not open.

"Wendy, please!" she begged, her back flat against the wall as she fumbled in vain to turn the knob. She glanced at Nicole as she approached, Pam at her side. Nicole was not insane like her sister. In fact, her clear eyes told Julie that Nicole was smart and reasoned. "Nicole, don't do this!" she pleaded, her panic readily apparent as her voice cracked. "Wendy is crazy, this makes no sense, don't let her—"

"Crazy?" Wendy frowned, but her bright eyes betrayed her good humor. "That hurts. I don't think I *will* forgive you."

Pam and Nicole each grabbed one of Julie's arms. They half dragged her to the spirit trap, and holding her still for the demon to inspect.

Like a deer trapped in headlights, Julie froze, enraptured by the woman's—the *demon's*—beauty. But when the stranger smiled, her breath reeked of death; and her hair wasn't flowing with silk, it was moving on its own, each strand a living snake, impossibly thin but braiding with the others, reaching out for her.

This wasn't a demon inside a human body. This was a demon incarnate, in full human shape.

The demon spoke, her voice deep and seductive. "Julie," she cooed, "you should be afraid. Very afraid."

Julie knew she was dead, no matter what happened, but if she was to have any chance at survival, she couldn't let this demon touch her soul.

The guilt for all the men she'd participated in killing weighed heavily on her heart. She'd never considered that what she was doing was all that wrong until she saw what had happened to Nadine. The horrible way she'd died. Julie had tried to help her friend but couldn't, and now she didn't know how to save herself. Grant would die. There was no way Julie would be able to save him trapped in her own body with this vile creature!

She didn't have time to think, and only one idea came to mind. Astral projection—temporarily removing her spirit from her body.

As the demon reached out for her, her spirit leapt silently from her body. She'd never been able to shift directly to the astral plane without a calming and purification ritual, but she'd been practicing, and had gotten faster and better and could survive longer on the astral plane—the invisible layer that enveloped this world, separating the living from the underworld and the heavens.

Her body collapsed between Pam and Nicole.

"She fainted," Pam said.

"Too bad. I wanted to watch her soul being shredded, the traitorous bitch." To the demon, Wendy said, "She's yours."

As a spirit, Julie watched from outside the house. Her unconscious body was drawn into the spirit trap by the demon's psychic power, no hands touching her. She was placed next to Ike. He tried to stand, but couldn't, and again lay still.

The demon lay on top of Julie's body. For a brief moment, Julie thought the demon was having sex with her. But the house shook, and the demon turned to a thick, dark gray cloud that wrapped itself around Julie's body. Ike screamed, unable to move, and Julie's body rose from the floor. She smiled.

"I like this body," the demon said. "It's very comfortable." She stripped and lay down on top of Ike.

"No, please," Ike begged, his voice rough.

"Now I can finish what I started," the demon in Julie's body said as she kissed him.

Julie watched in horror as the demon raped Ike even as he screamed, even as he begged Wendy to help him. But Wendy just watched, a half-smile on her face.

The evil bitch. How could she be so cruel to Ike? Someone she'd known for years? What had happened to Wendy that made her so vicious?

Julie couldn't stop the attack. She couldn't stop the demon from sucking Ike's soul out of his body. Julie watched in horror as the demon drew out a visible soul, a smoky gray mist, from Ike's mouth. The creature breathed deeply, draining Ike's life, an expression of ecstasy on her face as if on the brink of orgasm. Her entire body darkened and shimmered for a moment, then went back to looking like Julie, except for the darkly glowing aura surrounding her.

"I am satisfied," it said. "Release me, and I will finish."

Julie didn't wait around for the demon to be let out of the trap. She didn't know whether it would be able to see her or not, or what it would do to her if it did. Julie flew away, her spirit soaring over the valley, over the highways, but she didn't know where to go.

All she knew was that she didn't have much time. The longest she'd been without her body was half a day. She didn't know if she'd survive beyond that.

And she didn't know what would happen to her afterward.

There was only one person she could ask for help, and she didn't know how to do it without a body.

But dammit, she'd find Moira O'Donnell.

TWENTY-THREE

Rafe stood outside the police station to talk to Anthony on his cell. He didn't want anyone listening in on his conversation, though any eavesdropper would be more confused than worried.

It took him ten minutes to explain to Anthony what had happened since they'd arrived in Los Angeles yesterday morning. He concluded, "So you can see that we're at an impasse. When we tried to exorcise the demon last night, it didn't work."

Anthony said, "But you said the demon left its victim."

"Yes, but it happened fast, as if it was the demon's will. Since we're dealing with one of the Seven Deadly Sins, we know they have far greater powers—as fallen angels—than most demons."

"You're certain?"

"Yes."

"What does Jackson Moreno think? He's very knowledgeable."

"According to both Jackson and the witch who's trying to save her boyfriend, when the ritual is complete, the psychic leash is supposed to snap the succubus back into the chalice. The completion of the spell then sends it back to Hell. But Moira thinks because we're dealing with the demon Lust, it's too powerful to send back through a traditional exorcism. We'd hoped to trap it in the chalice, then melt the thing down, hoping that would incapacitate the creature.

"We're nearly out of time. The cop on the case has a demon mark. Jackson has the chalice in his vault, and we need to know what to do. If we destroy the chalice, will that free the demon, or will it force the demon back where it came from?"

When Rafe was done explaining their situation, Anthony was so quiet that he wondered whether the international cell phone call had been dropped.

When at last he spoke, his voice was tentative. "This is just a theory based on what I know of how demons are summoned and sent back. Occult rituals are in balance—meaning they need to come full circle or there's the potential for chaos. So a demon summoned through a physical vessel—such as a human body or an inanimate object like the chalice—must return the same way. That is their doorway."

Rafe frowned. "But when the Seven Deadly Sins were released, they came through Abby Weatherby. She's dead. They can't return through her."

"Correct. Because Fiona aims to change the balance of power. But she had Lily there. Lily is the other piece of the puzzle, the balancing *arca,* and thus would have given Fiona control over the Seven, and the ability to return them when she got what she wanted."

"Is that what Dr. Lieber told you? But won't it kill her?"

Anthony said, "The theory of balance isn't new, and I believe we can send them back through the portal opened on the cliffs in Santa Louisa. But it's not going to be easy, and we still have a lot to learn. Dr. Lieber's papers are a mess, and—"

"Ask him. He can tell us right now if he knows."

"Dr. Lieber is dead. He died in his sleep before I arrived."

"In his sleep? He has information for you, but suddenly he drops dead?"

"Rafe, we'll talk about Dr. Lieber's death and what it means when I return to Santa Louisa." He paused, and Rafe wondered if Anthony didn't feel he could speak freely. The idea that someone at St. Michael's couldn't be trusted sent dark chills down Rafe's spine. St. Michael's had always been their sanctuary.

"First things first," Anthony continued. "Dr. Lieber has both facts and theories and examples, but his organization is lacking. I'm trying to put everything in order, and obviously I wish he were here to explain it. That's probably why he wanted to see me in person, because his writings are all over the place. He has documents and journals in four different languages, and putting them together is cumbersome. I can do it; it's just going to take time."

Rafe was skeptical, and he didn't know if he could trust the information Anthony now had. It made anything that came from Dr. Lieber's papers suspect. "Are you bringing everything back to Santa Louisa?"

"Yes. I'm hoping to leave Italy tomorrow."

Moira walked down the steps with the attorney, Nina Hardwick. Rafe caught her eye. She pointed to a Starbucks on the corner, across from the police station, and he nodded and pointed to his phone. He watched the two women cross the street, Moira discreetly surveying the people on the street, analyzing potential threats. She never stopped, he realized. She was always on alert, always tense, watchful, in motion. The only time he'd felt her relax noticeably was after they made love last night and she fell asleep in his arms. She practically melted into him, showing complete trust.

His heart quickened at the thought of losing her. Their lives were a balancing act, and it wouldn't take much to knock either one of them out. He wasn't going to let it happen to Moira.

"Rafe? Hello?" Anthony said. "I asked if you can trust this witch who came to you this morning."

"I'm a pretty good judge of people, Anthony. Years of psychology. She's scared, and she doesn't want her boyfriend to die. And she didn't fake any remorse for the other deaths—I don't think she'd really considered the consequences of what she's done until now. And Julie wasn't casting any spells with Moira in the room." Anthony didn't say anything, and Rafe's hand tightened on his phone. This cold war between Anthony and Moira was putting a wedge in Rafe's lifelong friendship with Anthony. "We're stuck, Anthony. The demon has possessed another woman, and Detective Nelson is going to lose his soul if we can't find it."

"Well, you know one thing—you know the demon is going after the cop. Do you know where the cop is now?"

"Yes."

"Follow him. When the demon comes for him, you'll have to trap it."

"That's why I called. How? Another tabernacle?"

"Possibly, but it would have to be special, like the one we used in Santa Louisa. I'll research the matter and get back to you."

"Research?" Rafe lost his temper, even though he knew Anthony was doing what he could. "We don't have time!"

"Don't you think I know that? I'm halfway around the world, Raphael! I'll contact everyone I know who might have an idea, but we're playing with the unknown here and I don't have all the answers! I wish I did. Dear God," he added quietly, "I wish I did."

They were all under pressure. "I'm sorry," Rafe said. "I know you're doing everything you can."

"I'll call you as soon as I know anything. I can tell you one thing: before sunset, you need to get that cop into a strong spirit trap. In a church or another sacred area. The building itself should weaken the demon some. Keeping the victim in a double trap will buy you some time."

"Should we destroy the chalice now, since the demon isn't going back that way?"

"No—destroying the chalice now will sever the demon's obligation to the coven, and it will be freed. You'll have to wait until it's trapped. Then do it quickly."

"You want me to use the cop as bait."

"I can't think of any other options. You didn't create this situation, Rafe. This is your best chance to stop the demon before it hurts anyone else."

"Will Jackson's church work?"

"It should. Grace Harvest used to be a Catholic church, and I believe that Jackson kept the relics under the altar. Create a reverse spirit trap and put Grant inside."

"He's not going to come willingly."

"You'll think of something."

He might have to resort to kidnapping, Rafe realized.

"I hope to have more answers before sunset," Anthony said.

Hope. We need a lot more than hope.

"Be careful, Rafe. Godspeed."

Anthony put aside the papers he had been reading. He had to search for the answers Rafe needed to stop this particular demon.

But what he had been learning from Dr. Lieber's research was far more frightening than he had let on to anyone here at St. Michael's, or to Rafe. His brothers would learn the truth in time, but until Anthony understood what it all meant, until he had all the pieces of the puzzle, he couldn't tell anyone what he was discovering.

Only Rico had given a hint of what Anthony might find. But even Rico didn't realize what they would be required to do to save mankind.

Many of them would die. It might be, in fact, the end of days for St. Michael's Order and all they represented, whether they successfully sent the Seven Deadly Sins back to Hell or not.

TWENTY-FOUR

Moira and Nina Hardwick settled down with their coffee at a table in the far corner of the Starbucks closest to the police station. Several cops were on break, and Moira supposed that most people would feel safe surrounded by law enforcement—but cops made people like her, who often crossed the legal lines in the fight against supernatural evil, nervous. Moira had her back to the wall so that she could see the entire room, including the door. She and Skye had had several arguments when they were out together about who got that seat—cops, it seemed, also hated having their backs to a door. Moira always won, but she played hardball—she either got the seat or she didn't sit.

Nina blurted out the question, "Are you really psychic?"

"No." *Dear God, I hope not.* "But Detective Nelson was becoming annoying and he didn't believe anything I said."

"I hear you there, but Grant is a good cop. Honest, I wouldn't tell him this because he has an ego *this big,* but he's one of the best detectives I've worked with."

"You're a prosecutor?"

She shook her head. "I work for the Board of Supervisors, but my specialty is labor law, so I deal with the unions. I hear about all the cops, and Grant has a stellar reputation. Except for his reputation as a tomcat."

She frowned. "Tomcat?"

"He strays." She winked.

"Oh." Moira hadn't heard that expression, but it made sense based on what Julie had told her. *If* she could believe anything Julie Schroeder said. After seeing Julie's astral at Nadine's suicide, Moira had several things she wanted to say to that witch, and most of them were four-letter words.

"So why were you talking to Grant? Because you tried to help that poor girl yesterday?"

"Partly." She weighed how much she should tell this woman. "Can I ask you a couple questions first?"

"Anything. I might not answer, though. I have confidentiality and ethics laws to consider."

"Fair enough. What files were you talking about that you gave the detective?"

"Files that a private investigator gave me. Carson Felix—he was one of the best in the business. I've used him in the past, and he often helps law enforcement, sharing info and that sort of thing, so I knew I could trust him. He allegedly committed suicide two months ago, but I think he was killed to keep quiet."

"Quiet about what?"

"You wouldn't believe me. Grant sure as hell didn't."

"You'd be surprised at what I'll believe."

Nina eyed Moira suspiciously. "Who are you?"

"I'm an expert on cults." Might as well go along with the party line, she thought. And it seemed to be working well.

Nina leaned forward. "Really? You're a psychologist? Psychiatrist?"

"No. Former cult member."

The attorney raised an eyebrow in disbelief. "You certainly don't seem the type to be easily manipulated."

"My mother was the cult leader. I ran away years ago. But I don't want other people to fall prey to her lies."

Nina nodded, her face a mask of sympathy that Moira didn't want. She averted her eyes and sipped her tea. Not as good as home-steeped, but tolerable.

Nina said quietly, "I was having an affair of the heart with George Erickson. Well, it had progressed beyond the *of the heart* part, but we fell in love long before he broke his marriage vows. Such as they were."

Julie had said the open marriage was one-way, but Moira didn't know what she could believe from the woman who had lied to her, so she commented, "Nelson said he had an open marriage."

"Open for *Pamela* Erickson, but not for George. She wanted a possession; that's how she treated George. He was wealthy, had genuine stature and respect in this town. And that is not easily achieved, let me tell you. Everyone liked George. He was a terrific attorney and advocate for his clients."

"And his wife is . . . ?"

"A bitch?" Nina leaned forward and whispered, "Or rather, a *witch*."

Nina was feeling her out. Moira sipped her tea and said, "Do you mean that figuratively, or that she's a spell-casting, broomstick-riding witch?"

"I don't know about the broomsticks or spells, and I don't know that I believe in witches *per se,* but she's definitely into the occult, and I know some of the extremist types do some bad things—criminal things."

Nina reached into her briefcase. "I made a complete

copy of the file I gave to Grant, but that's in a safe in case I end up dead before my time. *This* is what I'm talking about."

She slid a photograph across the small round table.

In the photo, Wendy Donovan was watching two women having sex with a man in the middle of a spirit trap. Moira recognized the Luciferian symbols painted on the floor. The tea in her stomach turned acidic.

Moira also recognized the room from Wendy Donovan's house—from which they'd barely got out alive last night.

"Who's the man?" she asked, trying to hide her horror.

"Don't know. Grant said he'd look into it, and I'm sure he will, but he's overworked and I don't know how much time he'll devote to a case that he thinks is closed."

"What do *you* think happened?"

"I think George's wife conspired with Nadine Anson to kill George. I *know* she was involved. She's a whack job. I want justice—for George. Why should she get everything that was his? The house—his before they married. His money—he has a substantial financial portfolio, the majority earned before their marriage. She was involved; I don't want her profiting from murder."

Rafe walked in and sat down next to Moira. He was preoccupied, and Moira wondered what his conversation with Anthony had been about. "This is Rafe Cooper," Moira said. She didn't quite know how to introduce him—partner? Friend? Lover?

"What's this?" Rafe picked up the photograph. "This is Wendy Donovan's basement."

Nina leaned back almost imperceptibly, but Moira

sensed a shift in the woman from easy to restrained. Damn, Moira was trying to play her cards close to the vest, and now Nina had her antenna up.

"Who?" Nina asked.

Rafe glanced at Moira and looked sheepish.

Nina said, "Okay, don't play me for a fool. Who *exactly* are you and how are you involved in this case?"

Moira glanced at Rafe. How much should she say? Most people didn't believe in witches, or that witchcraft at its core was trouble. They liked their witches kind and good, like Glinda the Good Witch and Samantha Stevens. That most witches looked like Glinda but acted like the Wicked Witch of the West was generally unknown.

Nina grabbed the photo from Rafe and said, "I'll take this with me."

"Don't go!" Moira frowned. She was torn.

Rafe leaned forward and took Nina's hand. "Nina," he said in a low voice, "we need your help. But what we have to tell you is difficult to understand."

Moira shifted uncomfortably. Rafe caught her eye and raised his brows slightly. He wanted her to trust him. She leaned back and let him run with it.

Rafe said to Nina, "Moira is worried you won't believe us, or worse."

"Worse?"

"That you're one of them. That you're here to set us up or send us down a false path."

Moira knew Nina wasn't a witch, and she almost said as much to Rafe, except at the last minute she figured out what Rafe was doing. He was seducing Nina. Not sexually, but using his quietly commanding presence, his attractiveness, his overwhelming masculine appeal—

which went far beyond simple sex appeal—to lull Nina into compliance. And while he didn't *act* like he was consciously doing it, Moira knew he was being calculating.

She admired Rafe's ability to use his charm and psychological background to open people. Moira was often too blunt and sharp-tongued, but Rafe was smooth and calm. He understood people far better than she did. While she recognized a witch on sight and could physically feel energy and emotions that no one else did, she didn't understand the *why*. Why did Wendy's coven want money, power, *things* so much that they were willing to not only kill men but subject them to eternal pain and suffering?

Maybe she didn't want to know why. Nothing could justify their actions. Their victims didn't deserve their horrid deaths, and Moira had no sympathy for those who hurt others for personal gain.

"I don't know who you are," Nina said. "When I came to the station today it was to talk to Grant about the investigation into George's murder. And you're the one who asked me to coffee," she pointed to Moira. "I'm not here to set anyone up."

"I'm going to tell you the truth," Rafe said. "It's hard to take, but I am not lying to you."

"I'm listening."

"Nadine Anson was a witch. When I say *witch*, I mean someone who uses spells to draw on demonic forces for personal gain. Most witches are innocuous"—he put his hand on Moira's leg to keep her from arguing that point—"because they don't have access to or experience with ancient spells and rituals that summon demons into our world."

Nina stared at Rafe. She wanted to believe, Moira saw it in her eyes, but her logical, lawyerly self doubted.

Rafe continued. "We don't know exactly what happened with Nadine and her coven, but the manager of Velocity, Wendy Donovan, is the leader. The high priestess—the head magician, whatever you want to call her—is in charge. Most of the members of the coven worked at Velocity or were affiliated with it in some way."

Nina leaned forward, hands splayed palms down on the table. "Pamela is a supplier. She works for a food and beverage service and handles alcohol supplies for local bars, including Velocity."

Rafe nodded, though the information was news to both him and Moira.

"Though witches aren't all women—hardly, as most magicians in ancient times were men—Wendy's coven is all female. They are practicing a particularly vile form of sex magic."

Nina frowned and leaned back in her chair. "Sex magic?"

Rafe continued. "I just spoke with Anthony Zaccardi, the preeminent scholar in ancient demons. He confirmed our fears, and more. Wendy, and her mother before her, and likely women in their family for generations, have been the protectors of a legion of demons known as succubi. They are female demons who steal the souls of unfaithful men. In exchange, Wendy's family members are given favor on Earth and believe they will also have authority in the underworld. What they don't realize, and will never accept, is that fallen angels control the underworld. They will never allow a demon who had once been human to have any power in Hell."

Moira watched Nina's expression closely. She'd listened, but Moira didn't know what she thought about Rafe's revelation.

Rafe continued. "From what we've learned, Craig Monroe was targeted because he was a jerk who was cruel to his girlfriend, a waitress at Velocity. George Erickson was targeted because he reneged on his arrangement with his wife, namely that she could have sex outside of marriage but he could not."

Nina hit her knee. "That's what I told Grant! He told you that?" She glared accusingly at Moira. "You didn't tell me that. You said you thought it was an open marriage. You lied to me."

Moira shook her head. "I told you we heard he had an open marriage. Nelson didn't tell us it was one-sided."

Before Nina could become more irritated, Rafe continued. "That fits with what we know about witches. She would want complete and total freedom, and as a member of a sex coven, she would participate in a multitude of sexual activities in order to maintain her supernatural strength. The more they participate, the more they *need,* if you understand."

"Like drugs. You need more and more coke or heroin to get the same high."

"Precisely. Only with sex magic, the more you participate, the greater your supernatural power—your magic—is here on Earth. Spells and rituals are still important, as part of the big picture, but on the micro level, you can essentially wiggle your nose and gain small favors."

Wiggle your nose? Since when had Rafe watched popular television? Moira wondered.

"And Pamela Erickson was part of this *sex coven*?"

"That picture proves it. If you look at the symbols, you see the occult, correct?"

Nina stared at the photograph. "Yes. It looks sort of like what I see in the movies."

"Sort of?"

"It's more . . . simple. Almost a parody."

"Because these rituals *aren't* elaborate. In fact, they are a lot easier than most people think. Because most of the spell is done up here." He tapped his head. "The circle there is called a spirit trap, or a devil's circle, or any number of things. Practically? It's a portal. It's a place where the layer between Hell and Earth is thin, and demons can be summoned and controlled. The picture your friend took is of a classic demon trap. We were told that they have one sacrifice a year in order to keep favor with the underworld. We know that they planned three victims this time. Only, when they changed the ritual to give the succubus more power, they trapped the wrong demon."

Nina didn't say anything for a long minute, and Moira thought she was going to laugh at them and leave. Then she asked, "And Pamela had a *demon* kill George?"

"Yes."

"But Nadine's fingerprints were all over his bedroom."

"Nadine volunteered her body to the demon and then killed George."

"But Nadine *died*."

Rafe was somber. "We're not exactly sure why, but the demon left Nadine's body."

"Okay, I've been a good sport. And I can almost believe you—*almost*. But why would the demon care if anyone saw it? From what you just said, it's powerful! Why not just kill Moira or you or everyone? Why aren't we overrun by demons?"

"Like any spirit, they have limitations."

"But you said they were fallen angels. Are you saying they're not superhuman? They don't have special powers?"

Moira felt Nina begin to close up, questions rolling off her tongue like those of a prosecutor. She leaned forward and took Nina's other hand. At first the woman tried to pull away, but Moira held tight. "Nina, everything Rafe said is true. I saw a death imprint of Craig Monroe in the alley. That means that after it happened—two days after it happened—I saw him die. Nadine is the one who killed him. And yes, regardless of what you saw on the video about how freaked out she was, it was her fault. She allowed herself to be possessed by the demon because she thought that she'd gain something from it. So while we might feel bad about what she went through—because dammit, I want so badly to believe that she felt awful about what she did—she was still responsible. When I saw Nadine on the street near Velocity, the demon knew I'd spotted her. It knew its time in her body was limited. Because that's what Rafe and I do—we send demons back to Hell."

Moira considered what she'd just said—it was the truth, but why would the demon be fearful of her? *Was* it vulnerable when it was trapped in a physical body? She needed to talk it out with Rafe. There was something they were missing.

"You're an exorcist?" Nina looked skeptically at Rafe. "You don't look like a Catholic priest."

"Not all exorcists are priests, or Catholic," Rafe said.

Nina stared at the photograph, her brows furrowed, thinking.

Rafe took Moira's hand under the table and squeezed it. Something else, something beyond this, was disturbing him. Moira wanted to ask, but it would have to wait.

"What do you want from me?" Nina asked quietly.

Moira opened, then closed her mouth. She had wanted to see the file Nina had. But the picture was enough, and she didn't want another outsider involved. It was too risky.

"We want you to know so that you're diligent in protecting yourself against them," Rafe said, "and because you know these people. We need a little help because we're not from here."

"I know Pam, but only through George." She frowned. "I know of Wendy Donovan. And Grant's girlfriend—she's not part of it, is she?"

"She is," Moira said, "and she's a fucking liar, so—"

Rafe squeezed her hand so tight she almost said *ouch*.

"We don't know everyone who is involved, only that Wendy recruits out of Velocity," Rafe said.

"The club has only been around for two years."

"Do you know where Wendy was before then?"

Nina shook her head. "I can find out. What do you need?"

"We need all the background information you can get on Wendy Donovan, and her fiancé who died—" Moira glanced at Rafe. "What was his name?"

"Kyle Dane," Rafe said.

"Kyle Dane? You think she killed Kyle Dane the musician?"

"We don't know," Rafe said at the same time Moira said, "Hell, yes."

Rafe rubbed the back of his neck. "We can't prove it. His death was ruled a heart attack. He was ill and went against doctor's orders."

"You know she was involved," Moira said. She was tired of Rafe pinching and squeezing her leg to signal she was being bullheaded.

Rafe ignored the comment and told Nina, "Wendy has a sister, Nicole Donovan. She was involved in a coven in Santa Louisa that resulted in several deaths, including a teenager. Their mother was Susan Donovan, and she was raised in foster care."

"Here in L.A.?"

"Yes."

"I can get anything you need. Not necessarily legally, but I can find it."

"We don't want you to get into trouble—"

"I know how to cover my ass. I want to help. *If* you think this will help get George justice. I don't want him to die in vain."

"It will not only help George, but it will help us in our battle against these people for years to come."

Nina tapped her finger on the table. "I'll admit, I don't know how much of this I believe, but I do know that Pam is bad news and I'd convinced George that he had to leave her. I loved him so much—but I didn't care if he left her for me, or just left her. I just wanted him to be happy. So I can't help but feel responsible that I had something to do with his death. I—" She stopped and frowned.

"Nina?" Moira asked.

"I'm thinking." She paused. "You said that Nadine stole his soul. What exactly does that mean?"

Rafe was torn, but Moira wasn't going to lie to the woman who was about to help them put together pieces of a puzzle they couldn't complete on their own. "When a demon steals a soul—meaning, not a soul the owner promised in exchange for favors, but an innocent or cursed soul—they suck it into their body, trapping it. The person dies, because without a soul you have nothing keeping you alive. Your heart just stops. That's why his death is being ruled cardiac arrest, though he didn't have a heart attack."

Tears leaked from Nina's eyes. "George wasn't a religious man, but . . . does the soul have feelings?"

"No," Rafe said as Moira said, "Yes."

Moira glanced sideways at Rafe and frowned. He was as angry with her as she was at him for sugarcoating the truth. Did he think that ignorance was bliss? Ignorance was right up there with lying to yourself. Nina asked for the truth, and she was going to tell it to her.

Nina said to Moira, "I believe you. Is he hurting?"

She didn't say anything. She didn't have to; Nina was smart enough to figure it out. If she believed that a demon could steal a soul, she had to believe in Heaven and Hell. Demons didn't go on the "up" escalator in the afterlife.

Rafe said, "We really don't know what happens to stolen souls." Moira was about to argue, but Rafe turned to her. "You know we don't. I do not believe that God allows innocent people to go to Hell."

This was a point Moira took no comfort in arguing, so she remained silent.

"Where's this damn demon now, and can I get George's soul back?"

"You can't bring George back to life," Moira said.

"That's not what I mean. I want to put his soul some-place safe. To rest. I don't want him suffering for eter-nity!" Nina shook her head. "I can't believe I said that. But that's what you mean, isn't it?"

"His soul is with the demon who took it," Moira said. "And until it goes back to Hell, it'll still be trapped there. It's feeding her, keeping her strong."

"Can you get it back?"

"I don't know," Moira said.

"George didn't do anything wrong!"

Rafe said, "We have to believe that God will protect innocents who die."

"Believe. Faith. *Bullshit,*" Nina said. "I want to know that George is safe. I want to give his soul a proper bur-ial, and if you want my help, you'll tell me how to do that."

Nina was right. George deserved a level playing field for the Powers That Be to decide on the merits of his life whether he should get a shot at Paradise. In St. Michael's world, George was collateral damage, a sad case that they would pray for but not do anything else to help.

Moira couldn't live like that. She couldn't stand back and do nothing, not if there was something she could do. She didn't believe her prayers were going to do squat, though she prayed in her own way every day. She had been around demons; when they got a soul, they never let go. And she'd never heard of an avenging angel swooping down and reclaiming an innocent victim. If it happened, Rico would have told her, because this was one of the subjects they argued about the most.

What upset her more than that, however, was that Rafe wasn't automatically on her side. What did she expect? He'd been raised at St. Michael's; he had faith on his side. Faith that the innocent would be saved at the end-time.

But what about the decade, the century, the millennia between then and now?

Moira said, "There's a way, but it's dangerous."

"Tell me," Nina said. "I don't care how dangerous; I will do anything."

"Moira, no—" Rafe began.

"I can't let George Erickson suffer any more than you can," Moira told Rafe. "He had nothing to do with this, and *damn* I'm not going to wait around for the end of the world before he's saved. We know how to get his soul back."

Rafe abruptly stood, knocking over Moira's near-empty cup, his jaw tight. Through clenched teeth he said, "I won't let you. You'll get yourself killed."

"You won't *let* me? Since when did you become my guardian angel?"

Rafe was furious and deeply hurt. From the minute he'd seen Moira two weeks ago, he knew she'd been sent to save him. She was *his* angel, and he was hers. It came to him as clearly as she sat in front of him: he had to protect her. Every day, every minute. She cared too deeply for everyone but herself, and she was going to die if she didn't accept that she couldn't save everyone.

The only way to take back a soul that had been stolen by a demon was to exorcise the soul from the demon while the demon was contained in a spirit trap. But that entailed great risk to the exorcist, who had to get far too close to the demon to ensure that the soul had an escape route, as well as the very real possibility that the soul—disembodied from its own physical self—would claim the exorcist's body as its own, resulting in a possession. Then a second exorcist would have to convince the soul that it was dead, and to willingly leave. There was also the risk of the soul being forever lost, stuck between this world and the afterlife, becoming a ghost or vengeful spirit.

It was physically and emotionally treacherous for everyone involved, but the risks to the exorcist were the greatest. Too many of Rafe's friends at St. Michael's Order had died performing just this type of ritual to save one of their fallen brothers.

"Moira, it's too dangerous," he said quietly, sitting back down.

"I'll do it," Nina interjected. "I don't care what the risks are; I want to help George."

Rafe turned to Nina. She was sincere. "Why?" he asked.

"I love him. I would do anything for him, even die. I couldn't live with myself if his soul was lost forever and I could have prevented it." She grabbed each of their hands. *"Please."*

"All right," Moira said. "Get the information Rafe needs about the Donovans. We'll get what we need for the exorcism."

She smiled. "Thank you. I'll get right on it." She slid over her card and took down Moira's cell phone number.

"If you can't reach me, call Jackson Moreno at Grace Harvest."

Nina looked at her, surprised. "Pastor Moreno?"

"You know him?"

"Everyone knows him. He's the dot-com genius who made a fortune, sold his company, then became a minister and lives very modestly. An enigma in this town."

"He's a friend," Moira said. "Give him the information if you can't find me; he'll know what to do with it."

Nina stood to leave, took both their hands, and said, "Thank you. I really mean that."

When Nina had left, Rafe turned to Moira. "You lied to her. She can't do it!"

"She doesn't know that."

"You're not going to."

"Of course I am."

"I will not let you! You could die."

"I can die every day. Our lives aren't exactly safe. But if we can't help people like George Erickson, why are we doing this? Revenge? Fuck that. George was imperfect, like the rest of us, and we both know there is a limited window of time to reclaim his soul and give it proper last rites. We know the demon is possessing someone. I hope Julie figures it out fast, and I hope she's not lying, or we're really screwed."

"Moira—"

She interrupted. "We take back George's soul first. Then we trap the damn demon Lust and put it up with her evil brother Envy at Olivet."

"Don't you understand that I can't lose you?"

A flash of Moira dying in his arms came and went so suddenly, Rafe would have missed it if it weren't so vivid that it etched itself in his mind. Fear gripped his throat, then an overwhelming sense of loss, of Moira being physically torn from his hands.

"I'm good at this," Moira said, reaching for him. "Trust me."

Rafe took her hand and kissed it. "Anthony is working on answers, but he says by sunset we need to have Grant Nelson protected in a reverse spirit trap. The demon will find him whether we use him as bait or not." But that didn't make Rafe feel any more confident. "I have a bad feeling about this."

"You can watch my back, okay?" She was trying to make light of the serious situation. Rafe took her face in his hands and kissed her softly.

He'd do a lot more than watch her back.

TWENTY-FIVE

Grant tried to ignore his partner, who was watching him too closely. Grant felt as if he were onstage. He rubbed his head and finished filling out the report on his interview with Moira O'Donnell.

Witness claims she's a psychic and saw deceased kill Craig Monroe in Velocity alley. Called it a death imprint.

He tore up the report into tiny pieces. This was ridiculous. No one would believe her; *he* didn't believe her. He didn't know what game Moira O'Donnell was playing, but he had to stop thinking about her because all he wanted to do was screw her brains out.

He froze. Where had that thought come from? He squeezed his eyes shut and rubbed his forehead.

Johnston said, "Hey, Nelson, you're exhausted. I'll take care of the rest of the paperwork. You should head home."

He shook his head. "I just didn't sleep much. Julie was upset about what happened to Nadine and we stayed up half the night." More like all night. And he still didn't feel satisfied. When Moira O'Donnell walked into police headquarters, all Grant could think about was taking her to bed. Hell, forget the bed. He just wanted to have sex with her. Grant had always enjoyed sex—too much sometimes—but he'd always put his job first. Now he couldn't get sex out of his mind. It was making him physically and mentally uncomfortable. He felt like a randy teenager who wanted to convince the head cheerleader that if she didn't put out he was going to die in agony, just to get in her panties. Only now, he had the uncomfortable sensation that he *was* dying.

Impossible. No one died because they didn't have sex.

Grant wanted to divert Johnston's attention from his physical condition to the case at hand. "Did you get anything on the man in the photograph Nina gave us?"

"Nothing. I sent his pic to Missing Persons and maybe they'll have something. I looked into the P.I.'s death, talked to the responding officers. The witnesses were solid; his staff reported that he was acting paranoid and skittish, and more than one thought he was on drugs. He had a drug problem years ago, was clean, but as you know it just takes one time to go back."

"What kind of drugs?"

"Cocaine."

"Did they find the dealer? Evidence of cocaine during autopsy?"

"I said that the witnesses *thought* he was on drugs—it went to his state of being."

"Do you have the autopsy report?"

Johnston sighed. "No."

"I need to contact the morgue anyway. Find out about our frozen waitress, and Nadine Anson's autopsy. Maybe I'll go down; sometimes showing up gets more answers."

"I'll go," Johnston offered.

"You hate the morgue."

"But I like that cute pathologist."

"Fern?"

"Yeah. The one with the sexy little nose ring."

"Maybe you should let me talk to her for you."

"I can hit on a woman all by myself," Johnston said.

"Yeah, but I've known Fern for years. Come on too strong and she'll knock you down."

"I wouldn't mind that too much." Johnston grinned. "I like women who stand up for themselves."

"Fine, come with me."

"You should go home. You look like shit."

"Fuck you," Grant said without animosity.

"Right back at you."

"If we split up the workload, we can both be home in time for a late lunch."

"You want the morgue," stated Jeff.

"Yep. And I have seniority. You can interview Pam Erickson again, feel her out about how she really felt about her husband's relationship with other women and see if you can push her a bit, without letting on that we think she had something to do with it."

"So does this mean you believe Nina?"

"I don't know what I believe. But Nina is a straight shooter, and I'm more inclined to trust her instincts than I am to trust a woman who was having sex with her ex-husband while her otherwise healthy current husband died. And then after Mrs. Erickson, talk to Marcus Galion about both his brother and Nadine Anson. Both his brother and girlfriend dead within a week?"

"Don't you want to do it?"

"You're good at making people comfortable. Feel him out. If you think we should bring Marcus in, we'll bring him in."

Grant just wanted Jeff to leave, because it was getting harder and harder to keep up the act that everything was fine. In fact, he couldn't. He shut down his computer and stretched. "I'm going to take a leak, then head to the morgue. We'll touch base this afternoon."

"Roger that, Boss."

Grant knew he should go home. He was in no condition to talk to anyone or go to the morgue. Events were spiraling out of control and he didn't know what to do about it. What the hell was wrong with him?

In the bathroom, he locked the door. Though the police station never closed, it was midshift Saturday morning. Quiet. He'd seen something this morning in the mirror—thought he'd seen something—but in denial, he hadn't paid much attention to it.

But he hadn't been able to get it out of his mind.

He stripped off his shirt, hoping the mark was a figment of his imagination and lack of sleep. The bathroom had one long mirror above the sinks, and if he angled his body right he could look over his shoulder and see most of his back.

On his lower shoulder blade was the mark. He could lie to himself and say it wasn't *exactly* like the odd tattoo-like marks on the two dead guys, but he didn't. It was as close to being identical as he could remember. Red, like a port-wine-stain birthmark. The edges seemed to bleed into the surrounding skin, but there was a fine red line, like a blood vessel, that created an odd image.

He didn't need to see more. He pulled his shirt back on and walked out.

How the *hell* had he gotten that thing on his back? It hadn't been there yesterday morning. It didn't hurt. The skin was slightly raised when he felt it, so slight that he might not have noticed it if he hadn't seen it.

It was not possible—but it was there. He considered

calling Moira O'Donnell, the cult expert. Psychic or not, that woman knew a hell of a lot more than what she'd told him.

He drove to the morgue while contemplating bringing in Moira O'Donnell to help. His head ached in spite of the milk, the coffee, and an untold number of aspirin. The bright sunlight burned his eyes and he fumbled for his sunglasses on the visor, nearly hitting a parked car. Though he had only drunk one beer last night, he felt hungover.

One beer. At Velocity. He could have been drugged. He'd gone home with Julie. He couldn't imagine that Julie—whom he'd known for two years—would have done anything like drugging him or tattooing his back. But he'd been at her place, and his memory was spotty. Those dead men with the marks were all connected to Velocity, and so was he. Had he stumbled upon a criminal activity where someone would kill a cop to keep it secret? Was Julie part of a conspiracy?

A ghost of Julie's image on the YouTube video of Nadine's death seemed impossible, but right now Grant could almost believe she'd been there. Right now, all he knew was that something was wrong with him.

He flashed his badge to the guard at the morgue parking lot and called Moira O'Donnell.

"Hello, Detective, miss me?" she asked, exaggerating her Irish accent.

"Meet me at your hotel."

"What's wrong?"

"I have questions."

"Okay, when?"

He looked at his dashboard clock. It was nearing the lunch hour. He had the morgue, then needed time to cross town and find food somewhere, though the thought of eating made him ill. "Two o'clock. Your room."

"We checked out—"

"I told you not to leave town!"

"It was a little pricey for me. We'll meet you in the Palomar lobby."

"Fine."

"What's going on—"

He hung up. Her voice was so damn unique, so seductive with that Irish lilt, his penis began to throb painfully and he reached down to adjust it. Grant had the overwhelming urge to jerk off. He was so hard that he was afraid someone would see, or that he'd have some sort of waking wet dream.

"This is ridiculous," he muttered to himself as he got out of his car and walked in through the employee entrance, flashing his badge to the receptionist. He found the bathroom; there was no lock on the main door. Fortunately, no one was inside. He went into the stall, slid the lock in place, and pulled down his pants. His penis was large, red, and painful to the touch. Damn, this couldn't be natural. Something was wrong.

What could he tell his doctor? That he had a perpetual hard-on all day? Maybe someone at the station spiked his coffee with Viagra or something. Some sick joke because he'd stepped on some asshole's overly sensitive ego. Not Johnston—but there were a couple of cops who didn't like Grant. He *wanted* to believe it was a prank, but he knew it wasn't. More likely he'd been drugged at Velocity last night, and his rock-hard cock was a side effect.

He couldn't live like this. He reached down and, embarrassed and angry and in pain, he jerked off. He pictured Julie last night and the things that he'd done to her, and he felt ashamed. He'd never been that callous before, that unconcerned about pleasing her. He closed his eyes and pictured himself fucking her, over and over, and then Moira O'Donnell's face replaced Julie's and Grant moaned, then bit his tongue so hard his mouth filled with blood as he spurted semen into the toilet.

He stood there, head down, flushed, ashamed at what he'd pictured, what he'd done, and what he wanted to do. He spat into the toilet, a bright red wad of saliva.

Still feeling ill, Grant washed his hands and face with icy water, then went to the main morgue level and asked the desk to page Fern Archer.

While he waited for Fern, he called Julie on her cell phone. No answer. He hoped she wasn't angry with him about last night. She had every right to be. He wanted to make it up to her, but didn't know how—or if he could. *Fool. She's the one who most likely drugged you. Have Johnston pick her up for questioning.*

How could he do that to Julie?

How could he not? He was a cop first.

He called Jeff. "Hey, Johnston, I need you to track down Julie. I have some questions for her."

"About what?"

He couldn't very well tell Jeff the truth because he didn't know what the truth was, and his theories were insane. Sure, tell his partner that he'd been drugged and assaulted last night. That he practically raped his girlfriend. That he was so sick he jerked off in the bathroom and was still hard and uncomfortable.

"Don't tell her why, just find out where she'll be this

afternoon. Tell her we need to ask her some follow-up questions."

"What are you thinking, Grant? I'm your partner—tell me what's going on."

Fern walked into the lobby. Grant used her as an excuse. "I'm at the morgue; I can't talk now. It's about Nadine and drugs," he added to get his partner off his back.

"I'll let you know what I find out."

Grant hung up. "Hello, Fern."

She smiled, her nose ring of yesterday now an emerald green stud. "Hey, Detective, what can I do for you?"

He glanced at the receptionist and said, "I wanted to ask you some questions about the woman who was brought in yesterday, as well as Erickson. And I need an older autopsy report."

"Sure." She hesitated. "I could have faxed you a report. You didn't have to come all the way over here."

"I wanted to take another look at the marks on the bodies."

"Whatever floats your boat. Right this way." Fern handed him disposable cloth booties for his shoes and he slipped them on. "We finished the suicide yesterday."

"She was a suspect in the death of George Erickson."

"Yeah, I saw the video on YouTube."

"Shit, who hasn't seen it?"

"No one in L.A., that's for sure. It's rare that you get such a fabulous, public confession."

"What did the autopsy reveal?"

"She died from massive internal bleeding—a no-brainer since a bus ran over her. She didn't live through it, which I suppose is lucky for her. She obviously was suffering enough before she went over the edge. Her ribs were crushed. A mess, really."

Grant didn't need to know the details. "Blood tests?"

"Not back yet. We ran a few in-house—no alcohol in her system—but the biggies won't be back until the end of next week. We've been sending more than our usual number of blood tests to the lab, and they've been complaining, damn lab bureaucrats." She shook her head. "We have a pool going here among the pathologists. PCP is leading, though without the alcohol chaser I don't see it having the effect I saw on the video. She was paranoid and panicked. I think it's a newly engineered LSD, probably made in some kid's basement, and she tripped. She was lucid and disoriented at the same time. She spoke clearly, but she sure wasn't acting sane. She was also dehydrated and hadn't eaten in more than twelve hours."

Grant really didn't care about the morgue's betting pool. "Did she have the same mark on her body as Erickson, Monroe, and Galion?"

"No, but I found a tattoo."

"You're certain it's a tattoo?"

Fern glanced at him as she stood outside the crypt. "Of course I'm sure. High-end, too. Quality ink, intricate design. Gorgeous, really. Almost makes me wish I were white." She laughed. "Not."

She opened the door to the crypt. "Monroe's family is taking possession of the body today. It's being shipped back to his home state; the transport company will be here this afternoon." She pulled off the sheet. Grant stared at the mark on the pale body, dull but still red against Monroe's skin.

"Have you figured out what that mark is?"

"No, but the coroner is going with a tattoo." Fern frowned. "His theory is that it's a new kind of process that uses an organic ink."

"That's bullshit. We'd be able to know whether it was a tat or not."

"I agree, but he didn't want to hold up the body when it's clear Monroe died of cardiac arrest."

"You're certain."

"Well, we know his heart stopped. We have the initial drug panels back. We've sent the blood for additional screens, and the coroner is agreeing to cardiac arrest with a possible secondary cause unknown narcotic since his endorphin levels were high. Which makes sense. If your suicide victim comes back with something else, we have enough of Monroe's blood samples to run more tests. Some labs have been engineering Ecstasy with LSD and other drugs. Nasty shit, and we've seen teenagers come through here pumped up with drugs that are variants of what's popular. They end up in the hospitals, too. Some are brain-dead; some just die. I promise, we'll keep at it. We want to know, and I know your Narcs want to keep up with anything new hitting the streets."

"Any other bodies come in?"

Fern tilted her head. "We're a morgue; we get dozens of bodies a day."

Grant rubbed his temple. "Bodies with marks like Monroe and Erickson."

"Actually, yeah. They weren't my cases, but I've seen a couple marks like this over the last week."

"Can you send me copies of the files?"

"Sure. On one condition."

He raised an eyebrow. "What condition?"

"Put in a good word with your hunky partner for me. I'm calling him my first day off."

Grant smiled even through the pain in his head. "He wanted me to do the same with you."

"No shit?"

"No shit. He's receptive."

"Screw that then, he can call me. But if I don't hear from him by tomorrow—I have Sunday and Monday off—I'm calling."

Grant handed her Jeff's cell phone number. "Can I see Nadine?"

"It's not pretty. We call her Humpty Dumpty."

"I want to see her tattoo."

"That's easy, I took a picture. This way."

Grant followed Fern to her small cubicle near the intake area. Her space was filled with photographs of the morgue and the dead. Though all were eerie and bordering on the sick side, they were quite phenomenal. "You're talented."

Fern grinned. "Thanks. I know, it's a morbid hobby—can you believe Takasugi tells me that *I'm* morbid when *he's* the one with a *mummy* in his living room?" She shook her head and handed Grant a picture. "You can keep it; it's a copy. I have another in the file."

But Grant barely heard Fern. He stared at the tattoo. It was a perfect circle, with an intricate pattern that was the same if you looked at it from the top or the bottom. It had been on the small of her back.

Julie had the identical tat in the same location.

TWENTY-SIX

Wendy gloated as she strode through Velocity casting a protective spell. She smiled, pleased that everything was coming together better than she'd planned—considering the disasters that had occurred over the last twelve hours. Losing Rachel as a vessel had been devastating, and having Raphael Cooper and Moira O'Donnell steal her chalice—Wendy was more than a little furious. That chalice had been in her coven for generations. If her mother were alive, she'd be irate that her precious chalice had been stolen by another coven.

Nicole emphatically believed that Moira wasn't practicing magic and intended to destroy the chalice, and even the *idea* of destroying such an immensely powerful and valuable tool was lunacy. Moira was likely rogue, not aligned with any of the loosely knit covens, which was why Fiona O'Donnell wanted her head on a platter. Dead or alive was the word on the street, with rewards either way.

Living prisoners made better bargaining chips. There was no doubt in Wendy's mind that Moira had valuable information on how to gain power to leverage into a high position within Fiona's growing circle of covens. It would be fun to play with Moira, torture the information from her, use Wendy's newfound talents to make up for the embarrassment of losing the chalice, for having to make another agreement with her new demon.

Nicole was weak; no matter what her sister said, she'd obviously been banished and had come running home. Wendy had never been weak. She didn't need her sister, but it would be nice to use her.

Wendy finished casting the protective spell around the empty club so that she would be forewarned if anyone drew near. Only a few more hours and the demon would be able to locate Grant Nelson, but Wendy wanted him in a special place. She'd spent half the day preparing Kent Galion's house for the ritual. Wendy needed space to give the demon what she wanted—an agreement she wouldn't have had to make if Moira hadn't stolen the chalice. And Moira wouldn't have been able to steal the chalice if Julie hadn't hidden Grant Nelson from them last night.

Wendy did not like being made the fool. Julie deserved everything she got. If she survived the night, when the demon left her body Wendy would call on an incubus to deal with the traitor. She'd watch Julie suffer until she begged to die.

Wendy had wanted to die many times. Her mother, Susan, was not a kind woman. Punishments were never as simple as spankings and time-outs. When Wendy was sixteen, she'd been raped by an incubus when her mother found out she'd been practicing sex magic outside of the coven.

Susan Donovan didn't tolerate betrayal, insolence, or anyone in her coven seeking power outside of her authority.

But Wendy grew up and got strong. She seduced the

men in her mother's coven—weak fools, every one of them—even seduced the magician who'd taken her virginity on her fourteenth birthday. She'd been a sex slave for them, but she'd had her retribution. Wendy practically glowed with pleasure remembering her mother pleading with her to stop the ritual that ended with her grisly death.

An eye for an eye, a tooth for a tooth, Mother dear.

Nicole walked onto the empty dance floor as Wendy finished the protective spell. Nicole the ignorant. Nicole the stupid. Nicole the baby. Her sister had never appreciated all she'd done for her, freeing her from their horrid mother's control. Nicole had wanted to simply kill Susan, but where was the fun in that? What was the fun if Susan didn't suffer what Wendy had suffered *times three*!

Nicole asked, "What are you doing?"

"I cast a protective spell." *Stupid.*

"Pam called. Grant Nelson's partner just drove up in front of her house."

"Pam knows what to do," Wendy said.

"But—"

Wendy put up her finger to silence her pathetic younger sister. "I'm going to show you how easy and enjoyable victory is when it is properly orchestrated by a talented magician. Maybe you'll learn something."

Julie couldn't find Moira O'Donnell. She'd checked out of her hotel and Julie had no idea where she'd gone. She thought Moira must have a powerful protective spell around her aura, because Nicole had said that even Fiona O'Donnell couldn't locate her, and rumor had it that Fiona could find *anyone* practically at will.

She might not be able to find Moira, but she *could* find Grant. She focused on his image. His name, his face, his energy signature. She relaxed her spirit, floated, and soon she was moving directly toward him. She let herself be carried along the astral plane, the freedom intoxicating, even with everything that had happened.

Without her voice, Julie didn't know how to communicate with Grant. Though she had great control over astral projection, she'd avoided communicating with anyone, living or dead, because of the inherent dangers to her life. Communicating took extreme focus and energy that could be replenished only once her spirit reunited with her body.

The astral body was always attached psychically to the physical body. As long as her astral projection had energy, she would be fine. But if she lost her strength, or if her spirit *or* physical body was injured, she'd snap back into her body—the invisible, indestructible thread pulling her back. If the demon still had her body when she returned, she'd never get out. And she wouldn't be able to stop the demon from killing Grant.

Julie continued to concentrate on Grant. Pictured him, imagined touching him, kissing him, being with him. Her body flew without conscious thought over the city. This complete and total oneness with the air could not be replicated inside the confines of a physical body. No one who hadn't experienced astral projection at its purest could possibly understand or appreciate true inner balance. It was as if the symmetry between being human and being a goddess was achieved only when Julie was a spirit. The more she participated in the natural oneness with earth, the more she craved it. Except for the not insignificant fact that her physical body was vulnerable when she was separated.

She shivered as if wrapped in a cool breeze and found herself floating above the Los Angeles County Morgue.

At first, Julie thought her reflections had turned her melancholy, but she was dangerously wrong.

The closer she got to the morgue, the more apprehensive she became. Her spirit kept fighting her will, trying to fly away, and she fought back, knowing Grant was inside.

For a split second she thought he was a corpse. Ignoring her instincts, she descended into the morgue.

Everyone looked at her.

There were specters here, remnants of the dead who had come through. Certainly not all of the dead; otherwise the place would be overrun, since hundreds of bodies came through the morgue each week. But even a dozen apparitions were fearsome, and they saw her. They not only saw her, but they knew she was alive.

One ghost walked toward her. It was a girl in her early teens, and she looked sad.

Why are you here? she asked Julie.

I'm watching that man. He's in danger. She gestured to where Grant was talking to a petite black woman. Julie was relieved that he was still breathing.

The girl looked at Grant and frowned. *He is dying.*

Julie shivered and resisted the urge to go to Grant. *How do you know?*

Look. You have to look for the colors. He's dark. Dying.

Julie took the ghost's word on it. *Why are you still here?*

The ghost looked around at other apparitions. *I don't*

*know. I've been here awhile—my body is in the other
room.*

She motioned, and Julie saw the deep freezer. On one
slot was a small sign:

DOE

They don't know who you are.
She shook her head sadly.
Everyone here is unknown?
*No. Most spirits come and go. They're attached to
their bodies, can't seem to leave them. When their body
goes, so do they. Most of the bodies who come through
don't have spirits with them. I have no friends anymore.
I want to leave but don't know how. I'm scared. Can
you help me?*
I'll try. What do I do?
The girl looked as if she was about to cry. *I don't
know.*
When I get back to my body, I'll figure it out, okay?
Julie didn't know if she'd survive, let alone be able to fig-
ure out how to find peace for this girl, but she'd try.
What's your name?
The girl brightened. *No one has ever asked me before.
I'm Amy Carney.*
I'm Julie.
The others hate you, you know.
I'm not going to bother them.
The girl shook her head. *They don't care. You're alive.
They're not. I'm not. I just don't know why I can't
leave. I don't know why I can't go to Heaven. Is it be-
cause I'm bad?*
Of course not.

This girl could not possibly have done a fraction of the bad things Julie had done over the years. More than anything, Julie wanted to fix everything, starting with saving Grant's life.

You need to go before he sees you.

Was she talking about Grant? Julie looked at him. He was viewing Nadine Anson's body. A chill ran through Julie's noncorporeal form.

He saw you. Julie, go! Now!

Julie had no idea what Amy was talking about, but all the ghosts disappeared, including Amy. All the ghosts, except for one.

It was a man, old and deformed, and it stared at her. For a moment she was frozen, but then she thought, what could a ghost do to her?

Mine, he said.

Julie didn't want to find out. Whatever he thought he could do, Julie realized she was vulnerable. The ghost could see her, but she had no way of defending herself. She rose to leave, but the ghost rushed at her. She flew as fast as she could out of the building, but it chased her. Faster.

She thought she was clear, blocks away from the morgue, and she stopped flying, fearing having expended too much energy. She needed to calm down or risk not having the strength to communicate with Grant.

She felt the spirit rush at her.

Mine.

Its icy darkness wrapped around her like a snake, squeezing her, trying to mingle its dead energy with her living aura. Julie was drifting, helpless and terrified.

Her fear fed the entity, and it whispered darkly: *Mine.*

No! She gathered all the psychic energy from the air

around her, used all her magical strength, and repelled the evil spirit. Like a slingshot, it flung back to the morgue, to whatever tangible item or body it was attached to.

Julie drifted down to earth, weakened. She'd had no idea what she would encounter at the morgue, or that the dead could see her. It seemed impossible, but of course it wasn't. She had once thought so much of what she was now able to do was impossible. But nothing was; she could do anything. She could be anything.

Yet she would be nothing if she couldn't get her body back.

She didn't dare go back inside the morgue, but she floated lazily to the parking lot until she found Grant's car. Inside it, she relaxed for the first time since leaving her body. She'd wait here for him, and hopefully figure out how to save him.

He is dying, the ghost—Amy—had said. Dying.

Please, whoever's listening, help me save him.

TWENTY-SEVEN

Moira and Rafe sat in Pastor Jackson Moreno's sunny kitchen, where she explained her plan to trap the demon Lust and save George Erickson's soul from eternal suffering. He didn't seem to like it any more than Rafe did, but Moira was certain she could pull it off. She had to try.

"Your plan is not only dangerous," Jackson said, "but the chances of success are next to nothing."

Moira said, "Others have been successful. It has worked before. And I'm good at this."

"Arrogance—pride—is one of the deadly sins," Jackson said.

"You don't have to remind me," she snapped. "You want to check my back? See if I'm marked?" She began to lift up her shirt, but Rafe grabbed her arm.

"You are good, Moira, but Jackson is right. You can't ignore the inherent dangers," Rafe said quietly.

"I know," she said, equally quiet. "I promise, I'm not being a hotdog. I have to at least try. I won't do anything rash."

She and Rafe had been through this earlier at Starbucks and again in the car after she'd spoken to Rico.

He hadn't wanted to share the exorcism rite with her because it put her in too great a danger.

"Why are you risking your life for this man?"

"It's the right thing to do. It's the only way to save his

soul, or are you going to tell me I am more important than he is?"

Rico didn't say anything for a minute, then said, "I emailed you the exorcism prayer."

"Thank you."

"Moira, you are more important. But you are also correct that it is the right thing to do. Put Raphael on."

She didn't know what Rico said to Rafe, and Rafe didn't tell her. His response to Rico was simple: "I understand."

They'd picked up the necessary supplies—more holy water, several bags of salt—then went to Jackson's place to fill him in on their basic plan and ask for his help.

Moira said, "All we have to do is stick Detective Nelson in a reverse spirit trap and wait. The demon will come to us." She glanced at her watch. "We're meeting him in an hour at the Palomar. I'm going to lie through my teeth to get him here, or knock him out and kidnap him." She was only half joking.

"Sunset is at five forty-five," Rafe said. "We only have a few hours to set the traps and bring the detective here, and then there's the waiting to hear from Anthony about trapping the demon."

"What about the chalice?" Jackson asked.

"We don't know yet. We can't use it to send the demon back to Hell, but we might be able to use it as a trap."

Moira frowned. "I'd be very wary of using any occult vessels. We don't know enough about it."

"For now, we'll keep it in the vault," Rafe agreed.

"Will the demon even come inside the church doors?" Jackson asked.

"The demon thinks it's invincible," Moira said. "And it's driven to find Detective Nelson. But it isn't stupid. It will sense a trap, so timing is important. As soon as the demon is in the church, you have to finish sealing the outside walls with salt, and mark every door and window with the blessed oil. That will complete the reverse trap and weaken the demon. We hope."

"Nelson may not be thinking rationally," Rafe said. "We can't count on him being cooperative."

"It's not like I'm going to tell him," Moira said. "I don't think he'll believe me until he sees it himself. He wants to ask me questions; I'll see what he has to say, then come up with a fabulous excuse to bring him here."

"That's not exactly what I meant," Rafe said.

Jackson said, "I think Rafe is concerned that Detective Nelson may act on his base impulses."

Moira raised an eyebrow. "I would hardly let him."

"We need something to melt the chalice once the demon is trapped," Rafe said. "Jackson, can you find a kiln or something?"

"I'm already ahead of you on that one. One of my flock has a ceramic shop. She's bringing a portable kiln over and will help me set it up in the sanctuary behind the altar. It'll be fired up before you return."

"Perfect. Jackson, are you going to be able to do all this alone?" Moira asked. "Rafe, do you think you should stay here—"

"Absolutely not," Rafe said. "We don't know what condition Grant Nelson is in. He was already showing signs this morning of being affected—the headache, for one, and he was preoccupied."

Rafe was right. "No sense delaying the inevitable. Ready?"

Rafe grabbed his bag and checked his knife.

"Let's go."

TWENTY-EIGHT

Grant was more than a little worried about Julie.

For a few minutes the jackhammer in his head slowed to a steady pounding. Maybe the aspirin he'd been popping finally kicked in. Or maybe it was just focusing on something other than his own problems.

Grant couldn't get the image of Nadine's tattoo out of his mind because it looked exactly like Julie's tat. It was uncommon, and exquisite. He remembered kissing the small of her back over and over, savoring the soft, unusually erotic spot.

For a detective, he realized he was an idiot. He didn't know much about Julie Schroeder or her friends. Everything Fern said made sense. Designer drugs. Julie had never seemed as though she'd been on drugs, at least when he was with her, but Grant also knew from his two years on Vice that major dealers rarely used, and never the heavy junk. They were in it for the money and power, not the drug high.

Grant could not believe that Julie was a drug dealer.

But he also realized that he hadn't asked her or Wendy the hard questions about Nadine. Why? Being tired was no excuse. Was he worried, maybe subconsciously, that Julie was involved with something illicit? Was he worried that she wasn't who he thought she was? Why did any of that matter when they were just off-again, on-again?

But it *did* matter. He cared deeply for Julie. Hell, he might even love her, but it was a warped kind of love wrapped in physical lust, not emotional need. Normal? Hell, no, but he wasn't normal. Never had been, not since he lost his virginity with his eighteen-year-old babysitter when he was fourteen. He'd told his twice-divorced mother he was too old for a babysitter, but when Sylvia Nelson went out of town on business, she refused to leave him alone overnight.

Little did she know what he did with Monica Jergens those nights. Monica had seduced him at the beginning—he'd been a mature kid, responsible for his little brother because of a busy single mom—but he'd also been a kid who liked video games and sports. But after the first time, Grant had never looked back at his childhood. Surprisingly, this fact now saddened him.

He drove down Sepulveda, where even now, the lunch hour on Saturday, hookers strolled. He wasn't a child anymore; he'd seen too much in life and on the job. These hookers were women who didn't care how hard he fucked or how long he took—they'd take it because they got paid to take it.

Grant slowed his sedan to a crawl. The hookers glanced over, but he looked like a cop and they moved on. He *was* a cop. He couldn't screw around with a hooker. He'd never paid for it before, so why would he now? Why did he have this overwhelming urge to fuck someone—anyone—without thought of the repercussions? His career was no small thing, and neither was his health.

All he could think about was sex. And it wasn't normal. He was a guy, he thought about sex many times a day, but not this constant barrage of images, these fantasies that wouldn't leave his mind. Fantasies he'd never lived out because they were illegal or because he'd never get a woman to agree.

Agree? Why ask? Just take what you want. Take it.

He slammed on his brakes, almost running a red light and nearly hitting two teenagers in the crosswalk. Grant barely noticed when the shorter kid flipped him off; he was frozen and distraught. He'd never raped a woman in his life, never came close until last night, but that was Julie, his Julie. He hadn't raped her. He'd just . . . been rough. Uncaring. He hadn't cared about whether she was comfortable or enjoying it, he just wanted to take. The idea that he was so close to finding it *acceptable* to force a woman made sweat bead on his brow, had his hands shaking.

He put his head down on the steering wheel. Something was wrong with him. He was sick. Maybe he had a fever and was hallucinating. That might explain his foul, perverted thoughts.

Cars honked behind him and he jumped, looked around. The light was green. He spurted through the intersection and pulled over to the side of the road, breathing heavily. He had to get it together. This sense of unease, of pain, the migraine, the visions of his first lover, of hookers, of Julie, of Moira O'Donnell—this wasn't him.

Grant rested his head back on his steering wheel and willed the pain to stop. His penis was still hard and uncomfortable; he squirmed in his seat, but that only made his migraine worse.

Home. He just had to go home and sleep this off . . .

whatever it was. He needed to meet Moira in . . . the digits on his clock blurred. It was already two; he was late.

What if Julie was really in trouble? The idea that she'd die in a horrible, gruesome way, like Nadine, terrified him. He didn't want to lose her like that. He didn't want to watch her rip her hair out, falling apart in front of him, flailing about until being run over by a bus.

He called her. Maybe if he talked to her, she'd meet him at her place. He couldn't walk into the Palomar feeling like this.

On the third ring he almost hung up; then she answered. "Grant."

It wasn't Julie's voice. He frowned. "Who's this?"

"Wendy. Julie is really upset with you. She doesn't want to talk to you."

Acid burned in his stomach. He knew it. He'd hurt her, no matter what she'd said earlier.

"Please put her on. I need to talk to her."

"She's working. Leave her alone."

"Dammit, put her on the phone!"

Wendy hung up on him. *She hung up the damn phone!*

But at least Grant knew Julie was at the club, so he could go talk to her in person.

His cop instincts told him something wasn't right about this—the close circle of people who were dead, the others involved with all of them. Except for George Erickson, though his wife knew Wendy Donovan. The pictures. Which made it all . . .

His head exploded in another burst of pain. The evidence was all right here—he felt it, but he couldn't put it together.

He looked at his reflection in the rearview mirror. His

eyes were bloodshot, as if he had been drinking all night. His face was haggard and pale, his light brown hair dark with perspiration.

His phone rang. It was Moira O'Donnell. He didn't want to talk to her, but dammit, he was supposed to have been at the Palomar five minutes ago.

"Nelson," he said.

"On your way?"

"I'm running late. We can do this tomorrow."

"I have information you need. Just ten minutes."

He didn't want to do this. "Fine," he agreed, "but I have a stop to make. It'll be another hour." He hung up before she could protest.

"First, I need to find Julie," he mumbled to himself.

Without looking, he started his car and abruptly turned into traffic. The horns of cars he nearly hit didn't faze him. With the thought of seeing Julie, his headache began to ease, from intolerable to simply excruciating.

Her astral projection invisibly resting in the passenger seat, Julie listened in horror as Grant believed what Wendy told him. That bitch was leading him into a trap, and using Julie's possessed body to do it! Julie had been trying to talk to Grant ever since he had gotten into his car—to communicate *somehow* without her body, without her voice—but he didn't hear her, he didn't feel her.

He was dying, his face hard and grim, unable to mask the pain. While Moira O'Donnell was waiting for him, he was playing right into Wendy's hands.

His cell phone was vibrating in the passenger seat, but Grant was either ignoring it or didn't notice. He was so focused on whatever dark thoughts filled his mind that Julie feared he'd crash, killing himself and others.

Julie used the intensity of her emotions to gather enough energy, then she pushed a directed pulse to move the cell phone. It flew across the seat and hit Grant in the arm.

"What the fuck?" he exclaimed as he swerved, corrected the car, then picked up the phone.

The simple telekinetic trick wore Julie down even more. After the ghosts at the morgue, and now using her limited energy reserve, she was growing weaker with each passing moment.

She didn't want to die, and she especially didn't want to die like Nadine.

Grant answered the phone on speaker. "Johnston?"

"Where the hell have you been? You haven't answered your phone for two hours."

Two hours? Julie frowned. Had that much time passed?

"I was at the morgue."

"You left at noon. It's nearly two-thirty. We have a problem."

"What?"

"I ran Moira O'Donnell's prints. The report came back. She's bad news."

"What did she do?"

"For starters, she's illegal. Her visa expired years ago. Her prints popped up in six open investigations of grand theft auto, and get this—Interpol has her passport flagged. If she attempts to fly to any European country, she's to be brought in for questioning."

"For what?"

"It doesn't say. She's a 'person of interest.'"

"Shit. I'm in the middle of something, but—don't put

out an APB on her. Call that sheriff from Santa Louisa and see what she has to say. I'm meeting O'Donnell at the Palomar in an hour or so—I have to stop at Velocity first."

"I don't like this, Grant. Something is going on."

"Head to the Palomar and keep our friend company until I get there."

"Will do." Johnston paused. "Are you okay? You don't sound well."

"I'm fine," Grant snapped. "This has been a fucked week. Why is everyone asking if I'm okay? I have a migraine from hell and a girlfriend involved in God knows what and a new dead body every day, connected to the last dead body."

"Grant—"

"Just meet me at the Palomar, okay?"

"Alright. One hour."

Grant jammed the off button and tossed the phone on the backseat.

Julie knew he was going to die if he showed up at Velocity, but how could she tell him to go straight to the Palomar and meet with Moira?

At least now Julie knew where Moira was. But there was no way Moira could intercept Grant before he reached Velocity, where Wendy—and very likely the demon in Julie's body—waited for him.

How could she stop him? They were approaching the on-ramp to the Ventura freeway. Twenty minutes and he'd be at Velocity. Twenty minutes and his fate would be sealed.

Julie ascended from the car and flew above it, looking for anything she could control to stop Grant. She didn't want to hurt anyone, and she didn't have enough energy or control to steer his car off the road. Moving the cell phone had been difficult enough.

They were approaching a park where kids were playing baseball. The idea came instantly—when the kid at bat hit the ball, Julie sent out a pulse of energy that pushed the ball off its intended course. The velocity of the ball coupled with her energy directed it, and it slammed directly into the windshield of Grant's car.

He slammed on his brakes and skidded, hitting a parked car. Stopped. He wouldn't be driving to Velocity now. That bought her time.

With a final glance at the tortured man she loved, her spirit flew to Moira's hotel. By the time she arrived, she had almost no energy left. She felt her body trying to pull her back, the psychic leash strong. She used her remaining energy to stay rooted on the astral plane.

She had one chance to save Grant, and that was to lead Moira to him. Find some way to communicate. The effort would likely kill her.

And maybe, Julie conceded, she deserved it.

TWENTY-NINE

"Where could he be?"

Rafe watched Moira pace the main lobby of the Palomar Hotel while he sat on the couch, keeping an eye on the main doors. He didn't like this situation any more than Moira did.

"Sit down," Rafe said.

She stopped walking, but she didn't sit. "He set the original meeting for two; it's nearly three. We have less than three hours. Hardly enough time to put this together!"

"Calm. Down."

She sat. "I have a bad feeling."

"Is that your nerves or a true premonition?"

She stood. "I don't have premonitions!"

Rafe wondered but didn't comment. Moira wasn't receptive to considering that she might have psychic abilities. She even made excuses for her visions, blaming them on her past. And while it was possible that her upbringing had initiated her visions, it was equally possible they were God-given. Why Moira couldn't see that, Rafe didn't understand—but he was beginning to.

She tried calling Grant again, but hung up in frustration.

"We should go to Velocity," she said.

"He said he'd be an hour late."

Rafe watched outside as a familiar sedan drove into the roundabout, driven by a broad-shouldered black guy. Why was Detective Johnston here? A police car pulled up behind him, but the officer didn't get out.

"Go to the bathroom," he told Moira.

"What?" she asked, but she'd already started walking, glancing over her shoulder. "Shit," she mumbled and walked nonchalantly around the corner. Rafe discreetly observed where she went. She was hiding just out of sight, but within earshot.

Rafe kept his eyes on Johnston as the detective spoke briefly to the cop outside before entering the lobby.

"Mr. Cooper," he said as he approached, his eyes scanning the area.

"Detective. I thought Nelson was meeting us."

"He's on his way, had a stop to make down the street."

Down the street. Velocity?

"Why is he going to the club?"

"Police business," Johnston said, not realizing that Rafe was making a guess. "Where's your girlfriend?"

"Upstairs. I'll tell her you're here."

"I can go up with you," Johnston said.

"I'll text her."

"That's not necessary."

Rafe sent the message to Moira. *Grant is at Velocity. I'll meet you there. Be Careful!!! Something's up with the cops.*

"Already done," he said, pocketing his phone. "What's with the police officer?"

"Nothing." Johnston glanced around again, rocked almost imperceptibly on his heels. Rafe thought cops would make better liars.

Rafe! Help me!

Rafe glanced around. He could have sworn he'd heard a distant female voice. No one was paying him much attention. There were few people in this part of the lobby.

Rafe, please, it's me, Julie, help me.

Julie? Where? He stepped back to get a better view of the hall, but didn't see the woman.

Johnston eyed him suspiciously. "Is something the matter, Mr. Cooper? You seem distracted."

"No, just tired." Rafe couldn't come up with a better excuse. The voice whispered again. It sounded like she was speaking directly in his ear.

They're going after Grant! Help me, Rafe, I'm dying. Moira is in trouble.

Moira?

"Wait here," Rafe told the cop. "I'll check on Moira."

"I'll go with you."

Rafe whirled around, every muscle tight and ready to fight—or run. "What is it? What do you want with Moira?"

Johnston raised an eyebrow. "Do you know that her visa expired?"

Rafe grew more suspicious. "That's it?"

"No, that's just the beginning. How long have you known Ms. O'Donnell?"

Rafe's stomach sank. What did they have on Moira? What kind of record did she have? Some of St. Michael's men had to stay in hiding, take new identities, or remain at the sanctuary because they were tied to an alleged crime. With Moira's drive, Rafe wasn't surprised that something might have popped up in the criminal database.

"I've know her two weeks," Rafe said. But it was much longer, in his heart. He wasn't going to let this cop take her in for questioning.

Rafe, I'm fading. I need you.

He didn't know what Julie's game was, but she knew something about Moira. He strained to listen, thinking of the YouTube video of Nadine Anson's death. The split-second image of Julie Schroeder near the bus. Moira had said her image was astral projection. But when your spirit left a living body, few people could see it except other spirits. How could he hear her but not see her?

"What do you want?" he said out loud.

Johnston stared at Rafe, his jacket parted to reveal his sidearm. "Are you talking to me?"

Rafe said, "I need to take a call." He put his phone to his ear and focused on Julie's voice.

"Okay, tell me what's going on." He stepped away from Johnston, acutely aware that the cop was scrutinizing him. He turned away and spoke softly to Julie. "Why's Moira in trouble?"

She's going to Velocity. I tried to get in her body to stop her, but I bounced off. I couldn't even get close enough to talk to her.

"Where are you now?"

Right in front of you. I'm touching you.

Rafe couldn't feel anything. He glanced at the hall mirror in front of him and saw only his worried expression—and Detective Johnston's sharp stare behind him.

Let me inside. Trust me, I won't stay. The demon has my body and it's almost too late. We have to get to Grant before Wendy finds him. Please, please, please!

"You know where he is?"

Wendy tricked Grant into thinking I was at Velocity, so I made his car crash. He's okay, but we have to hurry!

A trap at Velocity? Moira was walking right into it!

"Moira first." He kept his eyes on Johnston, who was inching closer to listen to Rafe's hushed conversation. The uniformed officer who was waiting outside had entered the lobby and was going up the stairs. Dammit, he needed to get rid of Grant Nelson's partner, get to Moira before Wendy did, and find Nelson before the demon.

No! Grant's in danger.

So was Moira. And without her, their plan to save Julie's boyfriend wouldn't work.

"Mr. Cooper," Johnston said, "we need to talk now. Your girlfriend is in serious trouble, and I don't want to have to bring you in as well."

The detective didn't know the meaning of the word trouble. Rafe held up his finger to buy time and said to Julie, "What is Wendy's plan for Moira?"

"Cooper," Johnston warned.

Let me in and I'll share everything. Please. I don't want to die.

Rafe hesitated. If Julie's physical body died, she wouldn't give up his body without a fight. Yet he didn't want her to die. Moira thought Julie had betrayed them and she didn't believe the witch, but maybe she'd been telling mostly the truth. He would know for certain if he allowed her spirit to share his body.

We have to hurry, but I can't do it alone. I tried. I can't. I'm fading, Rafe, I need you.

Moira would be furious if he let Julie's spirit inside. So would Anthony and Rico and everyone else at St.

Michael's. But what choice did he have? Julie had information about Wendy and the demon that they needed. More important, she knew where Grant was.

"All right. You can hitch a ride with me."

Rafe felt Julie's spirit touch him. Her fear wrapped around him—she was terrified. As he relaxed, she merged with his aura, then slipped inside his consciousness, but made no move to squash his thoughts or seize physical control.

She blended her thoughts with his, and for a minute he was disoriented and unsteady on his feet. She shared what had happened to her with him, dumping the memories in his mind as if he'd lived them. The demon Lust, taking her body. Killing Ike, the bartender. Wendy's plans to turn Moira over to Fiona.

Thank you, she whispered from deep inside his mind.

Rafe wobbled on his feet. Johnston grabbed him before he fell. "Hey, do you need a doctor?"

"I'm okay."

"Why don't you sit here awhile? My officer is checking on Ms. O'Donnell. She seems to be taking a long time."

You have to get rid of him! Julie demanded.

But Rafe might need a cop with him. He said to Johnston, "That was Moira—she said she's at Velocity."

Johnston couldn't hide his irritation and distrust. "What?"

"Your partner called her, said he was there and asked her to come down."

What are you doing!

Trust me, he told her. Honestly? He didn't have a plan. He was winging it. But he wasn't going to leave Moira to face Wendy and Nicole Donovan without backup.

"I'll follow you," Johnston said. "Straight to Velocity."

"Yes, sir."

Rafe half walked, half ran to his truck. As he started the ignition, his phone vibrated.

It was a text from Moira.

Hurry. There's a spell working. If you have to bring the cop, bring him.

"I'm already ahead of you, sweetheart."

Moira sensed magic as soon as she approached Velocity, but she couldn't discern what kind of spell was at work. She closed her eyes and focused on her sense of touch, lifting her arms slightly away from her body as if reaching out to a timid animal. The faint energy slithered up her hand, under her jacket, caressing her skin. It had taken her a long time to hone these skills, but she blocked out sight and sound, allowed the magic to touch her so she knew exactly what she faced. Her skin tightened, her heart rate quickened, and she could almost see the energy seductively reaching for her. Its tendrils wrapped around Velocity, rolling out of the club's foundation as an ocean wave stretches up the beach, its liquid reach long but losing potency with distance.

A powerful spell protected the club. She didn't know if there was a demon inside the building, but she had to assume Lust was here.

Cautiously, she walked around to the alleyway. She didn't see Grant Nelson's car, but she didn't know what he was driving today. Personal car or cop car. She pulled out her phone to text Rafe.

Hurry. There's a spell working. If you have to bring the cop, bring him.

A dark breeze brushed over Moira's skin as she pressed *Send*. She closed her eyes and focused. Primal fear gripped her and refused to let her go as she suddenly felt a thousand eyes watching her. Whoever was inside knew of her arrival. The magic told them.

The heavy metal employee door leading into Velocity slammed open and Moira jumped to the side, pulling out her dagger, angry with herself for not sensing the spell earlier, before it revealed her. Nicole Donovan stepped from the doorway and said with thick sarcasm, "Moira O'Donnell. What a surprise."

"This round is over," Moira said. "We know how to trap Lust. Good guys two, bad witches zero. Now where's Grant Nelson?"

Nicole laughed. "You are so far behind us, Moira. You don't even know what demon you're battling."

"It's you who are out of step, Nicole. You brought Lust with you to L.A., and Lust is who you sacrificed Nadine Anson to. You of all people should know how powerful that bitch of a demon is! You summoned it."

"The Seven are spread far and wide," Nicole said with such confidence, Moira knew she believed the lie.

"Is that what Fiona told you? That you're protected from the Seven? That they won't hurt you? That there is no connection? That's bullshit. You are forever connected to the Seven Deadly Sins. You're a carrier of their demonic virus. Wherever you go, they will find you. Tell me where Fiona is and I'll stop this insanity."

For a split second, Nicole hesitated, considered what Moira said.

"Why don't you simply cast a spell and find her your-self?"

"Dammit, this isn't a game!"

"No one else believes you gave up magic, Moira. I wouldn't have believed it if I hadn't seen it with my own eyes. You're easy prey for someone like my sister. You cannot imagine what she has done, or what she will do."

Moira was not going to rise to the bait. "Give me Grant and I'll clean up your mess. If Lust takes his soul, it's freed from Wendy's spell. It will hurt more people, while you sit here and watch people you claim to care about die."

"There's your mistake, Moira. You presume that there are people *here* that I care about."

Nicole's plan suddenly became clear to Moira. She'd thought Nicole was a follower, one of the easily led. She was a lot more dangerous than Moira had assumed. "You want Wendy dead."

"I want what's mine. Give me the chalice and I won't turn Raphael over to Fiona."

"You can't touch him," Moira said, but fear rose in her chest. "You don't even know where he is."

"Fiona can get to Raphael whenever she wants. It's you that will solidify my position with her."

"We melted the chalice. It's gone."

Nicole shook her head. "You're a good liar, Moira, but I know you didn't because we're still in control of the succubus."

"You mean the demon Lust."

She shrugged. Too casually. She was too cocky, too confident. She had no weapon. What was going on? "The chalice, or you're going to die," Nicole demanded.

"*No.*"

Every pore on her skin burned as if on fire as magic energy increased rapidly and she barely got her dagger up in time to block the surge. She could see the magic in the area, a shimmering of light and dark, magically charged air a fraction denser than the air surrounding it. No one else would be able to see it. Not Rafe. Not even most practicing witches. Why her, she didn't know, but this gift—or curse—enabled her to protect herself and others.

She pulled out her backup knife and like two swords, had the dagger and knife extended, reflecting magic only she could see; but even more than sight, she heard each jolt of energy clash against the sacred metal blades as it went off in every direction but at her. She didn't want to hurt Nicole, but the woman made her angry.

Nicole was using battle magic, not curses or lengthy rituals. Battle magic could be summoned quickly, but it had no lasting power. In order to have the time to work a more elaborate, dangerous spell, Nicole aimed to zap Moira and render her unable to defend herself.

Moira couldn't let her get a shot in. She had to distract her until Rafe arrived. Grant might not even be here. Nicole may simply be a distraction to keep Moira from finding him. But if Grant Nelson wasn't here, where was he? Did they already have him? Were they holding him captive until sunset, when they'd turn him over to Lust?

Sweat beaded on Nicole's face as she worked her magic. Her voice began to rise, fervent in its urgency.

"You give me Grant, I won't hurt you," Moira said.

Nicole laughed. "Hurt me? *Please.* Nothing you can do will stop the ritual."

She smiled, and Moira had a very bad feeling.

Because all her senses were focused on stopping the battle magic, she didn't feel the person approach from behind until it was too late.

She whirled around, but the blow hit her squarely on the side of her head and she fell to the ground. Pam Erickson.

"Grab her before her boyfriend gets here," Pam barked.

"Gladly."

"Nelson hasn't showed yet."

"That doesn't matter. Wendy and her stupid games. We'll find him."

"How much time do we have?"

"Enough."

Moira struggled to get up, though she couldn't see anything but spots of light and dark. She tried to shout for help but failed. She tried to reach her knives that had fallen when Pam Erickson hit her, but couldn't see them. She felt her gun being removed from her holster.

The two witches pulled her up and half carried, half dragged her down the alley and around the corner to where a blue sedan idled. She was dropped unceremoniously in the trunk. The steel frame slammed down, wrapping her in darkness.

Her heart raced as Moira's mind clouded in panic. She almost wished she had been knocked unconscious so she wouldn't know she was trapped. She reached up, touching the cold metal of the trunk much closer than she expected. Her eyes were open but she couldn't see her hand. She saw nothing, nothing but black and shadows. Shadows . . . a hint of light filtered in through the hairline seams where the lid closed. No real light, just a shadow, but she focused on it as if her life depended on it.

Moira wasn't scared of the dark, even though she knew of monsters that lurked there. In the dark, she could fight, she could run, she had room to battle. But here, trapped, as effective as the bars her mother kept her behind, no room to maneuver, there was no escape.

Hadn't Rico locked her in a dungeon so she could conquer this fear? Was her suffering for nothing?

It's just a car. Just a trunk. Just two magicians who have a fraction of Fiona's power. Think, Moira.

She focused first on even breathing while staring at the shadow, the promise of light when she got out. Her heart rate shifted from full throttle to fast. They hadn't tied her up, but she couldn't find a release in the trunk to pop it open. She couldn't hear Nicole and Pam in the front of the car; either the sound didn't travel over the noise of the road, or they weren't talking.

The car picked up speed and the exhaust fumes filled her lungs, making her gag and light-headed. Still, she felt around the trunk. Nothing except rough carpet on a board.

A board? Didn't cars have a spare tire in the trunk? She didn't know enough about cars—she'd never owned one, and none of the cars she'd stolen had a flat—but it made sense that the tire would be in the trunk. And with tires came things like tools and bolts. Anything that she could use as a weapon.

She shifted in the tight confines, the pain above her ear coupled with the movement and fumes making her nauseous. She waited a moment for it to pass, then rolled over to her stomach and felt along the carpet for a seam or handle or something that she could pull up.

There it was, a small chain. She tried to lift it up but the board didn't budge—she was on top of it. No matter how she moved, she couldn't find a way to pull up the floor to reach the spare tire and the possible tools inside.

The panic rose again, an overwhelming sense of helplessness that had her shaking uncontrollably. How could she let her claustrophobia defeat her? She was no shrinking violet. She was Moira O'Donnell, and dammit, that meant something! What would Rico say if he could see her now?

"Your fear will get you killed."

But it wasn't fear that would get her killed, it was inaction. Letting her emotions win over her training. Healthy fear was a good thing; healthy fear would keep her focused on what was important.

Stopping Wendy and Nicole. Meeting Rafe at Grace Harvest Church, saving Grant Nelson, trapping the demon Lust.

What would Rafe do? He'd tell her to have a plan. Be ready to improvise. Not to act blindly, but to act smart.

The car slowed. She didn't know how much time had passed, but not more than fifteen, twenty minutes. She stretched as best she could, moving her ankles and wrists in circles, working out the kinks, shifting her arms over her head and touching her shoulder blades. She flexed and relaxed, not letting her muscles fall to sleep.

The car stopped, someone got out, but she didn't hear a door close. A moment later it did and the car moved forward. Slowly. Excruciatingly.

Then it stopped one last time and the ignition turned off.

Moira waited. Her first reaction would be to come out

kicking and fighting as soon as Nicole opened the trunk. But she didn't know how many there were, where she was, and she would be off balance coming out of the trunk. Her head was still fuzzy, now more from the fumes than the attack.

She would bide her time, seizing the best opportunity to fight back.

Waiting. Definitely not her strength.

Velocity wouldn't open to the public for another hour, and the main doors were locked. Rafe ran around to the alley but didn't see Moira. As he approached the employee door he saw her knives on the ground, one partly obscured by the dumpster. He picked them up and pocketed them.

"Where is she, Julie?" he demanded of the spirit inside him. "Tell me or I'll send your astral self back to your body so fast you won't know what hit you."

Don't, please—I don't know where they took her!

"You knew she was in danger." Rafe kicked the dumpster, then tried the door.

No. Only that Wendy was luring Grant here. I didn't want Moira to get caught in the middle! Please, you have to find him before Wendy!

"I need to find Moira first!" He took a deep breath. They hadn't killed her—they likely wanted to turn her over to Fiona. He had time. He had to think, be smart. If he had Grant, he could offer an exchange. "She could be inside."

The code to the door is 65601.

Rafe typed it in and cautiously entered the employee break room. Two women were putting on makeup and stared at him.

Tell them you're subbing for Ike. They're not witches.

Rafe smiled. "I'm filling in for the bartender. Is Wendy around? I was supposed to check in with her."

The taller girl said, "We just got here. She's not here yet."

But she was here! Julie cried.

Rafe smiled and crossed the room as if he knew what he was doing. "Where's your security tape?" he asked Julie.

Reggie's office. He's the bouncer, but he doesn't come in until five.

Julie directed him to the bouncer's small office. Several security screens showed the club inside and out from various angles. He focused on the screen that scrolled through four different angles of the alley. He looked at the equipment, noted it was digital, and replayed the last fifteen minutes.

He watched Moira stride slowly but purposefully down the alley, then she halted, on full alert. She appeared to be listening—with all of her senses. Nicole came out of the door a moment later. Moira had her knives out so fast Rafe almost missed it. They began to argue.

A voice behind him said, "You have some explaining to do, Mr. Cooper."

He glanced over his shoulder at Detective Johnston, who had his hand on the butt of his gun.

"Watch this—Moira's in trouble."

"I think—" Johnston stopped, watching the silent replay. Moira moved her knives in front of her with surprising speed as Nicole held her hands up. Not in a defensive posture, but almost as if she were conducting an orchestra. Every step Nicole took toward Moira, Moira took a step back.

"What the fuck?" Johnston stared in disbelief at the screen. "O'Donnell is the one with the weapons, but the other woman is the aggressor?"

Rafe said, "Nicole Donovan is a witch. She's using magic to attack Moira."

He threw his hands up. "You think I'm an idiot? If—" He stopped midsentence as Pam Erickson walked onto the screen and hit Moira from behind while Moira was focused on defending herself from invisible energy waves. The women removed Moira's gun and half carried, half dragged her from the alley.

"What's going on?" Johnston asked, his voice low.

"You said Grant was coming here. Where is he?"

Johnston pulled out his phone and dialed. "Nelson, it's me—" Johnston frowned, turning his back to Rafe. "Detective Jeffrey Johnston, Pacific Division, Badge number 455599." A moment later, he said, "Nelson, what the hell is going on? . . . Tell me you didn't hit a cop. . . . I'll be there in twenty minutes. I—" he glanced at Rafe. "It appears Moira O'Donnell has been taken against her will by Nicole Donovan and Pamela Erickson. She seems to have been running her own investigation. Cooper is with me. . . . I don't . . . Right . . . but . . . I don't think you're in the position to make demands right now. I'll be there ASAP."

He hung up, then whirled around to face Rafe. "What's going on, Cooper? Grant is being detained for assaulting a police officer. He had a traffic accident and refused a field sobriety test. I need to get over there."

"He's sick," Rafe said. "Not drunk. I need to get him to Grace Harvest Church."

Johnston barked out a gruff laugh. "I doubt Nelson has ever stepped foot in a church."

"I'll tell you once, and you have to believe me. You saw that tape. Magic is real. Witches are real. There is a demon on the loose and it wants Grant's soul. The marks on your dead bodies? Demon marks—Grant has one on his back right now."

"You're insane."

"I've been called worse. But I'm not a liar. Julie Schroeder, Grant's girlfriend, is a witch. Remember the image you saw of her on the YouTube video?"

"It was a reflection; it couldn't have been her."

"It was her astral projection."

"Whatever. I have to get to Grant." He turned around.

Rafe stepped forward and grabbed his arm. Johnston slapped his hand away and pulled his gun out. "Back off, Cooper."

"Grant will die if you don't believe me."

"Keep your hands where I can see them."

Rafe complied. "Julie, right now, is separate from her body, just like she was on the video. She's right with me; ask me something only she would know about Grant. Like where they met or why they broke up—something!"

Johnston was skeptical, but Rafe had to convince him. He had to find Moira, dammit! He didn't want to waste time arguing with a cop.

"Please!" Rafe pleaded.

"When is Grant's birthday—and where did Grant and Julie go for his last birthday?"

Rafe listened to Julie, then said, "His birthday is July twenty-seventh. But they'd broken up a week before. She'd bought them tickets to Hawaii, and she went by herself. Grant showed up halfway into the week and said it was the best four days of his life. A month later, they broke up again."

Johnston was swayed by the details.

"You can ask me anything, Detective—but let's get going. We have no more time to waste. We have until sunset before the demon will attack your partner."

"Sunset? Thought that was vampires who can't go out in daylight."

Rafe despised being ridiculed. "It's an ancient ritual, and I don't care if you believe me, but sunset is only ninety minutes from now and if we don't get Grant to safety, he's a dead man."

Johnston stared.

Rafe added, "Julie just told me where Grant is right now. He's on Washington Boulevard approaching the Santa Monica Freeway."

"How do you know that?"

"Because Julie was with him when he crashed. She forced him off the road to stop him from walking into a trap."

"I'm driving."

"I need my supplies. And Detective—"

"Call me Jeff. I think we can be on a first-name basis about now."

"Do you have a Taser?"

"Why?"

"You might have to subdue your partner. He's not himself."

Jeff's jaw tightened. "I was aware of something different about him this morning, but I didn't do anything."

"This isn't your fault. But you can help stop it."

* * *

Nina Hardwick was pleased with herself. It helped being a staff attorney for the Board of Supervisors—one call and most county employees were willing to work on a Saturday getting her information. By five Saturday evening, she had a complete dossier on Wendy Donovan, Nicole Donovan, and even their mother, Susan. If they weren't responsible for killing George, she might have felt a sliver of sympathy for the children of Susan— that woman was a nutcase. To be raised in such a horrid manner . . . but Nina didn't allow herself sympathy for the mother or her children. Someone's upbringing, no matter how horrific, didn't justify murder.

It reminded her, however, that she needed to push the Board of Supervisors to conduct a complete audit of the troubled foster care system. It wouldn't solve the problems, but if Nina could help a few children who'd slipped through the cracks, she'd feel that she'd done something.

She drove toward the hotel where Moira had told her they were staying, and tried Moira on her cell phone. No answer. She flipped over the card where she'd scrawled an emergency number.

Jackson Moreno 818-555-8860
Grace Harvest, Burbank

No one picked up that phone, either, but Nina knew that church. It was near the Warner Bros. Studio. She was closer to the church than to the Palomar.

She made a quick decision as the ramp to the Ventura Freeway came up. She merged onto it, then took the second exit into Toluca Lake and Burbank.

Rafe Cooper had asked her to send along anything she could find that would help them take down Wendy Donovan. Knowing they were dealing with a woman who'd been institutionalized on and off most of her childhood—and then killed her mother when she was sixteen—was important. Nina was set on getting Rafe that information.

THIRTY

Whether we fall by ambition, blood, or lust,
like diamonds we are cut with our own dust.
—JOHN WEBSTER

Grant sat in the backseat of a patrol car on Washington Boulevard, waiting to be bailed out of this mess. He
wasn't drunk, he wasn't high, the baby-faced uniformed
cop had *no fucking right* to ask him to come down to
the station for a blood test simply because he'd refused
a field sobriety test. His word should mean something—
he was a near-twenty-year veteran of the LAPD! Who
was this uniform, anyway? A rookie? A year under his
belt? The baseball hit *his* car—he hadn't been driving
drunk.

If he didn't have the sick sensation that his brain was
melting and about to leak out of his ears, he'd have been
able to talk himself out of the situation. A ball hit his
windshield. He swerved, hit a parked car. End of story.
He'd been furious and in pain and the patrolman had
rubbed him the wrong way. But he hadn't decked him
until the novice had called in the incident—on an unse-
cured channel where everyone and the press could hear.
The gawking bystanders had finally left, but passersby
kept looking into the car, watching him.

Worse, the longer he sat here doing nothing, the more
apprehensive he became about Julie. What if she pressed

charges against him? He'd bruised her—sure, the sex was consensual, it had always been wild between them, but he'd never left marks like he'd given her last night. He hadn't meant to hurt her—he didn't even remember, only flashes of screwing her and the disturbing feeling that he was losing his mind.

Grant caught a glimpse of himself in the patrol car's rearview mirror. Hair matted from sweat. Blood on his scalp from when the young cop had thrown him against the hood after Grant had hit him. His eyes were more red than white, and his pupils were dilated.

No wonder the uniform thought he was on drugs. He looked like he'd been on a bender for a week. He should have listened to Jeff this morning and gone home to sleep off this headache. But sleep was the last thing on his mind. He had to find Julie.

An unmarked black pool car pulled up behind the black-and-white. Jeff got out of the driver's seat, and— Grant almost couldn't believe Johnston's audacity!— Raphael Cooper stepped out of the passenger seat.

What was his partner doing with that prick? Where was Moira O'Donnell? In the back of his mind Grant remembered Jeff saying that the Donovan sisters had kidnapped her. Kidnapped? Ludicrous. As ridiculous as Nina Hardwick's accusation that Pamela Erickson was a witch. Or Moira O'Donnell's claim that she was a psychic.

He reached for the handle only to remember he was in the back of the patrol car and trapped. He saw his partner talking—arguing—with the cop, but he could hear only indistinct voices and isolated words.

Stress. Difficult case. Girlfriend.

"Ex-girlfriend," Grant mumbled.

He didn't know why he insisted that Julie was his *ex*. He still slept with her. He still sought out her company. He still called her in the middle of the night when he had insomnia. When he'd had a rough day. When he had to tell a mother that her son was dead.

He stared at his hands. He'd calmed down enough to convince the uniform not to cuff him, even though he was still trapped in the back of the patrol car. He'd been there the day the sheriff had come to the house and told his mother that Brian had died. That Brian had died a hero defending an elderly couple in a twenty-four-hour convenience store during a holdup didn't matter. He was dead. Grant's little brother was dead, and his mother had never recovered. And she never wanted to look at Grant again, since Grant was the one who had told Brian to go to the store. Brian always did what Grant said. And Brian was dead.

Julie had listened. God, he missed talking to her. He just wanted to make everything up to her. Maybe there was more to *them* than he'd realized. Maybe he should have tried harder to make the relationship work. He didn't want to be with her 24/7, but when he wasn't, he missed her.

He wanted to fix everything. With Julie. With *them*. With their future.

The door opened and the uniform said, "You can go. But I'm writing this up."

He wanted to deck the prick—again—but relief over getting out of this damn car won over vengeance.

Grant stepped out, saw Cooper again. "What's he doing here?"

He hadn't meant to sound so gruff or ungrateful—he was damn humiliated, but he couldn't think about that now. Raphael Cooper stared at him as if *he* were a problem. *He* was a cop.

Jeff put a hand on his forearm. "Grant, let's go back—"

Grant shook Jeff off. "I need to find Julie."

"All right," Jeff said, then glanced at Cooper.

"Why are you looking at him?" Grant asked. "Is he in charge now? Is he your senior officer?"

"Detective," Jeff said, sounding stern but looking uncertain, "I think we should talk about this in private."

"Fuck that. I'm going to Velocity—Julie is waiting for me, and I need to talk to her about this case." That sounded lame, but he couldn't think of another reason for this overwhelming need to see Julie. Now. Passing cars on Washington Boulevard slowed as the drivers turned their necks to see what the commotion was about. The kids from the park were watching from the field. Grant's humiliation made him want to fight, to regain ground. To do something to fix this. But the only thing that would fix it was Julie. He had to see her. Only thinking about her made the pain fade enough so he didn't think he was dying.

"I'll take you," Jeff said quickly. Too quickly.

"What's going on?"

"I could ask the same about you," Jeff said.

Jeff was acting like *he* was the problem. "Shit, Jeff, I have a migraine the size of Dodger Stadium, that's what's wrong. Why the fuck is Cooper here? Why'd you bring him? Where's O'Donnell?"

"We'll talk in the car," Jeff said.

"I'm not going anywhere with you. There's nothing wrong with the engine in my car. I'm getting my keys—"

"I have your keys, Grant. You're in no condition to drive."

"I'm not on anything!"

Cooper said, "Detective, you're sick—we don't have a lot of time, I'll explain on the—"

Before Cooper could finish his sentence, Grant charged him. He would not tolerate a civilian giving him orders. He was *not* sick.

Then why is your dick hard as a rock and your head is about to explode? Why were you thinking of picking up a hooker? Why'd you hurt Julie during sex?

Something was wrong with him, but he couldn't focus.

He tackled Cooper, but the larger man pivoted and Grant went down hard on his right arm. Cooper was down, too, but he rolled away and jumped up, as fluid as a prizefighter.

Jeff grabbed Grant by the arm and pulled him up. "Stop," he said in a low voice so only he could hear. "You're making this worse. I can fix it, but not if you don't calm down."

Grant let Jeff walk him to the pool car. Cooper got into the passenger seat. "I'm not sitting in the back like a criminal," Grant said. His vision was blurring and he shook his head to clear it, but that made the migraine pound. He grabbed his head and squeezed as if trying to hold his skull together. He stumbled and would have fallen to his knees if Jeff hadn't held him up.

"It's going to be okay, Grant. I promise. We're going to see someone who can fix this. You're going to get through this."

"We're going to Velocity. To see Julie."

"Sure," Jeff said. He glanced at Cooper and refused to look Grant in the eye.

"Where are you taking me?"

"Grant, I think—"

Grant pushed Jeff hard against the car and ran in the other direction. What was wrong with everyone? Why wouldn't they give him a straight answer?

A sharp pain exploded in his lower back and his body vibrated violently as he fell to the sidewalk, twitching and dazed. His last clear image was of his partner standing over him as he lay nearly paralyzed from the Taser.

"I'm sorry, Nelson, but I didn't have a choice."

Moira assessed the situation pretty quickly, coming to the conclusion that she was screwed big-time.

She'd done exactly what Rafe would have told her to do: wait for an opportunity. But so far, there had been no chance to escape. And now, Wendy had her tied down in a spirit trap. She'd been stripped down to her bra and jeans, her leather jacket and turtleneck shirt tossed to the far side of the room. There was nothing sexual about her partial nakedness—Wendy had searched her completely and found all her goodies. The sacred oil, the holy water, the salt lining in her jacket, the iron in the pockets, the devil's cuff—everything that could have helped Moira fight demons. All gone.

Yep, she was screwed.

"Where are we?" she asked. She'd only seen a small portion of the mansion Nicole had brought her to—secluded, opulent, and empty. They were in the dining room. The table had been pushed to the side, all the chairs had been removed, and a spirit trap was painted on the wooden floor. Pam Erickson watched from one of two doorways, and Nicole had laid out her tools on the table: an asthame, glass bowl, and a variety of dried herbs. Moira also noted a vial of blood.

"Kent Galion's house," Wendy said. "It's perfect. Rape, murder, violence—perfect to complete the ritual. I like the balance."

She sounded so much like Fiona, except for one major difference. Moira had never doubted Fiona's sanity—she was simply evil and selfish. But Wendy was a magician *and* crazy. A dangerous combination.

Moira said, "As I told Nicole, you're a fool. You don't have a succubus in your power, you have the demon Lust, and she's only playing along with you until she completes your demands; then she's free."

"You know nothing about *my* magic!" Wendy lit all the candles in the room with a simple incantation.

Moira laughed. "Parlor tricks."

"I didn't believe Nicole when she said you turned your back on your heritage. I'm shocked it's true."

"I know more about magic in my little finger than—"

Moira sucked in her breath involuntarily as Wendy delivered a psychic punch to her chest. She couldn't speak as she recovered from the jolt.

"Yes, *please* be quiet."

Julie Schroeder entered the dining room. She wore a thin, flowing red gown. As she sashayed past the flickering candles, Moira noted she wore no underclothes.

Moira found her voice enough to say, "Lying bitch."

Julie laughed and Moira frowned. She'd closed off her senses when she'd been kidnapped, out of fear and self-preservation. Now, she slowly opened them.

It only took a few seconds to realize she was facing a demon.

Not just any demon. Lust inhabited Julie's body.

"Where is my soul?" the demon asked.

"We'll begin the ritual and find him." Wendy glared at Moira. "You screwed up my plans when you showed up at Velocity. I couldn't wait for Grant."

"I feel just awful about that." Moira feigned a yawn, keeping an eye on Nicole's ritual.

"It doesn't matter because I know how to find him."

The three women circled the demon and held hands. The demon closed her eyes, a secret grin on her face.

Wendy spoke an ancient Latin incantation that at first Moira didn't recognize. She listened, unable to translate it quickly. Then she heard one word, *oculus,* eye. It was an all-seeing spell, for the witch to locate someone. Eye . . . blood . . .

My eye, his eye. My blood, his blood. As it is above, so it is below.

Wendy held up the small vial of red liquid that Moira knew in her heart was Grant's blood. She twisted off the cap, and for a second Moira thought she was going to drink it. Instead, she held out her wrist and the demon cut it with Nicole's asthame. Wendy gasped, then poured a few drops of Grant's blood on her wrist. The demon put her finger in the mixed blood and wrote a symbol on Wendy's arm.

The intimacy of the ritual astounded Moira. Even Fiona would not have risked her life by allowing a demon to cut her skin, even for added power.

Wendy held her arms out and the demon spoke the language of the *Conoscenza,* the ancient book written by demons that Fiona had found. The book Moira needed to destroy to prevent the Seven from being summoned again. Unable to translate the words, Moira didn't know what the demon Lust was saying, but the rhythm and tone chilled her until she couldn't stop shaking. The ground beneath the house shook slightly, barely enough to feel, but magical energy flowed around them until on a breath of stirred air, the spell left in search of Grant.

"I see him!" Wendy cried. She laughed and didn't sound sane.

A cell phone trilled.

Nicole said, "That's Julie's phone."

Wendy, eyes bright with demonic magic, answered the phone.

Moira heard Rafe's voice on the other end.

"I have Grant Nelson. You have Moira. Let's trade."

Wendy laughed until tears ran down her face, then hung up without answering Rafe's question. She faced Moira with a glowing smile. "I hope you said goodbye to your boyfriend because you won't see him until you meet again in Hell."

The demon, Wendy, and Pam Erickson left.

Nicole smiled at Moira. "It's just you and me." Moira felt the energy building again. "I can't kill you yet, but I can have some fun."

THIRTY-ONE

Rafe had Grant Nelson restrained in the reverse spirit trap. They were in Jackson's church, in the large area where the altar had been. A twenty-foot-tall empty cross hung on thick wires from the ceiling, the base eight feet overhead and behind them.

A thick line of salt circled Grant, as well as a nearly invisible circle of sacred oil. Rafe hoped they weren't making a mistake using the church as their last stand—it had once been a Catholic church, and Jackson said the relics beneath the altar had never been removed. They were safe in a wooden box beneath the floor. Maybe it was overkill, but Rafe tied Grant to a chair directly above the relics. If the cop didn't calm down and listen, Rafe wouldn't be able to free him, and if Grant couldn't defend himself it could put him at greater risk.

He hoped he was doing the right thing—and he wished Anthony would call him back with answers. They were cutting it far too close. If Anthony didn't know what to do, then they would have to wing it. Which might well get them all killed. Rafe tried not to dwell over Moira's captivity otherwise he'd lose his edge. Wendy's laughter had been borderline hysterical, and Rafe expected the demon any minute.

He didn't know if he could do this without Moira, and prayed she was safe.

"I'm sorry," Rafe said as he checked Grant's restraints.

"You kidnapped a cop. Sorry isn't going to cut it." Grant glared at Jeff Johnston, who stood to the side, his eyes red with restrained emotion and uncertainty. He'd been the one to Taser his partner. "I'll have your badge, Johnston."

"I'm sorry, too, Grant, but you're not yourself." Jeff asked Rafe, "Is he possessed or something?"

"No. He's infected. The demon Lust did a number on him, and now she's coming to finish the job. Steal his soul, then end his life."

Grant fought his restraints. "You're both fucking insane! I'm going to kill you!"

"I want to cut you loose," Rafe said, "but you'll only endanger yourself if you leave this spirit trap."

"I'm going to throw the book at you," he growled.

Jackson Moreno brought the chalice from the sanctuary. "I don't think we should bring that out," Rafe said. "Not until Anthony calls."

"I'll keep it with me."

"But—" Rafe was unsure. Moira had been adamant about keeping it well secured until the demon was trapped. "I'm going to call Anthony now," he said. "We can't wait."

"What's that?" Grant demanded. He was obviously in pain, but not from the restraints. His hair was dark with sweat, his face flushed, his eyes bloodshot. He was fighting the lustful urges, but Rafe suspected he'd be vulnerable as soon as the demon arrived. Rafe couldn't free him; Grant Nelson wasn't in his right mind.

"I've been telling you the truth, Detective. Wendy Donovan is a witch," Rafe told him as he called Anthony. "She summoned a succubus—a demon who steals the souls of men during sex—in order to gain favors. But this time, she trapped one of the Seven Deadly Sins, and it's not as simple to get rid of it."

"You're all fucking lunatics!"

Let me talk to him.

There was no way Rafe was letting Julie take over. Moira was already going to be livid that he'd let the witch's spirit inside him. Rafe couldn't give up even a sliver of control.

Anthony answered his phone on the third ring. "Rafe."

"I'm desperate for answers, Anthony. We have the cop, the demon is on its way, and the Donovans have Moira somewhere."

"What? Who has Moira?"

"Wendy and Nicole Donovan plan to turn her over to Fiona."

"You can't let that happen!"

Rafe hesitated. For two weeks Anthony had been berating Moira, doubting her, and arguing with her. It had developed into a huge problem between him and Anthony as well, and now he was suddenly concerned about her safety? Not simply concerned—but panicked. "I have no intention of letting them harm her. But it's nearly sunset here and we're out of time."

"Where's the chalice?"

"We have it here."

"You need to contain the demon in the chalice and then melt it. But you won't have much time."

"And how do we do that?"

"That, I'm not as certain about."

"You're not helping, Anthony."

"What do you want from *me*? I'm seven thousand

miles away, and I've been reading handwritten notes in four languages for twenty hours straight. In one book I've found reliable, it states that any physical portal— that is, an object and not a place—into the underworld can be used to trap a demon using a binding exorcism prayer. In my experience working with artifacts, I believe this is correct."

"Have you done it?"

"I haven't had cause. I've encountered demons trapped in physical vessels like the chalice during archeological excavations and have successfully sent them back, but I've never handled a demon as powerful as Lust."

Rafe considered Anthony's experience. "Right now the demon is in a human body. Do I need to draw it out of the body first, then bind it to the chalice?"

"I would suggest just that. You'll need to be in the reverse trap to protect you."

"And the chalice?"

"Nearby, outside the trap."

Rafe could think of a half-dozen things that could go wrong. "I hope this works."

"I'll be praying for you. As soon as possible, find Moira."

"I plan on it." Rafe hung up. He wasn't certain whether Anthony's concern was for Moira's ultimate safety or her value as a tool, and it made him uneasy.

Rafe said to Jackson, "Put the chalice under the altar, to the side so Wendy won't see it."

"Does Anthony have a plan?"

"One plan. If Plan A doesn't work, we'll improvise."

Jeff was trying to talk to Grant. "I saw some things this afternoon that I can't explain."

Grant strained, his lips curling. "They drugged you! It's a hallucination!"

Jeff glanced at Rafe. "Can't you do something for him?"

Rafe shook his head.

Julie said, *Please, Rafe! Let me talk to him.*

He mentally told her, *"Feed me information. I'm not giving you control."*

She was too weak to fight him, and reluctantly agreed.

Rafe said to Grant, "Wendy was jealous because you kept going back to Julie. Wendy didn't want you; she just didn't want Julie to have you."

"You bastard, if you touched Julie I swear I'll kill you—"

"I haven't hurt Julie, but Wendy gave her body to a demon. That demon has been around you—you've been infected. The symptoms of being infected? Headaches worse than any migraine you've ever had. An overwhelming urge to do things you know you shouldn't, but you still want to. *Need* to. Julie came to my hotel room this morning. She had bruises on her arms from where you held her down. She said you weren't acting yourself, then told us about the mark on your back. The same mark that's on the backs of the demon's victims lying in the morgue." Recognition crossed Grant's face. "You saw it with your own eyes," Rafe added.

"You son of a bitch!" Grant pulled and strained at his restraints.

Jackson tried to calm him down. "Grant, it's true. I know it's hard to accept, but there are demons that walk the earth. Wendy is the head of a powerful coven—"

"If I hear that word one more time!" Grant stared at

the ceiling. Veins throbbed in his neck as sweat flowed down his back.

"Detective Nelson," Rafe said, "Julie is trying to save your life. Her spirit—her astral self—is right here with me. She knows you don't believe in any of this. If it helps, she wants to remind you that she's the only one who knows about your brother."

Rafe didn't feel comfortable sharing the private information, but the comment had Grant frozen. Then he went off. "I don't know *who* the fuck you are, but if you mention Brian I will beat your brains out! You know *nothing* about him! You're not fit to be in the same room with him! I hate you!"

Rafe's compassion went out to Grant. He let the comments stand, not elaborating. Grant was losing his steam. Rafe didn't want to beat the guy down, but he had to get him to at least comply.

"We want to untie you, but you have to stay in the spirit trap," Rafe said. "The demon wants you. It wants your soul. There is also the not-so-little problem of the mark on your back. Remember Galion? Everyone who is marked dies unless we trap the demon."

Grant had nothing more to say, but he glared at Jeff.

"Hello!" A female voice rang out in the church.

Rafe pivoted with his dagger out. It was Nina Hardwick.

"What are you doing here, Nina?" Rafe asked, angry. They didn't have time for this. Wendy was on her way.

Nina frowned. "I tried Moira, but—" She stared at Grant. "What happened? What are you doing to him?" She ran toward Grant and Rafe intercepted her.

"Nina." He grabbed her arm and made her look at him. "You have to go."

"Why are you hurting him?"

"I haven't hurt him—he has the mark of the demon. He's going to die if I can't stop Wendy. And so will Moira."

Nina looked around. It was all too incredible; impossible to believe. "Where is Moira?"

"Wendy kidnapped her. She set Grant up, but we found him first. He doesn't understand what's going on."

Grant said, "I understand perfectly well that you are a fucking loon and will be in prison for a long, long time."

Detective Jeff Johnston approached her. "Nina, Grant isn't himself right now. He assaulted a cop after getting into a minor car accident. He's lucky he wasn't hauled to the station and placed on administrative leave. Something is wrong with him."

"Nina," Rafe said, "you need to leave before Wendy gets here with the demon."

"I found the information you wanted."

For a minute, Rafe didn't know what he'd asked for. Nina elaborated. "Wendy and Nicole's background. Wendy was in and out of mental institutions for years. Their mother, Susan, was in foster care from the age of six. Susan's parents were grossly abusive, and she was forcibly removed from their home. They went to prison, but not long enough if you ask me, and Susan was raised in a series of—"

"I appreciate this, but now you need to leave."

"But—"

"Please, Nina."

"Wendy killed her mother. No one prosecuted her because she had proof that her mother set her up to be raped repeatedly. Wendy was finally released for good when she was eighteen, and hasn't had a problem with law enforcement since. Her records are sealed."

"How did you get them?" Jeff asked.

Nina straightened her spine. "I have my sources. I don't th—"

Rafe smelled a hint of sulfur as soon as the demon stepped into the church.

"Get behind me," he ordered Nina while pushing her back.

The demon—in Julie's body—was flanked by Wendy and Pamela.

Rafe caught Jackson's eye and mouthed, *Go! Now!*

Jackson hesitated. Dammit, he knew the plan! He didn't have time to panic.

Wendy said, "You lose, Raphael Cooper."

"Where's Moira?" He hadn't expected them to bring her, but he prayed she was still alive. They wanted her for Fiona, not themselves.

"You think I'd bring her *here*? Give me Grant. He's already marked. He's ours."

The demon growled, "He's mine."

Every door in the place slammed shut. They'd been sealed inside. No one could get in or out.

THIRTY-TWO

Another jolt of magically charged air hit Moira in the chest. Stunned, she stopped fighting against her restraints until she caught her breath. Nicole Donovan smirked down at Moira's half-naked body.

"You are pathetic. From what your mother told me, you used to have power. Where is it, Moira? Where's your magic? It's there somewhere, weak, unused, but magic is in your blood. You can't escape. Why don't you find it? I would have more fun in a fair battle."

Moira drew in a sharp breath, her lungs aching from having the wind knocked out of her repeatedly. "I can beat you without magic," she whispered.

Nicole laughed. Not the half-insane hysterical laugh of her deranged sister, Wendy, but an I-have-a-secret laugh, low and full of humor.

The witch held up her hands and chanted a spell. Moira closed her eyes and used mental tricks Rico had taught her to battle the curse, repeating a Psalm in its original Hebrew. It must have been working, because Nicole stopped speaking. Moira slowly opened her eyes and was surprised that Nicole had knelt next to her, her asthame in hand.

Trapped, Moira was not going to let this bitch see her panic. She said, "You won't kill me. You don't have the courage."

Nicole took the blade and broke the skin on Moira's forearm, an inch long. Blood seeped quickly through the cut. Nicole grabbed her arm and squeezed. Moira bit back a cry as her arm exploded in pain. Nicole twisted her arm so Moira's blood would drip into a small glass jar.

"Fucking bitch," Moira ground out through clenched teeth.

"I already contacted Fiona. She's waiting for you."

Panic bubbled in her chest, but Moira forced it down and said, "Why doesn't she come for me herself? Too scared?"

"I'll tell her you said that."

Her mother was the one person she feared more than anything. Even more than demons. Demons didn't play around; they were just bad. They were, in fact, predictable, and could be dispatched with exorcism prayers that differed from witchcraft in one fundamental way: they didn't ask for favors. Sure, demons were fearsome—and Moira didn't enjoy battling them. But Moira would rather face down the demon Lust than her mother.

Because Fiona knew her greatest weakness. Fiona didn't want to kill her. She wanted Moira to suffer for eternity.

Your fear will kill you.

Shut up! Moira wanted to strangle Rico for his pithy sayings and devout wisdom. Why shouldn't she be afraid? Why shouldn't she fear demons *and* her mother? Rico was a hunter; he'd never been hunted. Not the way she'd been. In life and in her nightmares, she'd been the prey. She'd died a thousand deaths in her mind, and still, she lived. She'd suffered the pain of others and still she survived. The mere mention of Fiona's name, of what she was and what she'd done, was enough to grow panic in Moira's soul.

When Fiona imprisoned her, she'd play with Moira because that's what her mother enjoyed. But the best way to hurt Moira was to take what she loved. To kill that which made her feel human. To destroy the only thing that gave her hope for a future.

Rafe.

No!

She trusted that Rafe had a plan—though Lord knew she had no fucking idea what it was. She had to get out of here and get to the church before it was too late. She had far more important matters to concern herself with than when—or if—Nicole delivered her to Fiona.

She didn't have her daggers. Wendy had stripped her of her jacket, with her other tools hidden inside. But she had her mind.

"So, Wendy left you to babysit me."

"It doesn't matter," Nicole said smugly. "As soon as the demon takes Grant's soul, she'll take Wendy's body—*and* her soul."

"That's your brilliant plan? Kill a cop, then your deal with the demon is to give her your sister?"

"Wendy thinks she and the demon have an understanding. She has no clue. Wendy will finally know what it feels like to be used and manipulated."

"Poor little baby sister Nicole. Manipulated by Wendy, manipulated by Fiona, a fucking doormat for anyone and every—"

"Shut up, Moira. I know what you're doing."

"What? I'm half naked and you have me tied up in a spirit trap waiting for a demon to come get me and deliver me to Fiona. You think I'm manipulating you? Are you that pathetic?"

Moira continued to work at her binds and wished Nicole wasn't so damn efficient with knots.

Nicole paced. "You don't know me."

"I know that you seduced Hank Santos to get information from the Sheriff's Department and to keep an eye on Lily when her mother couldn't. I know your mother was a bitch who killed two innocent people to get that damn chalice back. I—"

Nicole whipped around. "What? You—who—I knew it!"

"Knew that you're a sociopath? No, that would be your sister. Hell, it runs in the entire Donovan family."

"You're still a witch. You hide it well."

"No," she said, "I'm not a witch; I don't summon demons or cast spells. What I know comes from . . ." She looked pointedly at Nicole. "A *higher* authority."

Nicole burst out in laughter. "Oh! Oh!" She couldn't talk, hysterical that Moira would imply that God had something to do with her abilities.

At first, Moira was irritated at Nicole's reaction—but then realized she could take advantage of Nicole's funny bone. She wiggled around to sit up, her tied hands behind her. Tears ran down Nicole's face, blurring her vision. Moira worked her binds frantically.

"That's. So. *Wrong*." Nicole giggled and wiped her eyes.

Moira was getting pissed. "Excuse me? You summon demons and you don't believe in God?"

"Oh, I'm sure He's around . . . *somewhere*. But like He cares? And even if He does, what does that matter to me? The power I get from my contacts down under, it more than makes up for anything that *might* happen because some distant God is oh so sad."

Nicole stared at her, shaking her head, and added, "You can't believe that anyone in the Heavens cares about *you*. After everything you've done."

Moira inwardly grimaced, swallowing bile-filled guilt. She'd hurt so many people . . . how could anyone forgive her? How could anyone love her?

She closed her eyes and pictured Rafe, the man who had chiseled an opening into her hardened heart. The man who gave her the will to find a way to survive even after this battle was over. The man who gave her hope for tomorrow.

How could Rafe love her?

God has already forgiven you. But you haven't forgiven yourself.

Moira's eyes shot open. Father Philip's voice as clear as a bell—but he wasn't here. She'd heard him, but he wasn't here! He'd died, because he'd come to Santa Louisa to save her, to give them all a chance at fighting the evil Fiona had unleashed. She would not let him down.

She worked her restraints.

Nicole sighed. "I see what you're doing, Moira, and it's not going to work."

Nicole strode over to the spirit trap and reached down to tighten Moira's binds.

Moira leaned back then kicked Nicole in the chest and jumped up, her balance off because her hands were still bound. She twisted her arms as she stumbled back, the ropes falling to the floor.

"I don't want to kill you—"

Nicole ran toward her, an asthame in hand. The ceremonial dagger was sharp as Nicole had proven when she cut Moira's arm. Moira pivoted, but the tip of the dagger nicked her shoulder.

Moira leapt out of the way and ran over to her jacket in the far corner. She didn't have her daggers, but she had something up her sleeve—the devil's cuff, a thin lead chain usually used to protect the possessed from hurting themselves during an exorcism. Moira could use it in other ways.

Nicole hesitated, then laughed again, though a little less forcefully. "You think that can hurt *me*?"

Nicole began an incantation. Considering the spirit trap had been laid out, Moira didn't know what would be brought forth.

"Where is Fiona?" Moira asked. She knew she should just run. Run and steal a car and hightail it to Jackson's church. But she needed to know. "Where has she been hiding?"

"Just wait a few hours and I'll take you to see her, up close and personal."

The offer was tempting. Moira didn't know where Fiona was hiding out, but Nicole did, or would find out. If Moira could figure out a plan that would enable her to get close to Fiona, close enough to put an end to this insanity—

But now was not the time. Lives were at stake, and Rafe needed her.

"*Ominae ominae de—*" Nicole began a summoning spell.

Moira rushed Nicole, then faked right, spun around, the devil's cuff extended like a whip. The thin wire sliced Nicole deep in the arm.

The witch grabbed her bleeding wrist and cried out.

"Fiona!" Moira shouted, cracking the devil's cuff in the air. "Where is she?"

"Fuck *you*!"

Moira backhanded Nicole so hard she fell backward and hit the wall. She wanted to kill this woman. Nicole had stood there only feet from Father Philip, watched him suffer, watched him die. Father didn't deserve it, but Nicole did. Dammit, she deserved to die!

Moira couldn't do it. Dear Lord, she wanted to, but to kill Nicole Donovan in cold blood would make her no better than any of them.

Before she changed her mind, or Nicole recovered enough to work up a spell to stop her, Moira grabbed her things and ran out.

Rafe watched as Wendy led the way down the aisle. He glanced over his shoulder and saw Jackson round the corner behind the sanctuary. How was he going to get out of the church to finish sealing the trap?

Grant stared at Julie as she sauntered over to him, her red gown swirling around her obviously naked body. "Julie! Thank God you're okay."

"God?" Wendy sounded bemused. "How about thanking me?"

Grant ignored her and said, "Julie, are you okay?"

The demon in Julie's body approached Rafe with long, languid strides. He could stop this now by stabbing the body with his blessed dagger, but Julie would die and he didn't know if the demon Lust would be dragged back to Hell. Weaker demons, yes, but Lust? The Seven didn't play by the same rules.

But more important, the Order was forbidden to kill

people, whether possessed or evil. Only God should have the power to decide who lives and who dies. Their charge, their sacred duty, was to stop the spread of demons on Earth—not to kill those who summoned them. Perhaps it would be more expedient to slaughter witches like Fiona and Wendy, but it would relegate St. Michael's Order to the same Hell they were fighting.

Everyone deserved the chance to repent.

"Raphael," the demon hissed in a low voice. She touched his cheek, her manicured nail drawing blood. Rafe showed no reaction to the pain. "Someday," she added ominously.

The demon then approached the spirit trap and frowned.

"You put a barrier between me and mine," she said. "Remove it!"

Wendy strode down the aisle. Rafe stepped in front of her. "The demon can't pass through the sacred chrism."

Grant pleaded, "Julie, I'm so sorry about last night; I don't know what's wrong with me. I need help. Please forgive me."

Rafe! Julie cried in his head. *Help him! He's in pain.*

"You forget who I am!" Wendy said. "As it is above, it is below, I call on the power of Sammael for strength over my foes!"

The demon said to Grant, "Of course I forgive you. All you need to say is you want me."

Rafe shouted, "Grant, don't!" If he said yes, he was giving her his soul. The other men—they'd had sex with her. She'd asked and they agreed, not knowing what they were agreeing to. "Grant, say no!"

The demon turned to face Rafe and raised her hand,

palm out. She pushed her palm forward, and Rafe flew across the aisle until he was pinned against the wall.

Screaming, Nina ran forward to help Rafe. Pam stepped in her path and scowled. "You bitch. I suspected it was you who seduced George. You will pay for sleeping with mine!"

"You hypocritical slut!" Nina shouted.

Rafe shouted, "Nina, you need to find a hiding place. Now!"

She disregarded him and said to Pam, "You seduced him with your magic and spells. You forced him to marry you."

Pam laughed. "Hardly. George liked our sex games. But they were *our* games. He wasn't allowed to play with anyone else."

"You killed him!" Nina cried, stepping toward her.

"Nina!" Rafe called out, trying to pull himself off the wall. The demon's power was too strong. He began an exorcism, but it was difficult pulling the words out of his chest as the demon's force had him frozen several feet off the ground.

From the corner of his eye, Rafe saw Jeff moving toward the demon. Rafe tried to call him off, but the demon turned slowly to face him just as Jeff pulled his Taser out. Rafe saw that the demon wanted to kill him—and it would once Grant gave it the answer it wanted. But right now, the demon needed Grant's positive response. Killing his partner wouldn't help that cause.

Instead of breaking his neck, the demon used a pulse of energy to force Jeff to Taser himself. He fell to the floor in convulsions, hitting his head on the end of the pew. When he stopped convulsing, he wasn't moving.

Grant stared at him, stunned. The demon said, "He's fine. And he'll remain fine as long as you tell me you want me."

"Don't!" Rafe shouted with as much force as he could muster.

The demon ignored Rafe and knelt in front of the circle. She spoke in a seductive voice. "You're in pain, Grant. I can see it. I can help you. You love this body." She moved her hands down the front of the filmy dress. "You crave release. I see the sweat pouring from your body. Why deny yourself ecstasy? Why deny yourself anything? You want me. You need me."

"Julie—" Grant said, his voice low and pained, sweat soaking his clothes, his eyes glassy and intoxicated. Grant had been fighting his urges, the same primal urge that had pushed Kent Galion into raping and killing one woman and attacking another, but he was losing. Rafe tried to warn him, but his throat constricted and he could barely breathe.

"I want you!" Grant cried out.

Wendy laughed.

Nina pushed past Pam and screamed, "No, Grant!"

Without looking, the demon pushed Nina up against the wall next to Rafe.

"I guess this means I win." Wendy continued to laugh as she walked around the church. She approached the altar, mumbling something inaudible.

Then she smiled. "It's here. I knew it would be."

She picked up the chalice and approached Grant. She placed the Satanic bowl on the ground in front of him and held her hands up.

"Let the games begin!"

THIRTY-THREE

When Moira arrived at Grace Harvest she found the doors sealed shut. Not locked, but sealed by supernatural force. A faint, warm stench of demonic sulphur seeped from every crevice in the old church.

"Dammit!" She glanced up into the sky, the sunset tinting the blue with red, pink, orange, and purple. For a moment, just a split second, she was awestruck by the magnificent, serene beauty of the atmosphere above. So vibrant and hopeful. She said, "I could use some help down here."

She squeezed back her frustration and fear, and focused on the evil within these walls. Rafe was inside, and she wasn't going to let him die. Nor anyone else, for that matter. She ran around the entire perimeter, looking for a way in, and ran right into Jackson Moreno who was wet and muddy.

You took something from me last night. I want it back.

At Galion's house Moira had thought Wendy was talking about the chalice, but hadn't she mentioned the chalice separately? Jackson had been alone for several minutes while she and Rafe were breaking into Wendy's altar. What had he done?

"Jackson—" But she stopped herself. Now wasn't the time.

"They sealed the doors. I broke a window in the basement."

"I need to get in that way. Show me."

"I haven't finished the reverse trap—"

"Show me the way, then finish. They're in trouble. Nicole is double-crossing her sister. If the demon succeeds in killing Grant, everyone in there dies. I have to stop it." Not to mention that the demon Lust would be free—again.

Jackson led her around to the back of the church to the narrow basement window. "Careful," he said. "I tried to push the glass away, but it's all over the basement floor. It's a six-foot drop."

"Finish the trap, Jackson," she said. "And don't come back in."

"But—"

"It's too dangerous, and I can't worry about innocents."

"Nina Hardwick is inside. She arrived right before Wendy. Told Rafe something about Wendy and mental institutions and killing her mother—I don't have the details."

That didn't help Moira now. She started through the window on her stomach, then realized she was going in unarmed. Stupid! She had to think, be smart. Her fear for Rafe and the others had propelled her to act without planning.

She pulled herself back out and called out to Jackson as he poured a thick line of rock salt along the base of the church.

"Do you have an iron dagger?"

He looked sheepish. "Rafe told me to get my weapons—they're in the old sanctuary behind the altar.

But the only way you can get to the room is through a door on the altar. That's where I put the kiln as well to melt the chalice—it's on, but it hasn't had time to heat to the required temperature."

"Is the sanctuary locked?"

"No, but the door is one of the wood panels and the handle is camouflaged. On the left side, facing the altar."

"I'll take my chances." She had her jacket back, but that wouldn't do her much good if Wendy started zapping her with magical jolts.

She slid back through the window. Like Jackson, she had gotten wet sliding along the muddy grass outside, but the basement itself was dry. A dim bulb in the middle of the small room showed that this was used for storage—several pews, extra chairs, Christmas and Easter decorations. It certainly wasn't a full basement, as the church above was at least ten times bigger than this room.

She found the door Jackson had indicated and went up the narrow stairs. As she ascended, she smelled the sulphur of Hell, stronger here than outside. Dark energy slithered over her skin, making her hair rise. She forced her heart rate to slow, focused on her senses. Where was everyone? If they were going with the plan, then Grant should be in a spirit trap on the altar.

Her hand began to throb where yesterday Nadine had clawed the healing wound from her battle with the demon Envy. Moira continued up the stairs, hearing voices now. It was an incantation, Wendy and Pam reciting a vaguely familiar spell. It wasn't exactly a summoning ritual, but . . .

She took a chance and skirted around the edge of the

back of the altar, trying to see what was happening. Wendy, Pam, and Julie—or rather the demon possessing Julie—were standing around Grant, who was protected by the reverse spirit trap. What were they doing? She glanced down: the salt had been disturbed, but the sacred oil was doing its job for the moment, soaking through the red carpet in a wide circle.

Grant was writhing in pain, his body twisting in the seat. He was trying to talk, but couldn't. Trying futilely to break his bonds.

She looked around the unlit church for Rafe. Thirty rows of twenty-foot-long oak pews framed either side of a wide aisle. The rapidly descending darkness made it more difficult to see, except where swatches of light were coming in from the streetlights.

Her eyes narrowed when she saw Rafe suspended against the far wall. Nina was pinned beside him.

He appeared unharmed, anger and concern clouding his expression. She wanted to get him down but couldn't yet risk exposing her presence.

The group of witches in front of her was only ten feet from the door to the sanctuary. The altar table had been moved to the side so that the reverse trap could be laid out to protect Grant. There was nothing for her to hide behind, nothing to shield her from being seen. But she couldn't wait for a distraction; Grant might not live long enough.

As she watched, Julie's body collapsed. Her body lay motionless in front of Grant, outside the circle. A revolting stench filled the church—fouler than anything Moira had smelled before. She looked everywhere, at Wendy and Pam, Rafe and Nina—who had the demon entered? Dammit, where was it?

Moira's heart skipped a beat when she saw the chalice was on the floor in front of Grant. Wendy stared at it, excitement brightening her face.

"Pamela! It worked!"

Worked? What the— Moira bit back a scream. The glass ball at the top of the chalice had turned dark gray and smoky. Then the smoke began to leach from the glass into the cup below. It flowed out of the cup and filled the space within the trap.

Wendy had used the chalice as a portal—not to Hell, but into the trap—in order to fulfill the agreement she'd made with Lust for Grant's soul. Now the demon was contained in the spirit trap, but so was Grant.

While Wendy was enraptured by the transforming demon, Moira ran across the altar, searching for the door. No, no, no—shit!

"Wendy!" Pam shouted. "It's O'Donnell!"

Wendy first glanced behind her toward Rafe, not knowing where Moira was. Moira sprung the latch and jumped inside the sanctuary. It was a long, narrow room filled with boxes, crosses, some chairs, and several remnants from the previous church, including an old baptismal font. She found a whole array of weapons on the shelf next to the door and grabbed two knives similar to her own. Now wasn't the time to try something new.

She also saw a Glock and briefly wondered whether it was Grant Nelson's. She grabbed that, too, and stuffed it in her pocket.

The sanctuary shook violently. Supplies crashed down around her and she fled.

Wendy grabbed her as soon as she emerged, but Moira was prepared. She elbowed Wendy, then spun around and kicked her in the stomach, propelling herself with her momentum until she was several feet out of Wendy's reach.

Grant cried out in pained surprise, and Moira glanced at the trap. She needed to get him out of there, but the demon was swirling around, beginning to take form.

Pam stood outside the circle, staring at the darkly glowing clouds. A deep rumbling built within the church, growing louder until it sounded like a thousand bats in flight. The thick mist took shape and solidified into the form of a stunning woman.

"Wendy—what's happening?" Pam asked.

Wendy stared at the demon, an odd smile on her face. "We did it!"

"Did what?" Moira shouted. "You don't understand what this thing is!" Moira saw the demon beneath the skin; in its shiny eyes she saw the fires of Hell.

Wendy looked almost giddy. "Yes! I do! I gave the demon life! It doesn't need a human body anymore."

Moira wanted to smack the witch. "You did nothing! That's what it is—that is the demon Lust!"

Wendy turned to her, eyes narrow. "You're jealous because I have far more power than you and your pathetic mother!"

Pam was staring, unable to take her eyes away from the beautiful creature walking slowly around the circle.

The demon stopped and looked at Pam, who was only a couple of feet from the edge. In a seductive voice, she asked, "Are you scared of me?"

Pam said nothing.

"Pamela, tell me the truth, do I scare you?"

Obviously terrified, Pam shook her head *no*.

The demon raised her elegant hands, palms up and out, and released a wave of unseen energy that pushed Pam across the church with such force that her body slammed the building's far corner, a hundred feet away, causing the plaster to crack. Pam's body hung there for just a second, embedded in the wall, before it dropped unmoving to the floor.

Wendy stared, wide-eyed and stunned.

Moira assessed the situation. Wendy wasn't surprised at the demon taking corporeal form, but she hadn't expected the demon to kill Pam. Why had she thought they were safe?

Moira remembered Nicole's comments about paying back her sister. Being used and manipulated. She pushed that with Wendy.

"Nicole betrayed you," Moira told her, knife out. "She's safe from this demon. She was in the protective circle two weeks ago when Lust was summoned. Nicole wants you dead. You have to help stop this insanity!"

Wendy laughed, her eyes wild. "I'm not falling for your tricks. That's an old one, divide and conquer."

Moira glanced over to where Rafe had been trapped against the wall—but he was gone. Where was he? Then she caught a glimpse of movement, low, between the pews.

She had to neutralize Wendy or she could do nothing to help Grant. She glanced over and saw that the demon was looking at Grant with pure lust—lust to kill.

"You're mine, darling," it said to him.

"Julie," Grant moaned. "Where's Julie?"

The demon grew frustrated. "I'm far more beautiful. Far more powerful than *her*."

Lust sounded jealous. Did Lust need Grant to want her? Craig Monroe, George Erickson—they had acted on their lust, and she'd stolen their souls.

But how had the demon changed the game? It was trapped—Moira shot a glance to the chalice in front of Grant. The demon could use the portal to possess any of them, or escape the trap. And if the demon succeeded in killing Grant, it would be freed.

Keep fighting, Grant. It'll buy us time.

The demon grabbed him by the throat and kissed him as her body slowly moved up and down in a seductive lap dance. Its shimmering golden hair moved as if on its own. A scream from deep in Grant's chest sent chills up Moira's spine.

Grant turned his head away and the demon growled. It turned toward Julie's body and made the unconscious woman stand.

"You want *her*? This weak vessel? This *human*? You are a pathetic man."

Moira couldn't let Julie die the way Pam just had. She began an exorcism that Rafe had been teaching her—the one he'd used in Santa Louisa on the demon Envy. It hadn't stopped Envy, but it had slowed it down. She prayed it would work on Lust.

"Avertet mala inimicis meis in veritate tua—"

At the sound of her voice, the demon turned to her with a scowl. "It is you. You are a problem."

She felt her body rise from the floor. She shouted, *"Avertet mala inimicis meis in veritate tua disperde illos! Voluntarie sacrificabo tibi confitebor nomini tuo Domine quoniam bonum!"*

Fury twisted Lust's expression as Moira broke the

demon's hold on her, just for a moment. But that was enough time to pull the holy water from her pocket and squirt it at the demon.

Steam rose from its skin where the droplets of blessed water hit. Lust hissed in annoyance more than agony. From past experience, Moira knew it wouldn't stop the demon, but anything holy and pure would weaken it. With its full power, she'd never be able to stop it.

She glanced around the church but didn't see Rafe or Nina. Jeff Johnston had regained consciousness and had crawled weakly to hide between the pews.

The demon's voice had Moira focusing on the danger at hand. It said to Grant, "You are mine. I broke the spell; I will break you all!" Lust sat on his lap.

What did Lust mean about the spell being broken? The demon had to be talking about the ritual where Wendy and Pam sent it into the chalice so it could breach the reverse spirit trap.

She whirled around and shouted to Wendy, "Who gave you that ritual? Who taught you how to use the chalice to violate the trap?"

Wendy had regained her feet after Moira knocked her down. She was holding her stomach, and Moira suspected she'd cracked a rib.

"Dammit, Wendy! This is important or you're going to die."

"I'm not going to die!"

"Who gave you the fucking spell?"

Wendy refused to answer, but her eyes flickered toward the trap. Dammit, the demon had used the witch and Wendy hadn't even suspected it.

But her sister Nicole had.

Moira had no idea how they were going to trap the demon, but she knew she had to get that chalice—the portal—out of the trap or the demon would be able to move freely back and forth. Out of the trap, it would be unstoppable, but its lust for Grant—its craving for his soul—would keep the damned creature occupied. And she also needed to get Grant out of harm's way before Lust finished with him.

Wendy rushed toward her as she moved to the trap. At the same time, from the corner of her eye she saw Rafe, an odd look on his face, jump up from behind the first pew and run up the aisle, leaping up the five stairs to the altar with one stride.

No! No! She pictured the demon throwing him across the church, just as had happened to Peter, her first love. The lover she'd killed when a demon possessed her seven years ago. She would not lose Rafe that way. She wouldn't lose Rafe!

But he didn't even acknowledge or look at her. He was focused solely on Grant. What was wrong with him?

In Moira's hesitation, Wendy hit her hard in the lower back. The excruciating pain brought her to her knees.

"I will not let you ruin this for me!"

"The demon"—Moira took a deep breath, blinking back tears while pushing the pain from intolerable to barely manageable—"will kill you."

"You know nothing about the underworld!"

"I know more than you."

Moira pulled the gun from her waistband and rolled over. Wendy held a knife above her chest. Moira lowered the barrel and shot Wendy in first one calf, then the other. She didn't want to kill anyone, but she had to get Wendy out of the picture.

Wendy collapsed with a scream, a hand on each calf. One of the bullets had skimmed her, but the other went in deep.

"You fucking bitch!"

The gunfire halted Rafe just as he was about to foolishly leap into the circle. He looked at Moira, as if seeing her for the first time.

"Moira!"

Whatever had gotten into him was gone. Thank God. She didn't have time to ask him what his plan had been, because it simply couldn't have been smart. Not if it involved rushing a demon. Moira raced to his side. "Are you okay? What were you doing?"

He said, "Julie took— I'll explain later, okay?" He glanced at the demon who was sliding up and down Grant's agonized body. "Did you see how the demon used the chalice?"

"Hell, yeah. We need to melt it immediately. We can't use it as a trap. I have no idea how to contain the demon and it broke the spell Wendy had bound it with."

"Then what are we going to trap the demon with?"

Anything holy and pure would slow it down.

Suddenly, Moira had a thought. "I know. The baptismal font."

"This isn't a Catholic church."

"But it *was*. Jackson is one of us; he's going to keep tradition. In fact, Jackson kept everything in the original church, except the crucifix. The font has a cover. It's in the sanctuary. Do you have holy water?"

"About a quart."

"I need it."

He handed her a large water bottle. "What's your plan?"

"I'm kind of making it up as I go along. Do you have
a better idea?"

"No." Rafe kissed her quickly. "Be careful."

"You, too."

But she wasn't taking any chances. She took her dagger and cut her arm an inch, wincing at the sting of the
blade as it reopened the wound Nicole had inflicted.

He stared at her. "What are you doing?"

"Rico wanted my blood, so there must be something
to it—like when we slowed down the demon Envy." She
rubbed her blood on Rafe's arm. "Sorry, this is kinda
sick, but I can't think of anything else."

A scream from the spirit trap had them jumping. Julie
was regaining consciousness, and slowly rose from the
ground.

"No!" Rafe shouted. "Julie, what are you doing?"

Moira ran to the sanctuary. The font was portable,
but damn heavy. She was surprised to find Nina hiding
in the corner.

"Nina!"

"Rafe told me to hide in here."

"I need your help moving this."

"Why?"

"Questions later."

Together, they slid the baptismal font along the floor.
When they reached the doorway, Moira told her, "Now,
go back to hiding."

"What are you doing?"

"I'm going to try and trap that demon in here. But I
have to force it out of its corporeal form to do it." She
bit her lip and glanced over at the spirit trap. Julie was
stumbling, much like Nadine had after the demon left

her body. Rafe was trying to help Julie, but she was shaking her head and fighting him.

In the trap, Lust was touching Grant. His face, his hair, his chest. One hand went down to his erect penis and squeezed until Grant screamed.

The chalice was next to Grant. Moira needed to get it out, but to do so she had to trick the demon.

She swiped her finger over her still-bleeding cut and made the sign of the cross on Nina's forehead.

"I'm Jewish," Nina said.

"Good."

"But I don't believe that—"

"I don't care. Do you believe in God?"

"Of course, but—"

"Do you believe in demons?"

Nina frowned, glancing over at the trap. "Today I do."

"Then push this font directly under the cross, take off the lid, and pour this holy water into the bowl." She handed Nina Rafe's container of holy water. "Then hide."

"You'll save George's soul, right?" she asked quietly.

That had been the last thing on Moira's mind but she remembered her promise. "I'll try."

Rafe watched as Julie's astral self fully reclaimed her body. She stumbled for a moment, weak on all accounts. When the demon first touched Grant, Julie had surprised Rafe and took over his consciousness. He'd fought her the entire time she had control, but she'd panicked. Now, she had little strength left.

"Julie!" he yelled. "Get out of there! Please!"

Julie ignored him. She staggered into the circle and

grabbed the demon by its neck, trying to pull it off Grant's body. "Leave him! Take my soul instead!"

Julie had no strength to move the demon. Lust slowly, sensually, rose from Grant's trembling body and turned to face the witch, bemused.

"You," it said. "Where were you?"

Julie took a step aside, not answering the demon, looking only at Grant.

To distract the demon from Julie, Rafe crossed himself and began the Lord's Prayer.

The demon growled, then said, "Oh, you again."

Rafe felt his body twist as the demon pushed him with its will. He shouted a prayer he'd never heard before. It came from deep in his memory, a place he couldn't access when he wanted to, a place that opened for him only when he wasn't trying.

He didn't dwell long on the situation; it had disturbed him since the Seven Deadly Sins had been released in Santa Louisa. Now, however, he used the force of the prayer he barely understood to stop the demon from hurling him across the church the way it had Pamela Erickson. His feet came back to the floor and he crouched, bracing for another attack.

But it didn't come. The demon saw that Julie was untying Grant's restraints and it grabbed her with hands that turned into talons. She screamed as two marks burned her flesh.

"You displease me. You trapped me here, and now you won't give me my due!"

Rafe leapt into the spirit trap and kicked the demon in the stomach. It didn't loosen its hold on Julie. Rafe jumped out again and started the exorcism. The demon

hissed, throwing Julie to the ground. It kept rubbing it
arm as if something burned. Rafe glanced down. /
smear of blood—Moira's blood—stained the demon'
forearm.

Grant slowly rose from his chair, shaky and weak
"Leave me alone!" Grant cried at the demon. "I'm no
yours!"

The enraged demon howled and stepped towar
Grant.

Moira leapt into the circle and wrapped her cut arm
around the demon's neck.

The demon became paralyzed. Its eyes bulged an
then it lost shape and form, turning from a woman to
snake to a deformed centaur-like creature. Moira hel
on even though Rafe saw she was in agony, her grip o
the demon slipping. The demon tried to shake her of
but Moira clung, her blood forcing the demon back t
its noncorporeal form.

The demon turned to a thick black cloud and Moir
fell to the ground.

Rafe rushed to help her, but Moira screamed, "Th
exorcism! Keep going!"

He did, stopping just short of the demon trap. The an
cient words rolled off his tongue though he didn't kno
exactly what he was saying—deep inside he knew, but a
soon as he concentrated, all meaning was lost. He let th
words flow from his lips without conscious thought, a
if he were speaking in tongues.

Grant was carrying Julie from the trap and Moir
grabbed the chalice. "The kiln!" Rafe told her.

She wasn't listening. She had begun her own exorcism
She was trying to draw out George Erickson's soul fror
the demon.

"Moira, stop!"

"I have to, Rafe! I promised!"

Rafe wouldn't let her. The danger was too great. And the only thing Rico had commanded him during their conversation was to keep Moira alive.

"Or the world is over as we know it."

He stepped into the circle and commanded the demon, "By the power of St. Michael's sword, a faithful servant to the Lord, release the souls you stole!"

The demon took partial form, the head of a snake, the body of smoke, and hissed in his ear, "Take them *allllllll.*"

An inhuman screech had Rafe on his knees, his eardrums near bursting. Dozens of spirits whipped around him, trying to get inside, the demon hurling the souls at him one by one, pummeling him with the pain of their collective suffering.

Rafe couldn't think; he could scarcely breathe. The assault continued and he held up his hands to ward off the attack. He knew the exorcism, but he couldn't get any words out.

Moira screamed his name. The snake turned to her and she held up the chalice, then turned as if to leave.

"Noooo," the snake hissed and turned again into the smoky mist. It wrapped around Moira, then dove into the chalice, filling it. Just as Moira had hoped. The chalice was its escape route from the trap—she'd nabbed the demon's portal.

Moira ran from the trap to the baptismal font, hoping—praying—this would work. She had to get the demon to the font before it escaped the chalice. She glanced back at Rafe, who was on his knees, battling spirits she couldn't see but felt with every cell in her body. These weren't ghosts—they were raw spirits, human souls, released from bondage. The good, the bad, and the downright evil.

"What's happening?" Nina cried. "Is that George?"

"It's all the souls the demon stole!" Moira had to help Rafe. Tears streamed down her face as she knew exactly what he was facing, trying to keep his own soul intact as the spirits fought to get inside. Why had he done it? Why had he risked himself? The demon had been busy this week—or were these all the souls who'd died since it was released from Hell two weeks ago? How many had died that they didn't know about?

Moira placed the base of the chalice in the baptismal font. The holy water steamed, and the chalice became so hot it burned Moira's hands. At this rate, the water would dissipate in minutes! What else could she do?

She grabbed the small vial of holy water from her pocket. It was nearly gone. She poured it over the glass. It steamed, and the ground shook beneath her. She and Nina held on to the edge of the font to keep from falling over.

The lid wouldn't fit over the font with the chalice inside. "Nina—go to the sanctuary and look for bottles of holy water."

"How will I know?"

"Jackson said he put his supplies in there; he has to have some!"

The ground shaking, Nina did as Moira commanded.

Moira's cut had started to clot. She squeezed her skin and drew out more blood, which she smeared on the top of the glass ball. The shaking stopped. She didn't know what to believe, but right now she didn't care—saving

Rafe was the only thing that mattered. She'd figure everything else out later.

The spirits had beaten Rafe into a fetal ball. He was praying fervently, but Moira couldn't hear him over a rumble she couldn't identify.

She began her own exorcism and saw from the corner of her eye Jackson run into the church. "The doors are open," he said.

"Help me!" she cried.

"What's happening?"

"They're souls trying to possess Rafe. Give them last rites."

"I'm not—"

"Are you a man of God or not? What do you do when someone dies? Do it!"

Jackson raised his hands and began a prayer.

"The Lord is my shepherd, I shall not be in want. He makes me lie down in green pastures, he leads me beside quiet waters, he restores my soul."

Good enough, Moira thought as she stepped forward.

"What are you doing?" Jackson asked.

"Keep praying, dammit!"

She feared opening her senses would give the souls a way to enter her body, but she needed to discern how many they were dealing with. As Jackson prayed, Rafe gained strength. He rose to his knees. She was about to step into the trap when he ordered, "Stand back, Moira!"

She hesitated, not wanting to obey, but she had to trust Rafe.

Rafe rose from the floor. He saw the souls moving around him, confused, suffering, none of them knowing where to go. None were pure, but many had color, some light, some dark. Some black as night.

"Dear Lord, help me help them," he whispered in Aramaic.

The ground violently shook. Moira almost ran into the trap again, but Rafe couldn't risk it, so he put up his hand to ward her off. She stumbled back as if hit, but he barely noticed. One by one, each soul spun away as he spoke, finally disappearing. He didn't know where they were going, but they were gone from here. Rafe had opened a gateway to the astral plane, where all souls go on their way to Heaven or Hell.

Their passage through him to reach the astral plane weakened him. Pain tore at his mind, pain so great that he thought he would die. As they pushed through him, they deposited their shackles in his mind, leaving with him their last wish. He couldn't do this. He was going to die. And still they came through him and departed, a never-ending line of souls searching for peace.

A crash sounded outside the trap, though it sounded far, far away. Rafe forced his eyes open, and through blurred vision saw that Wendy had knocked over the baptismal font. The chalice crashed to the ground, the glass ball splitting clean in half.

Moira ran toward the font. The demon rose from the broken glass.

"Moira!" Rafe cried out, sounding as though he were far down a tunnel.

Rafe flexed his mind—he couldn't explain it any other way—and pushed every soul through to the astral plane. As he crawled from the spirit trap, he said the closing prayer, sealing the split between their world and the spirit world.

Jackson helped him up. "What the hell was that?"

Rafe shook his head and stumbled toward Moira as she righted the font.

The demon grew into a monstrous-sized creature. Wendy laughed hysterically as she crawled away, insane or in shock. The demon took its claws and picked her up, squeezing her body until Rafe heard her back break.

Nina rushed from the sanctuary with two bottles of holy water. She screamed at the sight of the huge demon that continued to grow.

Rafe ordered Jackson, "Grab the chalice! Melt it! I'll distract the demon."

Jackson didn't argue. Rafe, still weak from his ordeal with the spirits, stumbled over to Moira's side.

She stared at the creature. "What's Plan B?" she asked with a nervous laugh.

"I didn't know we had a Plan A," Rafe countered. He took her arm; she was bleeding profusely. "You're losing blood."

"I might have cut too deep."

"Dammit, Moira." He ripped off his shirt and wrapped it around Moira's arm.

"No—" she said, pulling the shirt off.

"I'm not letting you bleed to death!"

"We have a bigger problem here," she said. She stared at his black shirt as her blood darkened the fabric. "Take the shirt—hit the demon with it."

Rafe unwrapped the shirt, wet with Moira's blood, and rushed the demon. Its claws reached for him, and he dodged.

Moira ran in the other direction to distract the creature. She shouted an exorcism and the demon laughed, a low, sick rumble that terrified Rafe. The demon Envy was bad; this demon seemed to have even more power. A thought dawned on him: all those souls—what if the Seven grew more powerful the longer they were on Earth? A pit formed in his stomach. If they got any stronger, they'd never defeat all of them.

He slapped the demon with the bloody shirt. It hit and the demon cried out as if shot, shrinking away from Rafe. He slapped it again and again. The demon bellowed and reached out for Jackson, who had picked up the chalice.

Nina grabbed one of the bottles of holy water, took off the cap, and threw it at the demon. The demon flinched, but it was enough time for Jackson to get into the sanctuary with the chalice, pulling Nina with him.

Hurry up, Pastor! Rafe rushed toward the demon, and it grabbed him with its huge hands.

"You will suffer, Raphael. You will know the truth and you will die forever!"

Moira watched in horror as Rafe was lifted off the ground by the demon, who'd grown to over twelve feet tall with snakes in its hair and black wings growing out of its back. Its clawlike hands were more like talons on a bird. It moved as if walking on air, the lower body still smoke, as if it couldn't completely take shape. If this was its weakened state, they were as good as dead.

She ran to the two perfect halves of the glass ball. She picked them up and dropped them into the baptismal font. The demon flinched. This was its connection to the underworld. Wendy's spell had bound it somehow to the chalice, and because it couldn't fulfill its mission—Grant's soul was still intact—it wasn't completely free. Even though it had gained power, it was still tethered to the chalice.

Nina had dropped the other bottle of holy water. Moira grabbed it and poured the water into the font. The demon cried out and dropped Rafe.

Suddenly, the room became hot. So hot Moira felt her skin burn.

Rafe ran over and grabbed her. "Run!"

They ran into the sanctuary and Jackson closed the door. The heat in there was nearly unbearable, the oxygen being depleted.

The demon thundered and screamed shrilly. They covered their ears with their hands. It swirled around the church like a tornado, the eye drawing it back into the glass now sitting in the baptismal font.

And then, as fast as the air had heated, it cooled. The demon was gone, trapped in the font.

They didn't move for several minutes.

Jackson opened the kiln. Inside, the fire had gone out. The chalice had melted completely into the mold. With gloved hands, he removed it.

He'd picked an appropriate mold. The chalice had become a cross.

THIRTY-FOUR

"What happened to the glass ball from the chalice?" Jackson asked.

"It's in the baptismal font," Moira said, her voice fading as she leaned against Rafe. He wrapped his arm around her. "Trapped in something pure and innocent. We'll have to be careful transporting it—I don't know how secure it is."

Rafe frowned as he felt Moira's arm, slick with blood. "Moira—you're still bleeding." There was only dim light in the sanctuary. "Dear God, you're covered in blood."

"You're exaggerating." Her voice was so weak, it pained him to listen to her. "Just take me home."

"You need stitches." Rafe laid Moira down on the floor, then ordered Jackson, "I need towels—bandages—anything."

"My bag," Moira said. "In the corner."

Jackson retrieved her satchel and Rafe looked through it. He found a water bottle. "Holy water?"

"Drinking water," she said.

"It'll clean you up."

"It looks worse than it is," she said, but closed her eyes.

Rafe took a soft cloth and doused it in water, then

gently wiped her arms. She was so pale. "Moira—don't do that again."

"I don't remember half of it."

But Rafe did. He remembered how she'd cut her arm and bled on the demon. How she'd smeared blood on him, on Nina, protecting everyone she could. And she would have continued to do it until she bled dry. The risk to her far greater than he'd realized—until now.

She had two deep cuts, both on her left arm. He bandaged them—she'd scar, no doubt. He kissed her forearm. "You really should get stitches."

"I don't want to go to the hospital."

"I have a good first-aid kit in the house," Jackson said. "I'll get it." He left the sanctuary. Nina walked out with him.

Alone at last, Rafe wanted to simply hold Moira. For just a moment, to put the night behind them. Moira started to get up, but Rafe pulled her down. "You need to rest."

"I need to make sure the font is as secure as it can be." She looked up at him, her expression worn and worried. "What happened with those spirits? You were under attack—I didn't know what to do." She reached for him and he took her hand and kissed it repeatedly.

"I'm okay." He wasn't, the last wishes of each soul weighing heavily on his heart. The guilt, the pain, the fear. He hoped they'd found peace on the other side, but he didn't know any of their fates.

"Rafe, what really happened?"

"It went so fast. I tried to draw out the soul of George Erickson alone, but the demon threw all of them at me. Hundreds."

"Hundreds?"

"It felt that way—I don't know how many. They wanted me to help them . . ." His voice trailed off.

Moira took his hand and kissed it. "And you did."

"I don't know."

"How did you send them to the afterlife?"

Rafe hesitated, and this time Moira brought his hand to her lips. "It was another one of those memories," he said. "I wonder, have I been speaking in tongues? So rare, but there's nothing else to explain how I know the right exorcism at the right time. The languages—I'm okay with languages, but nothing like Anthony. Yet I spoke Aramaic like it was my native tongue, and I did not know what I was saying. I understood it in one way, but I wouldn't be able to translate. I had control—it wasn't a possession—but in some ways it happened on its own. I could stop it—but I couldn't direct it." He took a deep breath, then let it slowly out. "I'm not making sense."

"You're making about as much sense as my visions—especially what I saw yesterday."

"I—" He hesitated. There was so much he wanted to tell her, but right now wasn't the time. He couldn't explain exactly what happened with Julie Schroeder, or how he fought her spirit after she took over his body. He couldn't explain even how he got himself off the wall when the demon had him pinned. It was with another prayer, and not for the first time he was terrified. Of the unknown, of not knowing whether his words came from above . . . or below.

"Rafe?"

"I thank God that you're alive," he said, looking deep into Moira's eyes. "That we're alive."

"Me, too." She touched him again, as if to confirm his words.

He kissed her again, lightly, on her lips, her chin, her neck, back to her lips. He murmured, "My love," before he realized he'd spoken.

"Where's Nicole—?" he asked.

"Probably long gone. She wanted Wendy dead. I wonder how much of what happened tonight was partly Nicole's doing." Moira slowly rose to her feet.

"Don't—"

"I have to. The font, Grant—there are going to be serious consequences. We'd better call Skye and clue her in."

Rafe steadied Moira as they walked out of the sanctuary.

Jackson's church was filthy, the pews half destroyed, the altar smashed. The only thing intact was the cross hanging from the ceiling.

Rafe and Moira approached the baptismal font cautiously. The glass had fused together and turned black. Moira's heart quickened. "It's in there."

"But the chalice—"

"No—the demon is trapped in that glass ball."

Jackson and Nina walked back in. "Jackson," Moira said, "can you get that iron box you had for the chalice?"

"It's in the sanctuary," he said as he handed Nina the first-aid kit.

Teary-eyed, Nina looked from Moira to Rafe. "Thank you seems trite."

"Don't," Moira said. "Thank you for your help."

"Is—are—well, after everything I hate to ask, but . . ."

Rafe took Nina's hand. "George's last wish was for

me to tell you he loved you and he'll be watching to make sure you're happy."

Moira's head whipped around to Rafe. She stared at him, eyes questioning.

Rafe said quietly, "When the souls left, I had a sense of their final thoughts."

Nina said, "Grant, Jeff, and Julie are on the portico outside. Jackson called an ambulance. I don't think Julie is going to make it."

Jackson returned with the iron box. Moira found Rafe's shirt stained with her blood. It was still damp. She wrapped it around the glass ball and carefully placed it in the box, leaving the shirt inside with it. Jackson added the melted chalice, then closed and locked it.

"Put it in your vault until Rico can retrieve it," Moira said.

"Nina?" Jackson asked. "Could I ask you to get the doors for me?"

Nina handed Rafe the first-aid kit and left with Jackson, while Rafe and Moira went to the portico in the front of the church.

Grant was sitting on the ground, his back against the stucco, holding Julie in his arms. Tears streamed silently down his face. Jeff sat several feet away, his head between his knees. The neck of his shirt was covered in blood, and he had a nasty welt on the side of his face from where he'd hit the pew. But being unconscious probably saved his life.

"Where's the ambulance?" Grant asked. "I called and called and it's not here. She needs help."

Julie was pale, her aura nearly gone. She was dying.

Moira knelt next to them. "You saved him, Julie. You helped save all of us."

Grant pushed Moira. "Leave her alone!"

Julie's eyes fluttered open. "Grant—" She swallowed. "Please."

"Don't talk," Grant told her.

Julie touched his face with one shaky hand, but said to Moira, "Thank you. I understand better now—what you said this morning at the hotel. I—I'm so sorry for the pain I've caused. What I did was so wrong."

Moira wished she could do something. "Rafe—can you help her?" Moira pleaded.

Rafe said, "I can give Julie last rites."

Moira kissed Julie's hand, then stood and gave Rafe some room. She walked to the edge of the portico and wiped away tears.

Rafe knelt next to Julie. "The ambulance will be here—I hear it."

Julie shook her head. "I—there's a lot broken inside."

Rafe anointed her head with oil and prayed.

"No! She's not going to die! God, no!" Grant cried, holding Julie close.

"Grant—" Julie coughed. "It's okay."

"No, we'll make this work. I promise. I love you, Julie. I love you! I'm so sorry for everything—please, let me make it up to you. Let me—"

"Shh. Please, Grant. I'm dying. I want to do one thing to help someone."

"I can't let you die."

Julie swallowed; her voice was weak. "I have a favor."

"Anything."

"There's a girl at the morgue. She's been there for years. They don't know who she is—her name is Amy Carney. Find her family; let them bury her. Her family doesn't know what happened to her, and the morgue doesn't know who she is. She just wants them to know what happened."

Grant's tears fell on Julie's chest. He held her close. "Julie," he sobbed.

Rafe finished the last rites, then took her hand. "Rest in peace, Julie. God is a forgiving God."

"I hope so," she said, a hint of fear in her eyes. She coughed and looked at Rafe, her eyes unfocused. "Thank you for letting me share your body. I explained everything to Grant; you and Moira should not have any problems." She coughed again. "Come closer."

Her voice was so faint he nearly missed it. He leaned over, his ear to her mouth. She whispered, "I wasn't the only one in there."

Moira slipped away to the far side of the church when she saw the ambulance pull into the parking lot. Cops would soon follow, and she wasn't confident she wouldn't be spending the night in jail. All she really wanted to do was go home.

But she didn't have a home. It hurt, an empty, hollow pit in the center of her chest. When she told Rafe she wanted to go home, she'd simply meant go with him anywhere. *Away*. Because she didn't have a place to call her own. She didn't have much of anything that couldn't fit in her backpack.

Rafe had changed all that. She'd found a place with him that wasn't a place at all, but a person. She'd found the one person on earth who wouldn't judge her, doubt her, or use her. The one person who could love her unconditionally.

Her heart skipped a beat. Love hadn't been good to

er. She didn't know if she could do it again. Whether
he could survive losing another part of herself.

She'd never thought about, never looked for, a love
ke the one she'd had with Peter. He had saved her,
ved her, cared for her. Yet—she'd been young. Naïve.
n many ways, foolish. But she had loved deeply. When
'eter died violently at her hands, she no longer wanted
o live. And had she been truly alive ever since? Or had
he merely survived?

Rafe wasn't Peter. What she felt for Rafe wasn't the
ure, innocent love she'd had with Peter. It was deeper,
ar more terrifying because of its intensity. She couldn't
dmit to these feelings, because she feared they would be
sed against her by her enemies. If Fiona knew . . . she
ould use Rafe against Moira. Another tool in her
nother's arsenal of weapons—the man she loved.

A woeful moan escaped her throat and she swallowed
. It was her secret for now. She had to keep it buried
eep. To protect herself. To protect Rafe.

Moira saw Jackson and Nina go into his house. She
ollowed, and caught up with them before he closed the
oor.

"Come in."

"The paramedics are here. The police are soon to fol-
w. We need to be on the same page."

Nina said, "I'll help take care of any problems. I work
or the Board of Supervisors—it might help."

"Skye originally told Grant she was investigating a
ult," Moira reminded Nina.

Nina nodded. "Grant said something about drugs. I'll
ake sure he's with us on this. Wendy and Pam sure
cted like they were high."

"One little thing—I shot Wendy in the leg wit Grant's gun."

"Oh."

"I'm not a legal resident. And, um," Moira looke sheepish, "I might be in the system for stealing car But," she added quickly, "I always left them undamage and with money for gas."

"Let's see if we can keep your name out of it alto gether, okay?"

Nina left, and Jackson took the first-aid kit fro Moira and took out the supplies.

"Let's get you fixed up here, since you're being stul born about the hospital," he said.

Moira let him clean her wound with antibacteri spray and seal it with medical glue before rebandagin it. She didn't know how to bring up the subject she" wanted to discuss, but finally said, "Jackson, did yo take something from Wendy's house?"

He repacked the first-aid kit. "Why?"

"Wendy thought I took something other than th chalice. I don't know what, but you were alone for least ten minutes. What did you take?"

He let out his breath. "Names. Contacts. I couldn pass up the opportunity to expand my information. Yo know how important it is to put the associations to gether, to be able to track these people through th country—"

"You're looking for Courtney."

Jackson's mouth tightened, but he didn't avert h gaze. "She's my daughter."

"I'm afraid for you, Jackson."

"I'm not blind."

"About this, you are."

"Don't tell me you wouldn't do the same."

"True. I don't have a daughter. But Courtney was over eighteen."

"You don't give up on your children just because they're adults."

"Jackson—"

"Don't. You won't understand. I'm not going to be rash. I need to know where she is."

His face was hard, but it was an act. He was hurting inside, and Moira couldn't do anything to help him. So she let it go. At least for now.

"Why don't you stay here while I talk to the police?" Jackson said. "I'll do everything I can to protect you and St. Michael's."

"Thank you. And thank you for your help. I'm sorry about your church."

"It is replaceable." He touched her lightly on the chin. "You are not."

Julie was dead by the time the paramedics took her from Grant's arms. Grant seemed to be in shock. He didn't speak to anyone, only stared straight ahead. Rafe looked around for Moira, but as soon as the paramedics—followed by a cop car—pulled into the church parking lot, she'd disappeared.

Rafe didn't want to talk to anyone about what happened. He wished they'd had more time to come up with a believable story.

Two uniformed officers approached. One spoke to the paramedics; the other approached Rafe, who was standing near the door.

"Sir, what's your name?"

"Raphael Cooper." He pulled out his wallet and iden
tification.

The officer looked at it, wrote down the information
and handed it back. "We need to remove you from the
crime scene if you're able," he said.

"Pastor Moreno's house is across the parking lot."

"This is Jackson Moreno's church?" the cop asked
recognizing the name.

"Officer?"

Nina Hardwick strode purposefully across the portico
until she stood in front of the cop. She was a mess, just
like all of them. There was blood on her white blouse
and two buttons had popped off, revealing a very white
stomach. The cop stared at her, as if trying to place her.

"Yes?"

"Nina Hardwick, staff counsel for Supervisor Vochek
I was here for this unfortunate tragedy, and I'm happy
to answer any questions. Have you spoken with detec
tives Nelson and Johnston?"

The officer looked at the two men sitting on the
ground. A paramedic was looking each one over. Grant
pushed the EMT aside. "Help me up," he told the cop.

"Sir—"

"Detective Grant Nelson." Grant held out his hand
The cop took it. Aided, Grant rose to his feet, his body
beaten and pale. "Pacific Division. You remember Ken
Galion died last week? I was investigating his death, and
my partner and I uncovered a drug ring operating out o
Velocity. It spiraled out of control today. We were
caught unawares. Ambushed. The two dead women in
side were high on something. The coroner has been
looking into designer drugs, but—" Grant shook his
head.

"Is Pastor Moreno under investigation?" the cop asked.

"Of course not," Grant said. "He had some information for us. I wish I could share with you all the details, but right now it's still an ongoing undercover operation and you'll have to talk to my boss."

He glanced at Nina. Rafe watched the unspoken communication, and Nina excused herself.

Rafe didn't know whether Grant's quick talking would get him out of trouble, but for now it had saved his and Moira's hides.

It was time for him to take Moira someplace to rest. They both needed sleep.

THIRTY-FIVE

Forty-Eight Hours Later

Anthony landed in Missoula, Montana, after traveling for more than sixteen hours. A thick blanket of snow covered the ground, eerily beautiful in the stunning moonlight. He watched out the window of the taxi that wound carefully through the mountains to Olivet.

He was exhausted. More than anything, he wanted to hold Skye. If he'd gone straight to San Francisco, it would have been a short five-hour drive to Santa Louisa. He'd have been walking into Skye's arms now, instead of facing Rico Cortese's grim face.

"Thank you for coming," Rico said, taking Anthony's coat and escorting him to a fire in the library.

"I didn't have a choice." Anthony stood in front of the grand stone fireplace, the heat unable to melt the ice in his veins.

"The cardinal said you found answers in Dr. Lieber's papers."

Anthony turned and faced the hunter. "Don't you find it suspicious that Dr. Lieber is dead?"

Rico sat down slowly, indicating that Anthony do the same. Anthony remained standing. Rico said, "He was elderly and infirm. The trip could have worn him out." Then he looked pointedly at Anthony. "Yes, I find it highly suspicious. But no one has been able to prove it. We must keep our information close."

Believing that someone had breached St. Michael's fortress—or worse, that someone inside was responsible—deeply disturbed Anthony.

"What did you find?" Rico asked quietly.

Anthony looked back toward the fire. "Father Philip believed that Moira was the only one who could destroy the *Conoscenza*."

"Yes. The *Book of the Unknown Martyr* clearly states that only a repentant magician with the proper lineage can forever destroy the evil book, through 'blood and fire.'"

Rico continued. "I tested Moira's blood. It is poison to demons. We know this is a sign."

Anthony slowly turned and sat across from Rico. "How do you know for certain?" he asked. "Could it be a trick?"

"It is no trick. It was Moira's blood that weakened the demon Envy in Santa Louisa. And you heard what happened in Los Angeles."

"In part. I spoke with Rafe right before I left St. Michael's."

"When Moira's blood touches the demon, it weakens the creature. Gives us time to trap or kill it. When I tested it on a demon—"

"What?"

"A possessed man. We confirmed it was a demonic possession. I injected Moira's blood into him. The demon was instantly exorcised."

"Impossible."

Rico raised an eyebrow as if to say *You doubt me?*

"I've never heard of such a thing."

"Humanity was formed in blood. Sacrifice. Jesus was tortured and crucified, a sacrifice of blood and His human life to save the world."

"Moira is no Christ!"

"No. But there is history. And Moira's blood is from the proper lineage. She's of Fiona, who is of the line of witches that dates back to the dawn of mankind, when the first humans forged an unholy alliance with fallen angels. And Moira is repentant—she has not used magic in seven years."

"How can you be sure?"

Rico stared at him. "I am."

The truth was hard for Anthony to accept. "You mean we must kill her."

"No." Rico stared him in the eye. "She must martyr herself."

Anthony closed his eyes. "Yes. That is what Dr. Lieber's notes say."

Anthony handed Rico a copy of the key page. He already knew it by heart.

The Book of Knowledge, *known by most as the* Conoscenza, *was written in demon blood by the first magicians. It can be destroyed only by the blood of a repentant magician. Martyrdom is the only guarantee that the book will be destroyed, but if not possible, the blood must still flow, followed by fire. The blood will wash away the stain on the pages; the fire will destroy the paper made of human skin. Only then will humanity be safe from the spells therein.*

"You agree," Rico said.

"I don't know. But—" He hesitated, handing Rico another page. "It seems destroying the *Conoscenza* is the only way to send the Seven Deadly Sins back to Hell."

Rico read the papers. "We don't need to trap every demon to succeed. Destroy the book and they'll be pulled back to the underworld."

"It should be easier to retrieve the book than to capture the Seven."

"I have many leads. In fact, I'll be returning to Santa Louisa in ten days to bring Moira back to Olivet for additional training." Rico looked pained, and turned away from Anthony. "She needs to be prepared for her fate," he said softly.

Anthony didn't know what would happen, but he said, "I have a difficult time putting my life in the hands of a witch."

"Forgiveness, Anthony. You need to work on that."

Moira bolted upright in bed, her heart racing. She looked around the room, frantically searching for something familiar, something that told her where she was.

"Moira."

Rafe took her hand and pulled her back down, kissing her. Rafe was familiar. They were back in Santa Louisa, but not at Skye's. Lily was still there, and there wasn't room for everyone at Skye's house, so Moira and Rafe had checked into a hotel. They needed the time alone after what they'd faced in Los Angeles. They needed the time to just be together.

Rafe held her close. "You had a nightmare."

"No, you did."

He held her face in his hands. "I wasn't having a nightmare."

"I heard you cry out in your sleep."

Or had she? Had she dreamed Rafe was suffering? Dying? She touched him, hardly able to believe he was alive. She didn't want to do this five more times, chasing after the sins that remained at large. She just wanted peace. She just wanted to live quietly. Alone, with Rafe.

He kissed her softly. "I don't remember what I was dreaming. For one more night, let's put everything aside. Everything but us."

"Us?"

"I love you, Moira. We're going to find Fiona and stop her. I promise. And then you'll be free. We'll both be free."

He touched her cheek, made her look at him. It was dark, and he could barely see her face, but her eyes glistened in what little light filtered in from outside. "Where you were is not where you are now. Who you came from is not who you are. You know that, I don't have to tell you, but sometimes you need to hear it. Whatever gifts you have, they're good. It might not feel that way . . ." His voice trailed off as he thought about the memories he had. He pushed those thoughts aside as a dull ache in his head threatened to break out. "But without you, we'd be at a loss. We need you."

I need you.

He swallowed, wanting to tell Moira exactly how he felt. He'd told her he loved her—and dear Lord, he did love her—but he feared if she knew how much he needed her—how she completed him, how she kept him sane, how she had saved his soul—she would run away. He refused to add any more weight to her load.

I need you. I love you.

Instead, he kissed her, smoothed the hair back from her damp forehead, erasing the remnants of whatever dark dream had her heart pounding. He could do this for her, every night. Hold her. Make love to her. Love her.

"Rafe—"

"Shh."

Moira sighed when Rafe silenced her with another kiss. Her nightmare faded as she let Rafe soothe her frayed nerves with his warm affection, the heat between them rising quickly. He made her forget the past and not think about the future; his touch told her they only had this day. Today was all that mattered. If tomorrow came, they would face it together.

Desire replaced tension, her need to touch every inch of Rafe grounded her, gave her humanity in ways nothing else could. Sex was primal, necessary, both light and dark, both good and bad. Sex connected two people physically, but what Moira felt for Rafe went far beyond simple lust. With every sigh, every touch, every need, she fell deeper into the abyss, a place she'd never escape. She didn't want to, because this abyss was love, and she would fight to protect this precious bond.

Moira ran her hands down Rafe's bare back. She'd memorized every scar on his body, all the damage inflicted on him in the past—days ago, years ago, decades ago. Her fingertips traced the ridges as the scars cut south, to the waistband of his boxers, then back up again, until she squeezed his shoulders. She whispered, "I need you." And she did, more than she'd admit to anyone, even Rafe, except for now. When they were isolated, alone, together in the darkest hours of the night.

She pulled off her tank top with one hand and tossed it aside, so now both of them were completely naked except for her panties and his boxers. Rafe's hand skimmed over her breasts. "Come to me, sweetness," he whispered, then breathed warmly into her ear, sending shivers along each nerve ending, down and back. She kissed his neck, ran her teeth over his jawline, lightly biting his earlobe when she tasted it. His long, hard body pinned her to the mattress and for one torturous, exquisite moment neither of them moved. Time stopped, the only sound their hearts and breath.

Rafe clasped her hands in his and spread them out on the bed. His lips sought hers, slow and firm, a long kiss she never wanted to end. Her skin basked in Rafe's scent, his heat, his love. She yearned for much more than this breathtaking kiss, but she didn't want to move.

And still he kissed her, his fingers entwined with hers, his arms pressed against her arms, his bare chest hot against hers. Now she squirmed beneath him, her passion fighting the restraints of Rafe's methodical seduction.

He tilted his head up, breaking the kiss, his lips curved in a half smile that alone would have knocked her socks off. "Is this lust, Moira? Or is it love?"

His eyes locked on hers and she realized he expected an answer. He'd been hurt the other day when she'd implied that maybe their passionate feelings for each other had been the result of the demon Lust, not their own desires.

She licked her lips and swallowed. The intensity of Rafe's stare had her heart quicken. He brought one hand to her breast and held it there, right above her heart, and waited for her to respond.

She leaned up to kiss him, but he leaned away, not taking his eyes from hers.

"Rafe—"

"Tell me."

"I'm scared," she whispered.

"I know."

Moira watched Rafe's expression, both patient and passionate. He wanted an answer and would wait forever to get it, even if he had to keep her lying here for hours. Days. She swallowed, wanting more time. Time for them. What if she loved so deeply that she couldn't think? That she couldn't fight? That she couldn't protect those she cared about out of fear for their lives and souls?

Then she realized that love wasn't something she could stop. Love couldn't be turned on and off like a faucet. Love existed between two people who valued each other more than themselves, who recognized that together they were stronger, not weaker. The depth of her love for Rafe couldn't be regulated or controlled. Her love, their love, simply *was*.

"It's always been love," she said, the words tumbling out before she could stop them, before she could reconsider the step she was taking. Maybe she thought too much, analyzed too much. "From that first moment I found you, it's been love. Each day it grows stronger until I feel like I'm drowning with these emotions. I am scared." Her voice cracked. "But I love you so much."

Rafe had been waiting to hear those words, even though he knew them to be true long before Moira accepted the fact. He kissed her, this time with the passion and urgency he'd been holding back, waiting for her to open her heart. He let go of her hand and her arms wrapped around him, moving up and down his back, her fingers pressing into his muscles inch by inch, as if memorizing every cell in his body. His lips moved from her mouth to her neck, his tongue tasting her salty skin, his nose breathing in the light, floral soap she'd showered with. But under the faint perfume, Moira shined. Her touch, her taste, her scent was so familiar Rafe could believe he'd known her for a lifetime.

He kissed the soft, delicate skin under her chin, moved down and painstakingly kissed every inch of her smooth skin around the base of her breasts, circling until his mouth reached her nipple. He drew the nub in slowly, held it until Moira groaned and tried to flip him to his back. She was strong, but he was stronger, and he pinned her back down with a grin. "I'm not done."

"You're driving me crazy, Rafe."

"Likewise, sweetness." He reached down and skirted his fingers over her panties.

"Take them off," she demanded.

"Or what?"

Her eyes flashed with sexy humor. "Or I won't play nice."

"I'm not playing."

He slid down her body, the blankets falling to the floor at the end of the bed. The room was near black, only a dim streetlight splitting the room in half through the slit in the hotel's curtains, wrapping them in dark and light shadows. Moira's body was long, lean, and full of energy she could barely restrain. He had to give her credit for the attempt; Moira was not a woman who laid around limply. She was life itself.

He took off her panties as she'd commanded and dropped them to the floor. He rubbed each of her calves in turn, his thumbs memorizing every curve of her tight muscles, every one of the soft spots, the tender points under her knees, the fine lines where one well-defined muscle met another. She squirmed, her hands grabbing the sheet beneath them, as he worked his hands up past her knees, parting her glorious legs as he kissed her inner thigh. First one side, then the other. She trembled, and Rafe smiled. She was trying so hard not to take control. It went against her nature, and he loved her more for it. For trusting him.

When Rafe's mouth skimmed Moira between her legs she gasped and pulled at the sheet, trying in vain to hold back her explosion. She thought she felt his smile, or maybe it was a chuckle, but she heard nothing except the hot rush of her blood. She might have cried out, she didn't know, she didn't care; all she wanted was this moment to never stop at the same time she wanted it to end. How could something that felt so wonderful be so agonizing?

Rafe's hot breath teased her, and then he kissed her at her center, his tongue mimicking lovemaking, and she did call out then as she lost all control, every muscle in her body tightening, then releasing all at once in a rolling wave of ecstasy.

She barely caught her breath and Rafe was doing it again, torturing her with his firm, deliberate kisses. She'd had enough of submitting to him.

Rafe wasn't surprised when Moira relaxed completely, then pounced on him, efficiently flipping him to his back. Except that he was too close to the edge of the bed and they tumbled to the floor. She ended up on top, her eyes narrowed, a small smile on her face. She was glowing in her passion and her love, and Rafe reached up to pull her down to him.

"My turn," she said and roughly pulled down his boxers.

Rafe closed his eyes, letting all his senses focus on Moira's touch. She was not as patient as he'd forced himself to be. She kissed his thighs, then nipped him, her hands moving from his legs to his stomach to his ass, where she squeezed at the same time as she licked the underside of his penis. He gasped, instinctively reaching for her head, her hair twisting in his hands. She slid her entire mouth around him and he was teetering on the edge.

"Make love to me, Moira," he said. "Love me, sweetness."

She rose above him looking like an angel, her dark wavy hair falling tangled around her face. She straddled him, directing his penis with her strong, slender fingers, until he slipped in. She pushed him deep inside with one thrust and froze. Her eyes closed, her mouth partly open, the narrow strip of light cutting across her breast, she was the most beautiful, sexiest woman Rafe had ever seen.

"Open your eyes," he demanded. "Look at me, love."

At first her gaze was unfocused with pleasure. He relished Moira's ability to do everything with intense passion, but it was here as they made love that she truly came alive.

He leaned up, the friction between them making them both gasp, but he had to kiss those lips. He had to taste her. He locked her in the kiss until she shuddered, vibrating deep inside where he felt it with the tip of his penis. Primal need had him thrusting, then he fell back to the floor and said, "I'm all yours."

Moira was momentarily overpowered when her last barriers collapsed, washed away in a flood of unconditional trust and love flowing from Rafe's aura. She hadn't realized until now that she'd been holding back her senses, but the last remnants of fear disappeared with her walls. In this one perfect moment she blended with Rafe as if she were sharing his soul, and he sharing hers. Their thoughts, their feelings, their bodies were one, a perfect union.

"Don't cry," Rafe said.

"I'm not." She wiped her face, surprised there were tears on her cheeks. "I love you so much."

Moira lowered her body onto Rafe's, kissed his chest softly as they moved together in a slow, steady rhythm. She let him roll her over, their limbs entwined, their separate bodies becoming one. In unison they encouraged the other, urging each other at the same pace, spiraling higher the faster their bodies moved. Hands linked, they stared in each other's blue eyes; Moira's bright, Rafe's dark, saw their love as they felt it.

Moira's lips involuntarily parted as Rafe brought her to the edge. She teetered there, and Rafe put his mouth on hers, kissing her as she gasped. He held himself deep inside her, his entire body rigid, then with a deep cry that bordered on a growl, he began to shake as he could no longer hold back his ecstasy.

Moira dove right off the edge with Rafe, holding him as a flash of hot, white light preceded an incredible orgasm, fueled by lust and love, trust and passion. Nothing existed except them, and they became one, holding still, the diminishing shudders that surged through their bodies touching the most tender spots inside and out.

Rafe pulled the blankets that had fallen on the floor around both of them. He held Moira close, their bodies still hot and slick with sweat. He didn't want to let her go, and kissed her again, lightly, tenderly.

"I wish we could stay like this forever," Moira said wistfully.

"We have now."

"Yes, we have now." She sighed and shivered.

Rafe reluctantly rose to his feet, picking Moira up with him. He laid her on the bed, covered her with the blankets and spooned his body around hers. She hugged his arm to her chest and breathed out a long, steady moan.

"Sleep, sweetness," Rafe said. "I will be here when you wake up."

She melted into his arms with a contented sigh. They lay wrapped together, unmoving, Rafe's hand over Moira's heart. He focused on her steady pulse as it slowed to a soft, even beat; he listened to her breathing as it evened out, rhythmic, calming.

Rafe watched Moira's face, surprisingly peaceful and vulnerable in sleep. She trusted him, otherwise she wouldn't be resting so soundly. His chest tightened painfully at what they would be facing over the next weeks, months, even years. But maybe this love was God's way of giving them something so good, so pure, so perfect that they could survive the future.

"It's always been love."

"Yes, Moira," he murmured, "it's always been love."

Rafe drifted into a light, troubled sleep.

I wasn't alone in there.

Julie's voice startled him and his eyes flashed open. She wasn't here. She was dead, but her words haunted him. He hadn't told Moira what Julie had said. But until he had more answers, he would keep the information to himself.

He tightened his grip around Moira, and she tensed,

then relaxed again, as if sensing his uneasiness. He had more questions than answers, and he feared he might be more a danger to Moira than her unknown future. But he would not hurt her. He would die first.

Perhaps Julie was wrong. Perhaps it was the memories that made her think she wasn't alone. Or the spirits that had flooded through him on their way to the astral plane. Moira would sense if something was supernaturally wrong with him. Her perceptions were extraordinary. All he had was memories, and there had to be a logical explanation. He would find it. He had to, for both him and Moira, and for their future.

He thought back to Rod Fielding's observation about the amygdala, the primitive core of the brain. The part that housed basic emotions. The foundation on which the Seven Deadly Sins fed. The memory center of the brain . . . primitive memories. Nothing was more primitive than fear.

Rafe prayed for answers that did not come, except for a deep—primitive—need to protect Moira at all costs. Moira's life was Rafe's responsibility. He knew it with as strong a certainty as he knew that he loved her. It was his sacred duty. Even if he had to die. Even if he had to kill.

Moira whimpered once in her sleep and Rafe whispered in her ear, "I'm here, sweetness. Don't be afraid, I'm right here with you."

Dawn broke over the Los Padres Mountains before Rafe slept again.

Read on for an excerpt from
LOVE ME TO DEATH
by Allison Brennan

Published by Ballantine Books

One Month Ago

This was Roger Morton's big chance. By taking the best practices of his criminal past blended with what he'd since learned in prison, he was going to create an amazing new life.

Staying off the main path, he cut through Rock Creek Park behind the Omni Shoreham hotel. The trails were officially closed at night, but the D.C. cops couldn't be everywhere at once. He wasn't worried about the few stragglers he encountered. Walking in pairs and small groups, thinning out as the hour passed nine, they were scurrying across the park after burning the midnight oil at work, or taking a shortcut on their way to a high-priced bar to play the eternal mating game.

He stuffed his hands in the pockets of his leather jacket, wishing he had a warmer coat. It had been cold all day, a depressing gray haze clouding everything in sight. He couldn't wait to grab his money and get out of this miserable town. He had a place already lined up in South America. Even after six years in prison, Roger had contacts. Once he had the money in hand, he'd be sitting pretty.

Six long years behind bars. His attorney had said he was lucky to get away with just that after the attempted murder of a federal agent and felony rape. *Six years in the federal pen was lucky?* He'd spilled his guts, gave the cops everything they wanted, admitted to practically everything—well, he had left out the crucial detail that he'd killed one of their own people. That fact he'd most certainly kept to himself, thanks very much. Anyway, the Feds didn't have anything implicating him—no gun, no witnesses, nothing. It had been easy enough to lay blame for that escapade on someone else

Six years of his life gone. For *cooperating*.

Everything had changed while he was in the pen, and he was damned if he was going to sit around and be a car mechanic making chump change. Not when he knew how to make real money. The kind of serious dough that would set him up in his previous lifestyle, the kind that bought freedom. In prison, his life had been on hold— now he had the chance to start over.

Adam had spouted off that Roger was the dumb one. Well, Adam was *dead*—how smart did that make *him*?

Roger cautiously approached the meeting spot. He wasn't an idiot; when there was this kind of money in-volved, he knew not to bring the merchandise without cash up front—or to tangle with someone who hadn't been vetted.

First show me what you got, buddy.

And damn, that pimp had been nasty. Roger had en-joyed the digital files of young women getting screwed every which way. Some were actual actresses, others desperate for a quick buck to pay for their next fix. Some of the recordings—or the best, in his opinion— were those where the chicks didn't even know they were being filmed. Amateur whores. Roger saw the marketing potential for that campaign, practically salivating over the dollars he'd rake in. Straight porn wasn't illegal, but the money was in edgier areas—hidden cameras, under-age teens, fantasy rape that wasn't necessarily consensual.

Roger had recently rented a small storage unit to re-create the operation he'd run with Adam. Only now, with Adam six feet under, Roger wouldn't have to split profits so many ways or take orders. He'd run the web-site, handle the back-end, and the pimp provided the pornographic content. A fifty-fifty split. Roger was confident the cash would stream in fast and he'd learned from Adam how to manage the credit cards of their cus-tomers and funnel money to offshore accounts. Best of all, without Adam around, Roger wouldn't have to worry anymore about the snuff films that had brought the Feds down on them. If Adam hadn't gotten his ya-ya's off strangling the women he screwed, they'd never have been busted. Rape was a crime, but murder was a whole other story.

All Roger needed was some up-front cash to set up the offshore operation. It didn't matter that he was on pa-role, he'd skip out and never again step on American soil. That took more money than he could make work-ing fifty-hour weeks at some suburban car dealership changing oil.

The trees were denser as he circled the meeting spot near a footbridge crossing a muddy stream. Roger made double sure it wasn't a setup—though he couldn't imag-ine how. He wasn't the one carrying the money, he was the partner with the know-how, the brains. Sure he was risking prosecution, but the potential rewards were well worth it. Besides, using his old contacts, Roger had tracked these guys down. It's not like they'd been looking for him. He'd kept a low profile since getting out five months ago.

He'd rather be dead than go back.

He spotted his new partner approaching the rendezvous point. The man was wearing jeans, a dark Windbreaker, and a Yankees baseball cap—just like he'd said. Roger glanced around, saw no one else, and approached.

"Hey," he said, sizing up the man he had yet to meet. "Morton?"

He gave a single nod. "Have my advance?"

"We got an agreement?" The man's voice was raspy, as if he'd been a two-pack-a-day smoker for years.

Roger was waiting for entrapment clues—such as having him explicitly say that he was using the money to set up an illegal porn website—but the guy didn't go into details. An agreement could mean anything in court. Sure, he was in the park after dark—a misdemeanor, and he could technically be thrown back in prison for even the smallest slipup—but they still couldn't get him on anything big.

Roger said, "Yes, we have a deal."

Tensing as the man reached into his pocket, Roger's hand moved to the gun in his waistband, but he didn't need to use it. His new partner handed him an envelope.

Roger frowned as he held the paper. "It's a little thin for twenty g's."

"Open it."

The flap was unsealed, and Roger removed a folded piece of paper. It was blank, with a faded photo between the folds: a beautiful teenage girl with long black hair and large, sultry brown eyes.

His instincts had him reacting almost before he recognized the dead girl, but not fast enough. He dropped the photo and paper and reached for his gun, but the man kicked his wrist before he touched the grip, and in the faint light from the trail Roger saw the man's face dead-on for the first time.

Another ghost from his past.

"I wish I could be the one to put the bullet in your head," the man said before shoving Roger down face-first.

He tried to rise, but the traitor kicked him between the legs three times with steel-toed boots. Excruciating pain froze him. Worse than when he was raped in prison. But then he'd had his revenge. Panic and self-preservation rose with the pain as he tried to stand, only to be knocked down again.

"Mr. Morton." The quiet, cultured voice didn't belong to his attacker. Roger hadn't heard another man approach, and the idea that two—or more—men stood over him made him shake even as he tried to get up one last time.

A boot in his balls had him seeing nothing. He almost didn't hear the slide of the nine millimeter.

"I wish this hurt you more, but in this case expediency is more important than my personal satisfaction at seeing you suffer. This is for Monique."

Roger Morton was dead before even registering the sound of the gunshot.

Present Day

Brad Monahan thought he had a get-out-of-jail-free card, but Lucy Kincaid would set him straight.

She glanced at the clock on her computer and frowned. It was already nearly six and she'd promised her brother Patrick she wouldn't be late after canceling their dinner plans twice last week.

"Come on, come on," she muttered as she split the large screen into six open chat windows she could monitor simultaneously. "You've been here every day this week at five, why are you late tonight?"

Out of the corner of her eye, Lucy saw Women and Children First! director Frances Buckley approach. She'd retired from the FBI nine years ago after putting in twenty-five years, and though she was nearly sixty, she looked and acted ten years younger. After Lucy started volunteering for WCF, Fran quickly became her mentor. She'd written a glowing recommendation letter for Lucy's application into the FBI and had helped her prepare for both the written and verbal tests. And for the last three months, Fran had helped Lucy cope with the anxiety of waiting to hear whether she made it to the final interview.

Lucy didn't allow herself to think that she could be rejected. She knew the process could take months, but not knowing either way was frustrating. For the last six years, all she'd wanted was to be an FBI agent. Everything she'd done—her double major in psychology and computer science, her internships with the police department and the D.C. Medical Examiners Office, her volunteer work at high schools and here at WCF—were all calculated to help her get into the FBI. She hoped the hiring panel could see that what she'd learned would make her a strong addition to the Bureau.

Fran put a hand on the back of Lucy's chair. "Tick-tock. It's six, Lucy."

"Five more minutes. Monahan isn't online yet."

"Life happens. You can't sit here all night waiting for him. You have a life, too. Don't you have dinner plans with your brother tonight?"

"Yes, but—"

Lucy, Monahan will be here tomorrow."

"I have some time—twenty minutes and I'll make it to Clyde's by seven."

"If you sprint to the metro."

"I'm a fast runner." Lucy smiled at Fran, deliberately flashing her dimple.

The older woman shook her head, but returned the smile. "I'll pull the plug if you're still here at 6:15."

Fran meant she would literally cut the power. She'd done it before. Lucy crossed her heart with her right index finger and blew Fran a kiss before she turned back to the fast-moving chat rooms.

WCF had a secure bank of computers, as secure and untraceable as any in the FBI, where they investigated illegal sexual exploitation of women and children. When they collected enough evidence to identify the victim or the perpetrator, Fran turned the files over to the FBI for further investigation.

But tonight, Lucy was involved in a more personal project. Brad Monahan. He'd raped two women, including her friend Sara Tyson, and had been sentenced to three-to-five years in state prison. But less than two years after his conviction, he'd been paroled, and now walked the streets free while his two known victims still faced the emotional devastation he'd caused.

Lucy had sat through the two-day trial. Watched both Sara and Maggie torn apart on the stand. Knew what they'd gone through. The remorse Monahan showed to the jury was an act: Lucy would prove it now. The terms of his parole were clear: he had to stay clean for three years because alcohol was a contributing factor in the sexual assaults. He liked the club scene, and it was just a matter of time before he started drinking again. And when he did? D.C. Police Officer Cody Lorenzo would be there to cuff him and haul him back in.

Justice would be *fully* served. All three-to-five-years.

After Brad Monahan's release two weeks ago, Lucy had created a profile that fit his preferences: a college-age blonde who liked running and rock music, and enjoyed clubs that played live music. Her screen name was "AKA Tanya" and she'd been chatting him up since he'd been released from prison two weeks ago.

Talking to him online made her physically ill, but it was for a greater good. She'd done her part, played both coy and sexy, never suggesting they meet, but always giving him the opportunity. He asked once, early on in their online chatting, about "hooking up" somewhere, but she'd declined. Always give them an out. Always give them a chance to say no. The second time he asked she declined, but hinted that she was interested, just busy. Another out, another chance to say no.

This was an important rule when dealing with child predators; Brad Monahan wasn't a child predator, but Lucy played by the same rules. Never suggest a meet. Always decline the first offer.

At 6:10, Lucy's computer softly beeped. "AKA Tanya" received a private message from BDM87. Brad David Monahan.

BDM87: You still there?

AKA Tanya: yep. studying. sorta . . . lol.

BDM87: You free tonight?

Lucy's pulse quickened, but she kept her breathing even as she typed.

AKA Tanya: ☹ i have a big test.

BDM87: Tomorrow night??

AKA Tanya: better . . . where?

BDM87: You pick.

Even though Monahan was on parole and Lucy wasn't a cop—so this wasn't technically entrapment—the conversation was moving into the gray area. Lucy had to get Monahan to pick the place.

AKA Tanya: i dunno—someplace fun good music good drinks

BDM87: Firehouse Grill? You know it?

Lucy rolled her eyes. She didn't hang at bars, but everyone under the age of thirty knew of the Fairfax-area bar that catered to the college crowd. Lots of drinking, too loud music, and crowded. Not a place for quiet conversation; definitely a place to hook up. It was perfect for men like Monahan, and perfect for this operation.

AKA Tanya: i'll be there . . . nine? eight?

BDM87: Eight.

AKA Tanya: ☺

Lucy smiled as she typed the online happy face.

Fran called from the doorway, "Ten, nine, eight—"

"I got him!" she called out as she typed a message to Monahan that she was logging out to study.

Then she shut down each of the chat rooms after sending her personal email the transcripts that had been copied while she was logged in. She then quickly sent Cody a message.

Monahan will be waiting for "AKA Tanya" at the Firehouse Grill, eight tomorrow. His choice.

"You got Monahan?" Fran looked over Lucy's shoulder. "Good."

"Yep, I accepted his third invite to hook up, changed the day so Cody has twenty-four hours, but he picked the time and place." She spontaneously gave Fran a hug. "Finally, I feel like I've accomplished something!"

"It's been awhile since we had a victory, but don't count your chickens before—"

"They squeak. Right." But nothing was going to diminish her good mood. Now she had something to celebrate with Patrick. She glanced at her watch. She was definitely going to have to run. "I wish I could be there when Cody arrests him."

"Lucy, you know the rules." Fran forbade any of them from getting involved in the field, even on the periphery.

"I know, I know." Lucy shut down her monitor and grabbed her raincoat and scarf. "I'll be satisfied with Cody's report." Not as satisfied as seeing Brad Monahan's expression when he realized his date was a setup, but it would have to be enough.